AN DA SHELLADH

A Novel

Dennis Gibb

NEWMAN SPRINGS PUBLISHING
320 Broad Street
Red Bank, NJ 07701

First originally published by Newman Springs Publishing 2024

ISBN 979-8-89061-274-8 (Paperback)
ISBN 979-8-89061-275-5 (Digital)

Printed in the United States of America

To my victims, I'm so sorry

PRELUDE

My name is David Joseph MacIntosh. David, not Dave or Mac. I'm very old, having lived far beyond the biblical threescore and ten. I've outlived my parents, as is typical. I have survived my wife. I have outlived my younger siblings and two of my four children.

As I sit at the computer, I look down at the joints of my fingers. They are gnarled by age, wrinkled and spotted. My ghostly face stares back at me from the monitor screen, deep age lines and furrows etched by the sands of time and the tears I have shed.

I also can almost feel the untreatable cancer eating at my spine.

Like many old men, I think back on the glories of youth, the joys of my life, but in my case, the events I'm about to recount crowd out the pleasant, with memories of decisions made or not made of love lost, of those who loved me regardless of my flaws and who are now gone.

Since I am of a logical cast of mind, my story must start at its beginning.

Chapter 1

In 1960, I turned thirteen, and everything in my life changed. At that time, we lived in Wheaton, Illinois, a small conservative town twenty-five miles west of Chicago. The town was dominated by its college known as the Harvard of divinity schools.

There were, of course, the expected changes. Hair appeared in unexpected places, body parts seemed to grow out of all proportion or reason, other boys grew taller, their voices changed, and girls got curves and breasts. I became clumsy; it seemed like nothing moved the way it used to. Then came the wet dreams. Sex education was hugely different in those days; it was at the school of Mom and Dad. They tried to offset the street teachings, which were usually wrong but certainly more exciting than the truth.

Girls became mildly fascinating, not because they expressed any interest in me but because they just got interesting. I still found them silly, the way they would scream and swoon when Elvis appeared, for example. They started to wear tight, more correctly, formfitting, revealing clothes as much as they could in a conservative small religious town (which wasn't much). Rumors would fly that "so and so had done it with…"

For me, girls were mysterious creatures, and I was not a fan of rejection, so I was not an active player in the developing adolescent sexual dance.

I also developed an affliction that plagues me still. I remember every clumsy action I took, every misplaced word, false start, and unsuccessful attempt. I couldn't seem to retain pleasant memories nearly as well, neither in volume nor lucidity.

Most of the curses of adolescence would pass but not the one that now arrived.

Summer passed, and as it ended, nature's soothsayers appeared. Vying for first were the woolly bugger caterpillars. According to old wives' tales, they heralded a bad winter if they appeared before the first leaves fell. The thickness of the black or orange bands held omniscient if you could remember the predictive sequence. Was it black smaller than orange or the other way around?

There were other signs: birds scoring the sky in long V formations, the Cubs falling out of contention. Fall always came, and the Cubs always folded.

School playing fields resounded with the symphony of the coach's whistles, the crack of football pads, sleeves got longer, dresses less sheer, zephyrs of cold brought horripilation. Sleeping got easier as temperatures dropped, and blankets were needed on screened porches.

The glorious trees arching over the walkways sensed the change. The colder weather dried the leaves, frost appeared, and leaves started to change colors.

We had the opportunity to view all of this without hordes of buses and color tourists who would become the bane of many small towns. Soon the area was a fabulous kaleidoscope of colors and hues. The wind became more persistent, rattling the leaves and branches like the bones in a dice cup.

Then without much warning—metrology at the time being a very inexact science—low pressure would form someplace to the south, and wind from Canada would scream down, seeking every crack and hole. Windows frosted and banged in their frames as the wind moaned around the corners of the house. The cold would soon seep into everything, and as you shoveled newly formed snowdrifts from walks and driveways, it seemed you would never be warm again.

In 1960, the winter in Chicago came early and hung around; the summer's heat became a fond memory.

It was a cold Saturday, two weeks before Thanksgiving. The snow was deep in the yard, the tree branches were heavy with snow, and stalactites hung from the gutters.

My best friend, Shamus, and I were in his front yard, throwing snowballs at passing cars when Joe and Josh Bruderman came by with sleds and a toboggan. They were heading toward the sled hill. I had my sled with me, but I called home to tell Mom and Dad where I would be. They reminded me to be home at four, and off we went.

On the way, Megan Forman joined us, her brother Stepan trailing behind. He was a huge, kind of stupid, clumsy ape-looking guy. Shamus called him (behind his back) a mouth breather or a knuckle dragger. We found our classmates, Steve Xanders and Evan Harris, at the hill. We were oblivious to the cold; we were working hard hauling sleds up the hill in the fifty or so layers of cotton and wool we were required to wear. After we'd finished a run and were humping up the hill, Shamus took his hat off to cool down, and I noticed an oval black mark two to three inches long from his left eyebrow to the top of his ear.

"You got something on your head—by your left eye." I gasped through the effort.

He wiped the area with his gloved hand. "Gone?"

"No, still there."

He rubbed again longer and harder, but the mark stayed in place.

"Still there," I said, and he rubbed harder, finally scrapping up snow and using it to rub.

"Still there," I said again, just as we reached the top of the hill.

Evan and Steve Xanders asked what was going on, and the others gathered around, but they all said there was no mark.

Shamus turned to me. "Damn, my ear is frozen off. You trying to give me frostbite? You're an asshole, MacIntosh!" He stormed off.

I checked the time and started home alone. It gets dark fast in the winter in Wheaton. It was near-total darkness as I walked. I had waited too long, and it looked like I might not get home on time.

I was wearing what I called my bumper riding galoshes, rubber boots of no insulating quality but whose soles had worn smooth. I found a car at a stop sign. I crouched down behind it so the driver couldn't see me and grabbed the bumper. As the driver moved off, the smooth soles of my boots slid over the ice and snow. I rode the bumper for four blocks and made it on time.

Mom and Dad were ready to leave, and dinner—mac and cheese, the only thing all four of us would eat—was ready. We were allowed one hour of TV before bed, which Eleanor and I took to mean Daphne and Peter had an hour together, and she and I got an hour each. Amid the TV noises, we heard sirens but paid little attention.

Around seven, the phone rang. A male voice asked for Dad, and I replied, as I had been instructed, that he wasn't available and could I take a number.

"I'll call back in fifteen minutes," the caller said.

Fifteen minutes later, the phone erupted again. This time a female voice asked for Mom, again declining to leave a number or name. The calls were weird because everyone who knew us would have known where my parents were. The calls should have been a clue, but I just thought they were strange.

Around eight, I heard a car crunch over the ice in the driveway, its lights briefly illuminating the house, then Mom and Dad walked in with matching frowns. Mom took Eleanor upstairs. Daphne and Peter were already in bed, and Dad and I went to the kitchen.

Dad looked at me with serious eyes. "Were you sledding with Shamus today?"

"Yeah. Shamus, me, Xanders, Evan, and a few more," I replied.

Dad swallowed hard. "What time did you leave?"

"I had to be home at four, so I left just after three-thirty. Xanders had a watch. It was great out there, the snow was so fresh, and we got going really fast. We made runs all the way to the woods at the bottom of the hill!" I bubbled on.

Dad looked down at the floor. It was as if he hadn't heard anything I'd said.

The door creaked open, and Mom entered without making a sound. Her eyes were all red and puffy. They didn't seem to care about the snow. I must have done something wrong. I went through a list in my mind of all the things I might have done to make them angry, and the only thing I came up with was the bumper riding.

The phone rang. Mom picked it up, but she couldn't seem to get the words out; her voice kept cracking, so Dad took over. I could hear the other voice, male and forceful, and my dad answered in monosyllables.

He hung up the phone and nodded to Mom. "I think you had better come with me, son," he said in a resigned tone.

I grabbed my coat, and we got in the car.

I took a shot in the dark. "Dad, I know I shouldn't have been bumper riding, but I was late, and everyone does it, and I don't think the driver even knew I was there."

"We'll talk about it later. Bumper riding wasn't the problem," he added gruffly.

My fears were growing, watered by the lack of information. I started to wonder if Shamus and the others had done something after I'd left, and I was getting caught in the net.

We drove the few blocks to Shamus's house in silence. There were two cop cars parked in the street and two civilian cars on the drive. One of the cop cars had its rack lights running, casting red and blue flashes on the snow and windows. I noticed people peering through their curtains from the neighboring houses between the flashes, but the flashers probably made it hard for them to see much. I started to sweat; this had to be serious if the cops were involved.

A cop was standing in the cold, blocking the path to the front door. He stopped us, letting us pass when Dad explained who we were.

A tall man in a gray suit, a black shirt, and a pastor's dog collar opened the door. He introduced himself as Reverend Smithy and ushered us in. We stomped the snow and ice from our shoes.

Mr. and Mrs. Cosman were seated on the davenport and, in a chair at one end, sat a police officer. Another officer stood beside the seated cop, notebook and pen in hand. The reverend took a chair at the other end, leaving Dad and me to stand. My worries ramped up a further notch.

Mrs. Cosman looked like she was made up for Halloween. She had been crying; her mascara had streaked down her face. She sniffed and cried in sobs; a handkerchief screwed tight in her hands. Mr. Cosman was stonefaced, staring straight ahead, neither acknowledging anyone nor making any movement. His eyes were showing only a fraction of the emotions working inside him.

"Coffee will be ready soon," the pastor's wife announced.

No one acknowledged her.

I have never figured out why people offer others food and drink in times of great stress.

The seated cop started. "Son, I'm Chief Fontent." He pronounced it slowly with emphasis on the first syllable. "I need to ask you a few questions."

There was no pause for me to ascent.

"Full name?"

Not a lot of kindness in his voice. My worry amped up yet again.

"David Joseph MacIntosh…sir," I quickly added.

"Were you out sledding earlier today?" This came rapid-fire from the second cop who was standing there, rocking back and forth, toes to heels.

"Yes, sir," I replied. "Shamus, myself…" At the mention of Shamus, Mrs. Cosman started crying, "And a few others. We were told it's okay to sled there."

"Dave," said the chief. "Can I call you Dave?"

"I prefer David," I replied.

"This isn't about being allowed to sled, so just answer the questions," the chief said, the flicker of kindness gone.

I guess it's an occupational hazard of spending all day dealing with criminals; you lose compassion and empathy.

"What time did you leave?"

"I had to be home at four, so I left a little after three-thirty."

"Went straight home, did you?" came a question from the second cop. He had a sneer on his face. "This kind of stuff wouldn't happen if people would listen and ban sledding on that hill!"

The chief coughed. "Sam, go help the pastor's wife with the coffee." He pulled a notebook out of his jacket pocket.

"I went straight home," I replied.

"And you didn't go back, maybe sneak away from the house, or see Shamus or the rest after you supposedly left, did you?"

I was not smart enough to understand the grammatical hash the chief made of the sentence, but I knew he was asking me to admit if I had done something wrong. I was beginning to get an understanding of the power of police authority. I was scared.

"I can confirm that, Chief," interjected Dad. "He got home around ten to four. My wife and I left for the symposium at the college at four, and he was still there."

The mention of Shamus brought on a new round of sniffling and crying from Shamus's mother and a look of compassion from the pastor's wife from the kitchen door. The police radios continued to crackle.

The chief's pen scratched notes in his book. He was winding up for another question when the pastor's wife and Sam brought in a tray of coffee and cookies. The Cosmans didn't respond, and no one asked me if I wanted anything.

The coffee was served in china cups and on saucers with paper dollies. The chief had to wrestle with his notebook, pen, and coffee. He was a mug man, and the cup looked lost and afraid in his paws. I also realized his gun belt was making a mess of the chair, scratching grooves in the arms and back.

The chief juggled, took a sip, complimented Mrs. Smithy, put his cup down, and started to say something only to be interrupted by the chirpy pastor's wife.

"Would anyone like any else? I can make sandwiches."

She got no takers, though, like most thirteen-year-old. I was constantly hungry and would have gleefully dispatched one or more sandwiches.

"Was Shamus"— more sniffling—"okay when you left him?" asked the chief.

"Yes, sir. We were tired from hauling the sleds, but he was fine." As I said those words, I made perhaps the first consequential decision of my life but didn't know it. I wasn't then or now a liar by trade or choice. In less foreboding situations, I would have bubbled on.

There was a creeping feeling of unease, of doubt, of concern that what I said now could mean trouble. Countering that for the first time, my conscience tried to direct my actions. My natural honesty and the teachings of my parents said, *Tell them*, but the dangerous sense of unease said, *No—danger*.

I didn't mention the spot or the harsh words.

The pastor suggested prayer. At that point, the chief said, "I have what I need," and he stood to leave.

The pastor's wife led him and us to the door.

Sam, the other cop, said, "I wouldn't leave town; there might be more questions," in a tone that was simultaneously arrogant, controlling, and accusatory.

What a jerk, I thought.

Given my narration, you might assume I connected all the dots: crying parents, cops, questions, the pastor and wife, and Dad's serious mien. Perhaps, I didn't want to make the connection.

On the way home, I finally asked, "Dad, is Shamus okay?"

He pulled to the curb, and we sat silently. I could almost hear his mind working. "I guess in all the agitation, no one told you." He paused for a bit, looking for a graceful way to say the horrible words. "As I understand it, Shamus went down the hill on his sled into the woods. He didn't get up, and the other kids realized he was hurt and called the cops. I'm so sorry, David. Shamus is dead."

My best friend was dead, and our last words were in anger. Nietzsche said the contemplation of death was the motivator of almost everything humans did, but few thirteen-year-olds in the West have any understanding of death. Fewer have any knowledge of Nietzsche. Few kids from middle-class families in small Christian communities in those days had a lot of knowledge about death, and the media didn't glorify it the way it does now.

When we got home, I was limp. I ached, my brain whirled, I wanted to cry, and so I did.

Mom was waiting for us, and she did those things that make moms so wonderful. She hugged me, rocking me back and forth, saying "I'm sorry" over and over like she wanted to transfer my hurt to herself.

I went to bed, but I knew I wouldn't sleep, and I didn't. I was allowed to miss school the next day.

When I did go back, my schoolmates pestered me for details I couldn't supply. One of the kids, Orlando Davidow, spun a typical teenage boy story: long on gore and short on facts. He hadn't been there. In his rendering, Shamus's head had split wide open, and his brains were all over everything, and the other kids should have been taken to the hospital because human brains were dangerous if they got into your mouth or eyes. He knew this because his grandfather was a butcher. I told him to shut up, and we got into a pushing match before I walked away.

As I returned home from school that day, I opened the door and let one of the great destroyers of the human psyche, guilt, into my world. It came from realizing my last words with my best friend had been harsh ones, and the thought of him going wherever dead kids went thinking badly of me weighted me down.

I began to realize that if the police talked to everyone who had been there, someone would likely tell them about the harsh words between Shamus and me and even mention that I thought I had seen a spot on Shamus's head. I had seen enough Perry Mason TV shows to know that lying to the cops would inspire more questions from the police and would make me look guilty.

My parents knew that death without perspective was meaningless. They also knew that expressed or not, I was suffering and that the sufferer most wants their struggle to be acknowledged. Mom took the position that Shamus's death warned us all that life could be short and that loss was unavoidable. For the first time, she acknowledged my brother's death and how she could have wallowed in her sense of loss but instead cherished the gift I represented. Dad unsurprisingly took a more academic view. He focused on death and suffering as a way to gain knowledge. To him, the gentle soul that he was, any death was a loss, but death was part of life. For Dad, death was a calling to refocus on the present and the joys of life. It was a reminder of the blessing life represented.

I left to go to my room and do my homework.

Dad followed me. "David, this is a big shock, and you probably don't know how to act or what to feel, but it would be better if you could talk to your mother and me about your feelings. It might give you a way to deal with your grief."

I really didn't want to talk about it, not because I wasn't grieving but because I didn't know what to say. It wasn't just the death that was affecting me, it was my foreknowledge of it, and I had no way to explain that. Emotions serve various functions in daily life, calling our attention to important events and motivating and directing subsequent behavior. But fueled by hormones, emotions in the teenage years throw up barriers to knowledge that seem insurmountable.

It took an easy way out—denial. Shamus's death still didn't seem real. Shamus wasn't dead. It was some cosmic joke. All I knew for sure was I felt numb inside.

It would be years before Elizabeth Kubler Ross formulated the stages of grief, but I didn't need her help. I have never forgotten how I felt, sitting there on a snowbound street, silver moonlight glistening on the snow, in the relative silence of the car, feeling lonely and believing that my loneliness was selfish. I was flummoxed. Shamus died of a cerebral hematoma or brain bleeding caused by a tree branch crushing his temporal bone. The coroner ruled it an accidental death, but I knew something the others didn't. Knowing what I had seen made me even less comfortable.

My numbness didn't last long, nor did my denial. I quickly moved to anger. I took it out on everyone—my siblings, friends, anyone who crossed my path. I wasn't sure why I was so angry. Was it that Shamus was taken at thirteen and I thought my life would be empty without my best friend, or was I mad at myself? My reactions represented an emotional upheaval far beyond a thirteen-year-old's pay grade. There weren't grief counselors and therapists on every street corner and no antidepressants. You had to get through grief, some did, and some didn't.

I had seen an indication of the death wound, but I did nothing other than try to get him to wipe it away. Could I have prevented his death if I had persisted? I didn't know how to answer the question, but it was there, and I became convinced if I had done more, he might have lived.

I had no resources to understand or contextualize it, so I did what most people would have done: I pushed it down inside me and went back to being lonely. I shut the door of my culpability but opened the door for shame to enter.

Over the coming decades, I would spend a ton of mental energy contemplating the difference between guilt and shame, two words frequently used interchangeably, promiscuously, and incorrectly. At this point, I had no way of separating the two, even if I knew the difference.

Guilt is an internal emotion stemming from doing something wrong or failing to do something. Its focus is on things and actions, not the self. The individual can deal with it, and resolution helps motivate and direct behavior. Unresolved guilt leads to self-doubt and loss of confidence. In my mind, I was guilty because I saw the spot and didn't do enough or really anything to change the outcome. I was also guilty because I hadn't told anyone, including the police.

Shame is about the self and a person's perception of themselves. When a person feels bad about who they are as a person because they have mistreated someone, that is shame. People who dwell in shame have a hard time forgiving themselves. The shame began to develop because I couldn't forgive myself for not stopping Shamus, and it reinforced itself when I started to think back on my past. All I could see were the mistakes and fumbles in my life. Shame interprets all things as bad. I exhibited a classic shame mechanism, and I was withdrawing and trying to escape my bad feelings about myself.

Even though I couldn't express it, my real concern was that something was wrong with me, it made me different, and I was so emotionally volatile that I needed to fit in and be accepted more than anything. Now to some extent, mostly in my mind, I would be the boy who saw death. I hoped what happened was a one-time thing, and everyone would forget about it.

No such luck.

The day after Thanksgiving was Shamus's funeral. Pastor Smithy tried to make sense of the senseless and failed, although he did use a sentence in one of his prayers that stuck with me.

He said, "Lord, thank you for this moment of death so that we can reflect on the joy of living."

Shamus's father tried to make sense of it and succeeded in making me feel worse. As his closest friend, I might have said something, but I couldn't do it, and I have always felt bad I didn't. If not for him, then for me.

They had lunch, and I left the service with only my appetite satisfied. I felt worse if anything. The bad feelings I had about myself increased. It cemented in my mind the fact that sometimes it takes years for people to realize that there is an end of life called death, and it's irreversible. The unchanging nature of death, especially if one feels responsibility, often directs a person to contemplate regrets, guilt, and remorse. It would be years before I realized the true impact of living with those feelings was a kind of death in and of itself.

The fight reinforced my shame. The Monday after Thanksgiving, we were leaving school, and Steve Xanders said, "Hey, MacIntosh, you asshole, how do you feel about killing Shamus?"

Everyone looked at him.

"Yeah, you told him he had a spot on his head right here." He pointed to the area where the branch had hit Shamus. "And that's where the branch killed him. You could have stopped him, but you didn't. His last words were him calling you an asshole. You were supposed to be his friend."

"What's up with him seeing a spot on Shamus's head?" DeBain Ellsworth asked.

"Apparently, MacIntosh thinks he's like that army guy on *Twilight Zone* who saw a weird light on people before they died. He said there was a spot on Shamus's head right here." Xanders pointed to his temple. "Whadya know, that's where the branch hit Shamus." He turned around to face me and opened his mouth ready to spit out more accusations. "You told him before his last run that he hadn't driven the sleds right; you could've gone further and broken the record. Then you ran away, he went down again to prove you wrong, and he got killed, asshole!" Xanders got right up in my face, poking me in the chest with his finger.

12

I had not seen the TV episode he was describing. You didn't just get the TV remote and go to on-demand. In those days, there were no remotes; on-demand was called reruns.

They were all looking at me, waiting for an answer. I didn't have one, so I fell on the age-old response. "Fuck you, Xanders, I didn't do anything wrong."

"That's right, you did nothing and got him killed, you shithead! He's dead because you killed him."

Another guy said Shamus was stupid and deserved to die because of his route on the fatal run. This jerk was blaming Shamus! It pissed me off even more than Xanders's stupidity. It wasn't much of a fight, just a lot of swearing, pushing, and threats mixed in with a few ill-directed punches. Xanders and I got detention. It was reported to our parents and became the talk of the entire school.

The fight soon faded for most but not for me.

As I look back on the situation from my current perch, I see how foolish I was. I assumed the guilt and blame for Shamus's death which was not mine. While I had seen the spot before the accident, I could not connect the two events. I should not have felt guilt or shame, but I did.

Often, we misunderstand what we are guilty of. We convince ourselves of our guilt for small things to avoid addressing our feelings about more significant issues. The result is we fail to learn the proper lessons, and our guilt continues, and we feel worse. If we learn from guilt and change, guilt becomes what psychologists call a positive affective emotion. When not addressed, guilt morphs into shame, especially when the guilt gets reinforced by others' constant reminders of your mistake.

I knew my classmates were condemning me, whispering about me, and making jokes at my expense. Others—bolder perhaps but, in my estimation, stupider—made fun of me, directly calling me all sorts of names. I believed I was poison; no one wanted to be around me. I withdrew, telling myself I needed not to put myself out there; it was better to be alone than risk criticism.

One of the hallmarks of depression is a feeling of worthlessness. I started to think I had no purpose on earth, and that it would have been better if I had died, not Shamus. I was ashamed of having done nothing. I walked through the remainder of the school year in a daze. I remember little of it other than the events surrounding Shamus's death. Your first death is like your first love, first sex, and marriage; it is always the first and most memorable for being premier.

*****

All people have secrets and demons. They push secrets down deep inside themselves and wall off the demons to prevent them from destroying life. Secrets lead to lies and lies to webs of deceit. When exposed to the light, you often wonder why this was a secret after all, and the demons become less intimidating, but to the person who has them, they are so horrifying.

In the end, I think what led me to wall off my secret and demon was fear of reprisal. The teenage years are years of conformity. A few branch off and uphold their own individuality, but most seek the crowd to give them meaning. I couldn't very well go around talking about seeing death. No one wants Cassandra or Jeremiah around.

In Wheaton's rather strait-laced religious environment, my visions would be viewed as some sort of possession by evil. I wasn't very bright, but I did know how cruel people, especially children, could be, even if unintended.

I sucked up my fears, pushed down my secret and demon, and went on feeling that somehow the world had victimized me by taking my friend.

American history is full of years and decades of consequence. The 1960s were a decade of consequence. It started with hope and ended in dismay. A new generation came of age; politics went from a noble calling to a collection of craven opportunists. Society discovered its ills but decided to solve them by turning to government and decadence. It was a decade Dickensian in contradiction.

The news media also began to change. We had the old war horses around like Walter Cronkite, Edward R. Murrow, and others who carried with them the honorable nature of the press. For some reason, the press began to report the news as a caricature, and they had a picture-perfect matchup for President Kennedy as he was young and handsome, and Nixon was older but also had a distinguishing nose and five o'clock shadow. It seemed to me that every picture of Nixon had him scowling or sneering with a heavy bread. He looked like a character out of film noir, but Kennedy always looked angelic.

Mayor Daly of Chicago, a lot of dead voters, and crooked vote counting led to the election of a new president in 1960. With the passing of the baton from the former general, a hero of WWII, to a younger man, we thought we were emerging from long years of somnolence into a new world. All presidential elections are impactful, but somehow the election of 1960 was deemed to be ushering in a new epoch. Perhaps it was the impact of television, maybe it was the last gasp of imagination, or it could have been an artful manipulation. The election of a young president with a beautiful wife and young children was cast as a return to the misty past of Arthurian myth, of Avalon, and of the magic of Camelot. It was crafted as a return to a time of stately people, of blemish-proof knights on virtuous quests, and of courtly love and chivalry. In short—Utopia.

The year 1960 was the high point of nirvana because events long in gestation were finally born. If anyone had been truly clairvoyant in 1960, they would have run away and hidden.

In June of 1962, the Supreme Court declared prayer in school violated the First Amendment. For most of us, prayer in school wasn't an issue. We never conceived people of other faiths, or no religion might be offended by prayer to a Christian God. No one we knew ever expressed any discomfort, including my anti-religious mother or her parents. Anton had written numerous columns advocating for prayer to provide a moral underpinning for youth.

In Wheaton, where the separation of church and state ranged from minuscule to nonexistent, the ruling was a thunderbolt. It was denounced in the local paper and harangued by every preacher and pastor who could find a pulpit. Earl Warren, the Chief Justice, was the devil's tool; lawyers were godless idolaters (that one might be true). They and all who supported this affront to God were irredeemably bound for hell; all said with the thundering certainty of self-righteousness, brooking no response.

Mom and Dad treated it as a teaching moment. They took the occasion to amplify our civics instruction in school and taught us about the framing of the Constitution, and the Bill of Rights, of the evils stemming from state-established religions. In Dad's view, life was not a right full of freedoms. Life was a privilege full of responsibilities.

One of those responsibilities was to be respectful of the rights of others. They pointed out that the phrase "separation of church and state" was not found in the Constitution or Bill of Rights but a letter from Thomas Jefferson.

Naturally, we children had discussions about prayer, full of the unfocused passions, imperfect knowledge, and flawed logic of youth. I approached the conversations using the concepts Mom and Dad gave me. Huge mistake!

I tried out the intellectual argument with some of my schoolmates, and a girl named Leslie Bennett took what I said badly. Leslie's father was the college's provost. He was ordained and had been a pastor before going on to be a full-time academic.

Leslie was adamant about the certainty of my habitation with Satan and shunned me, but she went one step further, she told her father I was getting these blasphemous ideas from my father, so Dad got a chewing out from the provost.

I was pissed off. Leslie had gotten my father in trouble solely because she wouldn't consider another viewpoint. Her shunning and condemnation combined with my continuing guilt over my part in Shamus's death fertilized the new shoots of my feelings that there was something wrong with me. Like many people faced with an audience ready to condemn, I stopped discussing things. The rigidity which often afflicts the religious mind suppressed the flowering of an inquiring young mind.

Dad bore no hostility toward the Provost or Leslie; he wasn't concerned about who did what they did. He was concerned about what we should learn from the experience. I, of course, thought the lesson was to not talk about things. He pointed out that silence in the face of evil endorses evil.

The real lesson was not to let emotion undermine logic and knowledge.

Later that same year, there was an indication the Lord might have been angry with us for banning school prayer. Lots of people who never prayed before wore their knees out. In October 1962, the U2 spy plane revealed that the Russians had installed missiles with nuclear warheads in Cuba, touching off the Cuban missile crisis.

We had bomb drills in school and frequent messages from civil defense, which convinced us we were just minutes away from being blown to bits. There was a mini-boom in people building fall-out shelters in their yards. The world held its collective breath as our inexperienced president confronted the Russians with an ultimatum that could have led to the commencement of a nuclear war. Since the end of World War II, we have never been as close to war as in those terrible weeks.

The road to Utopia is never smooth and is frequently a dead end. So it was with our route to Camelot. In early 1960, a group of people sat down at a segregated lunch counter at a North Carolina drugstore and refused to move in protest to segregation, and a new word and technique entered our lexicon's "sit-in." We had little knowledge of the fundamental issues, but how fast prejudice and hate came to the surface was amazing.

We were only gauzily aware of race problems. There were no blacks in our school. Most of us had never interacted with black people, even though the college had a solid record of helping slaves escape, and many people employed blacks as house cleaners, cooks, or landscapers.

Suddenly, our attitudes on race were challenged by demonstrations and films on television showing violence against people who seemed peaceful. We started to hear calls for black people to have the same rights as whites. We were so sheltered we didn't know they didn't have the same rights.

Another word had joined the lexicon around the same time, actually a spate of new words. Astronauts, the space race, missile gap, NASA. For all the civil rights crises and Cuban missiles, there were the dreams of going to the moon, into space, and of building a new world.

I stayed in the middle of the pack in high school and didn't play sports or do many after-school activities. I was perfectly happy not dating, although I got lonely because all my friends were, which left me with a lot of time on my hands. I found myself drawn to the space race. I remember how wonderful it was to go outside at night and see the traces of satellites across the sky. I thought I wanted to be an astronaut for a while, but my weakness in science and math killed that idea.

Many of us had embraced the Camelot concept to the disgust of our conservative Republican parents, but dreams are the bailiwick of youth. The nation was like a pot full of water, slowly getting ready to boil, and it boiled over. In June of '63, the National Guard had to force the Governor of Alabama to admit a black student to the University of Alabama. Two months later, Martin Luther King led a march in Washington and gave one of the greatest speeches in the English language, regrettably followed by a series of bombings of black churches in the South.

A few years in the future, Don McLean would record the monster hit *American Pie*, mourning the loss of some musicians. Regardless of its intent, it would quickly come to symbolize the loss of innocence our nation and my generation were experiencing. Death had come to us all, and Kennedy's death in 1963 would not be the last of the year. Before Christmas, news reached us that Donald Ober, a graduate of my high school and Wheaton College, had been killed in Vietnam. Reality grounded our dreams.

Chapter 2

My junior year in 1963 started with me still in the middle of the pack academically. I think I had been on three or four dates, so few I could number them. I continued to drift along through life healthy, reasonably happy, and not a problem for anyone. I began to work during the summers as soon as anyone would hire me. My junior year also marked the beginning of a coming-of-age event—the college bandwagon.

There was a new aspect to the college's decision. The war in Vietnam was heating up, and the draft was operational for the first time since the 1950s. There was a draft deferment if you were in college. While the world and the nation struggled with life and death issues and some people had to fight to sit where they wished on a bus, for us, there was one thing even more important. How were we going to get to Nirvana, a.k.a. California?

For all the tensions and crises, and likely because of them, the 1960s were wonderful for music. We had a folk period. We had the Four Seasons and Motown. The most popular, at least in my group, was the surfing sound of Jan and Dean, Dick and the Del Tones, The Ventures, and of course, the Beach Boys. Listening to them, California was Golconda. The girls were all beautiful, restaurants were all drive-ins with a collection of gorgeous automotive iron on display, all cars were convertibles, the sun shone for eighteen hours a day, even on rainy days, and living was easy.

The long, cold, dark Wheaton winters provided us with time to contemplate. Our dreams centered on Elysium. We had been fired by the ideals of Camelot, of a jump to the moon, of making the world better. While deeming ourselves sophisticates, our callowness provided fruitful ground for manipulating lyrics and movies to name our paradise California. We were sure of our knowledge and destiny, but the only thing we were was solipsistic.

I was among those determined to go to California, and I worked hard that year to make it happen. I even overcame my shyness to the point I scored a date to the prom with Juliette Chido. She was a cheerleader, an A student, and an Audrey Hepburn look-alike. In the prom picture, I look like an actor in a lousy movie, with my ill-fitting diner jacket, poorly tailored pants, and a shirt collar that didn't quite fit, while she looked radiant in a long, slim, white beaded gown with sparkles on it. I was the envy of my peers for thirty seconds.

Shortly after our junior year started, I was with Evan Harris, Sam Cepioda, and a guy we called Wizard. His last name was Wiza, and he came to the US as a refugee from the Hungarian uprising. My high school was playing our longtime rivals, and those games often took on an extraordinary degree of violence and hard-hitting. The buses taking us to the game let us off behind the home team's bleachers, and we had to walk past their fans and suffer their abuse.

Instead of walking around the track, we cut across the end zone. The home team was on the field stretching and doing warm-ups. They didn't have all their pads, jerseys, or helmets on. I noticed one guy in the rear rank, and on his neck, right above the top of his T-shirt, was a long black streak.

It had been almost three years since Shamus's death, a lifetime to a teenager.

I rationalized that the light was bad, the guy was too far away, and it had only been a glance, so there was every logical reason to believe what I had seen was some trick of light and dark. So I went on to my seat. The home team went into the locker room and then returned to the field.

I lost track of the guy with the black streak.

In the third quarter, the home team's number eighty-three went into the game. The center snapped the ball, and eighty-three sprinted about fifteen yards down the field and cut to the middle. The quarterback's pass was slightly high, and eighty-three jumped, catching the ball at full extension. While suspended, one of our defensive backs hit him on the backside of his legs. Eighty-three lost the ball, landed on his neck and shoulders, and didn't move.

Our side cheered loudly; the other side emitted a groan of disappointment. Eighty-three didn't move. I crashed; eighty-three had been the guy with the black mark.

I hoped I was wrong, but the gnawing feeling was hard to ignore. I pushed the sight of the streak out of my head. I didn't want to remember, but it was there knocking on the door of my mind, reminding me this had happened before.

The other players gathered around the unmoving eighty-three. The coaches and trainers ran out from the sidelines. The kid didn't move. The cheering stopped; an eerie hush fell over the field. A doctor was paged. Eighty-three still hadn't moved. There was a conference, and the coaches and players walked off the field, leaving the unmoving eighty-three, the trainers, and the doctor. The sirens blared. Eighty-three still hadn't moved.

The ambulance crew ran out onto the field and, with the help of the trainers and doctor, got the still-unmoving eighty-three on a stretcher. One of his arms flopped uselessly from the side of it, giving a momentary feeling of hope, but the doctor hurriedly tucked it back in. Eighty-three had not moved.

Both teams stood along the sidelines and applauded as they took him off the field. I looked down at our sidelines and could see the defensive back who had hit eighty-three crying and a woman I assumed was his mother held him.

I finally answered the knock of memory at the door of my conscious mind. I knew. I just knew he was dead. I don't know how, but I knew.

For some reason, I said to someone, "He might die," which got me a round of punches, shoves, and hissing from the adults, "How can you say something like that?"

The game recommenced, we won, but there was no news of eighty-three.

He never moved again. He'd broken his neck right where I saw the black streak. He was likely dead on the field. According to one of the girls whose father was a surgeon, death had been painless and instantaneous. That news didn't help me. I had seen the spot, and he died. The connection pounded home its message. The black mark had appeared twice, and twice, the person died within hours.

The defensive back quit the team. I went into a tailspin.

It doesn't take much for an adolescent to believe the weight of the world is on their shoulders. It's a price the young pay for their passions. Successfully migrating to adulthood is measured by how the youngster handles the weight. If successful, they grow to be functioning adults; if not, they end up carrying baggage either literally or metaphorically. My guilt and my building conviction that something was wrong with me now added a new concept: I was causing these deaths.

I was hyperalert to every little noise or motion. I was down all the time, finding no joy in anything, including the holidays. I withdrew to my room. I had rages—towering, monumental foaming-at-the-mouth angry. I punched, and I mean bashed, Eleanor and Peter, the first and last time I felt the belt on the rear.

Uncle Fergus, always to be relied on for sensitivity, told Dad to get me a hooker! The school suggested a psychiatrist, but mental illness was a form of leprosy in those days. So I moved on as well as I could and told no one as I slouched toward anhedonia. Even if I wanted to talk about what happened, I had no language to describe it. I shuffled along through my junior year and through that summer carrying uncertainty, doubt, and depression.

I took responsibility for Shamus's death—actually, my inability to prevent his death—and now I had taken responsibility for the football player's death. I never even knew his name. It ate at me, and it destroyed my self-confidence. Normal people didn't see spots indicating death, but I did, so I was different, and no teenager wants to be singled out as odd. My senior year started, and I continued to drift along without much adulation and without much disparagement.

At some point, most parents have been disappointed with their children. It was hard to believe any parent could ever have been disappointed with Mira Steblow. She was beautiful, a straight-A student, a homecoming queen with an incredible singing voice, and she was active in her church. She had SAT scores with commas in them.

Every college she applied to accepted her. She was recruited by other universities she hadn't applied to, including all the Ivies. In most cases, admission came with full-ride academic scholarships. She was Miss Perfect.

Mia's father was in the same department as Dad. Her parents, who never let an occasion slip by without telling you how wonderful their daughter was, decided to have a self-congratulatory party celebrating the fantastic Mira. The invitation we received included me. I would have rather had a root canal without anesthesia.

One of the women helping at the party was Iris Wagner, the second wife of Phil Wagner. The rumor was that Phil's first wife drank herself to death. Phil was the sales manager of the local New Holland dealer. Phil had two kids from his first marriage, one of whom was in my class. Iris was pregnant, which excited some comments and jokes. It was still a time when "bad girls" in high school got shipped off to have their babies so we wouldn't be "polluted" or think it was okay or even ask questions. Seeing an adult woman pregnant also reminded us our parents were having sex, and no kid wants to think about that.

Iris came out of the kitchen with a heavy tray. We had been taught that pregnant women were delicate and shouldn't exert themselves too much, so I broke off my conversation and hurried over to help her. After transferring the tray, a black stripe remained on her dress. She thanked me for the help, and I considered not saying anything about the black mark. But I thought it was the right thing to do, so I told her she had gotten something on her dress.

Okay, so this was the third time I had seen the black mark.

There were plenty of reasons to believe it wasn't the same thing. Iris had been working in the kitchen, and I knew how often I'd gotten stuff all over me when cooking. Second, death was not the first thing on my mind, and I felt a bit of trepidation that she might have overheard my jokes about Mira. Third, since the football player died, I had not opened the mental box of unexplained mysteries into which I had stuffed the memories of the spots. I didn't want to remember. The memory was too ugly and scary. I didn't attach any meaning to the black mark other than trying to be helpful. I pushed the sight of the streak out of my head. I didn't want to remember.

She thanked me, scurrying off to repair the damage. A couple of us were making jokes like how many minutes would pass before angels descended to crown Mira when Iris sought me out.

"David, you aren't very funny."

I didn't know if she had overheard our jokes, but I blushed in any case.

"About what?" I mumbled past the cake in my mouth, uncertain about what she meant.

"You said I had a stain on my dress, and there isn't one. Practical jokes are dumb. You should be ashamed," Iris said.

The memories of other black streaks and spots pushed their way into my mind all at the same time.

I was getting a bad feeling, and in my head, I could almost see a figure sitting there, pounding on a table to get my attention to tell me this was the same thing as I had seen before.

"I'm sorry," I said. "I thought there was a stain." I could have ended the situation right there, just by saying I was wrong, but I didn't.

"I can still see it on the front of your dress." I pointed to her baby bump, which wasn't a bump as much as a watermelon.

"You're a very bad boy to keep making fun, especially of a woman who is expecting. No one else sees anything there. It's not funny. I have a good mind to tell your parents."

I didn't know what to say. We were taught to respect our elders. We were at a party in someone else's home, which called for decorum, but I was getting mad. I got defensive at her accusation. For me, little else ignited anger more quickly than injustice. This wasn't going to end well. As in the case of Shamus, no one else could see the black streak.

Could it be happening again?

I was confused. If this was a sign of death, I should tell her, but would anyone believe me at this point? The situation was out of hand and not going to get better with me saying something like that. I was supposed to be respectful to adults, not challenging.

The anger of the injustice won. I was trying to help her. I was being honest; I wasn't lying. I dug in. "I don't care. I see a stain on

your dress. Tell my parents if you like, it's still there." I wasn't assertive. I was aggressive in tone and manner.

Phil steamed through the crowd a few minutes later like a
freighter with his tug, Iris in tow. Iris was in tears. I think Phil was
drunk. In any case, he grabbed me by the shoulder and shook me,
yelling at me about what a jerk I was.

Dad saw what was developing and came over. The situation got
ugly fast.

"You this jerk's dad?" Phil slurred, pinching my shoulder harder
and pushing me toward Dad to emphasize his point.

"Yes," replied Dad. "Let's take this outside and not disturb the
party."

Phil ignored the request. "This little shit," he said, squeezing me
even harder.

I tried to twist away to no avail.

"He's upsetting my wife, and you need to smack him."

"He will be punished as we see fit if we verify the facts," said
Dad.

People try to be rational with drunks and always fail.

"The only fact you need to know, bud"—Phil released my
shoulder, stabbing his index finger at Dad's chest—"is that your asshole kid is pulling some joke on my wife, and she's upset. You slap
him across the head, or I will."

"You do, and I'll have you arrested," Dad said as calmly as he
could.

I was not as calm; it was my head.

Phil raised his hand to slap me.

"Don't—you will get in real trouble," Dad said.

The large meaty hand sheered down and landed on the side of
my head like a thunderbolt. I saw stars and staggered off-balance,
almost falling over a chair. My head rang, my ear hurt, and my face
was stinging both from the impact and embarrassment. A party
focused on Mira was now fixated on our tableau. I had my hand to
my face. Dad was pissed off and fighting for control, Phil was smugly
smiling, and Iris was crying.

Then a terrible swift sword flew into battle. Mom, in full protective cry, flew out of the crowd. She let loose one of her tirades of choice language and epithets about Phil, his manhood, and general assholeness.

Dad physically restrained her from attacking Phil. The smart money would have taken Mom in that exchange, but Phil added gasoline to the fire. "You should slap the mouth off your bitch too!"

Luckily, Mira's father, Reverend Doctor Steblow, stepped in, taking Phil and Iris aside. Phil was still truculent and Iris crying. Mom was in full fury. We made our goodbyes and left.

Going home, we were as silent as three pissed-off people can be. I was physically hurt. My ear still rang from the impact, and I was embarrassed at being bitch-slapped in front of my friends. Mom was seething, making little sounds like a teakettle with the top on too tightly. Dad's hands gripped the wheel, knuckles prominent. All comments were short and sharp.

I knew the dreaded questioning and comments would come.

On Sunday, Dad called Phil and asked him to apologize. He refused with abusive language. Now Dad had to decide if he was going to take legal action, and what I had to say would be central to that decision. I was pretty stupid, but I knew things were about to get very complex.

Over the next several decades, I read and studied Viktor Frankl's book *Man's Search for Meaning*. Frankel talks about a place between impulse and action, the place where choice lies. Each action has costs. I was in one of those places. I had not told anyone about seeing the mark on Shamus, although Xanders had alluded to it. I had not mentioned the black streak on the football player, and only a few people heard me mention the black mark to Iris, so I was in this alone, and that was a scary place to be.

I was in an unusual position. The choice before me was to tell the truth as I knew it and face unknown consequences or lie and have it pass away after a while. My truth here would be less believable than the lie. The truth could and likely would bring reactions and consequences far greater than the lie.

My thinking in my emotionally driven, hormone-fueled bowl of unformed mush I was using as a brain was not so clear, but I knew I was in a difficult spot.

My impulse was to lie, to make it go away. To make my parents believe me about what happened with Iris, I would have to tell them about the other times, and they still might not—probably wouldn't—believe me. If I lied, it could all go away with some short-term embarrassment. I might even be able to spin it at school as a joke played on an adult like getting someone to page Mike Hunt on a public address system.

With a lie, I could control the outcome. With the truth, the results were unknown, which was scary to someone whose whole life had been hiding in the middle.

Lies and truth are opposite in obvious ways, but there is a hidden cost to lying. It's slow to develop and often ignored. The more lies you tell, the more you consume mental bandwidth. Lying is often justified because it spares others' pain, but lying transfers the pain to the liar. Building your life on a skein of lies rots the soul, creating the basis for real shame that there is something wrong with you.

Young adulthood is the time when a person begins to deal with right or wrong and good or evil, and that discernment has a real consequence when a person feels the impact of moral conscience. At eighteen, I could clearly hear the voice of conscience directing me toward the truth, but there was something indescribable gnawing at me, a strong force dragging me to lie.

When I contemplated what the truth might bring, I grew frightened. If I told the truth, my vision of the streak on Iris's dress, the issue would be my integrity, not Phil's actions. My statement would be taken as the creation of an overactive, sinister mind. If I told the truth and no one believed me, Phil would walk away with no consequences.

On the other hand, if I lied about what I saw or didn't see, my parents would be upset that I had dragged them into this, and they would press me for answers as to why I acted as I did, but that was manageable. Truth left me afraid and unsure.

Dad and Mom sat me down. "David, we need to go through the events at the Steblow's with Phil and Iris Wagner. Phil and Iris say you were pulling a practical joke on Iris. Were you? The truth is important here, son."

"It wasn't a joke, Dad, Mom. I saw a large black streak on her dress here." I ran my hands across my abdomen. "She thanked me at first for telling her."

"Then what happened?" asked Mom.

They were working a variation of good cop and bad cop, and I realized the lying route would end badly. One of them would figure out I was lying, so I didn't have to decide.

"She came out and asked if it was gone." I didn't remember her doing that, but it seemed fitting.

"What did you say?" asked Dad. "This is important."

"I told her it was still there."

Mom and Dad looked at each other.

Dad said, "We talked to Iris and looked at her dress; there's no mark on it anywhere."

For the first time in my life, I realized that when an authority figure asks a question, they usually already know the answer. The facts didn't support the truth I'd experienced.

I had a flashback to the day of Shamus's death; none of the other kids could see the spot, and I had just assumed other people could see it if I could. A lie would actually have been more believable.

There it was again; lies needed to be constructed when the truth was evident. But the truth wasn't apparent. I started down the path of truth with all good intentions, and now my truth was in doubt because the evidence of the senses did not provide corroboration. The voice in the back of my head was getting louder, telling me to lie, to protect myself, and to avoid branding myself a liar even though what I was saying was true.

"I saw the mark, Dad, Mom," I said pleadingly.

"Is it possible it was a shadow?" Dad asked.

"Or a wet spot?" Mom chimed in.

They were shaking my confidence in the path I had chosen. I jumped up from my chair and was standing behind it like it was a shield.

"I don't know," I said, "it was black across her belly."

"David," Dad said in a moderating tone, "you have to understand this is serious. This could end up in a lawsuit. You"—he emphasized with a pointed finger—"would have to tell your story under oath. Phil could go to jail, and if you"—he paused, the intellectual searching for the right word—"are massaging the facts, it will come out and be really bad for you. There is no evidence of a spot on Iris's dress. We aren't about to let Phil get away with assaulting you. He was wrong, but we can't take action without proof, and right now, we don't have any."

"I saw the spot. I'm not lying!" I was almost yelling, and the strength of my denial shocked them.

"Okay," they both said, edging away both physically and verbally, "we can talk about this another time when you aren't so upset."

I was scared and confused. Being patronized as an unstable teenager didn't help my temper. There seemed no way out.

Mom and Dad never raised the issue of Iris Wagner with me again.

There was some talk at school about me getting slapped, but it faded quickly, thanks to other distractions. College acceptance letters rolled in. I got into Illinois (they almost had to take me), someplace in West Virginia (West Virginia!), which I didn't remember applying to, and Chapman College in Orange, California. The jackpot!

Take that, Miss Perfect Steblow. You can freeze your ass off in Massachusetts. I'm going to California! And not just California but the home of surfing and the Beach Boys—Southern California! In our idolization of California, I don't think we realized there was a northern part of the state. There was no doubt where I was going. If I had to sell my soul, I was going to California. Which, when I started looking at the costs seemed like it might be the only way I could go.

In the mid-'60s, it was still not intended that everyone would go to college. It wasn't a hard class thing like Thomas Hardy described in Jude the Obscure, but going to college was expensive. Admissions were limited. There was no student loan program, so college was an actual out-of-pocket expense, and many people couldn't afford it. In those years, high schools did a far better job of preparing graduates for life than today, and there were admirable career paths open to those who didn't go to college. Mom and Dad knew a college degree would be essential in the future, so they expected us all to go.

Chapman was twice the price of Illinois, and the incidental expenses would be higher. Mom and Dad tried hard to convince me to go to Champaign, but the more they pushed, the more I was determined to go to Chapman. It was a lesson I took to heart when I had children. College is the first adult decision a child makes. Let them make it. If you try to influence it, they will do the opposite. My parents finally agreed, but I would have to find a way to bear more costs.

That same year, Dad was offered and accepted a full professorship at Northwestern, and the family prepared to move to Evanston. When the Korean War broke out, Dad had been an assistant professor at Northwestern when he was drafted Northwestern fired him. While the prestige and increased income were indeed welcome, the revenge had to be sweet.

I had one last summer in Wheaton.

I worked two jobs that summer, Monday through Friday. I was a laborer at a steel warehouse for eight hours a day plus occasional overtime, and I worked part-time at one of the hardware stores. I was in the hardware store one Saturday, and Phil Wagner came in. He looked like he had fought a battle with a whiskey bottle and been routed. He took one look at me, and the shit hit the fan.

His flaccid face became animated, and the distended veins around his discolored nose seemed to expand. His rheumy eyes suddenly became clear. His whole body tensed, his eyes narrowed to slits, and his lips drew into a snarl exposing yellow teeth. His fists balled; this was a man ready to release the rage which lay in him.

You can be angry for a long time; it does you no good, but it's possible. Rage, however, is hard to maintain. It needs to be released; both are soul-sicknesses, and both demand more of the mind and body than can be sustained. Anger is a churning, gnawing drive to address an injustice. Rage is a hand grenade with the pin out and the spoon gone.

Phil's was vibrating like the waves of heat off a road. His neck and face turned pink, then red, and finally scarlet as waves of rage splashed against the walls of his reserve.

"You fucking little shit!" He pointed directly at me, removing any doubt about who he was cursing. "You shouldn't be allowed out, you fucker!"

Everyone in hearing range was perplexed. I was terrified. Hardware stores in those days were as much social gatherings as places of commerce. The place was crowded, and here was a grown man, looking like a stroke seeking a home, yelling horrible words at me.

Phil was still screaming, "Don't look at me like I'm the crazy one here!" He paused to wave his arms to include everyone. "That little fucker"—he pointed at me—"killed my son and my wife, cost me my job, and my house. I'm gonna give you the beating you deserve." He grabbed a piece of one-inch pipe, raising it as he advanced on me.

I cowered.

Mr. De Angelo, the store owner who was about eighty, stepped between Phil and me. He wasn't going to stop Phil for long, but it was long enough.

An off-duty cop was there and pulled his badge and said, "Sir, you need to put down the pipe before this gets out of hand."

Phil's momentum toward me stopped, his hands wavered, and the pipe came down slowly.

Mr. De Angelo turned to me. "David, go home now."

I ran the entire two miles.

My parents never told me the rest of the story. There had been no need for Mom and Dad to take any action. One of the deputy county prosecutors had been at Mira's party. There were too many witnesses to ignore the assault. Phil pled guilty to misdemeanor assault. There was less tolerance in those days and less crime. New Holland fired him. He couldn't find work for a long time and lost his house in foreclosure. If the tale of woe wasn't enough, Iris's baby was stillborn. In her grief, she hung herself. Phil found her.

In small towns, stories spread fast. Soon the incident at the hardware was linked to Mira's party and then inevitably to Shamus's death. I felt a terrible sense of guilt for what happened to Phil, Iris, and their family. If I had not said anything, then Phil would not have hit me and would not have had to plead guilty. They wouldn't have lost the house, and who knows, maybe both Iris and her baby would have lived.

I was bearing the terrible burden of secrets and the knowledge that I was a bringer of death and had killed four people just because I existed. I was convinced everyone in town was staring at me. Any whispered conversation was about me, and not favorable.

One night at the movies, one of my classmates, Garrett Simpansky, saw me and said, "Hey, baby killer, there are seats in the front."

I went home after the movie and told Mom and Dad. They knew I was struggling.

"Kids can be very cruel to one another. They're looking for you to react. You need not let this get to you. If you give them what they want, they win, and they will do it more."

It was an excellent rubric and given with sincerity but incomplete knowledge. It didn't solve my internal conflict that something was wrong with me and that somehow I had done wrong. It was not a happy summer for me. I was carrying the weight of the world on my shoulders, and it merged with the sadness of leaving a place we had called home for thirteen years and the trepidation of leaving for college.

CHAPTER 3

I got ready to leave for California. California! I still had a hard time believing I was going. I thought I was ready. Combining my parent's contribution with my savings, I had enough money for my freshman year. Beyond that, I would have to hustle to earn enough. I was dedicated to my course and committed to living in California, but I started to worry.

I began to think about what would happen if I couldn't find the money, the humiliation of having to come home to go to Illinois, what my parents would think about me, and then what if I failed? I would spend the rest of my life working in a steel mill.

Just as my catastrophic thinking was reaching a peak and I was getting more and more convinced that I would not be able to live my dream, a windfall came my way. Mom's parents, Anton and Samantha, announced they would pay for my entire first year, tuition, books, and room and board. I was stunned. Of the two sets of grandparents, they were second in my order of affection. My financial worries were largely gone, and I started to kick myself for being so pessimistic and depressed. there was really no basis for it, but depressed people often can't see the potential good sides of things. After all my worrying, I had two years of college paid.

Flying was still an expensive luxury, and driving our wreck of a car was out of the question. It was so bad that even as a car-crazed teenager, I was ashamed to drive it. To drive 2,500 miles across the desert with four kids and where air conditioning meant rolling down a window, bordered on insanity. I took one of the last runs of Santa Fe's legendary Super Chief to Los Angeles and used buses to get to Orange. I thought Chicago was enormous; the LA basin made it look Lilliputian.

As I worked my way to Orange and the college, I saw the Hollywood sign up on the hills. I heard Spanish spoken in everyday commerce for the first time. I saw street signs with Spanish names and restaurants serving foods from nations I only knew from geography. It was exciting, mysterious, and strange. California hooked me the moment I stepped off the train. I would always be a Californian.

Chapman's campus is east of downtown Orange. The downtown looked like a Norman Rockwell painting. In later years, its quaintness would make it the backdrop for many movies set in the 1950s and 1960s. Five miles west was the now ten-year-old Magic Kingdom. Its nightly fireworks would become one of the background sounds of my life.

Chapman was growing fast. The college dated back to 1861 and was affiliated with a church, which apparently had slipped by Mom's gaze. Like Wheaton, it had always been a leader in admissions, and from its founding had admitted women and minorities. The college actively recruited students, reaching out to places like Chicago, New York, and Cleveland. In the depth of a Midwest winter meeting with people with seamless all-body tans, hair kissed by the sun was a highly effective strategy.

Driving Chapman's growth was an alumnus who was making a fortune mowing down orange groves and turning desert land into houses. I enrolled as a business major, having little idea of the curriculum and even less idea of a career path. It seemed to offer the best set of options.

In grade school, we did the hard grunt work of memorizing math tables, grammar rules, sentence construction, cursive writing, and of course, my bête noire penmanship. In high school, we learned more rote work and how to apply it to solve problems. College, however, was where you learned to think and think critically. Thinking, I have come to realize, is rarer than common sense. I bloomed academically. My mediocre high school grades improved to the high three-point range.

Chapman's drawback was competition; there was too much to do. If you wanted to screw around and not go to classes, there were plenty of places to do it. We were in Disneyland's back door, the golden beaches just beyond. To the north, Hollywood, the land of illusion, south San Diego, and Mexico. I had no trouble resisting the sirens.

Several fraternities rushed me, but there was no way I could afford that life, and it was unattractive to me. As I often did later, I missed the real story. While being in a frat meant great parties, girls seemed to prefer frat boys, and the frat boys seemed to have a confident, swaggering, boastful attitude. I missed the real upside of fraternity life, an orchard of contacts bearing fruit for the rest of your life.

Dating was another thing separating me from my classmates. Sex was like the national sport, certainly at college. It was all the guys seemed to talk about and seek out. I wasn't interested. My lack of interest wasn't due to an inability or orientation; I wasn't even remotely interested in men. I wasn't male model material, but I wasn't Quasimodo either.

I had not dated a lot in high school, and even though I had two sisters, I knew nothing about women. Dating, for all its wonders, is hard work. It exposes you to personal rejection and personal hurt. I had no wish to be hurt or rejected.

I didn't esteem myself very highly. I didn't know the truth of the statement that motion changes emotion, and that by acting confident, I could be confident. When I contemplated asking a girl out, I became fearful and rationalized my way out of it. She already had a boyfriend, she's a bitch, she's not very pretty, she would never go out with me, I'm not attractive, and so on.

Third, I wasn't then or now a fan of gamesmanship, subterfuge, half-truths, or mendacious behavior. From what my friends said, that was all that went on in dating.

The only valid reason was my low self-esteem. It came from being in the middle, never succeeding or failing added to my mediocrity. I was also concerned because I bore what was, at least for now, a secret curse.

Immunology counts on the idea of getting a little bit sick to prevent significant sickness. In other times, before we became so fearing of germs that hand sanitizer became ubiquitous, kids were always dirty, sticking their hands in their mouths and eyes, eating dirt or whatever, and all of it improved their immune systems.

You learn self-esteem. You learn it by success, which is tempered with a voice whispering, "All glory is fleeting." It's learned from failing and rising again after each failure, and the lessons it bore made you less likely to fail again. Failure was like a string of minor sicknesses. Success always brings forth many authors in our society, but failure is autobiography. I had always been in the middle. I was happy there. There is no demand on the average. There's a warm and comfortable feeling from being in the center of a flock of sheep. Teachers tended to leave you alone, happy you weren't testing them as you might at either end of the spectrum. I never took a risk nor understood the sweetness of risking and winning. I never experienced attempting and failing and learning how not to fail again. I was as much afraid of success as I was of failure.

The three sightings of death were still on my mind. Like all closely held secrets, it changed my personality and outlook. I was about to find out that my fears were well-founded.

In mid-November, my parents told me there would be a full family reunion in Chicago over Christmas, and a ticket for my first-ever plane ride was forthcoming. It would be quite an event with Mom's parents, Angus and Ruth, Uncle Fergus (a one-person crowd), my two aunts and their families, and my siblings.

I'd been home for seven days and was enjoying being with the family. One evening, we youngsters were playing games, and my cousin, Mark, pulled out an Ouija board. I had heard of them but never had seen or used one.

"It's really cool," said Mark. "We sit around, and one of us puts their fingers on the pointer, and it moves spelling out words. It also answers questions, and it can predict the future too."

I had a bad feeling about it, but the others wanted to see it work.

"I'll go first," Mark said, putting his fingers on the pointer.

Eleanor had a pencil and paper.

Daphne was the first to ask a question. "Will I marry a handsome prince?"

The pointer quivered and pointed to no.

Jeremy, another cousin, asked, "Will I be rich?"

The pointer said no to a round of laughter.

I hadn't noticed Grandma Ruth entering the room. The pointer started to quiver again and then started to point to letters.

I wasn't paying full attention as it pointed to D, then it moved to A, then jumped all the way to the other side to V before swinging back to I and then D again.

"David," said Eleanor, "it spelled your name, David."

Grandma Ruth had moved closer but didn't interfere.

The pointer moved to I, then S.

"David is," said Jeremy.

I was fully engaged now.

The pointer moved in jerky fashion to D, then E, then A, and a cold chill began to blow on my neck; and I got a very unsettled feeling. Somehow, I knew I should be afraid. The pointer moved to T and finally struggled across the board to H.

"David is death," said Eleanor.

Everyone looked at me, and I sat there, eyes wide and my mind reeling.

Grandma Ruth, with one smooth motion, swept up the board and threw it in the burning fireplace amid loud protests from Mark.

"There will be no more of that foolishness. Blasphemy is what that thing is. Pay it no mind, Davey. It's naught but a silly game." She was trying to make me feel better, but the silly game had spelled out part of my secret for all to see.

I was really upset. The Ouija board was rumored to connect the living and the dead, and now it had said that I belonged in the world of death. I started down my well-worn path of depression. I excused myself and went to the bedroom I shared with my brother and closed the door. I stayed there the rest of the night, refusing dinner and all questions about how I was feeling and what was wrong. I knew, but I couldn't tell anyone, in addition to all the other bad feelings I had been dealing with it appeared I had attracted the attention of the spirit world.

We—sans Mom, Samantha, and Anton—joined the rest of the C & E Catholics at Mass on Christmas Eve, and we did the standard holiday stuff. A couple of days before I was to go home—I was already thinking of California as home—there was a farewell dinner. It was an interesting group: three intellectuals (Dad, Anton, and Samantha), two farmers, my outspoken mom, two housewives (one married to an accountant, the other to a sales manager), a bunch of kids, and of course, after my half-semester of college, a possessor of all knowledge.

I never feared family dinners because our rule was all discussions were valid, and no censorship existed. Mom and Dad and Angus and Ruth viewed table discussions as teaching opportunities and were willing to allow us to argue and discuss so long as it was done with good manners and respect. No one was ever suppressed.

I had spent a lot less time with Anton and Samantha than with Ruth and Angus, so I was not as familiar with their attitudes and beliefs. Anton and Samantha took over the discussion and seemed almost to be bullying the group into talking about what they wanted to discuss.

Over the years, I had heard Mom talk privately to Dad about the changes in her parents. They seemed to be getting more and more full of themselves as the years passed and became more successful. Anton had parlayed the fame of his newspaper column into a stream of speaking fees and eventually book royalties. Samantha had the business sense. She had developed substantial real estate holdings and made herself and Anton a lot of money, none of which she shared with her daughter. As they moved in loftier circles and became more prosperous, they started to view the world and the rest of the family with increasing froideur.

Our table discussion at this diner was freewheeling. It covered a broad range of topics from politics to farming to children having trouble at school and who was dating to university politics. At one point in a momentary hiatus, Mark commented on the incident with the Ouija board and how it was telling the future. That, of course, led to him being questioned and admitting the message the board had spelled out about me. In my innocence, I believed I was amid a friendly audience. That was the impression I'd gotten from other gatherings.

I took a long breath and lifted my head. "I think I can see when a person is going to die." You'd thought I farted during a Papal Audience. Dead silence, heads turned to me. Dead accusatory silence, except for Grandma Ruth, who had a look of sadness in her eyes.

Grandma Sam was the first. "What do you mean? No one can see death."

"There have been three times when I've seen a black spot or mark on a person, and they all died shortly afterward."

"Halloween and April Fools are long past, David. You sound like one of those stories designed to distress a weakened mind," Grandma Sam said with a snort of derision.

There was a lot of head shaking in agreement, but not from Ruth.

Dad was having none of it. "Before we judge David's statement, we should at least hear him out. That's only fair."

Mom added, "I've never known David to make up stories. A couple of times, he experienced loss, particularly when Shamus died. There must be a reason he believes what he said. We need to hear him." Her father and mother shrugged their shoulders, waving their hands in a gesture of acquiescence.

"What makes you think you can see when someone else is going to die?" asked Mom.

Every eye riveted on me. I didn't want to be the center of attention, but here I was. Maybe that isn't entirely true. When you carry a secret for a long time, it becomes a burden, and there is a desire to share it and relieve yourself of the intolerable weight, so perhaps subconsciously, I was trying to ease the oppression of my secret.

I was frankly intimidated. This would be difficult, and my audience was already in a doubting frame of mind. I don't know what I expected, perhaps belief without question, but I was getting pushback here, and I had to defend myself. I had made a colossal mistake, and I wanted to slink away. I could have just shut up and let it go, and the conversation would have bounced onto other topics. The incident with the game had spooked me to the point I needed to tell someone and perhaps get reassurance that I wasn't crazy.

I began in a low voice. "You remember when Shamus died?"

Mom and Dad and my siblings knew the story, but Mom filled in the blanks for the others.

I continued, "What I never told you." I inclined my head toward Mom and Dad. "Just before I left, Shamus and I argued. I had seen a black mark on his head, right where the tree branch would eventually hit him."

There was silence. I scanned the family's faces, all of whom were looking back at me in disbelief except for Ruth, who seemed to have a look of horror on her face.

"It could have been a shadow. It was late in the afternoon, David," Dad said.

"More likely a story made up of partial memories, feelings of guilt, and repressed anger," said Anton.

"Why do you dismiss him so readily?" said Mom with a good deal of asperity.

"Then there was the football player."

"What football player?" chimed in Eleanor.

Again, all eyes bored into me.

"In my junior year, before the game, I saw the player who died, and across the back of his neck was a black mark right above the shoulders, right where he broke his neck."

All the eyes were now filled with nonbelief. Grandma Ruth stared at her wine glass as she spun it in her fingers.

"It was dark or nearly so, and the stadium lights were on, I assume, which creates shadows. Don't those people use all sorts of cosmetics to make themselves look terrifying? Maybe it was a mark from his clothing," Grandma Sam said.

"I know you're uncomfortable, David." Dad had the English gift for understatement; I wasn't uncomfortable as much as angry. I wasn't used to people doubting my word. "But there are logical fact-based explanations for all of this." He was trying to give me a graceful line of retreat. Of course, I didn't take it.

"Then there was Iris Wagner," I said a bit triumphantly.

Mom and Dad had firsthand knowledge of that incident, so I thought it would add credibility to my tale. Anton and Samantha and the kids looked at Mom and Dad to explain. Everyone ignored Angus and Ruth. Ruth was growing more and more uncomfortable.

"Are you claiming foreknowledge of that woman having a stillborn?" Grandma Sam said.

"What I am saying is that I saw a black mark on her dress right over the baby, and she had a stillborn and then hung herself. There was plenty of light, so the shadow argument won't hold up," I said forcefully.

Neither Angus nor Ruth said a word. Ruth was clearly troubled. She had filled her wine glass twice during the conversation, and she was usually quite abstentious.

Anton leaned forward and turned to them. "What do you think of your grandson's claims of prescience?"

In an almost dreamlike voice, quiet but firm, Grandma said, "And therefore as a stranger give it welcome. There are more things in heaven and earth, Horatio, than are dreamt of in your philosophy."

"Oh, the Bard," Anton replied with a mixture of sarcasm, dismissal, and derision. "A good place to hide when you have no answer. I wasn't interested in what others say. I wondered what you would say."

The insult hung like a fog. Civility was gone, and the conversation stuttered to a stop.

Dad tried to drive the conversation in a different direction. I'm not sure if Anton was drunk or just bloody-minded. I suspect both, but he had one final joust.

"The other night, Samantha," he pronounced her name with an exaggerated drawl, so it came out almost *saw-man-thaa*. "And I had dinner with an old friend, Arutro Walce. Walce is a psychiatrist and has done amazing work on delusions. Maybe he should meet David."

Anton continued, "It's obvious he needs to talk to someone. His beliefs about this are nothing but paralogism." He paused for a couple of heartbeats. "Imagine thinking you can foretell the future!"

There it was. I was some delusional fortune teller with all the carnival connotations that went with it.

The dinner ended, thankfully. I managed to be rude and not say goodbye to my college benefactors. I was angry about being handled so dismissively. It was also a warning I took to heart. The spots and their meaning were a secret I had to bear alone. Keep my mouth shut: That was the message I should have learned, but it hadn't fully cemented in my mind.

I did have another question that still confounds me to this day.

Anton and Samantha were intellectuals. Anton was a journalist who was supposed to seek the truth. They ran with a crowd of highly educated people who challenged accepted wisdom and dogma in their academic and professional lives, covering themselves in deep layers of self-congratulations for doing so. Why were they so closed-minded and abusive to my revelation?

I honestly believed those who loved truth would be open to new ideas and be ready to challenge dogma. Wasn't the position of science to challenge the hypothesis? Wasn't philosophy about arguing different points of view to arrive at the truth? Wasn't one of the elements of philosophical inquiry metaphysics seeking to explain how the world worked? It all seemed hypocritical.

As everyone was leaving, Ruth said to me, "I hope before you go back you can find some time to talk to your other grandmother privately." She put her hand on my arm and gave me a pleading sort of look.

I promised I would.

After everyone left, the younger kids were in bed. Mom and Dad said they needed to talk to me.

They questioned me deeply but gently. Mom was very irritated with her parents. Dad came from the direction that death and dying excited passions, and most people would rather not talk about death. It was a warning reinforcing my decision to never speak of what I saw again, and I clammed up. I had no desire for further abuse, but the decision not to talk about it felt wrong. They didn't judge me, which at that point was a huge relief.

The next day, the weather report predicted a big storm was moving in. To avoid being stuck in Chicago by flight cancellations, I left earlier than planned and didn't talk to Ruth. If I needed any further inducement to stay in California, it was that trip. I don't think the entire time the temperature exceeded freezing. The snow lay heaped in huge mounds along the roads and sidewalks. As we drove, the ashes, cinders, and salt rushed up into the car's wheel wells in a swooshing sound. In California, getting colder meant putting on a sweater. In Chicago, it meant cocooning yourself in layers of clothing only to have to take it off again.

The Los Angeles area is ramparted north and east by mountains. To the west lies the Pacific, the great weather regulator. In the winter months, the winds are primarily from the north, and the northern bulwark causes the air temperature to rise as the wind scaled the mountains, so we never got the full effect of northern winter blasts. The winds could be strong, blowing the smog and haze out to sea, leaving a cerulean blue sky scrubbed clean as if God on the first day of creation said, "This is my chosen land."

The winds would shift mainly from the west and veer southeast during spring and summer, giving rise to the legendary surfing environment. As it grows hotter, thermal inversions occur, trapping the effluents of all those people under layers of unmoving air. In the 1960s, smog was becoming a problem, and some days you could look north to see a haze hovering above LA. Under it, the sky was a gauzy gray. There was blue there someplace, but it was indistinct sort of like hope. It was nothing like Jimi Hendrix's Purple Haze.

When the wind came from offshore, waves would pile up at sea and roll in, irresistible in their power. Surfers would chevron both sides of the piers at Santa Monica, San Clemente, and San Onofre, waiting for the perfect wave to complete the California dream.

There were two significant pushes to California's growth: the Depression with the influx of the dispossessed from the Dust Bowl immortalized by Steinbeck and the aftermath of World War II. Many military personnel traveled through or trained in California, and when the war ended, they came back to stay. They brought pent-up buying demand, a desire for freedom, and living the ideal life. They also had the advantage of the reduced cost of cars and thus were born the car culture. As the car culture expanded, so did LA, and with it came the famous freeways. The freeways all had names: the Golden State, the Harbor, et cetera, but a true Angelino always calls them the I5 or the 405 or so on.

LA built up around the car and driving, and nothing was within walking distance. I was amazed to see major streets with no sidewalks, and you couldn't walk if you wanted to.

During my first years in college, I enjoyed some of the delights of southern California. Still, even with my college expenses paid, I had little spending money, and I lacked one of the essentials for a truly complete California experience: a car. Little did I realize in my yearning for more money, for a car, that I was really on the cusp of the authentic California life.

It was one that Montesquieu had in mind when he said, "If one only wished to be happy, this could be easily accomplished, but we wish to be happier than other people, and this is always difficult, for we believe others to be happier than they are."

The authentic California experience was one of a constant need for more, a constant fear of never having enough. The California experience was like the inspiration for its name, an illusion.

Chapman had an office of financial aid to help people who needed assistance with paying the bills. I went there even though I had funds for two college years. Why spend my money when I could consume others' money? However mendacious my intentions, I met Caesar Tovar, whose official title was chief of facilities management.

He was the first Hispanic man I had ever met. Caesar was about 5'4" and had to tip the beam at 350 or better. He typically wore shirts in primary colors and contrasting ties. There were times when you could feel your eyes crossing and uncrossing as they digested the divergent colors. Caesar controlled all the jobs on campus. For some reason, he and I got along well.

Regardless of my good feelings about him, I started the relationship with a partial truth. I told him my grandparents had paid for my first year, but I didn't reveal having enough money saved for the second. Caesar offered me three positions for my sophomore year. Washing dishes and dorm proctor (usually called dorm dick) and working on the campus cleanup crew. In all, they would pay for room and board and reduce my tuition by 25 percent.

I finished my freshman year in the upper half of my class, and I went back to Evanston for a summer job in a metals warehouse. I got a lot of overtime, earning a lot more than I expected. It was good. I worked so much, as all my friends were in Wheaton, and I was too young to drink. There was little else for me to do. It was a lonely summer. September 1966 found me back in California, ready to start my new job and my second year.

*****

People talk about flunking out of college in the freshman year when the freedom of college, parties, and events overwhelm good sense. It was possible to flunk out of college for non-completion of coursework or lack of attendance in those days. It had been my experience that the freshman flunkout mostly applied to the girls who were the subject of more intense social pressures. Freshmen girls were the meat of the upperclassmen's diets, and at registration, the wolves circled the herd of lambs.

The most dangerous time for the men was the second year when overconfidence led to overcommitment, and I walked right into the trap. I took too many credits, and the class and study time ran hard against the time I had to devote to the jobs.

I hated being a dorm dick. It's like being a cop without power but all the responsibility. People dislike you because of the position and don't want to be around you as it makes it seem they are sucking up. You had to live with these people, so resentment could come back to haunt you. Also, I am not a huge, imposing physical specimen, and confronting a drunk-as-a-skunk, loud, large football player usually didn't end well. It seemed my job was to make sure no one had any fun. I lasted a semester then quit. Caesar was cool and never told anyone else, so I never had to come up with more money.

I decided to stay in California over Christmas break. I got a job with the local utility helping dispatch electrical repair crews. It was the first Christmas I spent away from the family, but it was the hardest. There are few places as lonely as a college dorm over the holidays; you miss the music, the guy's snoring, and the lover boy and his latest conquest making love—actually, having sex. There was no love involved. The only compensation was it was easier to study and no debates about what to watch on TV.

Most of the dining halls were closed, so those of us left ate all together. One day I was eating the cafeteria's guess at what constituted a cheeseburger (it was a bad guess) when a woman's voice asked if the seat was taken.

What resulted was one of those perplexing questions of life: why do relationships seem to start when your mouth is full? Did Cary Grant or William Holden ever have that problem? I looked up, mouth full of burger, and not wanting to commit the ultimate sin, according to my grandmother, of talking with my mouth full, made a gesture by lifting my chin toward the chair that communicated it was free, and that I was irritated.

I had been trying to read as I ate, but it was proving an impossible task. I tried to start reading again, but the train of my thoughts left the station without me. The girl who sat down was quiet, then asked if I could pass the salt. I was just finding the place I had stopped reading, and now another interruption! The table was like four square feet, and there was nothing out of reach of either of us, but being well brought up, I passed her both the salt and the pepper.

"I'm not sure if you or I are above or below the salt," she said.

I had crammed the burger down my gullet like a cormorant with a fish, so my mouth was empty.

"What does that mean?" I probably said it more harshly than I intended.

"In the Middle Ages, salt was rare and expensive. When it was on the table, those above the salt, toward the head of the table, were nobility or considered more important than those below the salt. So here we are at a two-person table, and the question is, who is above or below?"

The clumsy metaphor carried a possibility of backfiring if I got pissed off at being considered below the salt or so dense not to understand it was an opening gambit. It also offered, I later reflected, a chance for a Cary Grant-like gallantry.

"You will always be above the salt as far as I'm concerned."

She had just told me something I didn't know, but it sounded like useless information. I'd like to say I had a courtly, witty response, but I didn't.

"That's great as long as the table is linear, not round. Then it would be one of those circular questions like the tree falling in the woods," I replied.

"It's also an interesting way to start a conversation. I'm Jean Cowel," I introduced myself, and we shook hands.

Christmastime alone is a slow time; I had no pressing engagements. She was the first girl I had had a social conversation with at college. She was from Ashland, Oregon, majoring in literature and education, so we had some common classes, and since my father was a literature professor, we had a common understanding.

Christmas break ended, and life resumed. A few weeks later, there was a social gathering, Jean was there, and we spent most of the party together. It would be romantic if I gave you a description of how when I saw her across the heads of the others, a thunderbolt struck me, and I knew she was the one. It was more straightforward: neither of us was a social butterfly. We didn't know a lot of people, so we gravitated together. For the rest of the year, we continued to go to parties and events together.

My time pressures lessened a bit when I stopped being a dorm dick. Perhaps with Jean's influence or because I was getting used to the load, my grades, attitude, and class rank improved with those changes.

Early in February, Jean told me she planned to stay at Chapman for the summer to take some courses at the University of California, Irvine, and wondered what my plans were. I had no desire to be lonely in Evanston, and in a passive-aggressive way, I had made no efforts to find a way home or get a job there for the summer. Thus, I took another step toward my destiny.

The first time a child takes a step, it's away from their parents. There are many steps, some bigger than others—going to college, getting married, or accepting a job in a distant location. Leaving Illinois for California was my first big step. Staying in California that summer would be another. Was it Jean? Was it just time? Was it my actual self-forming? It was likely a combination.

Jean and I started to study together and with others in the same classes, and usually afterward, we would go for coffee. This was before that was glamorous or a verb. We went to lectures when writers were on campus or nearby. The pace of social change was accelerating. Some of the lectures were by real radicals, talking about burning the place (meaning the country) down. It was the first time I'd ever heard a woman use the F word freely, and for some reason, it shocked me.

I had been taught that when anyone in a discussion resorts to swear words, it indicates they have nothing left to say and that swearing cheapened the rhetoric, and if you as a listener were upset at the language, you would likely miss the rest of the message. Again, I was offtrack. The purpose of the foul language was often precisely to hide the vacuous nature of the idea and the lack of intelligence of the speaker.

The fantastic Caesar stepped up and convinced the utility to hire me for the summer. The man was a godsend if there ever was one. I had no idea what I would be doing, but it didn't matter; the pay was okay, and if the previous stint were any clue, the work wouldn't be too demanding. So now I was set for the summer. Mom and Dad were bittersweet. My younger sister, Daphne, was having a lot of trouble in school and needed expensive private schooling. My parents had one in college, Eleanor about to go, Daphne in private school, and an anemic academic salary.

*****

The 1960s represented the jostling of one generation, the baby boomers, and its belief that it was ready for power against the incumbent generation's grip on power. Many thought the transition had taken place when Kennedy was elected even though he was of the earlier era, only to have that dream shattered. The strength of the vision inspired conspiracy theories. The conspiracies spawned a malignant genealogy seeking to find those responsible rather than seeking wisdom. The world fell into the clutches of the Masters of Suspicion.

Each generation brings its own set of notions about how to live. Large parts of ours postured themselves to be making decisions for the good of humanity, while others made them selfishly. The overriding concern for the men was the expanding war in Vietnam. What had been a minor disturbance in a faraway land had morphed at high speed into a full-fledged war. The draft was in full force, people were dying, and the deaths were getting personal. In July of 1967, two of my high school classmates were killed aboard *USS Forrestal* when it caught fire. Megan Forman from Wheaton had her brother killed near someplace called Na Trang.

Being a somewhat conservative school and associated with religious domination, we were partially shielded from the hothouses developing on other campuses such as Berkeley, but we could not escape. One day, Jean and I were walking across campus, and a young woman dressed all in black was standing on a wall shouting, without any sense of irony, W. B. Yeats's "The Second Coming," a sign at her feet proclaiming an antiwar, anti-draft event.

For those who appreciated them, Yeats's words powerfully captured what a lot of us were feeling, but the words which stayed with me the longest came from Simon and Garfunkel:

> and the people bowed and prayed,
> To the neon god they'd made
> and the sign flashed out its warning.
> In the words it was forming
> and the sign said the words of the prophets
> are written on the subway walls.
> and tenement halls
> and whispered in the sounds of silence.

June 1967 arrived, and the school year ended. We said goodbye to our friends. Couples made promises, soon broken, to continue the romance in the fall, and there were desperate grabs at relationships for those graduating and leaving the last four year's womb. In some cases, it was pathetic, in others, blatantly exploitative. One business grad had business cards printed and went around passing them out to everyone. He acted like he was endowing you with a crown jewel. Hundreds littered the campus.

I realized the irony of my existence that summer. I'd wanted to live in the California experience. I spent years in Wheaton's freezing winters dreaming of bikinis, surfing, and long evening rides in a convertible along the PCH of Venice, Redondo, Doheny, Santa Monica, and the other beaches. The reality turned out to be classes, studying, and trying to make ends meet during the school year. During that summer, I was stuck five days a week, eight hours a day, inside a concrete bunker dispatching electrical crews for the utility. The reality was far different from the dream, but I persisted. Maybe at some point in the future, I would be able to live as I longed for.

My work at the utility was terrible but well-paid. Everything we did was on huge, light-green accounting paper with pages taped together to make them larger. Trouble calls would come in, and we had to go through the sheets to find which crew was closest, then radio them. We had no real-time information, so some units had little work, while others were worked to death. They were all centrally located, so transit was often inordinately long, resulting in terrible customer satisfaction metrics.

Little did I know that the work I did that Christmas and during that summer would be the foundation for the rest of my life. At the time, it was just dull, inefficient, and thankless. Still in the off-hours and weekends, Jean and I were together and having fun. We went to the beaches, and generally acted like knowledgeable tourists and saw the things in California that most of the natives had never seen or done. What we didn't do was have sex.

Jean and I were growing closer as we spent more time together. Jean was not the California girl we had all dreamed about in the darkness of our Midwest winters. She was more handsome than beautiful. Her hair was a mousy brown with some black lowlights. her eyes were wide-set and black, framing what might have been considered a too-thin nose. She was average in height and slightly on the thin side. She was very smart and not shy about showing it, especially in public. Like a lot of us, she was sensitive to being compared to others. Jean disliked parties where the cheerleaders were in attendance.

*****

As August wound down, I made a trip to see Caesar about campus jobs for the upcoming year. Caesar had always been heavy—okay, fat—but during that summer, he exploded. I once pegged his weight at 350. Now he was way beyond that. His shirt strained at all the buttons, his collar was open, and his tie askew the way men wear them when they no longer fit. His pants were belted so far below his huge gut I wondered how they stayed up.

Caesar's face had always reminded me of a catcher's mitt, and it was usually a Latin brown. Now it was pale. His lips and fingernails had a blue tint to them. Even minor movement brought on panting and heavy breathing. That day he was wearing black pants, a bright-yellow shirt, a red tie, and a black spot.

There it was, right on his body: shoulder to shoulder and neck to waist. It rippled with his movements, and the light was bright enough to erase any shadow. Obviously, he was not feeling well because he was brusque and businesslike, not the usual fun and easy Caesar.

It had been almost three years since I last saw a spot, a year since the terrible Christmas diner/inquisition, and the spots had once again almost faded from memory. Seeing it now startled me and Caesar saw my reaction. He asked if I was okay, and I assured him I was never better. I asked him how he was feeling. He assured me he was getting over a summer cold, so we were both lying.

How do you describe the feeling of knowing someone close to you going to die? Soldiers can make assumptions that their fellow soldiers might die in battle, but it's an assumption, not knowledge. You can look at an elderly relative and know they're going to die because no one gets out of life alive. The same is true of being around a person with a terminal medical condition.

My seeing the spots was quite different. Caesar wasn't old, and he wasn't a soldier, but if the spots held true to past appearances, death was a certainty and would probably be sooner than later.

My conscience told me I should tell him. However, the memories of how my revelation of the spots had been taken in the past held me back. Deep inside was a gnawing feeling of disquiet. The voices in my head argued,

Do something.

Do nothing.

He's been good to you. You owe him a warning.

Don't—he won't believe you. Your grandparents didn't. Why should he?

You think he wants to know? I wouldn't.

Selfishness crept in. Was there a way to profit from this? I needed to protect what I had—my jobs. I never thought of myself as a mercenary, but here I was thinking about the effect of Caesar's death on me. Who would take his place? It was unlikely they would be as good to me as Caesar had been, and that selfish motive was the most honest thing my brain screamed at me. I was a mess, and I knew it.

I needed to talk to someone about my troubles but whom? Was I willing to risk my budding relationship with Jean? My parents were far away and at this point in my life, confiding to parents seemed like an admission that I couldn't solve my problems. I catastrophized. I convinced myself that this could mean losing my job and relationship and finding myself out of school.

The desire to tell Caesar was competing with my desire for self-preservation. I felt protective of him. I fancied myself to be a helpful person and thought giving him foreknowledge of his death might be the spur he needed to extend his life or to prepare his family better. The great enemy of human action—fear—loomed. I was afraid of ridicule, afraid of rejection.

My fears were the edge of the chaos lurking just outside my comfortably constructed everyday world. However, resist as I might, my suprasensory experiences were dragging me kicking and screaming to the frontiers of the known. It would take the acts of a hero, for heroes challenge the unknown, to pursue the meaning of the spots. Not ready to be a hero, I took the road most traveled, which is the easy route, and did nothing.

As the summer of 1967 ended, it was impossible, try as might, to ignore a world falling apart. It had been a long hot summer, both climatically and socially. Some have said that 1968 was the most pivotal year in American history, and I agree except to limit it to modern American history. As the young, we were heavily impacted by events. We were driven by passion, not logic. We were open drains accepting both wisdom and garbage without the filters of philosophy to tell us the difference.

On flags, pins, and signs, scrawled in paint on walls, all over the place was the trident in a circle symbol for peace. I thought again of the Sounds of Silence, about the words of the prophets. People dressed differently, and in their dress, we saw the contradictions of our time. Guys went to long hair and wire-rimmed glasses, but girls went one of two ways. Some wore baggy pants, prairie skirts, and braided hair. It was also the time of miniskirts, some so short that if the girl raised her arms, her panties would show.

Activism breeds trash, and as school started, I was busy as part of the grounds crew. The amount of trash rose exponentially, and it all seemed to end up on campus. I got really aggravated with one asshole. He was walking across campus, dumping trash on the ground. I followed him for a bit, picking it up before getting irritated at his obliviousness.

I called him out; he turned to me with a look of total disdain.

"Fuck you, shithead," he said. "I'm going to college, so I don't end up as a street sweeper like you. Loser!" He dropped more paper and started to walk away.

There might have been an earthquake at that exact moment, but somehow my stick, with its sharp point, missed the paper the asshole had dropped and instead got his foot. He screamed, hopping around on one foot, all the while calling down judgment on me, threatening to have me fired. I had acted badly and had guilt feelings, but damn it felt good to puncture that ass!

As we started our junior year, wars were brewing up, not only just the shooting one in Asia but also for a generation's soul. The battle, and our part in it, were elements of the intragenerational struggle and personified by ROTC. Reserve Officer Training Corps offered a route for many to go to college by providing scholarships in exchange for postcollege military service. It was a serious commitment because added to academic requirements, ROTC included military drills, classes, and uniforms. The military training and the uniforms were part of the problem.

As a group, we boomers had been raised in a sort of blessed world, largely at peace, with unparalleled prosperity, having every wish and need cared for by loving, doting parents who knew the cost of hardship and sacrifice. We knew little of sacrifice, only of taking. Our parents sacrificed because they believed there were transcendent ideas that they were willing to fight and die for. On the other hand, at least some of us began to doubt the existence of any transcending concepts and cared only for our immediate presence.

We were not monolithic; those born earlier in the generation tended to be more conservative, trusting higher authority and understanding sacrifices were necessary for life to continue. As the birth dates advanced, more hedonistic traits came forward, not as evident in the 1960s as they would be later, but it was certainly starting.

One of my legions of flaws is a failure to notice nuance in others. Jean was changing; it would have been impossible not to change; we all were, but a hard edge was developing in her. She became more activist, more involved in nonschool activities, hanging around with people I didn't like, and it seemed out of character for her. Frankly, I resented her lack of attention to me.

Early in October, she and I walked across campus and saw an ambulance and a crowd at the facility's building. My heart almost stopped. I knew what was going on. Like moths to a flame, we joined the group. I asked a woman what happened, hoping against hope. She turned to me, eyes red from tears, mascara running down her face.

Caesar was dead.

This was no Shakespearean play; it was real life. I want to tell you my first thoughts were charitable, but I'd be lying.

I frankly had no clue how to act. I had known Caesar would die and soon, and I had done nothing. I felt not only guilt over my non-action, but also the edges of that great destroyer, shame, appeared. What was wrong with me? What had I done to deserve this? I second-guessed myself. If I had told him, he would have changed, and the outcome would have been different. Jean knew Caesar and I were close, and she read my zombielike behavior as the trappings of a person's grief at losing someone close.

That night, I pitched and tossed, dreams pounding through my brain bearing images of horrible creatures, winged demons, or hags straight out of Macbeth, pushing me toward an indistinct figure surrounded by brilliant lights. I sweated and rolled. I must have cried out in my half-conscious state because I heard pounding at the door, which I ignored.

With the false dawn came some respite. I lay in my sodden sheets for an hour trying to sleep, but in the back of my mind, fear lodged like an unwelcome guest. Somewhere in all of that, I took ownership of my curse.

I personalized Caesar's death. His, along with the others, were my fault. How, I didn't know, but unquestionably it had to be my doing; there could be no other explanation. As many do when faced with a crisis, I cursed God for causing me to have this affliction, this sickness, for indeed it could be nothing else. I wondered if the indistinct figure of my dreams might be the devil seeking my soul.

I got up and did the morning dishes in the chow hall, stumbling along like a wraith. I went to class fortified with coffee and felt the acid burn in my stomach. I washed the lunch mess. I went to afternoon classes. If they had taught a method to turn stone into gold, I wouldn't have remembered it. I came out of business law to the sunken lawn or drunken lawn as we called it, and my day got worse.

A full-scale antiwar demonstration was in progress. At the far end of the lawn, a woman tonelessly sang "Masters of War." A forest of signs *ROTC out; make love, not war; end the senseless violence; and give peace a chance*, waved like palm trees in the wind. There were black people with signs for civil rights and an *Impeach Earl Warren* placard.

The frat boys talked to every girl around, the rumors of free and easy sex accompanying leftist demonstrations incentivizing them. I walked by a booth Students for a Democratic Society, a group most open about destroying things and whom I had come to despise, and Jean was passing out pamphlets. I didn't stop. If she was easy, it was news to me.

I stumbled along for the next few days, nothing sticking in my memory, nothing seeming to have meaning. Sleep was rare, the tension constant and draining. A week after Caesar's death, I had a meeting with my academic advisor, Dr. Ray Cromer.

Cromer looked old, I could never tell if it was old from the passage of time or the pressure of life, but he looked old. Cromer's back was hunched from a youthful accident. He wore one raised shoe, but the deformed nature of his spine left him slant-shouldered. Cromer wore wire-rimmed glasses, and his eyes twinkled with intelligence. He always seemed to dress like the archetypal college professor: tweed jackets, patches on the elbows, a smell of pipe smoke, a faint air of disorganization.

He had a fantastic memory for text, which he demonstrated once by catching four football players reusing papers written years before. Despite all his physical faults, perhaps because of them, he was a superb and passionate teacher. His history classes were the most popular on campus. He had once tried to convince me to major in history. He was leaving at the end of the year for a position on the East Coast, and I had been helping him pack up his office.

"David," he said, "pardon me for saying this, but you look terrible. Are you ill?" It was an interesting question.

Was I ill?

"I'm fine. I think, Dr. Cromer. I just haven't been sleeping well. Weird dreams and stuff."

"Well, okay," he said, not really believing me. "You know where I am if you need to talk to anyone. Get some sleep, you look awful."

Grief comes in many forms. As I was working the diner service, another kid went on about how Caesar was bound to die being so fat. He called Caesar a fat, greasy beaner. When another kid questioned him, his response was, "He killed himself really, eating all those tacos and other Mexican shit—he was asking to die. No loss, just another wetback."

Once again, there was an earthquake. The tub of dirty dishes was jolted out of my hands and into the jerk's lap. He jumped up, screaming that I'd destroyed his new *Brooks Brothers* sweater and shirt and that I would pay for it right after he beat the shit out of me. I stopped cleaning up the mess and grabbed him by his dirty sweater.

"Fuck you, asshole, you think Caesar deserved to die? You're a shithead. You're the one who should die, and I think I will just kick your Brooks Brothers ass!" I didn't yell the words; it was a forceful, reasonably quiet statement followed by me cocking my right fist back to clock him.

Millie, the kitchen boss, grabbed me and sent me packing to the dishwasher area. She made the asshole and his buddies clean up the mess and dismissed them. I found out later the only reason I didn't get fired was because Caesar had been Mille's boss. Of course, the guy and his friends spread stories that I was so afraid I had to have a woman bail me out. It was very out of character, but it was my anger and grief at not only Caesar's death but also my foreknowledge of the event.

I had arranged with Cromer to come by his office after dinner and help him pack. He complained endlessly about how he never realized he had accumulated so much stuff. Most of it was junk. However, as soon as I collected what he deemed junk, he would change his mind, deciding it was an irreplaceable expression of genius.

He didn't press me anymore, except to make a coy remark about controlling one's anger even when anger was justified, meaning the gossip channels were open, and he knew about the cafeteria incident. Then he really surprised me.

"David, I know you haven't been feeling well, and Caesar's death hit you hard. Maybe I can help you out before I leave." Not waiting for my response, he barreled on. "My colleague, Jack Pierce, you know him?"

I said I had taken Econ 101 from him.

"Well, he has been working on some research project. He tried to explain it to me, but it made no sense to these old ears. His research assistant is graduating, he's gotten grant money, and he mentioned he was looking for a new RA, and I hope it was okay, but I gave him your name and my strongest recommendation."

Due to his back issues, Cromer was shorter than me. He looked up through his frameless glasses, pipe in one hand unlit, with a hint of moisture in his sparkling blue-green eyes.

He reached out to put his hand on my arm. "You have a fine mind, but I would expect nothing less from a son of Joseph MacIntosh. You need to be careful of becoming hidebound, too inflexible in thought and action. Wisdom and true learning come only from asking questions unasked and seeking answers yet unspoken. Do you know the difference between a priest and a shaman?"

I answered a priest being an ordained minister and a shaman, representing a primitive society.

"No, David," he said, sitting down in his squeaky chair and waving me to another. "A priest is a functionary, a shaman has lived the experience. They may both have the same end in mind, but the shaman has opened him or herself to the experiences, while the priest more often than not recites dogmas created by others." He rocked back and forth, squeaking on both swings. It was irritating, but I wasn't about to interrupt him.

"We behave in certain ways because we have become accustomed to doing so. In most cases, we can't explain why we do what we do since we have more customs than experiences that justify them. We just accept those that exist. There are always experiences and customs at the edge of our lives and experiences we can't explain or understand because our lives never take us there, and we have no experiences to validate the customs. That is where new information lives, not only in those unexplained areas but also in the danger common to unexplored territory."

I nodded in agreement, although I didn't fully understand his points.

"David, we are living in great times. It might not appear so, but times of stress and anger can be very productive. This time we are in reminds me of the run-up to Civil War or WWI with the advancements in technology and social pressures. In those times, just like now, we couldn't fully explain why what is happening is occurring, and when explanations fail, you know something new is occurring. Once the immediate grief of those cataclysms passed—and I'm not just talking about the loss of death and destruction but of the death of customs—new worlds opened and heroes created. You need to keep your eyes open and your ear to the ground. Great things await you."

His words struck a chord deep within me, and they've stayed with me ever since. Cromer is long gone, but after seventy years, his wisdom still shines. The job was truly a magnificent gift, but the pearl of great price was the worldview he shared. I would refer back to it later in life many times, sometimes with regret that I did not fully follow the thread. It would take years before I fully realized what he was really saying to me.

RA jobs paid cash rather than offsetting a living cost, and if the research was published, you got mentioned, which was like the old English Army citation, "Mentioned in dispatches." RA jobs also allowed you to work independently and explore uncharted areas.

Since Caesar's death, I had not been with Jean and had not seen her since the demonstration. After thanking Cromer profusely and puttering around for another hour, he dismissed me to go and study. When I got back to my dorm, there was a note from Jean asking me to call her, so I trooped to the common phone.

It turned out that Jean's father was coming to Anaheim later in October and had invited Jean and me to dinner. I accepted, not recognizing in my innocence and idiocy that meeting her father was the next step in Jean and my relationship.

I never said anything about her hanging around with the SDS people, and she never shared her association with me. I didn't want to control her, and I really didn't want her trying to control me. She knew I was a conservative and non-activist. We disagreed on many subjects, but we got along because we allowed each other the dignity of their position. We could discuss without letting our disagreements get personal, and we never attacked each other.

The shock and guilt surrounding Caesar's death made me unwilling to get into new arguments. My unresolved grief had given me a short fuse of repressed anger. I was afraid I would blow up one day and destroy our relationship by transferring my rage. She was passionate about her course, and I was righteous in my belief.

A perfect receipt for disaster.

The Jolly Roger across Katella Boulevard from Disneyland is a small hotel, really a motel, and a restaurant. The motel tried to theme itself with a romantic image of pirates, and the restaurant's theme evidently was nighttime. It was so dark Jean and I bumped into tables as we moved toward her father. She introduced us, and Steven insisted I call him Steve. I appreciated the gesture of familiarity, but my conservative upbringing made it a struggle to use the familiar.

Steve was a bit over six feet, all legs. When he sat down, he was shorter than I. His hair, more brown than gray, hung almost to his collar. It must have been a recent affectation because Jean commented on his new haircut with an air of disapproval. He had a long face that made it look as if his eyes were not in the right place. His head was supported by a long thin neck, rising from extraordinarily wide shoulders, giving way to a moderate chest. His voice was high-pitched, almost feminine and his handshake was disappointingly sloppy.

We were seated in a banquette with Steve opposite me. It was so dark that it was hard to make out details once we were sitting. He was drinking, which seemed to annoy Jean. We had to use the table candle to light the menus. Dinner wound its way through salad, entrée, dessert, school, family, job ideas, and future plans. It was standard table talk, and the conversation lacked substance. Somewhere in the conversation, I realized I was being interviewed as a son-in-law.

He put me at ease. He was either a better interviewer than the substance of the conversation would have indicated, or I was less aware of the nature of the talk.

A week later, I met with my new boss, Jack Pierce. His current RA was a senior named Chadwick DeSalvio. It was a good thing Chadwick was brilliant. Being bright covered up his pomposity (he always insisted his name was Chadwick, usually with a lecture about your bad manners for not using his name correctly). He was monumentally ugly, so ugly that his nickname among the women was "Never Chad." He was on the short-timer's calendar, and the only thing he wanted from me was to learn the job as fast as possible so he could stop supervising me. He made it easy by being highly organized and keeping beautifully detailed notes.

The shock of Caesar's death passed more quickly than I expected. I wondered if the effect of seeing death wasn't jading me to an experience most people find emotionally gut-wrenching. My nascent shame, which I had suppressed, hung around like a lingering, low-level depression making me wary of human interaction. I didn't want to see more death, so I tended to avoid relationships. I was never a glad-hander, but now I was even less open.

One of the constellations of emotions surrounding depression is catastrophic thinking. I began to attribute terrible things to others, and the specter of Jean at the SDS booth rose. She continued working with SDS, never outright admitting it, but it was evident from our conversations. For me, SDS was the archenemy. SDS took noble ideas and wrapped them in lies, bringing them into disrepute. Most commentators did not take them seriously and advised others not to worry because the truth would win through. It didn't, and SDS quickly showed itself into what I believed to be a reprehensible hate group using immoral means for immoral ends.

I began to think the worst of Jean, and the destructive power of innuendo sank roots in my mind. I imagined her having a secret life of rampant drug use and sex. It was guilt by association. My concerns could have been removed by communication, but in the fevered atmosphere of the time, people's divisions around ideology became sufficient reason to disavow others. The unwillingness to respect others' views rots the structure of relationships. My guilt and shame combined to restrict me to a few close relationships, and I did not want to risk losing Jean by expressing my unfounded fears about her association with SDS, so I let it go.

Not really.

Cromer's gift to me was the cement binding all the elements of my life together. I would like to tell you I knew when he made his gift, that it was my destiny, but again, I'm trying not to lie. I was glad to have the work. It made things easier to have actual cash in hand. Jack was researching the use of computers to model data. He believed his models could be used to analyze management performance and project trends.

In the '60s, computers were expensive, large, mostly owned by large businesses or governments, and didn't have much utility for the common person. NASA was using many of them for the space program, but as we would learn later, most of the calculations were done by humans, many women. In fact, for many years, the term *computer* was a job description, not a synonym for a machine.

Jack believed that by rewriting the machine's instructions, which he called the software, it could analyze data and make predictions. As it acquired more data, it would improve its accuracy. Today this is machine learning; in the 1960s, it was cutting-edge stuff.

In a wonderful conjunction of need and means, Jack had had conversations with the local utility, the one I had worked for that summer, about getting access to their data to use in his project. As he worked through the outline of the project, I provided insights about where the data he wanted was and how it was currently being used and recorded. I also provided him with some hard facts about the utility systems, which significantly impacted the overall project structure.

One night after class, Jean and I walked together, me to Jack's office and she to some meeting (SDS?).

"Do you have plans for Christmas?" she asked.

I told her I was looking at helping the crew refinish the basketball court and planning on staying at Chapman.

"Don't you like being around your family for the holidays?"

"They're fine, I guess, but it's Chicago. I don't know anyone there. My parents have a small house and still have three kids running around, and it's expensive to go home. You think I'm eager to change this weather for freezing slush and snow?"

"You can't stay here; you did that last year," she said.

"Worked out pretty well. I met you, didn't I?"

"My parents would love to have you come home with me for the holidays. Dad really likes you, and I know my mom will love you. I won't hear of you staying here. You're coming to Ashland, and that's the last word."

It was. I was easily convinced.

Jack and I worked to lay out the plan's scope and anticipate the potential roadblocks, the first of which was that neither of us had ever written any computer code. In those days, writing code was complex and time-consuming. Jack arranged for both of us to get instruction on software and the interface to computers to reduce the need to hire programmers. We pounded away through October and November, and strangely, given the requirements were the equivalent of taking another six credit hours, my grades improved, and I found myself enjoying learning.

Steve, his wife Marho, and Hiram, their son, drove down to Orange. When we met, they talked endlessly about how fast they had gotten there. Steve calculated the miles per gallon they had achieved and seemed pleased. I had never seen anyone so excited about driving. The following day, they picked Jean and me up, and off we went. Steve acted as the captain of the ship, barking orders and asking for information. Whoever rode shotgun was responsible for having a map in their lap, knowing our location, and communicating it upon his nearly constant requests. Since there were four drivers, Steve decided we would make the trip in one hop and then started figuring out the location for driver swaps. I didn't tell him I had not driven a car in three years.

Once you leave LA, I5 is miles and miles of concrete through nothing. There were truck stops and rest areas inhabited chiefly by dust. One highlight was a huge cattle feedlot you could smell for miles. Jean's brother, Hiram, was eleven and a pain. He wouldn't or couldn't sit still, and he kept climbing over the seat and people.

When I was driving, he amused himself by turning on the wipers, lights, heater, or whatever. I wanted to slap him silly.

Ashland lies on the north side of the Siskiyou Mountains, surrounded by almost primeval forest. The arboreal environment means it rains a lot and is mountainous, and it snows more than a little. Often the clouds hang low, snagging in the treetops where the wind tears them into long cotton wool strips. Ashland in 1968 was a logging town. It didn't seem a joyous place to an outsider, with its unvarying color scheme of gray and green. The big rig logging trucks pounded potholes in the streets. There was the faint smell of desperation as if the town knew bad times would surely come and good times were merely a rehearsal for the bad.

Steve was a unit manager for a company called Crown Zellerbach or CrownZ. The company owned forests from the summit of the Siskiyou north beyond Klamath Lake, from the Cascades west to the coastal range. Over all, it was three million acres dotted with mills, sorting yards, and small towns.

Most of the land once belonged to a couple of Indian tribes. In a terminally misguided policy, the federal government decreed the local Indian tribes no longer existed, which was certainly news to the members of the tribes. The government took the land and sold it to logging interests. At least some of the money went to the now-non-existent tribal members. Crown Z got the trees at fire-sale prices and made huge profits supplying material for the fevered housing growth in the 1950s and 1960s. Steve's unit was 475,000 acres, about 200 square miles. He was responsible for all aspects of the operations in his unit; it was a big job without matching big pay.

Steven and Marho's modest house was surrounded by what I was informed were western hemlocks. They are the prototypical western tree that grows forty to sixty feet, ruler-straight, and the pyramidal Christmas tree is only on top. Among the hemlocks were pines, a couple of different cedar species, and Douglas firs, the kings of forest. All of which, according to Steve, the godless, son of a bitch environmentalists were trying to save and destroying the lumber business in the process.

Steve informed me that environmentalists were all communists, closely connected to the godless antiwar protesters, all enemies of commerce, the nation, motherhood, apple pie, and flag. He ranted on about how the forest products industry was the true hero in the morality play. The timber groups would preserve the trees because it was good business. Trees were renewable after all.

Jean rolled her eyes at the rant. Marho was silent as she was most of the time. I nodded and made what I thought were non-committal, thoughtful noises and wondered what he would do with Jean's flirtation with SDS.

At the house, the first complication occurred. There were three bedrooms. In 1968, there was no presumption of sex in a relationship, and unmarried people sleeping together was referred to as living in sin. The idea of Jean and I sleeping together under their roof was not even considered. When Hiram found out he and I would be sharing his room, he threw a tantrum. I volunteered to sleep on the couch, which seemed to satisfy both petulance and convention.

I was used to white Christmases, and most of the time in Ashland, it was cold enough to snow, but it didn't. It was mostly just wet and cold. It was a different cold. It seeped into your bones and stayed there. The worst was my feet, the cold and wet filtered up into my soles, and I had a feeling that all wasn't right, but I didn't know exactly why, but I was uncomfortable. It was vastly different and harder to take than the bone-crunching cold of Chicago. The cold and wet, the constantly gray sky, the wind, the unvarying green forest, and the lack of sunshine made me depressed. I had an overwhelming urge to eat carbohydrates and nap, and I felt down most of the time. Pretty depressing for a California boy.

My parents sent some of my presents out, mostly money, for which I was developing an inordinate fondness. It was still depressing watching Jean and her family enjoying their stuff. They'd gotten me a sweater, which came in very handy. I got them an electric can opener that Steve had told me that Marho wanted. Not a very personal gift, I will agree. I got Jean a scarf. Jean and I bought Hiram the new hit toy in California called Legos. He was a jerk and threw pieces around all over.

On Christmas Day, I made a call home. In those days and in many areas, long-distance calls required operator assistance and at holiday time, waiting for a circuit to be available. To make what today would be called a collect call, you told the operator to reverse the charges. It was one of those calls people my age hate: mushy and lots of interruptions as additional people wanted to talk and, of course, the one embarrassing question lobbed by Aunt Mary Stuart—when would we be getting engagement notices? There was a lot of awkward laughter, humming, hawing, and joking, but questions like that tend to fester.

I had not considered marrying Jean; I had not considered marriage at all. I was getting cold feet about even continuing to hang out with Jean. I thought at first it was the result of my working too hard or the restlessness that can infect a relationship. The reality was, and I would only learn this with age and experience, my whole approach to friendships and relationships was changing due to the spots. I couldn't verbalize it, but psychologically I was distancing myself from the potential of suffering and grief.

Overall, it was a pretty good holiday. I never read the books Jack had given me on computer language. Steve and Marho insisted on driving us back to Orange. There were some mercies; Hiram wasn't going.

We got back to campus, and as a final treat, Steve scored tickets to Disneyland. We stayed for fireworks, and Jean and I held hands as bombs burst. While we saw parts of the display every night from campus, we had never seen them from inside the park. Strangely, it was the first time Jean and I showed public affection toward each other.

The next night, I announced that I would take everyone to dinner. Since I would be paying the bill, we went to a Mexican place that was inexpensive, had great food, and had full illumination unlike the Jolly Roger.

On the drive south, I noticed a discoloration on Steve's nose. When I first saw it, any good feelings I had developed from the Christmas holiday vanished like vapor. I was able to suppress my concerns with rationalizations. He spent a lot of time outdoors, his face was not unlined or smooth, and so on. An average person might not have noticed it, but I was not normal.

It was almost as if some power forced me to see the spots. They occurred in scenarios where I had no option but to see them. The fates couldn't be or wouldn't be that cruel.

Would they?

Now as Steve sat across from me in the light of the restaurant, I could see it, right at the end of his nose.

A black spot.

CHAPTER 4

There was no doubt about it being there. I don't know if I was in love with Jean or not, but now I was sitting across from her father looking, if experience was any guide, at the mark of death. Even in my callowness, I realized this was something unique. I had seen the spot on four people, and death occurred soon afterward, but I had never been as close to the person as I was to Jean.

"You seem like you've seen a ghost, David," Marho said with unintended irony.

I paused, grateful for the mouthful of food giving me time to gain control and come up with a lie. "I'm sorry, I was just thinking about school starting again."

What I felt was a moral duty to tell Steve was opposed by a selfish impulse not to tell. Steve's death, like Caesar's, would have far-reaching implications for me. It could take Jean from me, and even if it didn't, it would undoubtedly change everything between Jean and me.

We do many things not because we have experienced them before and know what to do, but because it's what we believe we should do. I had read enough classics and religious tracts to understand that Western culture was rife with fear of death. People generally don't like to discuss or even acknowledge the mortality from which none of us can escape. Accepting death in others means acknowledging it in yourself. How do you, or even should you, tell someone they will die before their full time on earth has run?

The whole idea that the spots were some singular warnings of death was flawed. Who was to say what a person's normal life should be? Early death could be simply the luck of the draw.

Then there was the issue of whether he would believe me. Of those on whom I had seen a spot, I had only told two (Shamus and Iris), and neither had believed me.

I never said a word to Caesar, and I couldn't have said anything to the football player. The lack of success with early warnings gave me the rationalization that my prophecy would go unheeded, not believed, and be generally useless except to paint me as some sort of nut job.

What made me think Steve would believe me?

I had three choices. Do nothing, allowing my survivor's guilt and shame to increase. I could tell him not only about the mark on him but also about my history. The risk in that course was not being believed and possibly losing Jean due to being branded a fool. The final option was to find a way to tell Steve that he would believe. I had to make my decision quickly as this was the last night, we would be together with Steve and Marho, and what was going to happen might happen quickly.

I was distracted, running all those scenarios in my head and trying to figure out the right one. Sensing that something might be coming, Jean and Marho excused themselves to go to the ladies' room. It was now or never. I think they both attributed my confusion and distraction to an intention to ask Steve for Jean's hand.

"Steve, thank you and Marho for inviting me up to Ashland for Christmas. I had a great time, and your hospitality was wonderful," I began.

"Don't think anything of it," he said, waving his hand in motion of dismissal. "It was our pleasure. We're practically family, right?"

Already with the leading comments, I thought.

I put my finger on the tip of my nose and said, "You have something right at the end of your nose." Even as I said it, I was hoping against hope that the spot was an illusion.

"Oh. Must be salsa," he said with a laugh. "Thanks. Hope it hasn't been there long!" He laughed again as he wiped his nose with his napkin. "Gone?"

"Yes," I lied with a failing heart. It wasn't a total lie; the spot had transferred to the napkin as he wiped his nose. When he moved the napkin, it was back on his nose, so in a dishonest way, it had gone away. Weak justification for sure, but I was grasping at straws.

Jean and Marho came back, and Steve said, "David saw I had something on the end of my nose. Have I been going around with it there for long?"

Jean and Marho said they didn't see anything. I could still see it. Everyone was happy except me. Both Jean and Marho were disappointed that the big news wasn't an engagement ring.

I had made a half-assed attempt to change the outcome of Steve's life but failed, and now death stood at his door. I did what those in the middle do. I wanted to have it both ways. I didn't want to brand myself as some weirdo, so I didn't come right and say, "Steve, you have a spot on your nose, and I hope you have prepared for death because that's what coming, and soon!"

Then I made it worse.

What happened next did me no honor. After Steve and Marho had dropped us off with long goodbyes and hugs, Jean and I walked to her dorm. She had linked her arm through mine and was leaning in, pressing her breast against my arm. It was erotic. At the door of her dorm, I swung her around and kissed her. It surprised her, and we kissed badly. With school not fully open, there was time and place and soon kissing moved to touching and gasping and then stumbling up the stairs to her room, and then sex.

In our passion, we didn't even think about protection. It was just a long pent-up release of desire. It was neither pretty, touching, or particularly fulfilling for either of us. I think we were more surprised than anything. Of course, as a virgin, I had no benchmarks to compare the experience. Our relationship had been totally platonic, and suddenly there we were in a narrow dorm bed, naked in the half-light cast by campus lighting. We'd obviously been building to this point, but I felt guilty that I had exploited Jean.

I was terribly conflicted. I believed sex and its consequences were a man's responsibility. For me, there was no causal sex. Each time you had sex, it was with the understanding that there could be life-changing outcomes. I had been taught to respect women and not try to trick them into having sex. I'd just had sex with a woman I had no intention of marrying. We hadn't used any protection, so I started to worry about her getting pregnant.

There was a lot of anger in me, stemming from my powerlessness to control the spots and my belief that she was likely having sex with others, which combined, resulting in a weird form of revenge that said, "Get yours because others are." Anger can be a powerful aphrodisiac. All of those thoughts were bad enough, but then I made it still worse.

Sometimes in a football game, the offensive team fools the defense into jumping offside. Before the referee whistles the play dead due to the penalty, the quarterback will throw a long pass. If it's complete, the offensive team declines the penalty, and the play stands. If incomplete, they accept the penalty, and the ball gets moved five yards downfield. It's called a free play. In either case, the offense wins. Sex with Jean that night was almost a free play for me. I knew when Steve died, we would not survive as a couple. Did my anger, my late-teenage drive for sex, and the fact that I didn't have to worry about having a long-term relationship motivate me to initiate sex? Or was it simply the point in a relationship when sex was the next step?

It did change our relationship. Neither of us talked about it; we were shy about it, but in some magical way, those who were our friends knew we had had sex. There was crude teasing, some of which upset me but seemed not to trouble Jean at all. In fact, it seemed to make Jean more attractive to other guys in my eyes. I had not had competition before, but now guys were calling Jean and asking her out, or at least that's what she told me.

I felt not only protective of her, closer, and more desirous of being around her, but I also felt emptiness deep in my soul, knowing it wouldn't last. I finally convinced myself I had exploited her because I started something I was unwilling to finish. We never talked about it afterward, no languid après sex conversations wreathed in cigarette smoke. We didn't smoke, but another brick in my house of shame was set.

I think Jean wanted me to declare myself to her, to tell her I loved her and that she was the one, and I didn't do that. She never said it in that many words, people didn't talk that way in those days, but she wanted reassurance that I wasn't using her, and of course, I felt I was.

I will jump ahead here and confirm what your minds have already figured out. Late in January, Jean got a letter from her mother, and among other news was the fact that Steve was having crushing migraines, and the vision in his right eye was deteriorating. He was also having nosebleeds often twice or three times a day, which landed him in the ER. The doctors were at their wit's end.

The letters and phone calls spoke of deteriorating health as the weeks passed. Finally, some doctors in Portland diagnosed his condition as cancer of the vomer bone. Jean, of course, wanted to know all about it, so she went to see one of the doctors in the student clinic and asked me to go along. The doctor admitted that he didn't know much but told her that the vomer was one of the bones forming the nasal septum.

A couple of days later, the doctor called Jean in. She asked me to go with her for support. According to the doctor, this type of cancer was so rare he could only find one previous case in the medical journals. The doctor had the bedside manner of an ogre. There was no need to get treatment; Steve was a dead man, and the only thing left was to see to his financial affairs and prepare his family for his death. The doctor said he had months at best to live.

Even jerks are right sometimes.

Steve died in June of 1968, and all my predictions bore fruit. In March, Jean transferred to Southern Oregon University. Then I learned she dropped out of college completely. We traded letters for a while, and I got the impression things were hard financially. Then my letters went unanswered, and that was the end of it. I never heard from Jean again.

Before Steve's unfortunate death arrived, life continued.

Jack and I started to layout the project we agreed on some vital points. The first was that our access to computer time would be limited, arguing for a narrow focus so we could quickly see the impact. Second, the computers were likely to be less capable than we expected, and finally that our lack of knowledge of computer programing argued for a simple format.

The data came to us in box upon box of paper, colossal account-ing worksheets. Part of the problem was trying to discern what we had. Then we had to read it and understand what we were seeing.

I was doing most of the work for Jack in the evenings, so there were many late nights. I was tired, and I wasn't studying effectively. My grades were suffering. I found myself taking on Jean's increasing distress. In her distress, she wanted closeness, and often that close-ness moved to sex. The sex left me with a guilty feeling. I suppressed the guilt enough to enjoy it, but I still felt guilty afterward. The pres-sure must have shown up in my work because Jack noticed.

One night I went to Jack's office hoping he wasn't there. If he wasn't, I would sleep, not work, which added to my load of guilt. I wasn't doing my duty. I could have asked for time off or feigned ill-ness, which wouldn't have been far off the truth, but he was paying and depending on me, so I had a duty. As I think back on it, perhaps my going to work that night was an unconscious way of reaching out for help.

Jack was there with a full palate of work and information. As he laid out the job, he noticed I was distracted, and I'm sure I looked as bad as I felt.

"You okay, David? You seem out of sorts."

"Yeah, I'm fine. I didn't sleep well last night. Bad dreams," I replied.

"If you need to go to the dorm, this can wait," he said.

"Thanks, I will see how it goes, and maybe I will do that. I'll make up the time, I promise."

"I never worry about that with you, David. You always give a fair measure of work for the pay. I'm just concerned for you. Student burnout is a real issue, and you've got great promise. We are just getting started, and I really don't want to break in a new RA. If you need to talk to someone, the school has counseling services.

I stumbled through the work, making mistakes. There were some I noticed but was too tired to correct, and others I didn't see. I felt terrible for the poor effort. I started to think about Jack's sug-gestion of talking to someone. We weren't yet in today's therapeutic environment, but we were headed there. I was acutely aware of the stigma attached to mental illness or even the suggestion of a mental disorder.

When Jean announced her transfer to Southern Oregon, my emotions went on an elevator with only one way: down. While I knew it was coming, it still hit me hard. A couple of Jean's girlfriends offered consolation, but I wasn't interested. Sexual deprivation wasn't the issue. I was terribly sorry Jean was gone. It left a massive hole in my life, but it was a more profound and unresolved issue, knowing when someone would die.

I started to edge my way toward talking to someone. I had a classmate named Harrison Bell, who I thought was clever and a good guy, so I asked him a couple of questions one afternoon.

"Harrison, if you knew beforehand with 100 percent accuracy that someone was going to die, not of natural causes, but disease, accident, or violence, would you tell them?"

He thought for a minute or two, then replied, "No."

"That's it? No?"

"Yes," he replied, playing with me. "Actually, no. First, because no one would believe you. Second, no one wants to know that stuff. Everyone wants to think they're immortal. You start talking about anything doing with death, and they don't take it well."

I almost told him about my experiences but drew back for the same reason Harrison was using.

"I guess you're right," I said.

'You're acting really weird. Are you mooning over Jean?"

"Yes, I guess," I parried. I had gotten no consolation from the conversation. I wasn't asking the right questions and really didn't want the answer.

I knew I wasn't performing well for Jack. I was anxious, tense, grumpy, and had little energy, all classic signs of depression. We often only do what is right when something with meaning is threatened. I knew unless I got a handle on my problem, Jack would fire me. I told Jack I was depressed about Jean, and he once again recommended the Chapman Counseling Center and offered to reduce my workload or hire another RA.

I was getting possessive about the project. I apologized for the falloff in my work and decided I needed to act before I lost my job. What held me back from getting help was the fear of past rejection, which always lingers longest and most intensely in my memory.

I first thought about telling my parents but rejected that. Among the many things I have never understood is why people will quickly reveal the most intimate details of their lives to strangers, including strangers found on social media in modern times, but resist telling those details to their spouses and those who love unconditionally.

We were still far away from the time when trading the names of psychological counselors at cocktail parties was ordinary conversation, and admitting you were in counseling was a source of pride. The language of psychology was imprecise and derogatory. Terms like nervous breakdown and neurosis connoted weakness. We were still in an age that despised weakness of any kind, especially among men. In 1972, Thomas Eagleton would be forced off the Democratic presidential ticket because he suffered from and had been hospitalized for depression, so there was a real risk that seeking help would be an albatross around your neck.

Depression is a disease like a schoolyard bully, gaining power through lack of confrontation. It's a shipworm eating the timbers of the psyches' hull. Those who are saturnine have a magnetic filter that attracts the negative poles of events while filtering felicity, leaving them preoccupied with adverse outcomes. Like a paraphrase of Orwell, work becomes a burden; pleasure unknown; relationships a trial; fear triumphs over love; hatred replaces tolerance; foreboding replaces joy. Depression imposes a quarantine, and in its loneliness, the soul, like the single ember in a fire, grows colder, never warmer.

The great anxiety of depression is that it will never end and that life will never be the same again. That what was important is now trivial, and that all explanations are useless. It seems that self-destruction is the only course to stop suffering.

I had a solid A in depression.

I made an appointment with Lazlo Jacoby, PhD, who had a lot of experience in clinical settings. I wasn't sure what that meant to me, but it sounded impressive. Later in life, I developed the habit of scrutinizing a person's office, furnishings for clues about the person. If I had done that sort of analysis, it might have saved me from what followed.

I arrived at his office my usual five minutes early. I had to fill out reams of questionnaires. Jacoby kept me waiting for what seemed like twenty minutes, but when I looked at the clock, it had only been seven. When you are a precise person, it's hard to wait for others, and I was getting more stressed as time passed, so I was irritable when the secretary waved me through the door to his office.

Jacoby was very tall, six foot four or five, I estimated. Athletically thin, his long face had high, prominent cheekbones, and his cheeks were hollow. The word *aesthetic* sprang to mind. His rimless glasses perched at the end of his nose, far away from his pale eyes, topped by caterpillar eyebrows. He was plainly dressed, his hair matching his grays and whites, the dullness relieved only by a red-and-white-striped tie.

When he spoke, there was no warmth in his voice. His tone did not soothe. I was ready to find fault; I got the feeling I was more of a nuisance than anything else. He had my responses to the questionnaires, and he sat behind his desk, placing me in a subordinate position. The chair I was sitting in had been designed by the Spanish Inquisition, too short for my long calves, and the hard surface gave no rest to my butt. Now subordinated, irritated, and uncomfortable, I was not ready for the rest of the hour.

He asked a few questions, then said, "It says here you're depressed."

"Yes, I just feel like nothing matters anymore."

Then he asked one of those questions in the category of, "Where was the last time you saw it when you lose something?"

"What are you depressed about?"

I told him about Jean leaving.

"So this is all about your little girlfriend leaving? The ending of a college romance?" His tone was dismissive, belittling, and frankly infuriating.

Jack told me a therapist could only help if they knew all the facts, and there was a confidentiality restriction, so I should not be afraid to unburden.

I decided to follow Jack's advice, "It's not just her leaving. There…there were"—I paused for a second—"things that preceded her departure."

"Go on," Jacoby said, lowering his chin to look over his glasses. It was not a comforting move, more like a teacher about to issue punishment.

With the trust of youth in higher authority and the naivete born of lack of experience, I told him all of it. I was terrified. I never told anyone outside the family the whole story, but this guy was supposed to help me.

He listened impassively, except for his tell, a slight twitch at the corner of his left eye, and as I got deeper into the story, his expression hardened with disbelief.

After my recital, he said, "I see. I'm afraid we're out of time for today. We need to talk more about this as soon as we can. Let's say next week?"

I left totally disquieted. I had hoped unburdening would relieve me of the weight I bore. Instead, I felt worse.

During the next week, as I thought about it, I concluded that if I had heard the story for the first time, I wouldn't believe it either. We take for granted we have credibility. That what we say will be accepted. I realized no one had any reason to believe me, and Jacoby, who dealt with this sort of stuff daily, had an even greater reason not to believe it.

Catastrophic thinking appeared, and I began to worry about the consequences. Jacoby could, and probably would, tell Jack. I could lose my job. That could lead to him telling the school administration they could discipline me. I didn't know how, but depression is a great conjurer. Finally, he could tell the police I was unbalanced and needed watching. I started to beat myself up and work myself into a lather. Depression is a great creator of dire consequences.

The following week I presented myself at Jacoby's office with the joy of a condemned man. This time he sat on the same side of the desk. I felt better seeing him trying to get comfortable in his torture chair.

"David." He began. He was more animated than the last time. "Let me review what we talked about last time, to be sure I have the facts correct. Okay?"

"Sure." What else could I say?

"You told me that on four occasions—"

"Five," I interrupted. "There were five."

He stared at me with impatience at my interruption.

"On several occasions," he rephrased, dismissing my remark as meaningless, "over the last five or six years, you've had visions of someone's death and the person died shortly after that these...these visions." This was not an interrogatory; it was a declaration.

"Yes, sir."

"Have you ever had any other visions or delusions of any kind?"

Even in my youthful inexperience, I knew the importance of words and connotations. To have a vision, the word I had used to describe my experiences, was one thing, but the word *delusion* connoted falsity. A vision can be supernatural or supersensual sight, but delusions are false sights. If I let him continue to mischaracterize my experience, I was admitting my experiences were false.

"I used the word *vision*. I've had no other visions other than these five times." I emphasized the word *vision* when I spoke. "Each time I saw a spot or black mark, it was at the point where something was going to happen."

He seemed taken aback at my correction of his framing language. "Let's not quibble over the word. Spots, visions, delusions, manifestations, they all fall under the heading of delusion." He was excited, sitting upright, leaning forward.

I slumped in my chair, arms folded across my chest, trying to get as far from him as possible.

"Words mean things," I said meekly. "Delusions are false things; what I saw, I saw. It was a vision."

"Let's assume you actually saw these, these spots." Again with the dismissal. "Is it possible these delus...visions were some trick of light and shadow and so on?"

"My grandparents and parents asked the same thing, and I have asked myself the same question. I could accept it if it only happened once or twice, but five times seems unlikely."

He tapped his right index finger against his lips a few times before continuing, "Have you ever," he added quickly, pointing his finger at me, "heard voices, seen things no one else sees?"

My anger and fear were rising. Of course, I had seen things other people hadn't. That's what the spots are all about! I was essentially being asked, 'when did you first realize you were crazy?' at least that's what it seemed to me. He had a beatific smile on his face like he had it all figured out, was joyous at his knowledge, and I was just some crazy kid.

I summoned up my courage. "I continue to object to the word delusion, sir," I said, trying to sound in control and authoritative. "It's incorrect and has a negative connotation of mental illness, and I'm not mentally ill."

"The symptoms of mental illness, David, are often hidden. Denial is the first revealed symptom. What else would you call them? They aren't real. No one can see death. Can't be done, so there must be some other rational explanation. The mind is immensely powerful and can cause people to see things, and memory is fallible. Another issue is that you could be confusing correlation with causation; you see a spot that might be from a normal process, but because you have seen them before, and death occurred, your mind tricks you into believing the spots are warnings of death."

He looked at his watch. "Too bad...we are once again out of time. We'll set up weekly appointments so we can really dig into this." He leaned forward, patting my knee, which totally creeped me out, before he said, "We can get through this. We can make you better, David, we really can!" Then he sat back with a look on his face like he had just offered me the keys to a kingdom. I suppose in his mind, he had.

I had gone in with a feeling of dread, and I left with one of fear. I had sought help with something troubling and inexplicable, and now I was looking at the front end of a train. The concern that stopped a legion of sufferers from seeking help was staring me in the face. I was about to have a big C for crazy stamped on my forehead for all to see.

I did my classes that afternoon, went back to the dorm, did the dinner dishes, and then went to Jack's office for a short work period. Something felt different.

"David," Jack began almost before I stopped moving. "I know I have been asking a lot of you lately." He paused to light a cigarette. When a topic of conversation might be difficult, he had two tells, one was a cigarette, and the other was he stopped using contractions. "I hope"—more puffing—"that you know the last thing I want to do is cause you any problems that might"—he took a long drag—"hamper." He had been searching for the word, "What appears to be a bright future. You need to tell me if you need a break."

"Thanks," I said. "I'm fine." I placed a fair amount of emphasis on the fine. "I'm just a little on edge." And we left it at that.

I knew, however, what was different, and I thought, *Fuck, Jacoby has talked to Jack.* Now I knew the confidentiality agreement was tissue-thin, and my catastrophic thinking was correct. My fear amped up a notch. I should have canceled my other appointments with Jacoby and tried to nip the spread of the knowledge of my insanity, but I didn't.

It felt different when I entered Jacoby's office for the next meeting. Usually, his office looked like a monk's cell, with everything in its place and a clean desktop. Now prominently placed on the desk was a large cross, more correctly, a crucifix, and a Bible next to it.

Jacoby leaped right into the session, "David, I've been thinking about your issues, and we are in a position to help, but our success will depend on how much you trust me, your faith, and your willingness to get better."

The total weight of my recovery was on me.

"Can you have faith, trust, and confidence?"

How do you respond to a question like that?

"I'm not sure," I replied, "tell me more."

Jacoby leaned against the backrest of his chair, steepled his fingers, the middle fingers on his lips, then lowered his chin to look over his glasses. "David, in addition to being a psychologist and professor,

I'm a Baptist minister. After some research, thought, and prayer, I've come to believe that what you are seeing, and I believe you really are seeing them, are visions created by the evil one to capture your soul."

He delivered this extraordinary statement with no sense of humor or a hint that it might sound outlandish. He had a triumphant look the religious can get when they stumble on some gnostic concept or a soul in need.

"Your family is not religious, are they?" he continued.

"Not overly. My father is Catholic in name, and my mother has no denomination. We went to mass most of the time even when we lived in Wheaton."

"I expected as much, and this is where faith becomes critical. When a person's spirit is not focused on the Word and God's saving grace, there's ample room for the devil to work his black magic. We're going to be fighting for your soul and theirs! You have dwelled long enough outside the light of Christ. Satan has noticed and brought this delusional plague on you. We can in short order banish the Evil One and have you rise"—he made an upsweeping motion with one hand—"clean, free of taint and sin, in a personal relationship with Christ Jesus!" The intensity of his voice was genuinely frightening.

He reminded me of some of the more furious preachers in Wheaton or the television evangelists of the time like Oral Roberts. There was an almost maniacal light in his eyes. They looked like what I call Charlie Manson eyes, his face almost incandescent with emotion, holy mission, and eagerness to wage a righteous battle for my soul. It was scary.

"Well, I'm not sure," I started to say thoughtfully, but I never got it all the way out as he jumped on my uncertainty.

"You see! You see!" he said as if I had just proven his point, "that doubt, that's the devil working. You know the right path is baptism, washing away your sins, accepting Jesus Christ as your personal Savior, but the devil is working on you and in you."

He stopped his headlong rush toward my salvation. It had to be very exciting for him to have a devil-possessed nineteen-year-old to save. He took a breath and cleared the saliva collected at the corners of his mouth; the intensity of his purpose was undiminished. My heart was racing. Preachers use the cadence of speech to excite emotion. Jacoby had learned that lesson well.

I looked across the space between us, and I could see his eyes wide in anticipation, boring in, searching me. As he leaned toward me, I leaned back and looked away.

"You see, David, you just leaned away from me and broke eye contact. Both of those are symptoms of mental illness, and the devil does not like the truth I'm speaking. He's trying to prevent you from coming to Christ."

I was a rat in a maze; there were only two escape routes to go in his direction or continue in demonic possession.

I used what I thought was the perfect mode of escape. "I'm sorry, Dr. Jacoby, I have a class starting, then I have to work for Dr. Pierce."

Jacoby looked at me with a combination of pity, disbelief, and sorrow. We stared each other down for a minute. I didn't want to speak and make this worse, and he didn't talk because he was like a salesperson closing a sale. After the closing statement, the next person to speak loses.

Finally, he said, "Well, David, I was hoping we could reach some understanding, but you're very adamant that your delusions are real, and you are resisting my therapeutic design, so I think we are going to have to take some other steps to get you back on track. I'm going to recommend to the college that you go to regular counseling sessions. I'm concerned that your delusions are going to get worse and that you may become a danger to yourself and others eventually."

Now I was petrified, but then he went into tritheism. "Look, David, we are all in this together. We all need help once in a while, and I know you want help. No one likes to live a delusional and unbalanced life. You want to get better, don't you?"

There it was, after three conversations, this psychologist was telling me I was dangerously delusional or headed in that direction and unbalanced. After all, how could I become balanced if I wasn't unbalanced? I was being diagnosed as mentally ill. It was a diagnosis that would stay with me for the rest of my life and color decisions others made about me.

"Dr. Jacoby, I came here looking for help, and now you're going to sentence me to counseling, and the school's records will reflect that for all to see. It's going to say I needed help for a mental problem. How am I ever going to get a job when I graduate with that on my records?"

"It is what it is. I can't do anything about what happens to you in the future. You walked in here with some wild story, and you won't accept the fact that you're delusional. In my experience, delusional people don't get less delusional. You are either mentally unbalanced, either due to something from your childhood or a disease of the brain, drugs, or alcohol, or it could be that you are just looking for some attention. The real issue is that you are possessed by the devil who seeks your soul for his hideous purposes."

I sat there through his soliloquy, shaking my head in negation at every accusation growing increasingly worried about what he would do next. I found out later that the usual route of inquiry for a psychologist when they couldn't pin down the origin of a problem was to look at the parents.

"I know from your actions, the devil is working within you. Your resistance is not your fault. It's the devil resisting the will of God. You are aiding the devil in his work by not allowing the Word to fill you."

I ran, ran from his office so quickly. I left one of my books next to my chair. When I got outside, I had the shakes. I was angry at what I viewed as betrayal, depressed at the course this had taken, and afraid of what might happen if he followed through with his threats. I made a beeline for the nearest phone and called home to tell my parents I was coming home for spring break. Then I called a travel agent and made plane reservations to Chicago.

I stumbled through the next two weeks; certain word was spreading about my supposed mental condition. I started to interpret everything as aimed at me. When people stopped talking when I was near, I convinced myself it was because of me. I always felt people were staring at me, whispering, and laughing behind my back. The only good news was that Jack's grant was renewed and increased.

Mom and Dad were no fools, and my sudden desire to come home told them something was happening, so most of the usual *welcome homes* got cut short after they picked me up at O'Hare. I had worked myself into a state of utter desperation. Someone said you should never criticize yourself because there are plenty of people who will do it for you, but I was in full critical mode. I doubted my sanity, my place in the world. I had suicidal ideation.

Jacoby's proclamation of demonic possession shattered my confidence in professional help. The cumulative shock of seeing death five times was oppressive. The loss of Jean's father cemented the reality of what the spots meant; the spots could occur at any time on anyone, no matter how close they were emotionally. How could you ever have a successful relationship if you knew something that terrible?

All of my experiences with the spots and death were unexplored territory. I was being forced to deal with death, not just deal with it but also with the secret foreknowledge of death.

Carrying secrets is mentally very destructive. Jacoby had planted the idea that this was genuinely satanic. Based on that finding, I wondered if I might be able to cause the spots to wish a person dead. Where did Satanic power stop? My thoughts and emotions could be a death ray. It also appeared there was nothing the fated person or I could do to prevent the death once the spot appeared. My mind raced in all directions and raised lots of questions but no answers.

I was a student and the son of a scholar. I should have been questing for knowledge of the anomaly in my life, my ability to see death, but I didn't. I made no effort to gain understanding; I shoved it deep inside me as men tend to do. It became the demon of chaos riding inside, ready to devour me.

Nietzsche said when you look into the abyss long enough, it looks back at you. I was looking into the abyss of death, humankind's greatest fear. The abyss was changing me. When I thought about Jean and her father, I had not been what I considered honest. I wondered if I could ever be honest with anyone if I knew they or someone close to them would die. Good relationships, we were told, are based on honesty, and I might be bringing a vast element of dishonesty to any relationship.

*****

It had been almost two years since the family had seen me. Eleanor was off to the University of Illinois Circle Campus in Chicago in the fall. Daphne, now fifteen, was doing well in her new school. It turned out she had dyslexia, and Peter, fourteen, was all arms and legs, and full of questions about California, cars, girls, and surfing. When I finished telling them all I knew, I got Mom and Dad alone.

Mom took over right at the start.

"We got a call last Friday from somebody at Chapman, a Dr. Jacoby, who introduced himself as a psychologist. He said you had been in to see him about a problem. He was very concerned about your mental stability." She looked over at Dad, then continued, "This man, this Jacoby, said you were having delusions about seeing when people were going to die. He feels there was something wrong with you." She paused. "Is he a minister in addition to being a psychologist?"

"Yes."

"I thought so. He said that the devil possessed you, and if we were a more religious family, this wouldn't be happening. He suggested we should take you to church and, in his words, 'have the devil's work exorcised so you can get back in the good graces of God.'"

Few topics inspired my mother's passion faster than religion, and now add to her outrage over it, she was in maternal protection mode. Her voice had been gradually rising, and she was flogging her one hand back and forth on the table.

Mom and Dad looked at each other. Mom was ready to have a go at Jacoby, Chapman, and anyone else, and I feared for the damage she'd inflict.

Dad took her hand in a gesture designed to calm her down. "Okay, David, why don't you tell us what led you to go see Dr. Jacoby? Then we will all be on the same page. Is this related to that conversation we all had a couple of years ago?"

"Yeah," I said, my voice dropping in tone at the remembrance of that awful night. "There have been a couple of more sightings since then, and I'm starting to worry there is something wrong with me, as no one else can see the spots. I'm convinced they aren't just shadows and stuff like that. I told you at the Christmas crucifixion." The phrase got disapproving looks from Mom and Dad. "About Shamus, the football player, and Iris Wagner, but you don't know about Caesar Tovar and Jean's father."

After I finished, Dad said, "So Mr. Tovar died of a heart attack almost two years after you saw the spot on his chest and Jean's father died…"

"I don't know if he's dead, but the doctors said there was no treatment, so I assume it's a matter of time."

"Point taken, but you saw the spot, and he was diagnosed with cancer shortly after that."

"Yep, and Jean left. Chapman and I got the impression things were not going well."

"Oh, the poor woman," said Mom. "I should send them a note."

"Okay, first off, we believe you saw what you saw." His willingness to attribute truth first was one of the many attributes I admired about him. "If you think about it, you have to admit this is quite a story, and I hope you understand others might not accept it."

I nodded. "But it's true."

"Yes, but that doesn't mean it's believable," said Mom.

"How can the truth not be believable?" I asked.

"When it contradicts what's established truth in a person's mind," said Dad. "History is replete with people who've had visions, claimed foreknowledge, prophesized events. Usually, they're met with scorn, and sometimes worse. The results of some prophecies were realized in a contemporary period—the link between what they said and the actual events still hasn't been conclusively proven by science. Most of the prophecies can be explained by happenstance, lucky guesses, and synthesis of knowledge. Most of their prophecy has been judged to be true only long after its original utterance and then only with some creative rereading," Dad said. "Still, there are some cases where an explanation is still wanting."

"So people are just reacting to me like I was some old-time soothsayer like Nostradamus?"

"What's interesting in your formulation is that *sooth* is an archaic word for truth." He paused, working out a way to explain his ideas. "When a deeply held belief is challenged, most people are unwilling to believe the new. We all think in prescribed ways with rules of logic, behavior, and morals that determine our truth or reality. When new or unknown information appears, humans have to determine if it has value or should change the way we think."

"What's the reaction when you tell others about this, David?" asked Mom.

"It has always been negative," I replied.

"What about the effect on you, son?" Mom asked.

"Afraid, guilty, ashamed, mad, depressed. I don't know if the depression is from the reaction people have or knowing death or a combination. I was terrified of Phil attacking me, and I was really scared when Caesar died, and what scared me in the last two sightings was the lack of serious reaction. In the last two, my initial concern was how this would affect me personally, if I would lose my jobs, or if Jean would leave. The mercenary nature really scared me. Am I getting that jaded?"

"All are common to new and disturbing information entering the arena," said Dad. "If we want to be rational about this, we should begin to eliminate other causes for what you are seeing. If we eliminate other causes, what remains must be the truth."

"Sherlock Holmes would be proud of you," I said.

While all the beaches of California lay open, I was poked, prodded, hit, scraped, stuck, felt, touched, questioned, and hammered by a rotating cast of characters. After it all, I found out that I was slightly lighter and more anxious than a typical twenty-year-old. My vision and hearing were perfect, and there were no signs of tumors. The psychiatrist mentioned a form of hysteria that can lead to visions but was honest enough to admit he didn't think that was the case.

There was no physical basis for my having visions.

While it was helpful to eliminate any pathology, it was also unsettling in that if there was no organic cause of the spots, then the cause must be functional. Maybe Jacoby was partly right; I really was mentally ill. The psychiatrist in Chicago didn't have enough time to assess my mental health fully, so it was still a real possibility.

Grandma Ruth arrived in the middle of my break without Angus; supposedly, she came to shop in Chicago. It soon became evident that shopping was a cover. I was the real reason she was there. She was always trying to get me alone, offering to go with me to my doctor's appointments. I managed to avoid that, but one day she cornered me.

"We need to talk, Davey." She was the only one I allowed to use the diminutive of my name.

"About what?" I asked with feigned innocence.

"Your visions," said Ruth.

"Why? You want to see if I'm crazy? Everyone else does," I said as I opened two Cokes, one for her.

"I don't think you're crazy, Davie, but I need to ask some questions, and I hoped you would grant your grandmother some time without being angry. We are all trying to help," she said, shaming me.

I fell silent, so she carried on, "Tell me about what happens when you see the spots?"

"Not much, but I see them. There's a spot on Shamus, on the side of his head, the football player his neck, Iris her belly, Jean's father his nose, and Caesar his chest. It was just a black spot."

"When you saw it, were there others around?"

"With Shamus and Iris. I mean, there were always people around, but I didn't tell anyone about the spot, except Shamus. I think you are really asking if others saw the spot, and the answer is no."

"When you saw them did you see anything else, like with Shamus or the football player? Did you see them lying there dead, or was the spot the only thing?"

"No, nothing else. I had some horrible dreams after Caesar died like creatures were yelling at me in some foreign language."

"These may seem like silly questions, Davie, and you may have answered them before to others, but I was reading something a few months back about people who claimed to see manifestations of people dying, but what they saw was the person actually dead, not a spot on a living person. I wanted to check on your visions to see."

*****

I went back to Chapman physically healthy but still thinking about what Dad said about new information and still uneasy. I could avoid public censure by not talking about it, but I wondered if I had the strength to deal with my own emotions. I avoided Jacoby like the plague, but I still feared he would escalate things given that he had called Mom.

Another thing occurred to me about the most recent spot sightings. In both the case of Caesar and Steve, almost my first thought was mercenary. In the case of Caesar, it was the security of my jobs and financial outlook, and with Steve, it was my losing Jean. In both cases, my concerns ran over what I believed should have been my thought, that of charity and concern for the other person. I did not want the spots to turn me into a grasping, clawing jerk, seeking only my own comfort, but I feared I was going that way. Perhaps not so strangely, all the work in Chicago did not reduce my sense of shame.

I finished my junior year in the upper 20 percent of my class. I had taken a lot of hours in my first three years, so I only needed nine credit hours to graduate. I was going to have a lot of free time. I flew back to Chicago for Eleanor's graduation but returned to California for the rest of the summer. The utility had sought me out, and I had my job back, which was fortuitous as it helped me in the work I was doing for Jack.

During the summer, Jack and I prepared the data, which would be the basis of what the books told us was called a routine. In formatting the data, we used a machine like a typewriter to create punch cards with the instructions in a series of punched holes or solid paper. Each of the cards carried a warning, "Do not fold, spindle or mutilate," which, in one of those Luddite rebellions, was the motto of the new humanistic philosophy sweeping the world. If they had only known what awaited them.

In assembling the data, I noticed a couple of items that I thought we could use in the everyday world to make things easier in our dispatch. The county's growth had not slowed down. If anything, the war made it increase. The stresses on our antiquated system were intensifying, and service complaints rose. The chaotic work situation led to complaints and slowdowns from the crews' union.

I started making generally well-received recommendations to the others in dispatch. When I finally had what I thought was enough case-by-case analysis to warrant further study, I decided I needed to talk to my immediate boss.

Frank Cicilio, my boss, decided we needed to bring in the union since my ideas would involve crew changes and equipment utilization. The union and Frank were both helpful and eager to move forward. They got me permission to access past dispatch records. That involved climbing over stacks of dirty, dusty boxes, sometimes alive with spiders, centipedes, and rodents' droppings in a dozen forgotten basements. I undertook the task with the absurdity of youth and full of jejune arrogance.

My analysis convinced me, and eventually, Frank and Herb Zoller, the union rep, the utility could solve many of the issues we faced with a few changes. I wrote up a proposal, and Frank and Herb agreed to take it to their boss, Ernst Tiffin. Frank and Herb got more from their employees than any other managers, and they obtained the ultimate accolade of being considered one of us by the crews.

Tiffin wasn't anyone's us. Short and dumpy, his high, domed forehead gave a false impression of intelligence. He tried to cover his hair loss with a comb-over that looked like the stuff from a vacuum cleaner. Tiffin was a Navy veteran who never heard a shot fired in anger. He was staunchly pro-war, and proud head of the local chapter of the John Birch Society. Tiffin thought Ronald Reagan was God, saw a commie under every bed and blanket, and was free with opinions developed in a mind closed to new ideas.

Herb said Tiffin slept with the windows closed at night to prevent any fresh ideas from getting in. He was always drawing on some story of his lackluster Navy service to impart wisdom and diminish others.

He knew nothing of electricity or repair work and was determined to stay that way, meaning Herb and Frank would always have jobs. This towering intellect stood athwart the route my idea had to take to reach anyone who could see its value.

Of course, he shot me down with the comment that I was just a summer employee and still wanted seasoning. He talked like that, with a faux British syntax.

Rebuffed in my grand scheme to revolutionize the utility with resultant praise and glory, I undertook a project to prove my work. Herb and Frank supported it. They had no risk. Herb was the union head, and Tiffin couldn't operate without Frank.

The problem, in a nutshell, was that the utility stored all its equipment in one central location, but the calls for service spanned the whole county. As the population increased, the drive time from Orange increased. The available time for the crews on site declined. Unless the utility wanted to pay overtime as per the union contract, which it was loath to do, service levels were going to decline.

I constructed a spreadsheet, a cumbersome task then, and filled it with all sorts of data. Using my spreadsheet and my work for Jack, I made predictions about when and where trouble would likely occur, and Frank and Herb arranged for equipment to be staged near those locations.

Over the three months I was there, by the measures I used, the equipment utilization and work done skyrocketed, and with it came a considerable decline in service calls and complaints. As we operated, I made changes to the spreadsheet, and it became more and more accurate. It convinced me that it could save the company enormous sums of money if used system-wide. I was satisfied I had proven my concept and wrote it up again to take to Tiffin.

Tiffin, of course, knew better. Frank, Herb, and I were in his office. "What you have done is to go ahead and pursue this project"—he waved his hand at the document on his desk—"when I specifically forbade you to do so."

"All I did, sir, was take data, some from archives and some current data, and analyze it for inefficiencies to try to identify cost savings and improve working conditions." I stuck in the last phrase because it made it a union issue, and I figured Tiffin would respect the union's endorsement. "You should be glad I did because it shows you can save the utility lots of time and money," I said with the passion of youth threatened by ignorance.

What I didn't know then was the accusatory power of the word *you* in conversations. It's a lot easier to get an agreement if you don't say it. Marriage and having children would bring that lesson home.

It was the first time I would make this mistake but not the last. I believed that my knowledge, hard work, insouciance, and igneous presence would open all doors. Perhaps it was a romantic illusion. After all, I lived in the same area, which created most of the world's delusions, that my work, its benefits so apparent to me, would open the heavens and allow God's light to shine on the benighted. It would not be the last time illusion would be shattered.

I was wrong, and being wrong takes more effort than admitting it.

"So you are what?" Tiffin asked, waiting for an answer.

"Twenty," I said.

"Ah, yes, twenty," he said, smiling maliciously. "I remember when I was that age. I was never as ignorant or self-important as you. I guess that's all we can expect from someone fresh from the ivory towers of a socialist university. Frankly, what you have done is disloyal, the quality of this 'work,'" he said archly, "is so far beneath the standards I demand, it's disgusting and makes me question why we ever hired you."

I started to speak, but he waved me down. "I'm not done. Did you ever think that others have studied this? There are a few people here who have far more knowledge and seniority than you. Almost everyone, as a matter of fact."

I went headlong into the breach. "Has it really? I would love to see the work. Maybe I could learn from it. All I'm trying to do, Mr. Tiffin, is to help the company cut costs, make more money, and be more efficient, sir."

I took him aback. "Very noble, I'm sure, if true, which is unlikely. It has been thoroughly studied and rejected"—he paused for effect—"by better people than you. I have been with the company long enough to know what things work want won't. This is useless. People who show this sort of disloyalty are usually not doing their jobs very well. I will be watching you, MacIntosh. I can't believe the two of you"—he waved at Frank and Herb—"allowed this to go on. I'm very disappointed."

"The issue of the crew and equipment utilization has been around for a while, Ernst. I would like to see that study you mentioned," said Herb. Since he was the union boss, Tiffin couldn't blow him off.

"Well, well, well, I'll have to find it. It was a long time ago. I will find it and get back to you." Tiffin was fumbling and lying; that much was abundantly clear even to me. Just before we left his office, Tiffin looked up at me. "And, MacIntosh, no more disloyalty. Stick to your job and let your betters run the place." His voice was dripping with threat.

We left. I was pissed off, but Herb steered us to his car and drove us to a bar. He ordered three beers.

"Boy, that sucks," I said, "I thought we'd get a better reception."

"It won't suck as much as what comes next," Herb said.

I must have looked stupid.

"That hump," he said, waving his beer in a nonspecific way, "will bury it for a year or more, then he'll submit it to the management, and claim full credit. We've been trying to get this done for years, but you did the final piece in a way that made sense. He can't say it without giving up credit, but we will. Thanks."

We clinked bottles, and life moved on.

The senior year started with new tensions. It was impossible to ignore the war, although I had tried my hardest. It was a staple of discussion. As the war intensified, so did the tenor of the daily anti-war demonstrations. We had seen a sitting president chased from office by the war, witnessed open insurrection and police overreaction at the Democratic Convention, and an obscure senator mount a campaign on a single issue and fail because he attracted a better-known but nonetheless opportunistic competitor.

Like his brother, Robert Kennedy, the opportunist, fell victim to a bullet, leaving no one happy with the choice between Humphrey and Nixon for president. For the college crowd ending the war was the only issue.

Protests become potent, not necessarily due to the justice of the cause or the emotional content of the message. They gain potency with continued repetition of grievance and the organization of the advocates. In one of my classes, I learned there had been an infinitesimally small number of communists in the Russian Revolution compared to the total population of Russia. They won by superior organization, ruthlessness, and brutality of their tactics. The antiwar, civil rights, and feminist movements all discovered three things, the politics of envy, the wonders of intersectionality, and the power of media. The first two emoted, and the third possessed the channels to spread the grievance. Those three fuses would lead to explosions that would rock the nation and the world for decades.

In the real world, however, in ten months, I and thousands of others were going face four choices: run the risk of the draft, enlist, hope I wouldn't be drafted, or resist. Some of my contemporaries took off to Canada or Sweden. In the meantime, life still had to be lead.

We ran our program through the computers, solved some operational problems, and reran it. The results were far better than we expected. The machine demonstrated it could learn from mistakes. Despite limited computer time and capacity, Jack's hypothesis was proven. Jack's paper got great feedback, and in the introduction, he was fulsome in his praise of my efforts.

I really enjoyed my senior year. I had plenty of free time. I tried to grow a mustache, but it looked like my upper lip was dirty, so I ditched it. The year was everything I hoped college would have been, and only one thing would have made it better, someone to enjoy it with, but Jean was gone.

As June and graduation approached, I got two documents in the mail. One offered a full-time position at the utility. The second announced my reclassification for the draft.

Decision time.

I admit I found the draft notice inconvenient. I had a plan for my life. Perhaps not a plan but a series of events that didn't contemplate an unknown time in the service or death. My parents were of two minds. Mom favored resisting; she was antiwar but not aggressively so but would respect my decision so long as it was thoughtful. Dad did what intellectuals tend to do; he explained things. His explanation did little to quiet my concerns. I feared potentially dying, but I had finally seen *The Twilight Zone* episode Xanders had referred to years before. The guy who saw the lights on those about to die saw it on himself. I was concerned that would be my fate.

I had not seen any spots since Jean's dad. I had pushed them aside as I went on living my life. Now facing military service with its omnipresence of death, I wondered if I would be driven nuts by seeing the spots constantly. My concern almost led me to take one of the other courses. I couldn't get a deferment for conscience. I had no disqualifying diseases. The military wouldn't believe my tales of seeing the spots and medically refuse me. If I used that idea, I might be eliminated, but I would carry the stigma of mental instability with me forever.

That left me with the choice of going to Canada, going to jail for resisting the draft, or going into the service and hoping to be spared the torture the spots could unleash. In the end, it worked out better than I could have expected.

Graduation came, and the whole family came out to see me graduate. After they left, I went to the utility and told them I was grateful for the job offer but was going into the service. The personnel manager had the Marines' Globe and Anchor on his desk sign and said, "Good for you. We're going to hire you anyway and hold you inactive due to military service. We can't pay you, but you will be gaining seniority while you are away."

I accepted, signed the paperwork, went to the recruiting station, and signed up for the Navy. My concerns about the spots led me to choose a service where the risk of seeing large amounts of death would be minimal. The Coast Guard was my first choice, the Air Force the second, but they met their quotas with other kids trying hard to avoid combat.

CHAPTER 5

I resisted the blandishments of the recruiter of going to officer candidate school, as it would extend my service. Two weeks later, I was off. Navy basic training was at Great Lakes Naval Training Center in Chicago. After all my wishes and hopes to get to California, I was back in Chicago. Why the Navy trains its sailors so far from salt water is lost on me.

Ruth and Angus came up to Chicago to see me graduate, and since I had a few days before I was due for my next assignment, I went home.

Ruth wanted to continue the discussion we had a few years before. "Davie, have you had any more visions since we talked last?"

"No, Grandma, they seem to be taking a break or something, or I have been too busy to notice. The chance of seeing the spots is one of the reasons I went into the Navy. I hope they stay away."

"Okay, good, I hope so too. I was doing some genealogy work on the family, and I had a letter from the secretary of the Clan MacIntosh Society in Scotland. She passed on a story that there was a rumor that one of our sixteenth-century relatives might have had visions."

"What happened to him or her?"

"Don't know, but I thought it was an interesting story," she replied.

"It's interesting it might be fascinating to see if there have been others in our family history to see these visions, then we might know if it's an inheritable thing. The spots have had such a strange pattern that it's almost like some external force controls them. Sometimes I think Jacoby might have been right and that those who have the spots are cursed by whatever power controls them. It would be nice to know if it runs in families and if my children might be cursed.

"I'm glad they are gone" was all Ruth would say.

After basic, I was sent to San Diego and trained as a Yeoman. In Navy speak, a clerk. After Yeoman school, I was stateside for a year, then deployed on the *USS Kitty Hawk*.

After six months at sea, I was back in San Diego. With the unwinding of the war, I was offered early discharge in return for a commitment to the reserves. I took the offer.

My work with Jack gave me a different view of problems and showed me that computers could go a long way to making the world work more effectively. The *Kitty Hawk*'s battle group consisted of eleven ships. The logistics of supplying and maintaining a fleet at sea were staggering, and the Navy was an early adopter of computers. As I worked, I saw the incredible interconnections of the task force elements, and I realized how innovative the work Jack and I had done had been.

During my two-and-a-half years in the Navy, I was remarkably free of spots.

Not that death wasn't present. One guy walked into the propeller of a Hawkeye radar plane; another was blown overboard by a jet blast, one night off the coast of Vietnam, a badly shot up F4 Phantom smashed into the roll-up at the end of the flight deck, spewing fuel and aircraft parts down the deck. In addition to the two-person aircrew, three-deck crew died. It wasn't like death wasn't there. It was like the spots had taken a vacation. Hopefully, a permanent one.

It was a faint hope but hope all the same. I was glad for the break. The last spot I had seen was on Jean's father, and that loss still hung with me. There was one other possibility. The mind is very powerful and can force a person to see or not see what might be apparent. I would later learn there are syndromes such as hemispatial neglect, aphantasia, and schotoma, which can create blind spots and can account for not seeing what might otherwise be apparent.

Then again, there was the thought I had two years back that there was some extraordinary force controlling this, which for whatever reason was protecting me from an overwhelming assault on my mind. In the presence of so much potential death, it created a blind spot. In the movie Little Big Man, when Dustin Hoffman's character realizes that his Native American mentor is blind, he says, "Grandfather, you are blind," to which the chief responds, "I still see, it's just that the images no longer reach my heart."

Maybe that is what I experienced. I now added a question to the bits and pieces of data floating around in my mind. Did seeing the spots take a break, or was I developing a form of blindness? They were present, but I wasn't seeing them. Or was it that whatever power, good or evil, afflicting me had a compassionate nature and prevented me from seeing death and so preserved my sanity? Having had five experiences, I still hoped they would vanish as suddenly as they arrived.

After leaving the Navy, I took a month off just to decompress. The utility wasn't expecting me back for another four or five months, so I could finally enjoy California.

My time off also gave me a chance to really think about my future, a rare gift in our world.

I was a college graduate at the end of my formal education but at the early stages of my practical schooling. Rarely are we unique enough in thought to see the confluence of circumstances. Sometimes the right person exists in juxtaposition with the right circumstances.

A more factual statement would be plural, the right people, with the proper knowledge, connect with the right circumstances. Knowingly or not, I was at such a junction of circumstances. I didn't know the dimensions, but I thought I saw the opportunity.

California had tended to grow in bunches. The years of WWII made it the crossroads of the Pacific Theater, bringing hundreds of thousands to the Golden State. The growth of the '40s achieved critical mass, and development became internal, but as my story indicates, Golconda by the sea continued to have a loadstar effect.

While the sociology of demographic repositioning is the realm of academics, I saw the pragmatic realities of how the utility could manage its allocation of resources and capital.

I knew there was a role for large-scale computer-based data analysis to solve resource allocation issues, measure management effectiveness, and improve returns on investment. Several trends were working in my favor. Jack and I had been held back by scarce computer availability,

The space race and the war had driven technological improvement, and machine availability improved as costs fell.

During my absence and to no one's sorrow, Ernst Tiffin moved on. Rumor had it he was developing a filing system for the second copies of interoffice memos. My new boss was Al Jurret.

Al had the flair of a file folder, the sense of humor of a statue, and the voice of a crow. He looked like nature had taken a bunch of spare parts and given them to a committee of blind people, and the result was Al. He was tiny, and his narrow face was topped by subfusc hair.

I never saw him eat or get a cup of coffee. However, there was always a full hot cup on his desk. He was almost compulsively neat, his desk and office resembled a file drawer, and he never had a hair out of place, a wrinkle in his clothes, or a scuff on his shoes. He was always soigne.

Al was strange in looks and actions, but he and I seemed to get on well. He disguised his ambition well, combined it with a mind unburdened by convention. He knew I think that his appearance gave people a reason to discount him. Those who did so were often rudely surprised.

He was always better prepared than anyone. I watched him take apart swaggering bullies with an eerie calm and seemingly innocuous questions exposing the bully as a fool but leaving no rancorous feelings. He seemed to grasp the existential nature of the operating environment and knew changes were coming, and we needed to be in front of them instantly and completely.

Changes are always best when the alternative is chaos. Chaos forces us to examine the customary ways we have done things; chaos inspires fear, so overcoming it is redemptive. Chaos threatens paradigmatic thinking and changes assumptions of thought and action. Confronting chaos is terrifying, as is the failure to do so successfully, but we must do both to advance. Facing chaos is the route to new knowledge.

I felt Al understood the changes forced on us, and his ambition focused on being the one with the solution.

I could see little evidence that my original idea bore fruit. The changes in computers and my increased familiarity with systems integration gained in the Navy led me to believe my idea would work even more effectively now, so I prepared a presentation for Al.

Dad was a godsend to me here. I developed my thesis, and he treated me like a PhD candidate, testing my logic, trimming off the ragged edges of my thoughts, and prodding me to focus and avoid the flaw of trying to do too much.

When I presented the idea to Al, I was surprised at how fast he took to it.

"I see the fine hand of your father in this," he said.

"Do you know my father?" I replied.

"Of him, I know of him. When you look like me, David, you don't get asked to play football very often, and dating takes up little of your time, so you read. A lot. Classical literature has been an interest of mine. I thought his paper on Dante's *Inferno* was one of the best I've ever read. Fine mind."

"Thanks, I'll tell him you said so," I replied. "Where do we go from here?"

"You obviously know that not only the utility but also the entire county has been struggling with the correct allocation of resources for quite a few years. Tiffin, my predecessor, did you know him?"

"Yes, but not well," I replied.

"Said that he had been looking into a solution but never got very far," Al continued. "What you have proposed, only on a larger scale, is a big focus of the company. They have been trying to formulate a strategy to implement this sort of analysis. I think this has merit. I'm going to go upstairs with this." He tapped the folder containing my work and started pointing at the roof, speaking metaphorically since the building was one story. "In the meantime, I want you to start collecting data and doing what you can without computers, and what did you call it? Software, to make things go more smoothly. Send any questions my way."

"Good work, David."

In the ensuing months, I went to several senior management meetings and was added to the task force working on the issue. Things were moving faster than usual due to the presence of Arthur Andersen.

While we studied the project, I moved from Orange to Newport Beach. I shared an apartment with Lance Adderfelter, a salesman for the Irvine Ranch Company, which owned most of the land in the area, including Newport Beach.

Lance's extroversion was exhausting. His only interest in people was if they were helpful or posed a threat. He worked hard on me to quit the utility and join "the ranch," as he called it. Always with the glitter of money, parties, the good life, and as he termed them broads of every description. I was a stubborn Scot, and I was on a project, and I was going to see it through.

Newport Beach was the happening place, filled with clubs, bars, and restaurants full of young, single, career-based people dancing as fast as possible before they turned thirty, the end of life to them, approached. They seemed to be fatalistic and living unreal life. They knew the party had to end, and the horsemen of the apocalypse were waiting, so they partied on trying to escape reality for just a few more minutes.

A lot of the impetus for the lifestyle reflected substantial societal changes. The first wave of feminism helped women to become more assertive, and they started to break out of their formerly assigned roles—teacher, nurse, secretary stewardess, or mother. The new birth control pills opened up sex without consequences and made sex more available. Drugs, not just marijuana, but pills of various types, were becoming mainstream. There was an odd mixture of philosophy coming to the fore. It seemed to combine the nihilism of Nietzsche, the pessimism of Schopenhauer, the doubt of Sartre, the hedonism of Pan, and the self-worship of Narcissus.

We seemed to be moving pell-mell to what Durkheim called anomie, a social condition defined by the uprooting or breakdown of any moral values and standards or guidance for individuals to follow, and suicide rates began to rise. People were questioning their very existence, and there was nothing and no one offering anything other than placebos.

I felt out of phase, odd. I constantly thought I was the keeper of the flame of the old generation of philosophy. There seemed to be no belief or meaning. The government had proven itself to be untruthful. The news was alive with endless stories of government malfeasance and abuses of power. Politics seemed focused on envy of turning one group against the other. Rumor and innuendo increasingly became news.

In an echo of Orwell, public figures were held up to hate, none more so than LBJ and Richard Nixon. The new centurions of heroism were scoundrels like John Kerry, Abbie Hoffman, Howard Zinn, Daniel Ellsberg, Phillip Barringer, Daniel Sloan Coffin, Tom Hayden, and his wife, a traitorous actress who openly gave aid and comfort to the enemy during the Vietnam war and celebrated the deaths of her fellow countrymen. In another time, she would have been imprisoned or executed for her actions.

I have not spoken her name in over sixty years.

In this hothouse of lack of meaning, religion once again was offered the opportunity to prove its worth. In general, however, it capitulated to the mobs and became enraged at the world. Popular preachers added the power of unbridled invective to an explosive atmosphere. Not being able to command loyalty to their message of love, they substituted rhetoric and marginalized themselves.

I was not immune to the more open society, and I spread my wings a bit and got into a relationship with a girl we all dreamed about in Chicago. Her name was Sheryi, the dot on the *i*, a heart. No, really, I saw her birth certificate, and there it was; it was spelled that way on her driver's license. She was tall, taller than I was, all legs, bleached blond, deeply tanned with no tan lines, given to tight skirts, skimpy shorts, even smaller bathing suits, and drinking. She had no apparent job I ever discovered, which was the root of our breakup. She was perpetually broke, getting me to pick up a tab at a bar, buy her groceries, or whatever.

After nine months of "dating," mostly drunken sex and awful hangovers, she wanted to move in. She responded to my comment about sharing expenses by saying sex would be my payment, and I, in my usual suave way, equated that with the world's old profession, and the results were as expected.

I dated a few other women. I guess dating was a nice word for a few drinks, a couple of dinners, and then a few nights of grasping, gasping, sweaty sex before one of us realized it wasn't going to work, and we broke up. Usually, I got dumped for some blond surfer dude with white straight teeth, pecs and abs of steel, and a brain of mush, who treated the girl like shit.

In any case, the project moved along, and increasingly I was in contact with AA people. They were all beautifully educated, terribly, terribly, earnest, and intense. Although I was the inspiration for the project, I quickly realized I was the least qualified person on the team.

I knew so little of the programming languages, computer architecture, and software design I could not see if I was being handed a load of bullshit. So off I went to UCI, the University of California Irvine, which was then working up to its later nickname—the University of Chinese Immigrants.

In addition to my regular work, I was like Poe's narrator in *The Raven*, pondering over many a volume of forgotten lore.

It took three years, but finally, we had a computer-based system to help us allocate resources and capital. The solution to a problem often changes the problem, and the new system revealed things I think management would have been content to stay hidden. I kept asking why—when the machines found an anomaly—couldn't they detect and correct it? No one seemed to have an answer, at least a good one.

I was promoted along with Al and was now assistant director of system development with a proportional increase in workload and a non-commensurate increase in pay. Over the years, I had gotten close to the people at AA. I worked most closely with two people who I thought were a couple.

Ed Kelso was a Stanford grad and MBA. He had blond hair with black eyebrows and a small mustache. Even considering his 6'3" frame, his arms appeared too long, which made me think he might have been a competitive swimmer or basketball player. He was brilliant, quick on the uptake, and could quickly grasp and frame ideas without fully appreciating the details, leading to humorous results.

My life has been blessed. Jean Valjean sings in *Les Misérables* that to love another person is to touch the face of God. I have touched His face twice. The first was Ed's partner Suzan, the second, my beloved El, now gone like so many others. Even from a distance of sixty years, the memory of Suzan is fresh, powerful, and painful.

Suzan was perfect, not just to me. She was so perfect she was intimidating; even women could find no fault. Her entrance to a room was an event. There were times I conspired to arrive before she, just to watch her come in. She didn't have to make a scene; her presence preceded her. It seemed it was always a man who first noticed her. That man would stop talking and nudge another man, and so the notice spread. The conversation died away. Then women would notice, begin their laser-like appraisal, then lapse into embarrassed hopelessness when they found no fault.

Her five foot nine inches was crowned by a mass of thick black hair cascading effortlessly to below her shoulders. It gleamed, glimmered, and flowed with her every movement as if it was a separate living thing. She had a Botticelli face, the figure of a goddess. Her beauty was the kind that never faded. It would only mature into heart-stopping loveliness.

A Columbia, summa cum laude undergrad, a Dartmouth MBA with high honors gave her gravitas. Ed was the facilitator, but Suzan was the originator, and she did it with such grace that even in the chauvinistic world of the 1970s, no one seemed to mind her leadership. As time passed, I found myself interacting more with Suzan than with Ed. Finally, one day, I got a call from Ed.

"Hey, dumb shit!" he began. Getting no response, he continued, "I know as a Chapman grad you aren't very smart," this was a constant jab, "but the greatest opportunity you will ever see is staring you in the face, and you're blowing it!"

"I might be a Chapman grad and not have all the pretty paper on the wall," I replied. "But at least I have a real job and not some occasional gig."

"I make more at my gig than you'll ever make it your real job, butthead. But your present and future poverty isn't the issue. Have you noticed you're meeting more and more with Suzan? That's her choice. She's got the hots for you, stupid! Every man in his place is drooling over her, and I bet a lot of women too, and she's got her sights on some dumb-as-a-rock utility executive with a degree from a second-class college. There's no justice!"

Almost all my conversations with Ed were like that. Our insulting banter masked deep mutual respect and friendship. I never dreamed this movie star-gorgeous, intelligent, and capable woman would have any interest in me beyond a working relationship. At the same time, I was flattered beyond belief and frankly a bit scared. Was I good enough for her? My self-esteem when it came to women hadn't exactly soared.

Perhaps when men and women have worked together for a million years, things will change, and singularity between the sexes will occur. Until that magic moment, nature is going to have its way. Men and women working in close proximity, I think the term is propinquity, will often develop feelings for each other, and professional relationships will become personal. When they do, the rules change as the relationship deepens. Whatever boundaries the couple had established end up as porous as the US-Mexican border. Such relationships are fraught with risk for all concerned.

I was attracted to Suzan enough to make the next move. The next time I was scheduled to meet with her and Ed, I suggested coming to LA. I deliberately set the meeting late in the afternoon so it wouldn't reek of desperation when I proposed dinner. Plans are only good until they meet reality, and I was way too subtle.

I thought we would go to someplace in downtown LA. There actually is such a place, but Suzan had other ideas, and she and I went to her favorite restaurant, a hamburger joint at Sixth and Vermont. It was a simple format—you stood in line, reading the menu posted above the cook line. When it was your turn to order, they yelled at you, and you yelled back. The result was a giant hamburger to die for. I can still taste it. I watched people in the room trying to deal with the size of the burger. There was no way you could eat it and have any dignity. Eating it was an almost primal task. Suzan didn't cling to grace; she tucked right in.

Our relationship deepened quickly. Early on, we abjured sex. Working together while dating was one thing; adding sex to the situation would change everything. Without the complications of sex, we could develop intimacy and comfort with each other. I used an old saw I'd heard someplace. "Kissing wears out cookin' don't." She agreed.

As I said, she was perfect, and we had wonderful, long talks about history, art, and politics always without rancor. We took the time and effort to make it work. We both felt this was a lifetime commitment. We finally got around to our working relationship, and of course, she had the answer: "You come to Anderson."

"Won't that just complicate things? It will go from a client/consultant relationship to employer/employee, and there gotta be rules about that, and you would be senior to me, which has to complicate things more."

"Not if we're married."

"Kind of getting ahead of ourselves, or are you ahead of me?" I said.

"No," was all she said. She was right. She was committed and sure of herself; I was the one playing reluctant.

My parents, especially my mother, were all for it, and in her usual aggressive way, she said, "Go for it. All you do is talk about her. You're the only one that doesn't know you're in love."

Al Jurret was happy I was going to Anderson. "David, you have a lot of talent, too much to be stuck in a county utility for thirty years. Grab the shooting star. You have created Emerson's better mousetrap. Be a leader. With a partner like Suzan, life is going to be like a dream."

And so, it happened. What Anderson offered took my breath away and made my eyes water. They were even willing to pay for me to take classes toward an MBA and a degree in computer science. I told the hiring manager about my relationship with Suzan, and all he said was, "Congratulations."

Suzan's parents, Victor and Ella, came to LA to see Suzan's older brother, Gino, a priest at Loyola University. We laid out plans over dinner, and of course, it was no surprise to them. They were devout Catholics and wanted a Catholic wedding Mass. Of course, I was a non-worshipping Catholic but still a Catholic. I couldn't wait for Mom's reaction to her oldest marrying a devout Catholic.

After I moved to Anderson and we had committed ourselves to marriage, we had sex. I know books like this are supposed to have lurid descriptions of heavenly moments during lovemaking, embroidered with images of heavy breathing, gasping, tearing clothes, and so on. My time with Suzan was filled with beautiful, personal memories. Too beautiful to sully with that sort of stuff. I'm sorry, but I will not go there out of respect for her memory and decency. We decided to live together as soon as our respective apartment leases expired.

In the spring of 1976, Mom and Dad told me my twenty-one-year-old sister, Daphne, was getting married. I could read between the lines. It was a shotgun wedding. Suzan and I decided to go. I was concerned that our news would overshadow the bride, but everyone was all atwitter to meet Suzan. Of course, this meant the entire clan would show up, if for no other reason than to meet the future Mrs. David MacIntosh. I realized this would have all the dignity of a Scottish Games.

Angus, Ruth, Anton, Samantha, Uncle Fergus, and my two aunts were coming with their families. They would join Daphne's despoiler, his family, assorted cousins, and their families.

Suzan and I insisted on staying at a hotel rather than cramming into the house in Evanston. The first night was a dinner with our immediate family and Daphne's fiancé.

Before we all sat down for dinner, Grandma Ruth took me aside. "Suzan is a stunning woman and smart and very much in love with you, so she has good taste. Have you told her about your visions?"

I looked at my feet.

"I take that as a no?" Grandma got a stern look on her face. "What if this runs in families and one of your children develops this? Then you have to tell Suzan and the child that you knew all along. Starting a life together on a lie can be very dangerous, Davie."

"She would bolt in a second if I told her. She's so perfect she's taking a step down to be with me. I tell her something crazy like that, and she will be gone in a heartbeat. How do you think Grandpa would have reacted if you had told him something like that or that you were in some weird cult or communed with others telepathically? He would have thought he was getting a crazy woman."

Grandma's reaction was not much short of me slapping her. She retreated, and I could see tears in the corners of her eyes. Something I said had affected her deeply.

"Grandma, I'm sorry if I was rude or cross, but I just don't like talking about this. I appreciate you are trying to help, but I have decided to keep my own counsel on this."

We were rescued from further animosity by the call to dinner, but I had a distinct feeling of unease. Grandma would not meet my gaze for the rest of the evening.

Suzan, who had a streak of shit-disturber in her makeup, decided to tweak Mom and Samantha a bit. When the conversation of our wedding came up, she said, "David and I are going to have my brother, Gino, who's a Jesuit, preside at the mass. We're thinking of the Carmel Mission. Our kids are going to be raised Catholic and are going to go to Catholic school, so they get a good education."

Mom's head dropped in resignation, and Samantha's fingers tightened on her wineglass.

Anton cleared his throat, which was about as expressive as he ever got. Dad figured out the joke and was smiling along with Eleanor.

My mom struggled between explosion and grace, and I think grace won. Suzan apologized for the jest, and she and Mom chattered away like a couple of love birds. The next night was rehearsal dinner, and since I was an usher and Peter was part of the wedding party, I had to go.

In every family, tucked up in the leaves and branches of the family tree, there is the uncle or the cousin; ours was Fergus. He was a huge man, unmarried, but with a fine eye for the ladies, and a mission to ensure Scotland's distillers had ample reason to continue to work. He was a loud, funny drunk who never let an opportunity pass to wear his kilt and haul out his bagpipes, which he played loudly but poorly but with great gusto.

After one look at Suzan, he was a man on a mission: "Ta care for the bonnie lass and ta drive out da cold with a braw wet."

He reorganized the dinner seating to have Suzan next to him and me as far away as possible. Suzan's ariose laugh carried far and wide, bringing more joy to the room. Her laugh reminded me of an old saying, "One bell rings, and the others follow it." Her laughter seemed to spread contagiously across the room. I looked over at one point, and there were seven silver flasks in front of her and Fergus. My left-hand partner was some relative of Alexi, Daphne's despoiler, named George, who was as enjoyable as dust, Al Jurret had more flair.

On the right was a female cousin, and she and George talked past me all night. I offered to switch places with the woman, and she had not enough wit to accept the offer.

Alexi was apparently a stockbroker; he pumped me hard about investments as he did with everyone at the table. He drank like a fish and, as he did, became increasingly loud and crude. He seemed to be most interested in Angus and Ruth and their one thousand acres. I thought he was a jerk and felt sorry for Daphne.

On the way back to the hotel, I said to Suzan, "You had quite a time with Fergus."

"He's a real hoot. He's so uninhibited and fun."

"Looked like you two were sampling some of Scotland's best exports." There was an edge of reproach in my voice.

"David, I sipped. Since high school, men have been trying to get me in bed with booze, drugs, or lines of bullshit. I learned a long time ago how to stretch a drink a long way. You saw the flasks, but you didn't see the six glasses of water I drank. By the way, I have to pee. Fergus is just a hoot. He was simply happy to have a woman next to him and to be able to show off. He's harmless, but he really thinks the world of you.

"Your whole family is great. Eleanor will end up a nun. Daphne's fiancé is a jerk, as is his whole family. Your mom's folks seem to disapprove of everything, but they're interesting to talk to. Angus and Ruth, what sweethearts! Your aunts seem like wild and crazy women stuck in boring marriages. I love both of them. Peter seems very lonely, but he worships you. Having met them, I am prepared. After careful consideration of the evidence to state, unequivocally I love you too."

She had in her usual succinct way, summed up the family. They all loved her, and everyone was joyous over me finding such a wonderful partner. I was, for the first time in my life, happy. When we returned to the hotel, we realized how tired we were from dinner and jet lag.

Suzan had gone to the bathroom. The only thing not perfect about her was that she had TB (tiny bladder), and I was sitting on the end of the bed mindlessly flipping through TV channels. She came out and saw the stunned look on my face.

"I hope it will be the same when I am old and fat." She was, in fact, breathtaking. The light from the bathroom outlined her perfect figure, but that wasn't my primary focus. There, on the right side of her cream-colored sweater, just above her right breast but below the collarbone, was a dime-size spot. My heart stopped. Happiness fled.

She stood still. I sat still, and we both stared at each other. She was too perceptive to accept a lie, and she would soon understand that my look of astonishment was not due to desire. I fumbled, my mind racing, as I tried to make sense of the chasm of chaos opening in front of me.

Here was a woman I loved, and there was a spot that would take her away. My mind instantly dredged up the past incidents that told me it would take her away soon. There was no doubt that it would take her. The thoughts racing through my head conferred no honor on me; they were self-centered, offering no sympathy for Suzan, who would pay the price. I was so wrapped up in my agony I forgot my humanity.

I needed to explain my gasping shock. I had never told Suzan about my past history with the spots. Exactly how do you say to the person you love they will die, and you have this knowledge from seeing something no one else can see?

One side of my mind said, *You are in love. She will take it as an act of love.*

The other side, the side driven by my fear, said, *No, she's a rational person and will take it as a story of an idiot.*

No, fear said. *You will lose her*, a feeling confirmed by my low self-esteem.

No, idiot, my mind told me. *You condemn her to death without warning if you don't tell her. Everyone is entitled to a warning. You don't know if it's possible to fix what's wrong. If you don't tell her and she finds out you knew, you lose her for lying. If you tell her, you will lose her because she will think you are unbalanced.*

Nothing builds fear faster than untruth.

I eventually fell back on the shopworn excuse that I wasn't entirely well. It was a little white lie to cover my evident anguish. I don't think Suzan bought it, but she compounded my lie with her acceptance.

Deep in the night, with Suzan making mewing sounds just short of snoring, a positive thought found its way through all the negativity and fear, and I came fully awake. What if it wasn't a real spot? We had been to a diner, and it could have been a bit of food. For some reason, Scrooge's line in *A Christmas Carol* about there being more of gravy than grave about Marley's ghost flitted across my mind. I dropped food on my ties all the time. I assumed the spot on her sweater was a death indicator, but what if the simplest answer was correct? That it was food? I had never had a situation where the spot wasn't real.

I got up and padded to the bathroom, snagging her sweater on the way. There, under the light, was a dark dime-size, probably chocolate, spot. It was dark but brown, not black. Relief soared through me, almost to the point of tears. All those useless thoughts! All that unproductive rumination and self-abuse. The world's most fruitless exercise is second-guessing. As I lay back down, I started down that road. I hired the mental causality firm of "I woulda, shoulda, coulda, mighta." It's a vast organization specializing in second-guessing and recrimination with millions of remorseful people renewing their contracts daily.

Second-guessing is useless because it doesn't instruct. It mostly rationalizes. The only thing that counts is how you act in the moment of crisis.

All of us like to believe we will act in the highest moral and ethical plane, and that at every crisis, we will have seen the coming events, and because of our foresight, we will be able to choose the right path. Solomon said, "Vanity of vanity, all things are vanity," referring to pleasure. His wisdom is equally sound for those who attribute prescience to themselves.

The results of my past visions had been universally negative. Most of the time, our past decisions dictate our current actions. When fraught choices are at hand, what guides us are lessons learned from past decisions.

Like all people faced with something outside their experiences, I was at a hopeless disadvantage. The spots were at the edge of sensory knowledge and linguistic ability. The only method at hand to explain them was the past, and my precedents were all negative and, therefore, hindrances to my understanding. I was in new territory; this was unique, and this was not something that past experiences could frame.

I was all alone in it. I don't know if Suzan knew what happened. She was very intuitive. I suspected she sensed a profoundly troubling event. I wasn't that good an actor to have hidden it for long.

Daphne's wedding came off with only a couple of hitches. Daphne's despoiler, Alexi, was so hungover he looked like death, and the best man had to hold him up for most of the ceremony. The limo bringing the maids of honor got lost, and the priest dropped the ring.

We didn't care if Daphne was marrying someone with a Polish name. We considered this a Scottish wedding. Fergus, Peter, Dad, Angus, and Ruth, and my aunts and I were in full Scottish regalia. It was quite a show.

Today, as I write this, I finger a worn photo of Suzan and me at the reception. The memory haunts me.

A month after we got back, we moved into an apartment in Santa Monica and set a wedding date for October 1976 in Carmel. We were living the California dream of my youth in Wheaton. Sun, fun, in love, and employed in fulfilling work. I was deliriously happy, and I don't think it diminishes the love I had for my darling El to say I'm not sure I was ever that happy again.

Suzan and I were planning on having a large family, and we were practicing for impregnation daily, sometimes two or three times a day. Perfect practices make perfect, and we were going to be perfect. We had signed up for the company health plan.

The false alarm in Chicago still lurked in the back of my mind, and part of my consideration in signing up for the health plan was to catch problems early. I convinced Suzan that we should take advantage of the preventive medicine parts and have complete physicals to establish baseline data on our health. She, of course, rolled her eyes and made some crack about systems analyst thinking.

On the last weekend of summer, we went to one of the senior partner's houses for a party. Suzan was on the shortlist for selection as a partner, and this was a sort of show and tell. I tried to convince her not to wear the dress she chose not because I didn't like it, but I was afraid it would inspire nasty remarks from the partner's wives. She wore a sundress and dazzled everyone but me. There it was, right side, top of her right breast, just below the collar bone, dime-size, and it wasn't chocolate.

We finished our health examinations. Suzan was diagnosed with a lump in her breast. Right breast. Small. Dime-size. Just below the collarbone. Oh sure, we got the usual medical lines about how they got it early, high rate of survival, young and healthy, we'll go through this together.

It was all crap. I knew what the outcome would be, but I was irrational and hoped that maybe for the first time, fate would be different. Surely the world could not be so unfeeling that it would destroy our happiness? Surely God, who Suzan loved with all her heart, would protect his servant?

In all honesty, I have to tell you that I had dishonorable thoughts beyond my shock and terror of the diagnosis. I thought long and hard about dumping her, of moving away, of finding a new job someplace far, far away. I knew I didn't have the strength to go through this with her. I thought it would be easier for me to bear her bad thoughts about me than to go through the trauma to come.

It was a problem I thought I could run from successfully. She would be busy with the medical treatments and compared to those; my betrayal would not be high on the list of priorities. The real reason was that I was afraid, my love for her was challenged, and I had to respond to it. I was being asked to exert superhuman caring and commitment, and I wasn't sure I was up to the task. I was, of course, wrong.

My shame began to exert itself. I was still not convinced that the spots were not the results of my actions or thoughts. The fact that I was seeing them and no one else could see them or would believe me that I was seeing them in my mind was definitive proof of my flaw. Suzan's cancer was somehow my fault. I began to think that I wasn't ever to be allowed to have close relationships. I didn't want one because I didn't want to go through the pain. I knew my love affair with Suzan would end. Her diagnosis was another nail in the coffin of my shame. There was something flawed with me, and I was somehow incomplete, imperfect, cursed.

False senses of guilt and shame can make a person very selfish. Since shamed people believe something is fundamentally wrong with them, they tend to think only of themselves and how to assuage their sense of shame. Guilt, shame, and depression commit a great crime against those who suffer with them. They lock a person into their past by making them dissatisfied with their unchangeable past actions. The evil trio doesn't permit the lessons that should be learned from the past to be accepted. In committing the crime, the three of them change a person's future by denying progress.

I remembered every bad thing that had ever happened to me. I debated with myself about my course of action. I began to relive all those past events to create a picture of myself as always, a failure. Everything I had done was reduced to dust. Because I could not leave the past, I was denied the present and, therefore, the harmony that comes from being present-oriented.

In the end, I made the right decision and didn't dump her. I committed myself to the struggle, and in doing so, I realized the truth of the concept that decisions bring power, and fulfilling the decision unleashes wisdom and shows a person's depth.

Suzan attacked the cancer with all her formidable energy and intelligence. She worked and traveled until the chemo started. That went on for six or eight months. Then came a double mastectomy and lymph gland removal and the resulting psychological damage that can occur when a woman can feel that she is somehow less than a woman.

I was there every step of the way, holding her hair as she vomited, washing it if we didn't make to the bathroom or couldn't get it out of the way. Then the hair fell out. I packed the unique bag she carried with her medications and natural cures. I drove to Mexico to buy tons of laetrile, a naturopathic treatment. I held her in those dark, pain-filled nights when she cried in self-pity and pain. There were times when I imagined I could hear the aberrant cells eating her alive. I tried and failed not to let myself get lost in my self-pity.

It was months of a waking nightmare, endless medical visits, hospitalizations, vomiting, pain, sleeplessness, worry, anger, and fear. I prayed to God for the cup to pass, to pass to me, although I knew I had not the strength to bear it. I bargained with God endlessly to allow what little power I had to flow to her, even if it left me an empty shell. Cancer makes patients of loved ones too. It ate her, but it also ate me.

A year in, it was apparent, I think, to everyone, her chances were small. Still, her will was strong. She had lost forty pounds and was out of her mind with pain most of the time, but she fought on. You know cancer is incurable when someone with her spirit backed by the best modern medicine can provide can't change the outcome.

Suzan fought on implacably and prayed daily; her brother, the Jesuit, often came to see her and lead prayer. She prayed her Rosary and took Eucharist. When she was in her right mind, she questioned the medicos endlessly, and the tears rise in my eyes as I write this because still with all of that, Suzan cared for me, letting me know she loved me.

I told her constantly I loved her and always would. I could never imagine loving anyone again. My darling El understood and accepted my feelings for Suzan. I hope that over her and my life, I showed her the love she deserved. I told you Suzan was perfect.

The doctors and all the helpers we ran into stressed the importance of dealing with cancer to maintain a positive attitude, and Suzan had that in spades. I was the one with the doubts. No, not doubts, knowledge that everything they did was going to be useless. I convinced myself that I was canceling her positive energy with my negative stance, which made me even more ashamed.

I was not as strong as Suzan. I painted myself the victim, not her. I knew before she was diagnosed she would die. I convinced myself I was a particular victim not only of her cancer but also as the harbinger of death. I was letting the spots and the specter of death imprison me.

Whenever I met someone, I first looked for spots. I had no empathy for others because I knew that the spots might appear and take them at any moment, and I didn't want the sense of loss. I was angry and sad at the same time I cursed whatever malignant power infected me.

Mostly I pulled inward-focused on my loss. My loss, not hers. Amid my agony over losing Suzan and my curse, I began to contemplate and plan suicide; enough drugs were around to make it easy. I convinced myself I was causing the deaths. No longer could I hope the spots were a passing thing, aberrations of light and shadow, coincidences.

I was hanging on the pinnacle of three of the strongest emotions humans ever experience: love, hate, and fear. I loved Suzan so much I couldn't imagine a world without her. I was willing to do anything if it would save her. I hated the spots, what they did to me, and the news they would deliver to others. Hate is a caustic thing. It eats away at the soul, and it takes time and energy to hate, so an increasingly large part of my psyche was devoted to hating the spots and myself for being cursed. There was the fear that no matter what I did, I was fated to suffer constant sorrows of not only death but also the death of those close to me.

As I wallowed in my grief and victimhood, I started to think about fate and destiny. I could not understand how this happened and why. She was God's child, a believer. Was it simply some choice made by an all-powerful being that Suzan was to die a long-suffering death and David was to be devastated? I, of course, asked that most stupid of all questions. What kind of God did that? To me, someone who spent a lot of time with computers, it was illogical, and neither logic nor philosophy could explain it. I wanted an answer for which there was no answer because I was asking the wrong question.

Eighteen months after the diagnosis, Suzan died. I had been at the hospital almost constantly for five days. I was exhausted, sleep-deprived, angry, hungry, and sick at heart. Vic, Ella, and Gino were there a few hours before she passed, and they convinced me to leave to shower, shave, get some sleep, and eat. I did, and I wasn't there when she gasped her last breath.

I arrived back at the hospital to the smell of disinfectant and despair. Vic, Ella, Gino, and another priest were in Suzan's room. Suzan was still there, her husk anyway, still hooked to the now-silent monitors. The only noises were the squeak of rubber-soled shoes and the whispers of prayer. They all turned to me as I entered.

"David, I'm Father Altois, the hospital chaplain. She's gone. It's better now. All her pain is gone, the struggle over. She had last rites and is with him in grace."

Too bad he was first. "Grace! Fuck your grace!" I screamed. "How can you stand there and talk about grace? She prayed all the time, she did all that voodoo Catholics do, and she died in horrible, painful agony."

"David," began Vic.

"There can't be a loving God if this is allowed to happen! This is how he treats his servants?" I screamed, tears pouring down my face as a year and a half of fear and loss burst out.

Death is a leveler; it makes us all stupid. My statements were genuine if shopworn and trite.

Ella tried next. "David, we loved her too. I understand your anger. We felt it too, but she wouldn't have—"

"You don't understand shit!" I lashed out, looking from face to face. "You don't understand. I knew she was going to die, and I couldn't tell her. I killed her as much as the cancer!"

Some of the nurses had come to the room, attracted by the commotion. Everyone looked at me questioningly as I turned on my heel and stormed out.

CHAPTER 6

The wall heater rattled and banged, seeking to convince itself it still produced heat. I lay in bed, fully dressed under the blanket, towels, and bedspread. I had awoken out of a need for the bathroom. I got up, shivering. I looked out the window to see my Honda Accord drifted over by snow. The wind howled down the parking lot, and sinuous lines of snow susurrated across the pavement. On the way to the bathroom, I kicked aside a discarded food bag, one of many, bearing the name of a store in Havre, Montana.

How I had gotten there, I had no idea, but from the look of the room and the notices under the door demanding more money, I had been there awhile. When I turned on the TV, it told me a year had passed. Back at the window, I saw the world was white, but my heart was black.

I was gross, dirty, fat, longhaired, bearded, and drawn. My eyes were shrunken and red-rimmed. The taste of metal in my mouth told me I had neglected oral health as well.

My wallet contained little cash, but I had a checkbook and a gas card. Not seeing a suitcase, I gathered what I thought was mine, bundled it up, and went out to cram my stuff in the car. As I did so, I realized Montana is colder than Alaska. The battery was dead, but a helpful guy in a pickup jumped it, and off I went. To where? I wasn't sure.

Like a lost duckling, I went home. Not to Evanston, there was little there but questions. Not to LA, painful memories. No, I went home to Culloden.

My Honda and I were on our last legs when we came to rest in front of the farmhouse. I'm not sure Ruth recognized me. They had last seen me as a happy young man in love, and now here I was, dirty and bloated from a steady diet, long on salt, sugar, and fat, and short on nutrition. They took me in, asked no questions, made no judgments, just loved me. I don't think I left the bedroom except for essentials for the first week. At the week's end, my parents arrived bringing clothes that no longer fit and more love.

After that weekend, Dad went back to Evanston. The term at Northwestern wasn't over, but Mom stayed. Both my grandparents and parents had the gift of patience; they waited me out. I was nearly mute, answering only in monosyllables, and I carried myself in the shambling, head-down attitude of the utterly defeated.

Angus developed a recovery plan—work. He had me up before dawn every day, mucking out the cows and horses, then fence repairs, and the other endless tasks a one thousand-acre farm generates. Farming isn't just hard work; it's just work that never ends. The layers of neglect came off, the dirt, the long hair, the beard, the smell, the fat, and the bloat, almost as if they had been layers of armor protecting me from my thoughts.

Anger and depression are sisters, true daughters of the mother of knowledge, chaos. Neither sister can exist without the other. Anger needs depression, and depression anger to rationalize itself. The sisters seek to seduce those journeying the path of truth. They hide the mother and her knowledge. They are jealous of the mother, setting up a Greek tragedy of rivalry. Both, however, blanch in the light of the present. They reside only in the past their only strength is the misty uncertainty of times remembered.

The mother demands the present and future, so chaos can teach you. The daughters are seductive, but the price of seduction is your soul. The prize of the mother's benevolence is salvific knowledge.

The key to overcoming long-term stress and trauma is finding how to tell the story behind the tension; if no one else, to yourself. Over time we edged up on it.

One night at dinner, Angus said, "David, when Fraser died, we had an awful time. He was our first, and that's a special thing for parents." He paused to see if he should continue. "We became part of the Gold Star families, and we got to talk to others who had sons die. It really helped."

I was about to reject the overture when Mom said, "For a couple of years after your brother died, I couldn't shake the depression. My OB introduced me to Hilda Gobath, who lost two children to stillbirth. Just talking to her helped."

I was stunned. I had suspected Mom had some issues with losing my twin, but Mom always seemed self-assured and confident, and I had never before heard her express remorse over my twin's passing.

"What Elise and Angus are saying, David," said Ruth, "is talking about what happened, however painful it might be, will help. I have a feeling there's more to tell than you're letting on."

I declined to open up then. I was frankly too tired from Angus's cure to talk, and I wanted more time to think about what to say or if I was willing to talk at all.

Dad came down that Friday, and he, I, and Angus worked our butts off on Saturday to complete everything that needed doing. Sunday had always been a day of rest on the farm. We all went to Mass, and then we had dinner, another farm tradition. It was after the meal I let it all out. It was the third time my parents had heard it, the second time for Angus and Ruth. I told them about the fake spot on the night of the rehearsal dinner. I added the spots for Caesar, Steve, and Suzan for their benefit. Not willing to make myself out to be a blasphemer, I left out the last hospital confrontation.

"I guess it was quite a scene at the hospital the day she died," said Dad. Seeing me start to color, he said, "Her parents, Vic and Ella, sent us a letter, David. They're actually very complimentary about you and how much you loved Suzan. They wished you had stayed so they could have grieved with you as a member of the family."

Not for the last time, I would be humbled by the forgiveness of people I wronged.

Scottish restraint is a legend, like French cowardice, and as I told the story, I could see my grandmother almost physically receding, almost shrinking. When I had finished, she jumped up and started clearing the table, which of course, was a signal to Mom to help, and for Dad, Angus, and me to get out.

"I'll bring tea and coffee to parlor along with some wee biscuits." Grandma was starting to affect a Scottish brogue. Although, to my knowledge, she had never been to Scotland.

When we had tea and coffee, Angus patted Dad on the knee while looking into Mom's eyes. "Joe"—he tossed his head toward Mom—"she's a bonny one, but the lad and I have to be up early to take a load of timothy to town. Don't be keeping the house awake all night with your carrying-on." He winked at Mom, whose face was Ferrari red.

"Yeah, Daphne mentioned the noise to me at the wedding!" I said, laughing at my parent's discomfort.

"Well, she obviously learned a lesson well," Dad said. "She's working on number two already."

"Honestly, I'm going to bed!" said Mom in high dungeon. An hour later, the rodeo in their room went on loudly. I laughed for the first time in two years.

Dad and Mom stayed two more days. Dad shared some research he had done about people seeing visions of death. He had found several references to the Brahman Seer in Scotland, some incidents in Homer, and other ancient texts, but nothing to help me understand my curse. They were trying to be helpful, but like most moderns, they were having a hard time dealing with something that defied society's rules of logic and experience.

Ultimately, they were concerned with my health and did not want the spots to be an avenue leading to permanent disability. Dad pointed out that another occurrence like my year long absence would make me almost unemployable.

As I worked and lived at the farm, I got the feeling that Grandma Ruth knew more than she was letting on. Whenever I mentioned the spots or my concerns, she found ways to get busy or distract me from some other conversation topic. She was hanging back, spending a significant amount of time in a room she had set aside for "her things," as Angus said.

Every once in a while, I would find notes on the pillow in my room written in Grandma Ruth's precise handwriting. One day, the message was, *In the same way, you should remind yourself that what you love is mortal and that what you love is not your own; it has been granted to you just for the present, not irrevocably, and not forever...* (Epictetus, Discourses 3:24 line 84).

Her notes gave me more understanding that my grandmother was not a simple farm wife and that she had done a lot of reading and study over the years.

One of the others was from Aesculus: *"He who learns must suffer. And even in our sleep, pain that cannot forget falls drop-by-drop upon the heart, and in our own despair, against our will, comes wisdom to us by the awful grace of God."*

I stayed on, and as the weeks passed, I sort of healed, and with the extraordinary resilience of youth, I got better. I could, of course, stay and run the farm. Angus and Ruth needed help; they made a good living; it was prime farmland and increasing in value daily. The task of running one thousand acres, three hundred fifty cattle, with the attendant growing areas, and pasture was becoming more complex, scientific, and mechanized. The economics of farm life was changing, not for the better. Farming was not in my blood and never would be. The farm had been a good refuge at the end of my annees pelerinage. It was warm, loving, and safe and was always a refuge from the reality of life.

My destiny lay elsewhere.

Unless we—Eleanor, Daphne, Peter, or I—took over, Culloden would pass from the family. The farm was the touchpoint of my life. I was closer to it than the others, so the decision was mine.

As we were growing up, Mom and Dad tried to avoid telling us what to do when we had a decision to make. They tried to be sure we understood our options and the possible consequences of our choices but then let us make them. If the decision didn't affect our health or well-being, they supported us. I was weighing my options and taking input.

I knew Gramma Ruth had something to say, although every time she started to say something, she would pull back. She had quite a collection of books on Scotland, which she encouraged me to read, and often I found her pouring over one of them, but I wasn't ready for anything heavy. She would occasionally ask me what seemed to be off-the-wall questions, like did I ever see any future events, did I hear voices, or have bad dreams with mythical characters?

I told her yes after seeing a spot, and I had dreams of horrible creatures attacking me. I told her about the conflicting thoughts that ran through my mind every time I saw a spot telling me what to do or not to do. Her questions were burdensome, and I knew her well enough to know these were not idle queries, but I didn't want to talk about my experiences, so I told her I just saw spots and people died.

The depression lessened, although the heart still ached. I had little physically to remind me of Suzan, and that spared me the horrible loneliness which creeps in with finding some remembrance of theirs, or when the waft of a smell from a handkerchief reminds you of their fragrance.

The two sisters still hovered, but I think in some instinctual, nonrational way, I was beginning to appreciate that I would have to confront their mother (chaos) if I were to gain the knowledge of my curse. Few fears are greater than facing chaos, but fewer still are the ways to achieve a unique understanding; the risk is worth the reward.

I have alluded to the wisdom of my parents many times, but it was in this crisis their wisdom and understanding really showed. Once the term was over at Northwestern, Dad, Mom and the kids virtually moved to Culloden. Having the family around helped, as did visits by Fergus and my aunts, and gradually the pain eased. I'm not sure which pain went first—the pain of the loss of Suzan or the pain of my behavior.

One day, while we were milking cows, Dad said to me, "Have you ever read the Bhagavad Gita?"

I replied that I had not finished it but had started it several times.

"David, you are in pain, and you are suffering, but you have to remember that while your body is in pain, your self is indestructible. Arjuna is told the self-embodied in the body of every being is indestructible, and weapons do not cut, fire does not burn it, waters do not wet it, wind does not wither it. It cannot be cut or burned, it cannot be wet or withered, it is enduring all pervasive fixed immovable and timeless."

Dad recited the lines with a dreamlike voice and cadence similar to what you expect from a higher being. "Your pain will fade, and what will be left will be your inner self, and that will be undamaged by the pain. Trust yourself. All will be well."

One day, Mom announced that I was driving her to Kalamazoo to go shopping. What was in Kalamazoo was a mystery. Her real purpose, of course, was to get me alone in a captive environment for a lengthy discussion.

After we got on the road, she started, "How are you feeling?"

"About what?" I replied, knowing what she wanted but not taking my eyes off the road.

We drove through farm country and often shared the road with tractors and other farm equipment.

"Everything. You've been at the farm for months now, and you took a year to grieve, which is what your walk about was. After all that, how do you feel? Don't give me the standard male answer, 'I'm fine' routine."

I was silent for a few minutes as we rushed through the farms. "I feel a lot of guilt and shame. I'm convinced something is wrong with me. I'm ashamed of how I have acted around the spots, and I feel I could have done more to warn people, and perhaps I might have changed what happened. I'm a freak. No one has anything like this, and I'm not sure I can continue seeing spots and death any longer. I want it to end, and I have considered ending it the only way I know will work."

"You mean suicide? The cheap way out?"

"Maybe it's cheap, but it's more expensive and difficult for me to continue to live with this, and the only way I can continue to live and avoid seeing the spots would be severe isolation, which is a form of suicide."

"Good, I can see you've formed some answers, but let me tell you what's wrong with them." Not waiting for me to respond, she carried on. It was hard to stop Mom when she got on a roll. "First, you're framing this issue poorly. When anyone looks at another person, they see death."

I started to reply that her comment was ridiculous, but she hushed me. "To be alive is to die. What you are experiencing is seeing death for that person will be sooner rather than later."

"Okay," I said, "but even if I accept that as the proper framing, I'm still a freak. No one else can see what I see. I don't think anyone is supposed to see death. We are supposed to live our lives in the present, but the spots tell the future, and they are making me change my outlook on life and relationships, and not for the better."

"David, a certain number of people are going to die of accidents, violence, and disease every day. There was a tornado in Oklahoma the other day, and four people in a trailer park died. No one expected that."

"How do tornados always seem to know where the trailer parks are and land there?" I replied, and we giggled at my poor humor.

Mom continued, "If you were to go to Asia or Africa, you would see all kinds of spots. There is nothing you can do about who will die, and from experience, you apparently cannot change the course of events. So you are beating yourself up over what is fated, and worse, you are letting your inability to accept fate interfere with your destiny."

"Are you saying my destiny is something other than being a freak? I'm getting very jaded about death. Lately, the first thing on my mind has been the effect of the death will mean to me, not the loss. Like Caesar's case, my first thought was if I would lose my jobs. With Jean, I would lose her. With Suzan..." I had to pull over as the tears captured my eyes. "It was how could I possibly live without her?"

"David, son, death creates a sense of loss. The immediate effect is often confusion and unwillingness to accept the loss. Longer-term, it's the emptiness, the hole in the fabric of life. The strength of those feelings is related to the manner of death and the closeness of the relationship. It can move quickly from confusion to anger. When the relationship is close, the emotions will be stronger as those who are close live off one another and draw strength from each other. That is why when one partner of a long-married couple dies, the other usually follows quickly. What you've experienced in all these death situations is normal human emotion on display. Where you have gone wrong is to blame yourself and to take on your shoulders responsibility for something that is not yours to control."

We never did get to Kalamazoo. We stopped at Three Rivers, and Mom directed me to Moore Street and Railroad Avenue, where a small building looking a lot like an Airstream trailer sat. What came out of that trailer was the best popcorn and caramel corn I ever tasted. We loaded up for everyone back at Culloden, and Mom directed me to go back—she had had her say. She was content to let me drive and silently contemplate her thoughts, all the time being distracted by the delicious smell of the popcorn in the back seat, but the conversation had too much import to be cut off that quickly.

"I have always felt guilty that I didn't do more for Shamus or the others to try to prevent them from dying. I know I couldn't do anything for the football player or Iris, but I might have been able to change things with Shamus, Caesar, and Jean's father if I had tried harder."

"Not likely. It's been apparent that you had guilt about the deaths, and it all came to a head when Suzan died. I also know that you struggled because you had a unique ability that contradicted your lifelong self-placement in the middle. You could have done better in school, but you were more comfortable hiding in the middle, and over time you came to believe that was your place in the world. Having a poor or low self-image opens a person up for fear, and fear opens you up for guilt, and guilt opens you to shame, and shame is what you are dealing with right now."

She had hit me right between the eyes, no sugarcoating nice words, and it hurt to have what I thought was my secret be so obvious. "So you are saying if I were more self-confident, this would not affect me so deeply?"

"In a way, death is always going to be hard to take. There is no getting around that, but it's easier if you aren't convinced you did something wrong. That's why people bounce back from death in war but not from a car accident, for example. Your self-image was damaged by your inability to talk about your ability, and that is partly our fault for not providing you with a context or method to talk about it. I don't know what this thing you have is, but you have to understand that you are not causing this. Therefore, you should have no guilt or shame about it. Speaking of guilt, what do you say we open one of those popcorn bags? The smell is killing me."

It was good we were close to home; otherwise, we would have eaten all the Three Rivers Treasure.

Something was brewing between my father and his parents, particularly his mother. One day I was nursing a tractor with some mechanical illness into the garage, and I saw Mom, Dad, and Grandma standing in front of the milking barn in a heated discussion. The tractor was so loud I couldn't hear what they were saying, but they were pointing fingers at each other, and that was always a serious behavioral violation in our family.

Another time I came into the house, and Ruth, Angus, and Mom and Dad were in what Grandma called her room. Their voices were raised, and I heard Dad say, "Mom, you have to tell him. He's in agony and has been since he was young. He's trying to make sense of what is happening and what you know will help him. You have to tell him!"

Ruth replied, but her voice was quieter, and I couldn't make out the words. I wasn't about to listen further since that was another thing we were taught not to do as Angus said, "Gentlemen and ladies, neither read other's mail, listen at keyholes or to other's conversations."

In my healing, of course, life intruded. The Bible says, "Earth abides', and so does life. The intrusion was Ed Kelso. Grandma handed me the phone one afternoon, I didn't want to talk, but I took it anyway. "Hey, stupid!" came the booming jocular beginning.

"Ed, you haven't changed at all!"

"That's because the truth doesn't change. You're still stupid, possessor of a second-class education, and generally a dufus." He was quick with the insults. "Whatever powers are watching over you are working for you, regardless of your dumping us to go on a magical mystery tour. The firm still wants you, and they're willing to transfer you to a Chicago office. I tell you, MacIntosh, you live under the right star. If I did what you did, I would be pulling cable for the telephone company."

"It's a death star," I replied softly, reflecting the darkness still in my soul.

Ed was wise enough, despite his bombast, not to argue my definition of my star.

"I'll think about it," I said.

"Think fast, dumb shit, the systems practice is growing fast. We have a new partner, Sonny Kopinski, that's a hoot. His real name is Sheraton, Sheraton Kopinski. I guess his parents couldn't remember what hotel they were staying in when he got planted, so they used both."

I groaned at his crudity.

"He's like you, second-class education but reasonably smart, knows enough to leave us alone. We're growing fast. There's a place for you here and could be a partnership in a few years."

Ed was a nice guy but talking to him was exhausting. I rang off, but the seed was planted.

Ruth kept trying to get me to read books on Scottish history and legends. I tried some of them. Many had been written in the eighteenth century, and the writing style was complex. I made a mental promise to myself, which was as worthless as the paper it was written on, that I would read them later when I felt better about things.

One day, I was sitting in the living room, trying to read a book, but primarily using it as a cover as I thought about my next move. I could hear a faint noise rising and falling in a cadence. There was no radio or TV on, but the noise was still there, just loud enough to be irritating. I got up and walked around to see if I could find the noise. I stopped in the hallway outside Grandma's room and realized the noise was coming from inside it. I couldn't make out the words, but the voice was Grandma's.

I knocked on the door, and the sound stopped, and Grandma said, "Come in."

I opened the door. "I heard a noise in here and wanted to be sure everything is alright."

Ruth took the book she had in her hand on my entry and hurriedly put it in a drawer and then locked it.

"I was just reading some poems, and one of them seemed to need to read out loud."

"Stay, Davie, I'm glad for the company. Being an old lady means no one wants to spend a lot of time with you. Sit here by me." She waved to a chair next to her. "How are you doing? Are you feeling better?"

"I guess so, Grandma. I doubt I will ever be able to forget Suzan and her death, and I certainly don't want to see any more spots, but I'm coming to the conclusion that they will always be with me. Being able to come here was the perfect place for me. Thank you for taking me in."

"Nonsense! We're glad you're here. Where else would you go?" Ruth paused for a few seconds. "You will likely never forget Suzan, I can never forget Fraser, but you have to find a way forward. One time, you told me that you wondered if there was some sort of force or power that controlled the spots. Do you still feel that way?"

"Yes, I guess it's the only explanation that fits. There is no scientific evidence or explanation, and physically I'm well, so that avenue is closed. You know there is something else about them. They take breaks. I haven't seen one since Suzan, but I live with the fear that I will soon see them again. Whenever I have discreditable thoughts when I see them, I get a general feeling that I am unwell. It troubles me, and when I stop having those thoughts, things get better."

"Think back," she said. "I know it is hard for you to relive those moments, but is there any pattern of seeing more spots during the winter, for example, than in the summer?"

I thought for a minute reviewing each spot. "Well, Shamus was in November around Thanksgiving, the football guy was late October, Iris I think was in the spring, and Steve, Jean's father, was right after the new year. Caesar was in October, and Suzan was in September. Is that important?"

"Maybe, but it might just be an old lady thinking badly. In the ancient Celtic religions, there were times when the barrier between light and dark, or good and evil are the weakest, and during those times, evil forces could come through. One of those times was around the autumnal equinox, and it sounds like a lot of the spots occur around then. It was called *oidhche Shamhna toilichte.*"

"That sounds like the language I heard in my dreams. What is it?"

"It's Gaelic, the language of our ancestors," Ruth replied.

"I didn't know you spoke Gaelic."

"Nay, nay, I do na speak it, just a few words I've picked in these old books, think nothing of it."

She was lying. I knew her too well not to notice, but with the speaking of the Gaelic, she hurried to end the conversation. "I wish you would read somma my wee books, Davie. It might help you to understand."

She got up with more agility than one would expect and shooed me from the room, sending me to the parlor because she had to get dinner started.

I called Anderson and talked to Kopinski, who made no promises but indicated he would like to interview me in LA. The idea of returning to LA to my old haunts filled me with fear, but I needed to confront my fears. I started to worry about explaining my year of wandering and assuring them I wasn't some unstable nutjob who would run off at every crisis.

In the eighteen months I had been gone, the living thing that was LA had changed. Some said the city and areas were cancer, and as the plane set up for landing, I could see gouges in the earth for new suburbs as the city marched east across the desert. It was ugly. Further west was the endless white, gray blanket of smog that had come to characterize LA.

Kopinski turned out to be a grave-looking man, fastidious to the point of fussiness. He was always arranging perfectly aligned stacks of paper, picking at the razor creases in his pants for imaginary lint and examining the nonexistent results with disapproval like an ape picking nits.

He dressed more like an Eastern academic than an LA executive, a dark suit, heavy broadcloth shirt starched to immobility. A highly controlled, buttoned-down, very precise person.

"Ah, the famous Mr. MacIntosh." His speech betrayed a faux English accent. "I've heard of little else since I've been here. Naturally, I was anx…eager to see you in the flesh."

"I hope the reality is not too disappointing," I said, trying to match his formality.

"Preparatory to the interview." He paused, looking over his glasses at me with colorless eyes. "I reviewed your work before the erm…tragedy." He pronounced it with a vague sense of discovery. "I am impressed with what you did. Some of it frankly was revolutionary."

"Thank you," I began until he raised his hand, signaling a stop.

"However," he continued, looking professorial and stern, "as a firm with commitments to clients, we cannot countenance personnel abandoning projects"—he hurried on expecting objections and defensive responses—"however tragic the circumstances."

"Yes, sir," was my tight-lipped, hostile response. Those personal issues were still fresh; I was angry at what I perceived as his cavalier dismissal of my grief.

Then the whole tone changed. It was like he was an ice cream cone. He softened and began to melt. He took off his glasses and rubbed both palms up his face, softly grinding the heels of his hands into his eyes. He pulled his hands away; his eyes were glaucous and bore a look of infinite sorrow.

"David, I know this will sound like one of those patent nostrums we use at times of grief, but I know how you feel. A few years ago, I lost someone very close to me after a long, terrible struggle."

It seemed he was discounting me, and it was not making me feel better. Why do people need to make themselves relative in matters of grief? Can't they just leave it alone? No one's story could possibly be more terrible than mine. I was unique. I had the grief of loss and the misery of knowing death was coming. So deep was my own despair I couldn't see his remark as an attempt at kindness and creating rapport.

My self-absorption shattered when he fought back a sob, and I realized this wasn't an act. He was telling it from the heart. His stiffness was a cover for vulnerability. "Off the record, I almost killed myself. I thought…no, I was convinced that I could never be happy again. I can't tell you I'm happy, but the sense of loss does fade, leaving manageable emotions, but you will always have the memory of love and loss. The secret, David, is not to armor your heart to avoid grief, which only serves to make you unable to love again. Grief is as much a part of life as suffering and death. The real trick is to leave yourself open to grief and loss, not to block out love which is the rarest of all things."

We, two sufferers, bonded at that moment.

In later years, but only after more sorrow, I would recognize the depth of his wisdom. It had cost Kopinski much emotionally to say what he did to a virtual stranger, but my emotions blocked me from insight and relief.

There was something for which his wisdom was not salving; the guilty knowledge I had as a predictor of death was driving my emotions toward a deeply held sense of guilt and shame.

After I finished interviewing with Kopinski's boss, Mikhail Destrov, I interviewed Mikhail's boss, Cyrus Rosenthal (actually X. Cyrus Rosenthal the third). X cubed as he was known's chariot to the top had been drawn by horses named cliché and trite and whose communication relied on catachresis. I was offered the same job I had. Since I had lost seniority, I was lower in the pecking order, which came with a condition. I had to complete a degree in computational science.

I chose USC rather than the more familiar UCI. In the late 1970s, the leading-edge focus was networking and data storage. The size and cost of computing were sliding as the capacity of silicon chips ramped up. From rooms filled with big iron, computers found new places throughout organizations. As machines became accessible, more organizations began using them, and new users generated lots of data. As minuscule as the data was, computers couldn't store it all. The challenge was to store data and recall it in the future in a usable form.

My prior work history allowed me to challenge some courses, saving a ton of time and money. Like students everywhere, we formed study groups. Although I was standoffish at first, one of the fruits of shame, I was eventually included in a group. The groups found places to hang out. All the groups avoided bars frequented by the USC jocks, whom I found essentially dumb as a box of rocks.

Our place was Thinkers, romantically owned by Tom Tinker, an ex-IBM executive. IBM's motto was "Think." Tinker understood us and helped us formulate ideas. I credited him in several of my papers.

Given the newness of our field and the practical nature of the knowledge, most of our instructors were adjuncts. Jay Terlinski worked at Memorex, a leader in data storage. Jay liked to hang around with our study group, and he was generally welcome. He had a big mouth, and when he drank, which was often and a lot, he could get loud and obnoxious.

In the days before the curse of PowerPoint, professors used overhead projectors, and one night the bulb in Jay's projector blew up. I looked up from my notes as Jay turned on the room's lights, and I thought I saw a flash of a spot on Jay's neck. This time I pushed it aside as a trick of the changed lighting and my eyes refocusing. Deep in my brain, where conscious and unconscious join, the demon, quiet now for eighteen months, raised its hoary head and said, *It's real, and it's there,* laughing in its croaking cackle.

That night and each subsequent night in my dreams, specters appeared. First, the face of Shamus, speaking our last words. Then the football player lying motionless on the field, then Phil's face contorted with rage, Jean's father, Caesar, and the glorious Suzan in her final agony.

Each morning, exhausted by the emotion of remembrance, I stumbled along, asking the unanswerable. *Why, God? Why me? Why am I punished? What cross must I bear? What knowledge gained, what sin deserves this?*

This last idea that the spots resulted from some sin I had committed was a new intellectual wandering in my constant, ill-defined attempts to explain my curse. In Western religious thought, physical illness, misfortune, and early death were linked to sin. That kind of thought was one reason religion failed to construct a congruent message to the current generation, who did not want their actions to be connected to sin. Many of the miracles Jesus performed carried the admonition of 'go and sin no more."

With the rise of humanism's contention that all things are under the control of humankind, the link between sin and suffering broke. Sin arose from violating a moral imperative of a supreme being. If humans controlled all, then sin was not possible. Still, humanists, moderns, and postmodern thinkers' only answer to suffering is random chance, which offers no rational answer to why some people seem to have more than their fair share of sickness and troubles.

If the spots resulted from my sin, I needed not to sin, and not telling others of their eventual demise seemed to be furthering the sin. I knew those stricken would not take the information well, and the spots pointed to inevitable fate. I still didn't know if making the victim aware of the spot could change the outcome. Could the message be that I had to intervene and change others? Would that end the spots?

A few weeks later, we were at Thinkers. Most of us drank beer or wine, but Jay drank whiskey, doubles, and neat. He was on his third when a guy walked in who just radiated danger. Something about him gave rise to the description of Cassius in Shakespeare's *Julius Caesar*.

Jay went to buy his round, continuing to hold forth to us as he stumbled to the bar. He bumped into the lean and hungry one. They had words, and Jay walked back to the table carrying the drinks muttering about the asshole.

"Jay!" I almost yelled to be sure of being heard over the bar noise. "Be careful, that guy." I nodded my head toward him. "I got a bad feeling about him." I knew when Jay was in his cups; he had a violent temper.

"Fuck him!" Jay yelled loudly enough to hush the crowd for a second.

"Jay, shut the fuck up!" one of our groups said.

Somehow I convinced Jay to walk out with me. In the lesser roar of the street, I said, "Jay, a few days ago in class, I saw a black mark on your neck." I pointed to the area, two fingers breadth beneath his left ear, just below the jaw's hinge. It was a bad idea. He was drunk and mad, making him even more irrational, and I was telling him something totally alien. He looked at me with unfocused eyes, a disbelieving, perplexed look on his angry face.

"So what? It coulda been marker."

"I don't think so, Jay." I paused, my natural caution telling me to hold back, but I was too close to the edge, so I blundered on. "I've seen this before, and it always means death."

As I remembered each spot's occurrence in later years, I wondered if different words might have made a difference. If I had waited for a different time, he might have been more receptive and the results different. Such thoughts and what-ifs are useless, as almost all ex post facto thinking is.

"Fuck you! You didn't see shit!" he spat. Jay lost control of his temper and his language when drunk.

"Jay, I know it sounds like crap, but trust me, I saw it, and I have seen spots like this six times before and every time the person dies."

"You're an asshole, MacIntosh! You should be a writer." But he didn't go back in. He fumbled for his keys and headed off for his car.

I thought I had accomplished my purpose, and maybe fate could be postponed. Perhaps I had saved his life.

It doesn't like to stay dark for long in California. Like a rambunctious teenager, the sun always seems ready to kick away the cloak of night and go out and play.

My sleep was disturbed by a phone call at 1:30 a.m. which was followed by an eerie drive along almost empty freeways to a police station.

After the drive came the time in the waiting room filled with sufferers of various sorts, people trying to sleep in chairs engineered for maximum discomfort, of spare men and women chain-smoking, seeking relief via nicotine. Finally, I followed an officer back to the detective's area past officers in various states of rumpledness, finishing the late show as the midnight shift was called in police work. Finally, I left the police station, and I sat in my car as another golden California day started, less one life.

Jay returned to the bar and had words with the lean and evil one. Words became shoves, shoves, blows, blows became three fast punctures from a prison-made shank in the side of Jay's neck, left side, below the ear, just below the jaw. For the next six minutes, Jay's lifeblood was absorbed by the soiled napkins and scrapings of shoes and boots in the filth of Thinkers' floor.

One more cycle of life complete.

We were a callous lot, brutally judgmental, and untempered by age, but my group was shocked by the loss. I, of course, was the most shaken. I had known beforehand, and my intervention had been ineffectual. Depression stepped up to lead me to self-abnegation.

Often the route to discovery passes through well-formed questions. At the edges of my mind, queries were forming. My data analysis side directed me to look at the events, the precursors, and the results to see if they indicated causality or coincidence patterns.

What I was stumbling toward in my ham-handed way was an epistemology, and data analysis was the very opposite of the type of study needed. I was interested in occurrences, times, and outcomes. What I needed to understand were fate, destiny, and predestination. I studied data because it was accessible and available. I failed in epistemology because deep inside me, I was afraid of the truth and hiding was easier.

There had now been seven occurrences; one, the football player, was a total stranger; three, Shamus, Jay, and Caesar had been friends; one lover Suzan, one lover's father, and one casual acquaintance, Iris Wagner. I had strong emotional ties to five of the seven. The deaths occurred in bunches, three in high school, two in college, and two at work—one period of almost five years with no occurrences, another of two and a half years. The only pattern that appeared was that the spots were most likely to occur if I was close to someone, and the other possibility was they were random events, which was more frightening.

My rational mind and my training directed me to look for a pattern, but none appeared. The answers seem to lie in an unexplored country. I knew in my rational mind I wasn't the cause of the spots, nor could I wish a person dead, but my shame made me think otherwise.

Men might be from Mars, women from Venus, but my thoughts were straight from Saturn. I wallowed in misery and fear. I agonized over the unfairness of my affliction. Saturnine thinking can lead to wisdom as it provides the depressant time to reflect on the inner man, a rare occurrence in mass society. From that reflection can come knowledge if the person will accept it and, most importantly, can see it. The price, of course, is social isolation and emotional withdrawal. I had neither the willingness to accept whatever wisdom was coming my way nor the desire to find it. I turned my reflection into a pity party with me as the victim. I believed no one could understand me or my problem, and no one could help. The curse was mine alone, and I had to eat it and live the distress and pain, fearing any close relationship.

Victor Frankl would say that suffering was as much part of life as death. What gave meaning to the suffering was how it was handled. How a person deals with suffering can inspire others and reflect the greatness of the man's spirit. I was failing in being an example. I was convinced something was wrong with me. I was mentally flawed, covered in sin, and somehow not fit to be in society.

Consciously and unconsciously, I distanced myself from people, did my job, and attended my classes, but I was alone at night. I convinced myself I was like Prince Arjuna in the Bhagavad Gita, "I have become death. I am the destroyer of worlds."

I got my degree from USC. My final paper discussed a software model I'd been working on, allowing software to detect, learn, and correct mistakes making it more effective over time. It impressed people because the praise was fulsome, but I took no joy in the applause, and that's one of the hallmarks of depression.

Shortly after graduation, Anderson reorganized. The accounting side was significant, but consulting's growth was blowing the doors off. We were competing for talent with all the new tech companies; the firm needed to create a package to attract the people it needed. To do that, Anderson created a new class of junior consulting partners, and I was included in the new class. The elevation came with a nice raise and limited participation in the partnership pool.

Some didn't make it. To my great surprise, Ed Kelso was one, and he left to join a company called Printronix. Another one was a guy I had worked with and named by classically trained parents, Dante Mars.

Dante fancied himself a lady's man and flirted and frankly harassed women in the office. It was easier and less risky to do that in the still-patriarchal late 1970s and early 1980s. He did have the problem of being married, which he disguised by not wearing a ring. We rarely saw his wife of nearly twenty years. I had met her, and she was a terrific, long-suffering woman who loved him desperately. They had two delightful kids. Then he got the disease which often affects men in middle age. Fading *youthtitus*. One of its manifestations is a man's head going straight up his ass.

He started wearing clothing designed for younger, slimmer men, but his steady weight gain condemned him to look like look precisely like what he was, a middle-aged guy frantically trying not to be. He bought a Datsun 240Z, not a family car, and started wearing a hairpiece that looked like a skunk died on his head.

He couldn't afford the two lives he was living. It was counterproductive, making him unhappy and feeding his rationalizations, which led to more silliness. In the reorganization, he was let go. Rumor had it that he dipped his pen in the company ink once too often and in the wrong inkwell to boot.

Months passed. We would occasionally hear from or about Dante, me in particular. At first, it was the brave talk about his prospects and how good it was that he had been let go. Now he could focus on himself and do "his job," whatever that meant. The calls became less buoyant, more self-pitying, more desperate. I lost interest, being busy. That was easy, he was burdensome as dependent people are. He asked for solutions, then dismembered them. Finally, I stopped offering help and created ways to dodge his calls. Office relationships are hard to maintain once the daily interaction ceases. Once the fruit of residential propinquity, love and friendship shifted with societal transformation to nearness during employment, but once work ended, so did the relationship.

My apartment in Marina del Rey had a view of the marina and was full of single professional people. The sunsets seen from my deck were jaw-dropping. I abstained from the social life of the place, convinced as I was that my closeness to people inspired the spots. I lost interest in Dante Mars; he didn't lose interest in me. I was now living another fulfillment of the Illinois fantasy.

He called the office one day while I was multitasking, and I sort of acquiesced to getting together. I thought I had done so in a non-specific, socially meaningless, way but I was wrong. He showed up at the apartment that Saturday with all the grace and sophistication of a water buffalo, which he resembled.

"Hey, Mack!" He had resisted all attempts not to call me Mac or Dave. "Look at this place! Wow, look at all the broads!" He had a voice of brass. "Of course, you can't call chicks broads anymore. Dames really hate that." Now everyone knew the quiet guy in apartment 360a had an uncouth friend.

I was really shocked to see how much weight he had packed on his 5'10" frame, about forty or fifty pounds. The buttons on his shirt strained, and I thought if the clasp on his pants came loose, it would be with bullet-like force. He made it worse when he doffed his shirt and rolls of fish-belly white flesh leaped free. He landed noisily in the pool chair next to me before spotting the restroom and waddling across the pool deck, giving what he thought was a come-hither look at several women.

Dante had the idea of going out to dinner, then hitting some clubs. There was a great place, The Basement, in MDR, which was as he called it crawling with broads. Fortunately, I had plans, a platonic date, so he suggested lunch.

"Won't your wife wonder where you are?"

I don't know what I expected, but the question unleashed the litany of every unfaithful husband. Got married too early, she didn't get me, we've outgrown each other, men aren't designed for just one woman. As he finished his clichés, he said, "So we got divorced. Well, not divorced, actually. She calls it a trial separation, but the jury's back. It's over. Now I'm like you—footloose, fancy-free. So wadda say, the two amigos satisfying the needs of the LA babes!"

"Not really my thing Dante; I'm still getting over Suzan." I figured that would close it down. I was wrong. Having Dante as a wingman guaranteed a lack of success with women.

"She was a babe and a half for sure, but she was only one fish in the sea, Mac. There are ten chicks right here as good-looking as ole Suzan."

I was still in love with Suzan and her memory. To hear her so cavalierly dismissed angered me. I thought of blowing him off right there.

"Where are you working these days?" I asked.

"Here and there. You know how it is, Mac, Anderson really crushed me. All the years of loyalty, and they destroy me. I do some consulting, taxes, and stuff. Something will pop soon."

I managed to get away with only lunch, but I couldn't help noticing Dante ordered a lot of food and left with a well-stuffed doggy bag. He called a few times in the next few weeks, but I was fully engaged in a San Diego project and spent a lot of time there.

He finally ran me to ground at the apartment: same routine, more weight. The first time he came to my place, he looked like fourteen pounds of shit in a seven-pound bag. Now he had crammed an additional seven pounds in the same bag. However, this time, the fat rolls were marked by a large black spot on his back above the hips. No doubt, no light tricks, no shadows, no shifting chromatics, it was right there in the bright California sun. My heart collapsed, and I was rude in getting rid of him.

As I pursued what I thought was wisdom, I began to look at the issue from a more philosophical bent. I started to think about the moral implications of the spots, which were backward. I needed to create or find a theory to explain what was happening. I started at the wrong point. I couldn't explain what they were, but I tried to put rules around what they meant. Philosophy would have attempted to explain the first part. What I was doing was developing a set of ethics. I began to look at it from the standpoint of two long-lived philosophical schools, stoicism and spockism.

Scots are natural stoics. Wearing a kilt on a windy day, cold day, or in the presence of mosquitoes will do that. While the stoic's reputation is one of bloodlessness, they're more concerned with what they can control versus what is beyond their ken. Like most neo-stoics, my affection for the school most probably arose from a misunderstanding of Marcus Aurelius.

In the emperor's meditations, I read that peace of mind came from not dwelling on past troubles or future ones. It came from focusing on the present and which troubles could be born and which could not be endured. My guilt and shame, combined with my memory of what I believed were my past failures, created a fear of future bad outcomes, which in turn destroyed my peace of mind.

That rambling lead me back to a distant memory of a quote from Dumas about a man who doubts himself might as well enlist in the army of his enemies. I was holding my inability to change the outcome of the spots against myself and, in doing so, was destroying my peace and my ability to love.

I had no control over any of the aspects of the spots, so in stoic thought, they were neither good nor evil, and I should pay them no mind. But there's always a but in philosophy; the cold rationality of stoic thought fails when confronted with the emotions surrounding death, particularly the death of those close to you. Their deaths were just fate, and fate can be a troubling idea in a society that thinks of itself as shaping its destiny through choice. However, I had a feeling the spots pointed to some path to knowledge, belief, understanding, and even wisdom. The way seemed to be well hidden.

Spockism, like Christianity, is not a philosophy; but both are ethical systems. Spockism stems from the great normative teacher in the ethical canon called *Star Trek*. In one episode, Kirk, McCoy, and Spock go back to 1930s New York. Kirk, of course, falls in love (lust) with the female lead played by Joan Collins. Spock discovers that Collins's character forms a peace movement that prevents the US from entering World War II, allowing Hitler to win, thus changing the shape of the world. Spock tells Kirk that saving her will alter the arc of history and raises the right of anyone to do that, even driven by the greatest of all emotions, love.

Experience said intervention made no difference in the outcome, but like most people, the idea of not having control was troubling, but if I had power over the spots, could I affect the sweep of history? It was a breathtakingly arrogant proposition, and in my consideration of it, I ventured close to the edge of what the Greeks called hybris. We call it hubris, an arrogance so grand it touches on divinity.

While I debated pointy ears and eyebrows versus togas, I did what Christian ethics directed. I tried to prepare Dante for death. In doing so, I violated every rule of relationships and called his wife, Stephanie. She just broke apart, and I realized how isolated she had become.

Dante was the sole breadwinner, and she handled the family. To a large extent, her friends and acquaintances were Anderson people, and when Dante left, she was cut off. She was horribly worried about him; she still loved him, and the kids were all messed up. Money was tight, and she didn't want to divorce, but she couldn't wait forever.

I decided to try to show Dante what he was missing. Anderson had a membership at the Jonathan Club, and I invited Dante for dinner. I hoped getting dressed up, the white tablecloth, and the lavish surroundings might make him vulnerable, and he would listen.

I got there first and told the waiters no liquor at the table—the new, Anderson rule. The waiter looked aghast, no doubt calculating the potential decline in gross margins such a policy would cause. If you're going to lie, do it in a way that is immediately accepted and hopefully does good. It soothes the conscience.

Dante showed up in an unfortunate outfit. He had on an old sports coat worn at the cuffs and elbows, scuffed shoes, a shirt too small, pants unpressed and too tight, and a shirt and tie combination so mismatched it looked like the fading gentility in MacArthur Park.

"You must be doing well, Mac—here at the John club at the firm's table."

"Just a working stiff, Dante. Thought it might be nice to take advantage of the perk. Tax laws are changing, and it might not be around much longer."

The appetizers arrived and Dante fell on them like a dog on a steak.

"Dante," I said, waiting until his mouth was full, a trick I learned from waiters, "I had a call from Steph the other day, and I'm concerned."

His fork dropped.

"You know I care for you. I want the best for you. Right?" I wanted that line to carry sincerity. Instead, it seemed to drip with triteness. I hoped he didn't notice.

"Whad the bitch say?" he said loudly. "Blamed it all on me, right?"

The club's dining room was always a tranquil place, and with Dante's crudity, people were staring at us.

I was angry at his remark. "You might want to say it louder. I'm sure there's a drug addict in West Hollywood who didn't hear you!" My sarcasm ripped out.

"Sorry, Mac, she's always blaming me for everything, like everything's my fault, pisses me off."

"She told me she still loves you. Regardless, the kids are confused, she wants you back and doesn't want to divorce you, but she feels a need to protect herself and the kids." I paused for a second to let the litany sink in. "I got the impression money was very tight."

"Well"—he paused while salads arrived—"she should have been nicer to me and understood my needs. This would'na happened. You're a guy, Mac, we have needs and desires, and women just don't understand us."

With my nonexistent patience for self-serving bullshit, I could never be a therapist. I put my fork down harder than I expected, making a loud clatter. Then it fell off onto the tablecloth.

"Dante," I said forcefully, elbows on the table right fist held by the left hand, a hard stare at him demanding focus, "Suzan and I were deliriously all-encompassing in love, the kind you read about in chick books. We had a whole life ahead of us, and she was taken from me. Love, true real love that joyous is rare and shouldn't ever be let go." I don't know where it came from, but I began to quote scripture.

"Love bears all things, believes all things, endures all things," I said the words with all the intensity I could muster in the process, fracturing and misusing Paul's words. I wasn't talking; I was lecturing.

I needed to get through to him that he was dying; his time was short, he was unhappy, but happiness was a phone call away. Some inner voice told me that he would not see grace unless I found a way to reunite him and Steph. Once more, scripture came to me. From where? I had no idea. I hadn't read the Bible in twenty years.

"Be watchful and ready for no one knows when the master will return." I stopped but continued to stare at him. "You never know," I repeated.

Dealing with men in emotional crisis is vastly different than with women. No less dangerous, just different. Men define themselves into emotional holes, then armor themselves against internal and external pain. They use phony feelings as shields; their egos take control to prevent feelings of inadequacy. Interventions often cause misplaced anger and can come to grief on the rocks of egocentrism.

Before the dinner, I made some calls to Anderson's clients and found an independent film distributor looking for a part-time cost accountant. There was a chance the position would go full-time, and it came with health insurance. I presold them on Dante, and as dinner wound down, I gave him the contact information. We parted with quiet resignation. I wasn't sure I reached him, and I think he was upset at my intervention.

As I drove south in LA's eternal traffic jam, I should have felt happy. I'd helped a doomed man. If he got the job, the money and insurance would repair a bit of the damage and make his eventual death easier. If he blew it, which was always a possibility, I had done my best and more. I should have been happy, but I wasn't.

I didn't know what it was; there was some message I should have taken away. It teased at me from the corners of my mind, just out of reach. In my dreams, there was a figure waving me onward toward something. My peace of mind was also disturbed by the earthquake which occurred in the wee hours.

I called Stephane and told her what had happened. She gushed praise and thanks. It was the last time I heard anything from either of them. Dante died several years later of kidney disease.

Spots 8, MacIntosh 0.

Anderson landed a large contract with Princess Cruises to help them update and modernize their information systems. One of the perks was the team got some free cruises, to check out the software, of course. I took one cruise down the Mexican coast, and that was it for me. While I was on the ship, I was overwhelmed by spots. Cruising was still an older crowd. Many were already sick, and more would suffer accidents. It was too much for me. Even though I didn't know them, the signs of death were something I didn't want to have shoved in my face every second.

Two years had passed since Suzan died before I found the strength to write letters to her parents and her brother, Gino. I thought about writing to Father Altois, the hospital chaplain who had been there that terrible day. I needed to apologize for my actions when Suzan died, but an apology was only the apparent motivation.

Everyone knows Catholics are riddled with guilt, no one knows what they're guilty about, but it comes with the territory. Assuaging Catholic guilt wasn't what was happening here. I'd been more than rude at a time of significant loss and stress. Mom was a great fan of Eric Hoffer and often quoted us his line that "rudeness is the weak man's imitation of strength." I had lost control and disliked that in myself.

My rudeness insulted Suzan's and her parent's religious beliefs, which gave them solace during a terrible time in their life. That alone was unforgivable. The real reason I was motivated to mend fences was my growing maturity and my need to seek meaning in the events of my past. I was also growing tired of the falsity and mendacious nature of my existence.

While the California dream was beautiful, it came with accepting its narcissistic materialism. That materialism had treated me well, no argument, but it was a chimera. It was a series of accomplishments isolated from meaning. It was relative. There was always someone who had accomplished more, done it better, and made more money. You spent time thinking and worrying about the future, how you would be remembered, your legacy, about what you were doing now. You remembered everything you did and rushed to ensure you got credit for it because nothing in California lasted, and getting credit was the only way to be remembered. It was exhausting and self-defeating.

It created idolatry of symbols, houses, cars, clothing, houses, and trips, none of which had meaning. Dad used to say that when humankind lacks a source of meaning, they create one, and often that creation is a monster since most of our so-called reasoning consists of finding arguments for going on believing as we already do.

Vietnam and Watergate had killed our trust in the government. We didn't trust God, who couldn't provide empirical facts of existence, yet we had nothing else. The economy betrayed us as stagflation ate up our savings. Relationships unbridled by goals or propinquity became gossamer bits of ambition. The stem of unhappiness opened old wounds, which became running sores. Legends in their own minds, the press began to simulate, not inform. You couldn't put your finger on what was wrong; there were so many things you ran out of fingers, but you had to keep up; you were never right and were unhappy in distress.

There was a *dreath* of Sarahs, Ruths, Graces, and Elizabeths as the search for uniqueness created a plethora of Kaitlins, Brooks, Tiffanys, and Jeremiahs. Children became accessories to a lifestyle, driven to excel at all things by parents offloading their own hopes, dreams, wishes. They mostly wanted the kids to make up for their failures. Kids became tchotchkes of narcissism. So in a bloody-minded and incautious frame of mind, I tracked Father Altois down.

The hospital told me he had been posted to a parish in Garden Grove called St. Anastasia or, as the wags called it, St. Anesthesia. I always admired the cheerleaders at Catholic schools. It's one thing to spell out Central but try spelling out Immaculate Conception or St. Anastasia! I made an appointment.

It was neither a rich nor large parish, but it was a battleground. On one side was the enormous Roman Colosseum of churches, the Crystal Cathedral drawing thousands of nondenominational Protestants; on the other side was a Vietnamese Buddhist population arriving in the wake of the war. In the mix were Vietnamese Catholics, freshly arrived Hispanics many in the country without documents. Alongside them were Hispanics of earlier migrations and a few incumbent white folks.

Altois, whose first name was Germaine, didn't remember me, so I had to go through the whole remembrance process. "Father." I began, "I need to confess something." I meant to say apologize, but I guess Catholicism goes deep, and confession came out.

"Is this in the form of a regular reconciliation?" he asked with some irritation.

"No, sir, something happened between you and me a couple of years ago, and I've been troubled by it. I need to apologize and seek some guidance."

We were seated in his parish office, which was burdened by books and papers.

"Oh good. As you can see, I'm swamped saving souls," the twinkle in his eyes gave away his delight at having something to do, "and I would hate to be interrupting my afternoon nap."

I could have easily been put off, but the big smile on his face and the lightness of his voice belied his being bored to tears and seeking a challenge.

"What are you apologizing for?" he asked.

"As I said, a few years ago, you were at the bedside of Suzan Antonelli…" My voice cracked as remembrance welled up both for her and the memory of my actions. "When she…"

"Went to the Lord?" he finished hopefully.

"Yes, and I was insulting and defamatory to you and the Lord. It has always bothered me since."

"Your formulation is interesting. You are placing, least rhetorically, me before God in your concern."

Whack right between the eyes!

"Have you apologized to God?"

"No," I quickly replied.

"You should; it's called prayer and reconciliation. However, if you are sorry in your heart; contrite, God hears you and knows your remorse. The bigger thing is if you rejected God and turned away from Him as a result. I assume you haven't since you're here."

"I don't think I did, Father. I've never been a churchgoer. My father is Catholic; my mother is anti-Catholic."

"Oh, one of those!" Altois laughed.

"Yet you were poised to marry Suzan, a devout Catholic?" He steepled his fingers, a sly smile crossed his face, he was enjoying this. "If you wish to confess your sins, and be forgiven, I do confession—we call it reconciliation now, others, mind control—on Saturdays at four in the afternoon."

"I think what I did qualifies as sin under any religious doctrine." I noticed I was slipping into more formal and stilted language. "So thanks." I forced myself to be more casual. "I'll come back on Saturday. Can we talk about my need for guidance?"

"Most assuredly," he said, lapsing into biblical language, though continuing the gag he was running with from the confession discussion. "But verily, I listen better over lunch," he said, leaning forward and raising his eyebrows in a Groucho-like move. I was committed to a meeting later, so lunch, which I expected would be long, was out. I made an appointment for later in the week. He didn't write it down.

"My book is empty, but I won't forget a free meal."

I started to wonder if he might be too cynical for my needs.

The most remarkable occurrence of hive-like activity in large partnerships is around the partnership list. Each year rumors start to leak about who is on the list. The campaigns begin with hints, statements of worth, battles over who gets credit or blame for what, and careful calculation of the dollar value of the partnership. As much as possible, I stayed out of the office gossip, so I was surprised to be called to Kopinski's office and anointed as a partner. The first things I did were to take the rest of the day off and buy an ocean-view house in Pacific Palisades.

I was feeling good when I picked Altois up at the church, and for the first time, I noticed he walked with a cane and a brace on his left leg. I didn't make a mistake many fully abled people make and rush to accommodate those who are disabled, but he knew.

"Polio got one back, but the virus still holds the other one captive. Be glad you didn't have to deal with it."

149

One of the most irritating human actions, in my opinion, is when someone tells you of a personal tragedy they are experiencing, and the listener immediately relates one of their tragedies. I know it's supposed to provide context and bind people in joint suffering, but really, it's one-upmanship and diminishes the first person. It's a form of egocentrism. I have that habit, but this time I didn't follow the usual practice. I just said sorry.

"What are you sorry about? You didn't do it," he fired back, subject closed.

He directed me to a Mexican place that was owned by a parishioner, judging by the service and greeting. "You said you need spiritual guidance. About what?"

"I can see death."

His immediate reaction was hidden by the Margarita he was drinking.

"Big guy, black robes, scythe, or a Jesuit? Same thing." He laughed, but somehow the laughter didn't bother me since he laughed at his own joke, not at me, although I wondered at the possible irony.

I told the whole story.

"You see a spot on me?" he said.

"No, but I can't see all of you either. Seeing you naked would be way too much torture." I replied, wrinkling my eyes in laughter to match my smile.

He thought for a second before he said, "I've been a priest for thirty-five years, and I have to admit this is a new one. I have had Virgin Mary's, Jesus' face in peanut butter, angels at Disneyland, and God's face on TV. If you can believe it, I actually was getting a bit jaded and thought I'd heard it all, so thank you. Have you consulted with psychologists and doctors?"

I recalled the attempt to help Dante Mars. I told him about Jacoby, my family, and the other times I had taken action. He looked quizzical like he was forming a question or deciding how to question me. "I'm not sure what to tell you, David. Do you think you caused this? Have you ever seen anyone take action and change the outcome?"

"To the first point, I don't know. I intervened with Suzan manipulating her to get tested, which is how the cancer was discovered. I also tried to convince Jay not to go back to the bar, but he went anyway to his death, and I still don't know about Mars."

"So it is." He started using a favorite line from homiletics. "That it doesn't appear as if you cause the appearance of spots and perhaps no action on your part can change the outcome, so they are manifestations of fate."

"I'm not sure I understand why that is so important," I replied.

He looked past and through me, framing an answer. "If you could cause them, it would be an entirely unbearable condition. You could shoot death, as it were. Every thought could have the most disastrous effects." He waited to see if I had a response, then continued. "Second, since they seem to be all related to accident, violence, or disease, they are not the result of free will. Not chosen consciously and not by the person."

I was thinking hard as he rambled on.

"The pregnant woman, your high school friend, Shamus, Jean's father, and the sainted Suzan"—he made the sign of the cross, and I joined him—"did not choose to die, only two made choices—Caesar and your college teacher, Jay."

As he tucked into his bowl of menudo, I was confused, but his categorization was accurate.

"What I'm saying, David, is if this isn't some sort of pi shogue, they are a sign visible to you, evidencing of fate." He looked at me in a penetrating manner to see the effect of his words.

My mind was reeling. No one had looked at it this way, but something pulled me, a flaw, a tear in the logic fabric, maybe just resistance to an explanation based on a long period of self-exploration. Often, when we seek opinion, we're really seeking approbation. Had I fallen into that trap? I had gotten an explanation different from what I expected, which is always disturbing.

"The question you need to focus on as I see it, is not the outcome for the person but if there is a message and meaning to *you*." That's the key to finding knowledge or direction in your life."

"So are you saying this could be a sign of heavenly favor?"

"Not necessarily. Constantine saw a cross in the sky, Joan of Arc heard voices telling her to save France, the apostles had tongues of flame descend on them, and so on. Visions are common in the non-Christian tradition too."

"I'm being given a message. From God?"

"Maybe"—he shipped his drink—"you need to be careful with this, as it is very easy to discern the wrong message and act contrary to the actual message."

"Could it be, like Jacoby said, I'm demon-possessed?" I asked.

"Maybe, but I doubt it. You didn't burst into flame when we shook hands or cower before the crucifix. You don't act possessed. No, I don't think so; however, the devil used to be an angel, and is very clever and subtle, so it's something to be careful about." He finished his drink.

I paid, and we left.

The ride back to the parish was quiet except for one statement as we pulled into the parking lot. "David, you work in information theory, so I'll try to say this in terms that relate to that. Forgive me if I get the words wrong. I'm an old man. You face an anomaly disrupting the normal flow of data and logic. Anomalies point to flaws and disrupt paradigmatic thinking. Oh, how I hate that word!" he said with vehemence, "But it fits. Paradigms lock up formulas and channels. Anomaly breaks those channels."

"This anomaly, these spots, point to new knowledge. For a while, it's going to be disturbing, all new information is, but you must pursue it. That's how the world gets better. You need to pursue this information whatever the cost, just as Jesus had to pursue his course, and Joan and Constantine their destiny. Your destiny, not your fate lies along that path, and no other."

"I don't have a choice?"

"You always have a choice. If you have free will, but you choose another path, there will be costs, which will likely not be pleasant. Many who have struggled along the path laid out by the chaos caused by new information have found themselves falling into the abyss of disillusion, anger, and madness. You must have faith that this...this ability is ultimately for good and faith that God can set your feet on the correct path. We were silent for a moment, then he continued.

"At the same time, as you walk this road, be unhampered by guilt. You cannot have any guilt about those who die, and you cannot be ashamed of your ability. As far as you know, you did nothing to bring this on yourself other than being born. Guilt and shame and depression they bring will trap you in the past, in the distant and misty realm of nostalgia, guilt, and remorse, all of which are barriers to happiness."

I drove toward downtown LA my brain reeling. I was mentally exhausted, but I started to tease out the threads of the fabric of his arguments. I was like an automaton while driving, making me the same as the other eight million drivers in LA. I think, at this point, I came to one of my great loves. Those who spent endless hours in the inexorable traffic jams alongside millions of fellow humans, many of whom I was convinced suffered mental illness, find ways to escape.

In the days before cell phones, satellite radios, GPS, talking books, radio, AM, or FM were your only choices. The station scanner brought me to one playing classical music. Coincidences are clues. My finding that station at precisely that time might have been a coincidence, but it was unction for a troubled mind. From the speaker came something called the Nocturne in E flat major by Chopin. In later years, I would say there were several reasons to believe in God, and among them was the music of the tragic Frederic Chopin. One of my favorite movies would be Impromptu, about the love affair between Chopin and George Sand.

I resolved to learn about classical music. Now I had three resolutions: to go to Mass, find out about the spots, and learn about music.

CHAPTER 7

Andersen had a contract at Ames Labs in Mountain View through its government services division. Their systems were hodgepodges from the lowest bidder, with computers from different manufacturers working and communicating with other computers. The result was a digital cacophony.

I was appointed leader of the sub-team dealing with storage architecture. Ames Lab stands on the grounds of Moffett Field, then an active Navy base thirty-five miles south of San Francisco, right at the head of Silicon Valley.

The field was right next to Highway 101 and dominated by two structures. The most obvious was a gigantic hangar with curved doors at each end once the home of Navy blimps. Rumor had it that some hotshot pilot once flew straight through it. Just north of the blimp hanger was a giant wind tunnel for testing aircraft and missile design. There were two eleven thousand-foot runways. During the day, the air was filled with the sounds of PC 3 Orion anti-submarine aircraft leaving and arriving, helicopters, and the eerie silence of the U2 spy plane landing.

North of Ames was Palo Alto, home to Stanford, and the string of suburbs leading to Baghdad by the Bay, San Francisco. Across the Bay were Oakland, the poor sister, and its exurbs sprawling to the East. All are dominated by Mount Diablo and Mount Hamilton.

When the sun shone, the bay was dazzling, the air clean, and visibility unlimited. Every time I returned to LA through the smog and haze, I wondered why I lived there. Around us, Silicon Valley was humming, fed by the fecundity of Stanford and Xerox Labs. Intel, Fairchild, Advanced Micro, Xilinx, Intersil, and others appeared like mushrooms after a rain.

The literature I had been reading was full of the changes brought by the explosion of new companies with new technologies, and it was apparent that the rate of change would only increase. I was acutely aware that whatever we did for Ames would likely be obsolete in a couple of years unless we gave them solutions at the cutting edge. I got a fair amount of pushback with my idea both from Anderson and Ames.

NASA, in 1969, had put a man on the moon using technology unknown ten years before. They had created most of the technology, invented the names, and words to describe it. They should, at least in my mind, have understood the need for innovation. Anderson had more understandable objections. The Ames work was a consulting firm's dream. The client had the attention of Congress and was getting constant subvention. The present value of a long-term contract is higher than a higher payment for a shorter engagement. Anderson resisted the leading edge and sought something less capable to extend the revenue stream.

While we were still in the specifications stage, I politicked around Ames and got them to allocate more money to storage because I knew Ames would need it very soon. Several team members and I were in Mountain View getting ready for the first stage of the upgrade. When we were ready, we entered the commands and ran the programs.

I think everyone was surprised that it worked so well. We let it run all day and night with no incoming data. Then we allowed some input, and it held steady. Then we all went to dinner in Palo Alto to celebrate.

We had just finished salads when a tornado blew through the doors of our meeting room. This tornado was a five-foot-four-inch brunette—trim, tanned, and furious.

"Which of you, self-satisfied dumb shits, is in charge of this mess?" the tornado demanded. No one moved, although there were signs of discomfort.

"Somebody better answer me because someone"—she scanned the table with a terrible look—"has a real problem."

Finally, Alistair Carifear, an ex-pat Brit, answered, "What seems to be your concern, Miss Shackleton?"

"The problem is my team, and I have been inputting data for delivery to DoD next Friday, and you numbnuts threw a switch or something, and it's all gone! That Alistair is the problem, and it needs to be fixed. Now!"

"My dear, Miss Shackleton," Alastair began in his languid English drawl. His voice was both irritating and condescending. "I'm sure that something can be worked out. We have a lot of brain power here." He waved to all of us. "I know how distressing things must be. Still, it's hardly the end of the world, is it?" A rhetorical question. "Why don't you go home? Have some tea and a hot bath. Let us look into this." There it was the complete chauvinistic package, the torch into a barrel of gasoline.

"Not that is any of your business, Al, but I don't drink tea or take baths. I shower and drink black coffee, so I'm not going to be like you, and your brain trust here," she waved at us all before continuing sardonically, "and sit around and do nothing because I'm a woman!" She glared at us; arms akimbo. "Do something, or I go up the chain!" She stood there for a few seconds, spun her heels, and blew out of the room.

I expected the doors to slam shut and the windows to blow out with the pressure of the tornado going away.

People nervously drank, shuffled their feet, and cleared their throats. I was impressed. Alistair was about four levels above her, and the others in the room probably outranked her. She could have done real damage to her career.

I had an idea about what might have happened, so I said, "I think I might have an idea. It might solve the problem. Why don't I go back and see if I can help out?" I got a wave of dismissal from Al as if he had finished with his valet.

I headed out of the room, trying to catch the tornado. What was her name? I heard her heels clacking on the marble floor ahead of me.

"Hey," I called out. "Stop!" came out as a plea more than a command.

She whirled on me like a swordsman in an old movie, eyes like rapiers, determined expression, ready for battle. Seeing her, you could understand how small animals can bluff large predators.

"Why?" The word came back like a bullet.

"I might be able to help you find the data."

No response except a quizzical tilt of the head and neck.

"You got a car?" she spat.

"No."

"Come on then…something is better than nothing, I guess."

So being better than nothing, I went.

I was using an old male trick. I had an excellent idea of what happened. I knew the data wasn't gone, and I probably could have instructed the tornado on retrieving it. Still, I wanted to make myself essential and superior and create dependency.

I almost instantly regretted my tactic. She must have failed driving school. She threw her VW around corners in ways that violated the rules of physics. She would have been red-flagged at a NASCAR race. She said not a word. I was glad if her state of mind were as angry as her driving talking would make the ride more dangerous.

We barely slowed for the Marine guards at the main gate and then screeched to a stop at a building called Geospatial Information. Inside, a room full of people was milling around, waiting for something. They all looked up at us with aspects of hope as if all of their fates rested on Miss Shackleton; that was her name.

She sent the rest of the team home, and she and I sat down at a workstation. While the odor of anger carrying a mix of sweat and hormones was present, she also smelled good. It wasn't some frilly perfume, simply good clean, and healthy skin and hair. She explained what they'd been doing, where they had sent the data, and so on.

I experimented, asked questions, sent some data, had it fail, and generally worked through the operations. Around midnight, she fell asleep in her chair. I was wide awake and on the hunt. I put my suit coat jacket over her and finally found the data safe and sound.

I wrote some code creating a pathway to the data and renamed the files to be easily recognized. Around six thirty, she started making sounds like a kitten slowly coming awake. She unconsciously belched, which brought her fully awake with a start.

"Sorry," she said.

"For what?"

"Burping."

"That was not a burp. Burps are small and can be swallowed. What you did was more properly belch and loudly," I said, not taking my face from the screen.

"You trying to make me feel bad? I must look a fright."

"No, just being precise, you've been around Alistair too long. You're starting to pick up British syntax."

"Humph, you find the data, Mr. Precise."

"I think so, this part of it?" I moved my chair a bit, and she edged closer.

"Yeah, that's part of it. How did you find it?"

"I know how we set up the architecture, so I went looking. Why don't we wait until the team arrives? That way, I only have to explain this once. How about breakfast or at least some coffee?"

We walked to the mess hall at the Marine Barracks. We looked like a couple who stayed up late. The Marines assumed wild times and ribbed us both. She apparently had a standing invitation to the mess hall. Marines like pretty girls. They view them as a food source.

We went back to the lab, as she called it. It was a walk of shame. We both looked so disheveled that everyone assumed we had been out all night, likely having sex.

I showed them where the data was, how to retrieve it, and how the new systems would save them time. Someone asked her a question using her first name, and I discovered she was Elspeth Shackleton or El. Then El drove me to the Holiday Inn in Palo Alto.

"I owe you a drink, at least for saving our asses," she said.

I accepted. She picked me up at seven, and we went to a pleasant place on University Avenue called Henry's. We were both tired, so we had dinner, and I was back at the hotel by nine thirty. I got bolder than I usually am.

"I'm staying on for the next few days to monitor the systems. Can I buy you dinner tomorrow?"

"Sure, but if we're going to see each other, truth is important. Are you really staying on, or are you going to change your reservations based on my answer?"

She had me, and I responded in sort of a shamefaced way. I said, "I wanted to make sure things go well."

"With the data or us?" she was relentless.

"Is there an us?" I asked, thinking it sounded sophisticated and suave.

"Sorta up to you. See you tomorrow at seven." She screeched out of the parking lot.

She disconcerted me, and I failed to get her address or phone. In those days, working from home meant working little. I made some calls to the tech team to see if everything was still working and took a nap. In the afternoon, I rambled the length of University Ave. University is anchored at Sanford's campus and by Highway 101. The commercial portion was like Main Street Americana. There were shoe stores, a couple of drugstores, a scattering of restaurants, banks, at least three brokerage offices, one tall building, and next to a movie theater, a barbershop, and a hotel called The President.

I got my hair cut and asked the barber, Roy, the name of a good place for dinner. On the way west toward my hotel, I stopped at what used to be a grocery store divided into a series of small stores, almost kiosks, one of which was Mrs. Fields Cookies, the first gourmet cookie shop. The cookie was terrific, soft, gooey, and rich.

At the hotel, there was a message from El. She had forgotten I didn't have a car, and she'd collect me. I called her back and told her we were going to the Woodside Pub. She seemed impressed. I bought flowers and was brushed, trimmed, and ready at seven. She was on time to the minute. I had only seen her in work clothes, but now she was in a slinky shimmering blue dress, and what later I learned were slingback heels or, more crudely, fuck-me shoes.

Woodside is a small, very wealthy enclave in the hills west of Palo Alto and Menlo Park. The Pub is an institution, and while we were having a before-dinner drink, we got a glimpse of the singer Tennessee Ernie Ford and a good look at El.

While Suzan had been perfect in body, form, and lushly beautiful. El was cute. She was lovely, but it was a different kind. She was spunky and animated and held herself with a heart-stopping grace that infected every move. She emitted sexuality, and even her eating was suggestive. She radiated raw energy that welcomed discovery, but I sensed commitment was needed to be part of her world.

Like Suzan, she didn't quail or compromise in the face of men. She stood up when something was wrong; she didn't make herself weak so a man would feel strong. She was herself all the time. She was so utterly fascinating.

At about nine thirty, we started back down to Palo Alto. I was in a quandary about whether to kiss her. However, such was my inexperience that in my thirties, I still wanted to be sure I did things correctly. I wanted to be a gentleman, not make assumptions and not ruin the feeling by being overeager. I must have been quiet for too long.

"Yes."

"Yes, what?" I was confused.

"Yes, you can safely try to kiss me."

"You a mind reader too?"

"No, just thinking the same thing."

In the hotel's parking lot, I got out and walked around the car. I had decided not to try to kiss her over the center console, which was the method of old married couples and seemed cheap. There wasn't a lot of conversation. We both knew what we were about. We were the perfect height for kissing. I was six inches taller, so I had to bring my head down, and to one side, she had to raise her head. Her lips were soft, slightly moist, open, firm, but yielding.

Regardless of the yammering of a generation of romance novels, the first kiss is usually a mashup of passion, hesitation, surprise, and anatomical complications. Our first kiss was a mess, at least in my estimation. I quickly moved in for a second attempt, and this one stuck. So plastered together were we, a passerby yelled, "Get a room!" Both of us dissolved in laughter. We didn't get a room, but we both knew something special had just happened.

The next day, I called to say thanks, and we made vague plans about meeting again. I could hear from her tone that she was seeking assurance that what happened wouldn't end in a Holiday Inn parking lot. I hope I gave her that assurance. I spent the flight home looking out the window wistfully. When I got to the house in Pacific Palisades, it suddenly felt very empty.

Life changes rarely occur in isolation. My life changed as I added El to the equation. A month or so later, I got a phone call telling me that Angus and Ruth had sold Culloden. The news called up sorrow and reflections of long summer days in the sticky heat, bucking hay bales. I thought about the cow patty fights between us children, getting so filthy that we had to be hosed off in the yard before coming in the house to take baths. It was memories of summer evenings chasing lightning bugs, the sweet smell of new hay in the air, of early mornings crowded between the cows attaching milking machines amid steaming piles of manure.

It was sorrow felt at the passing of an icon of youth, of the memories, which give meaning to our lives. It was the realization that the steadfast rocks of our family were slowly returning to that of which they were made.

The farm had been a large part of my young life, and the summer with Shamus, a refuge when I came in from the wilderness, the trusting place I came to after Suzan's passing. It was the touchstone of tradition and connection to the old sod of Scotland and our forbearers. A place of myth and memory. It was a loss to us all except, of course, Angus and Ruth, who got $7,000 per acre from a dairy conglomerate. Good Scots, they owed nothing. They moved to a nearby retirement community, where Angus became a bit of a terror.

I'd been enjoying one of those blessed periods with no spots. Dad, prodded by my experiences, authored an article about the visible manifestation of death to the living for a scholarly journal and mentioned a monograph by the English intellectual, Samuel Johnson. Johnson and his ever-present chronicler, Boswell, went to Scotland to pursue people who had visions of death.

Dad's article was the first clue in what would be my story, but like Jesus's disciples, I didn't believe and understand what was said.

The article did get me thinking about two subjects. First, maybe my attempt to find common threads was too narrowly focused. Perhaps the area to study should be the periods of appearance versus nonappearance. Based on what happened with Suzan, the second was how to tell El. This thing could victimize me again, and my sense of shame made me leery of going the next step with El. Both Dad's article, which got rave reviews, and my need to tell El were unwelcome intrusions into an otherwise idyllic life.

Just running the sequence of events backward, the experiences would have dictated I was due to have a period with spots appearing. I won't tell you I wasn't afraid. I contemplated breaking off the budding relationship with El, and I remembered the quote from Marcus Aurelius that Grandma had left for me about not getting attached. It wouldn't hurt as much if I weren't close to someone who died.

Most people spend little time thinking about death, except they know, or think they know, it's to be feared since it's the end. Most Americans live in the present moment, and death is a mysterious time of eternal redemption or commendation to be avoided. It can't be avoided because the moment we start to live, we begin to die.

One of the great debates in philosophy and religion is if a man has a dual nature. Does humankind have a soul? Our present age is descended from the Enlightenment, emphasizing the value of knowledge coming through the five senses. The soul, if it existed, while immanent, it is not sensed; the humanist life stance rejects the concept of a human soul, focusing entirely on the present as the only real world.

What happens after death is unknown, and people fear the unknown. As the end approaches, many people focus on what they have ignored and beg more time from deities they disdained as death approaches. I had read a speech attributed to the Native American Tecumseh: *When it comes your time to die, be not like those whose hearts are filled with the fear of death, so that when their time comes, they weep and pray for a little more time to live their lives over again in a different way. Sing your death song and die like a hero going home.*

CHAPTER 8

For me, death wasn't a future event. I lived it every day, and it was my parasitic companion. It drew me to be concerned not only for my soul but also for those others' souls whose fate was going to be so different from what they hoped or planned. Death was making me a slave but was also driving me to knowledge. In another of my endless so far unexecuted resolutions, I decided to study how the ancients dealt with death and dying.

Did I want to continue the relationship with El? How could I tell her? She might not—probably wouldn't—believe me. She was a scientist after all. My victim's ideology started to rise, and I convinced myself that I could not enter the relationship because I couldn't stand to go through another situation like with Suzan. The loss now before we got more invested would be preferable to losing her later. I was worried about things yet to come while I had no means to control them.

I was slowly stepping into philosophy. At the time, philosophy was becoming strictly an academic pursuit. Tweedy professors, intellectuals smoking pipes in hushed rooms debating the fine points of Sartre and Hegel or debating if Heidegger's attachment to the Nazis amounted to a reason to shelve his intellectual output.

Very few people wake up one morning and say, *I'm going to find a theory of meaning and ethics that will connect all the points of my life.* Usually, it's more a subtle realization of things not being in accord, and then hearing of a system of ethics or theory of knowledge makes sense for the first time. That's why it is possible for people to suddenly become religious even though Christianity is not a philosophy but an ethical system.

Philosophy is the love of knowledge, and the first thing it must do is explain the world as it is. For the Greeks, Romans, and early Christians, philosophy was a way of being, blending myths and stories of creation to create morals and ethics. The 1970s and '80s saw the rise in pop philosophy and celebrity psychologists. Their teachings flourished if some numpty celebrity gave them credence by mentioning them in a TV show or book. When they flamed out, the next smooth opportunist with three- or four-word answers for the most complex questions of life stepped up.

That, of course, was not for me. I needed a more difficult path. I was on the way to one, but I resisted it and was not schooled enough to understand it fully. I was slow to move in that direction. In the meantime, I needed to answer some questions and make decisions. I was at the point in my personal development where the edges of rationality start to fray, where the empirical facts cease to be satisfying, the place where myth and faith lay.

I'd been going to Mass regularly most of the time to Altois church, and he and I continued to talk. Naturally, I brought my questions to him.

"Do you love the woman, David?"

"I don't know. I feel tremendous attraction, but that could be lust." I pushed back, trying to avoid answering his question because I didn't know the answer.

"Do you love her?"

"What is this, Father, like Jesus asking Peter in John 17?"

"No, although I'm impressed with your biblical knowledge. I'm asking because love imposes duties and responsibilities on both parties, which need to not only be fulfilled but also revered. True Christian love, true love of any kind, should not be entered into without understanding and commitment. Implicit in those duties is the duty of truth."

"What do I do if she blows me off the nut job?"

"Your fear is pre-staging your lack of faith in her. If she loves you, she may be shocked, but she'll rise above it. If you love her and enter marriage with a lie untold, you'll always bear the guilt and the responsibility for the lie." He paused to look out the window to the building across the street.

"Those walls are built of cinder blocks and mortar. Relationships are built of bricks and mortar. You must decide if the bricks of your relationship will be truth, honesty, and faith, or lies, desperation, and lack of commitment." He looked at me. "Love is a risk, David, always a risk. Still, love is worth the risk, but love is not empirical. You can't endlessly weigh the risks and evidence. You must have faith that the risk will be accepted as an act of love and treated with respect. If it's not, you have information, and perhaps this isn't where you need to be."

"You know, Father, you never give me answers. All I get are more questions," I said ruefully.

"Not my business, answers," he said dreamily and a bit wistfully with a mixture of irony. "I'm in the redemption business. Socrates only gave questions too."

The following Friday, a box arrived by Federal Express. It was from Ruth. Inside, well packed, and protected was an old book titled *A Description of the Western Islands of Scotland* by Martin. It was a first edition dated 1763. I started to read it, and it was printed at the time of long swooping Ss. The syntax and the style put it beyond casual reading. I set it aside.

My relationship with El continued to bloom. We talked by phone every day. We had a surprising lot to talk about since our work lives were similar. We traveled back and forth almost every weekend. I stayed at a hotel, her apartment being tiny, and she stayed at my house when in LA.

It was all very chaste. Then one night, it just drifted into sex. The terms for sex would transmute over the years, but the older crowd called it playing house. Later it would simply become sex. When we finally made love, it was unsatisfying at first. We were too anxious, certainly in my case. We worked on it, and it took on a rhythm, energy, and desire, the hallmarks of the perfectibility of human relationships when the partners commit to each other.

El was at my house for the weekend, and Mom called. It was like two sisters of the spirit connected. They rattled on for so long they forgot the message that inspired the call. That took a second call when we learned Mom and Dad were coming to LA. I knew then my fate was sealed. I had to marry her.

To give them even more to talk about, I decided to propose to El so we could announce it during their visit. First, I needed to tell her about my issue, so after dinner, I did.

"El," I said, "before I tell you my story, I need to tell you that I love you. You believe me, right?"

"Yes, and I love you, David." She knew something was coming, so she took my hand.

"I told you about Suzan, my time in hell, and Jean, but there's something I didn't tell you about. I need to say it now to be sure we start our lives with truth and honesty."

She began to say something, but I raised my hand.

"It's going to seem weird, but I swear it's true. Ready?"

"Please," she said with a nod and a look of concern.

"Since I've been thirteen, I've seen spots when people are going to die. It has been right 100 percent of the time. I don't know the method, time, or place. It's never natural death. It's always accidents, violence, or disease. The spot is always the locus of the method of death. In some cases, the death has..." I fumbled for words as the emotions, and memories rose, "happened very quickly, and other times it has been months or years before it occurs, but it always happens."

In the silence that followed, my conviction that I was a victim took me to the negative. *She thinks I'm a nutjob. She's going to laugh at me. She's going to walk away.* But she gripped my hand more tightly. The sun setting over the Pacific reflected sparkling light on her face making her blue-gray eyes shine, and the room sparkled in diamonds.

Her look was first quizzical and doubting. She was a scientist, after all. Then it turned toward amusement. Her mouth twitched as it can when a smile is forming. I was afraid she would laugh at me, and I couldn't bear that. Then she did something totally unexpected. She let go of my hand, and I realized how tightly we had been gripping. I was convinced she would walk away; I might have if she had told me a story like that. She did something so astonishing it floored me. She pushed away from the table and stripped right down to her glowing, healthy tanned skin.

"Look me over. Tell me if you see any of these spots."

Of course, as a red-blooded California male, I took a very long time in my examination. She was clear in every way.

Later, the sheets twisted and damp with exertion. We lay there in the lassitude of reflection, trying to remember what happened just before the sex. El propped herself on one elbow and tickled her fingers over my chest.

"I think we should get married on the beach and have four to five children." She had one of her sunshine radiant smiles, which made her irresistible. Three problems solved.

There were many things I grew to love about El, but at this early stage, her willingness to accept a new outlier occurrence, the mark of a true scientist, was one of them. She took my story and didn't ask for a lot about the spots until later. She was far better at that than I was.

Mom and Dad arrived, and after fifteen minutes of Mom and El together, nothing short of death would prevent our marriage. You might be expecting a lengthy description of the wedding, but like Frost's traveler on a snowy evening, I have miles to go before I sleep.

The wedding was fun. Dad. Fergus, Angus, and I were decked out in full Scottish gear, the women in MacIntosh plaids, and El had a MacIntosh sash showing that she was joining her husband's clan. We had it at the Jonathan Club's beach house with Father Altois presiding. I wanted my brother, Peter, to be the best man, but he couldn't get leave from the Army, so Dad suggested Fergus.

El's family, her mother (Deidre), her father (Simon), her sister (Annabelle), her brother (Eric), and their families all came, and the families blended almost seamlessly. The only discord was my sister, Daphne, who came with her three kids but not her husband. I got the feeling her husband was beating her and frequently, and that infuriated me. I tried talking to her, but she blew me off.

El and I didn't take an extended honeymoon. We took a few days in Cabo, but we both had work projects staring at us. One of which was a paper El was to deliver and a conference in Chicago.

Angus and Ruth were in town for the baptism of one of Daphne's kids. Ruth and I were in the kitchen cleaning up after one of the diners, and she turned to me and pulled the sleeve of her dress above her elbow.

There was a scar from a surgery and all around it was a black spot. Ruth said nothing just looked me in the eye and nodded toward the spot.

"That's what they look like," I said, fighting back tears.

"Don't cry for me, Davey. I've lived long and loved and been loved. My life is complete the fates have marked me for death, and I don't fear it." It was a vain request I couldn't stop crying, and finally we two walked into the backyard.

"Davey, you need to continue to study this ability of yours there are explanations, but you must find them yourself. It always seems as if we never have time to discuss this."

That proved to be the case again just as I started to ask her questions the door flew open, and kids came racing out chasing lightning bugs.

Ten months, two days after the wedding, our first child, Beatrice Ruth MacIntosh, was born. A year later, with El six months pregnant, Grandma Ruth died. Knowing ahead of time made it no easier to take. I had been down since she had shown me the spot. I told El about the exchange and she agreed we needed to find some answers. Now our best source was gone.

El and I flew to Chicago and drove down to Middlebury with Mom and Dad. The funeral mass was overflowing with Scots in full dress. Ruth had specified that in her final instructions.

The priest was from Scotland with a brogue so heavy I couldn't understand a word.

I was amazed to find that many people had come from Scotland itself. To my certain knowledge, Grandma had never been to Scotland. Many spoke to each other in Gaelic. Several American Scots were there, including a small self-contained woman from North Carolina who radiated energy and power and introduced herself to Dad as Ruth Lovat. El pointed out that the internment was on the Isle of Mull in the Inner Hebrides, which I found strange. I would have thought she would have wanted to rest next to Angus, her husband of forty-plus years. When I questioned Angus, he just said it was her wish.

My aunt, Mary Stuart, handed me a letter from Grandma sealed in an old-fashioned way with red wax, a signet ring, and a red ribbon bearing the notice, *Hand-deliver to David on my death, and to be opened only by him.*

I didn't open it.

The impact of Ruth's passing, following the sale of Culloden, was welling up in me, and I was not ready for any more revelations. My sense of loss increased by the questions raised at the funeral. Who were all these people? How did Grandma know them? Angus had little idea of who they were or the reasons behind Ruth's request for burial in Scotland.

I could see that Dad had something on his mind, even more pressing than the death of his mother. Finally, after we had driven back to Evanston, he took me out to the shore of Lake Michigan.

"David, I have something to tell you, and I am breaking a promise I made to your grandmother. It has to do with the spots and how you deal with them. How are you coping with the ever-present sign of death?"

I told him about my embrace of stoicism and my addition of spockism, and he laughed at the combo.

"David, for the Greeks and Romans, stoicism was a wonderful way to explain the world, which was composed of many things they had no way of understanding or expressing. They lacked language concepts and ways to understand events. To do that, they had to create gods and relationships between gods and men. It worked for a long time, and the key to stoic thoughts is that you worry only about what you can control and nothing else. The flaw of stoic thinking is that to embrace it, you had to give up your individuality." He paused for a minute, then continued, "In the modern post-Enlightenment world, stoic thought has fallen into disuse in favor of a philosophy that favors individual control, that is, humanism. In all, the world is full of unexplained things which defy science and seem to mock scientific efforts to prove or disprove them. Your spots are one of those things."

I waited for a moment before replying. With Dad, you had to wait to be sure he had finished his thoughts since he usually thought far ahead of you and pulled things from the various memory boxes in his brain.

He continued finally. "It really not only defies logic and science, but it also seems to defy any rational analysis. It does not seem you cause it, and it does not seem you have any control over the fate of the person."

"Your grandmother, rest her soul," he said, almost crying in remembrance, "knew something, but she resisted telling you or me. She took the secret to the grave, but we had several conversations about her knowledge to no result before she passed. I'm very uncomfortable keeping things from you, and the secret was made deeper by the details of the funeral and the interment on Mull."

"That bothered me too, and the fact that so many people came from Scotland was very strange. The other thing is that about a year before her death when we were at your place, she showed me a scar on her arm, and it was surrounded by a black spot. She acted like she knew it was there and what it meant," I said.

"Twilight Zone had a show about a guy in the Army who saw a light on people who were going to die. I finally watched the episode," I said. "It was one the basis of the fight between Xanders and me in Wheaton. When I was in the Navy, I never saw any spots even though death was not far away. That was one of the times when the spots seemed to take a long break. I thought maybe they had left me but no such luck."

"I don't think," Dad said, "that if you have this ability, it goes away. It's yours for life. I'm glad El has taken this in stride. It must have been a real shock for her. She's a remarkable woman. You are very lucky with women, David."

We went back to California, and life continued. Five months later, El resigned from Ames to tend to our now two children. The second was a boy who came to bear the name of Fergus Charles Edward Joseph Angus MacIntosh.

You can tell a committee had named him.

Like a lot of people, El and I had heard all the stories from our mothers and grandmothers about the terrible ordeal of childbirth. We had gone into the hospital for Beatrice's birth fully expecting a long difficult time. Once again, we were both wrong. I had left El's room to use the restroom. I couldn't have been gone more than five minutes but when I walked in there were two nurses, one of them holding a child wrapped in a blanket. A doctor hurried in and examined the child then El.

He turned to me. "Congratulations to you both you have a beautiful baby girl born with no assistance from us. If this catches on, I will be out of business."

"Then I can expect you won't be billing us since it was done without your help?" I said.

He laughed and left.

With Fergus, it took a bit longer he was bigger, but El popped him out after an hour of labor.

Having two children is really an exercise in juggling. One needs to be fed, the other changed, one needs to burp the other to sleep, and the two most opposite things are what's always going on. The other aspect of having children is how fast educated, well-spoken people descend into hypocorism and baby talk.

For all the noise, confusion, smells, and sleepless nights, I would not have had it any other way. El bloomed in motherhood, and I felt that I stood a bit more erect with pride when we were all out in public together.

Things could not have been going better. I was a father of two healthy children. I married an angel, was successful, grew more affluent by the day, was respected in my field, and had a wonderful house. In short, I was living the dreams hatched during those cold, dark winters in Wheaton. As you probably would have guessed, amidst all this bounty, the spots once again decided to make a mess out of my peace of mind.

The fly in the ointment was that I was not doing very well personally. I was having increasing difficulty sleeping, and what sleep I did get was after exhaustion claimed me or with the application of significant amounts of booze. I wrote it down to the high-pressure work environment and fatherhood, but there was a deeper reason, and it was another secret I had to carry alone.

While El and I were doing well our friends Will and Tammy weren't. They gave the appearance of success, but it was illusionary. I introduced the two of them when Will and I worked together at Anderson and Tammy worked with El at Ames.

There are people in the world who have the Midas touch and there are also people who can't seem to get out of their own way and everything they touch turns into crap, Will and Tammy were two of the latter.

Will left Anderson to join a startup disk drive company and invested every dollar he had, could borrow or get from anyone, some of it mine. The company flamed out in very short order. Will then jumped to another company and repeated the pattern, going so far as to take out a second mortgage on their house without Tammy's knowledge. The pattern of failure remained unbroken. Now with two failures behind him, Will was roadkill in Silicon Valley.

They maintained their lifestyle with as I would later discover the aid of a loan from a guy with a nickname of Two Fingers. When Will approached me, they were totally upside down and about to lose their house, and Two Fingers was promising that Will would lose a lot more.

I can be a sucker sometimes, and now I did one of the stupidest things I ever did: I cosigned his note to Two Fingers without telling El.

It was soon apparent that Will for all his protestations had no way to get out of his trouble and the terms on the note were such that it could never be paid off short of huge down payments on the principal, and Will was not going to be doing that any time soon. I started getting calls from Two Fingers whose real name was Gaetano telling me I had to pony up or...

I couldn't tap into our savings accounts or my partner's account without alerting El, so I had to find a way out without her knowledge. I had one thing going for me.

Since I could see death, why shouldn't I profit from it? My curse could become a blessing and bail out my ill-starred friend.

I had made the acquaintance someplace of a lackluster life insurance agent named Jorge Simpson who worked out of a disreputable office on the south side of LA. His specialty was burial insurance, largely for the black community and older people with health issues, the type of policy long known to be rip-offs. He dealt with some of the edge of the envelope life companies who were not too scrupulous about their due diligence on their insured.

I started to take out life insurance policies on people who had spots. I never took out insurance with a large payout, which might attract the company's attention, but five or ten thousand dollars would not. I set up a corporation as the beneficiary. That helped me skirt the condition that the beneficiary had to have a valid insured interest. If questioned, I could say that it was related to a loan or business deal from years past.

I knew that few insurance companies would not waste a lot of assets pursuing a ten-thousand-dollar payout; it was just too expensive to do so. Unless the person with a spot lived a long time, the premium paid versus the dollar received made it almost a riskless bet. I pushed away from my active conscience the fact that I was treating others' death as a casino bet. It didn't go very far, and I had frequent thoughts about wrongdoing. I was at the root of my being still too honorable to do it without pretty serious risks to my soul. The other part was that each time I did it, it grew easier to do it again.

At first, I pushed away all the bad thoughts with the salve that I was helping a friend, but then I started to feel it was my right to profit. After all, I had been cursed, and it wasn't fair that I shouldn't be able to benefit. Grandpa Angus used to quote Walter Scott's famous line about the tangled web we weave when we practice to deceive, but I ignored that and plunged on.

I told myself that the people I was insuring meant nothing to me and their death was immaterial and not my concern and it got easier and easier, and I started seeing more and more spots or maybe I was just realizing they were there.

Jorge was all-in and wanted to write more and more policies with larger dollar values because he was getting commissions. As the policies started to pay off, he figured out that I had previous knowledge and demanded participation. I agreed to let him reimburse me for a portion of the premium, and he would get a portion of the proceeds. Under California law, we were standing with only our toes over the line of legality. I checked with a couple of lawyers to be sure. Often what is legal is not moral, and what is moral is sometimes not legal.

That was a miserable excuse and not an excuse at all but a rationalization. It dovetailed nicely with my victim status. Something had cursed me, and my feeling that something was wrong led me to the stupid conclusion all too frequently in such cases that I had a right to be compensated for my bearing the curse. So the curse metastasized and became multiple curses.

I was wrong in so many ways.

The people died the insurance companies paid. Jorge got some money, and more importantly, Two Fingers got his; that part worked. What didn't work was my lack of comfort with what I was doing. I knew I was doing wrong.

Jorge started hinting, not too subtly—subtle was not a Jorge trait—that he had others who wanted to join the game by taking out policies. My greed and a misplaced relativistic sense of failure drove me to the scheme. I recognized he was talking about organized crime and perhaps money laundering, so I resisted. My self-hate grew, and I rued when I started the whole stupid thing. I was keeping it secret, but Jorge wasn't.

One day, I got a call at the office from a lawyer named Armen Maggossian. I didn't take the call, but he left a message identifying himself as a friend of Jorge's. I asked one of Anderson's lawyers who Maggossian was.

"Most lawyers know who he is and what he is, and he's one of the reasons people hate lawyers. Never met a scummy company or crooked clients he wouldn't represent. Rumors are, Anderson's lawyer pushed his nose out of shape, a pretty universal sign of mob involvement. Anything he is involved with, you don't want to be part of. It will be nothing but grief."

Now added to my self-hate was a real fear that Jorge was dealing with really dangerous people, and the risk increased and induced more tension with its resulting stress.

The bad dreams started. It was hard to describe, but I felt a weight on my shoulders from the time we got the first policy. It got heavier and heavier with each policy. I tried to suppress the ill feelings and dreams with booze, but nothing worked. It finally all came to a head in the usual traumatic fashion associated with the spots.

One of Anderson's old accounting clients had also become a consulting client. While the company was headquartered in New York, it had offices in California. They had been on a merger binge and recently closed on a deal for a company in Irvine. We had been systemizing their data processing and upgrading their overall systems. My team had the responsibility to make the new acquisition's computers talk to the parents.

The top management had flown in for the closing. The managers came to our office for an update on our efforts, and I had to make a presentation. My reaction to entering the conference room must have been obvious. One of Anderson's managing partners immediately wondered if I was ill. I was, and I nodded yes, bolting for the bathroom, where I slammed down on my knees and vomited.

The client's top five managers and five Anderson senior partners sat in the conference room. All ten of them were cloaked in black, covering the visible parts of their bodies. There was an overpowering and truly sickening smell that stuck to the hair in my nose. Its oily taste hung on even after vomiting, and I imagined my clothes smelled of it. It was a smell like frying bacon mixed with something else I couldn't place. I had sensed something like it before, but its identity was right at the edge of my mind.

I left the office, and some semblance of equanimity returned, to the extent it can ever return in LA traffic, as I drove home. I was kidding myself. The only reason I was able to drive was the act of driving forced me to exclude all else to avoid being killed. Once I hit my door, it all swept back on me.

I gave El no explanation. I just stormed into the room I used as a home office and locked myself in, violating our family rule—no locked doors. I knew it was the wrong thing to do. Robert Frost sprang up about being careful what you wall in or out. In the idealized scene, which never happens, I would have invited El into the situation and solved the problem through the power of two.

One of the hallmarks of victimology is that the person feels the hurt or wrong will continue, and they will have no control over it. If I ever needed confirmation of my victim status, it was that scene in the boardroom. Fear ruled me and fed my growing status as a victim. I was selfish, thinking only about myself, the old, "This is my problem, not anyone else's." What a crap! Of course, it was El's problem. When one person in a functioning marriage has a problem, both partners have a problem.

Trust is one of the most vital and challenging emotions. There are those you should be able to trust in all things and those you can't trust at all. Some you can trust with some things but not others. Some trust is more profound than others, but it's always rare, and the rarest is complete trust. One of the barriers to unconditional love is the fear the beloved will violate your trust or not return it. The opposite of love is not hate. Hate develops from fear. The opposite of love is fear.

Both trust and love are perishable. No spice or additives can preserve trust, only honesty, humility, and patience. While perishable, trust like love can be renewed with care, truth, forgiveness, and generosity mixed with a lot of time.

Now I was violating every rule of relationships with the one whom I should have been able to trust completely. I told El two years ago about the spots, and she believed me then.

Why was it so hard for me to share with her now? It was because I was ashamed of myself.

She was more intelligent than me; she knew it was something to do with the spots. I had never reacted this way to any other event, but then again, she had never really seen me experience the spots, and she knew nothing about the insurance scheme. Yet there I was with the sure knowledge that not only five of my partners but also the five top managers of the company would die. It would eviscerate the company and make a sizable dent in Anderson's culture. The size of the black shroud and the smell told me it wasn't a disease. They were going to burn to death. What was the correct course of action?

I assumed what El's reaction would be. She was also always so sure in her judgments and moral positions that I knew she would want me to tell the victims, but based on past experiences, it would not change the outcome.

I resisted because deep inside me, I feared what it could cost me. All I had accomplished, the idol I was worshiping, was at stake. I'd be the laughingstock of Anderson and LA in general.

My insurance scheme would collapse. Deep in the recesses of my mind where only God lives, His voice told me to tell them. But, like Bonhoeffer's Christian disciple, I realized the cost of my discipleship was too high to bear. In the end, I furthered my moral destruction.

The client company was publicly traded, and the loss of the top five executives would devastate the stock price. I called my broker and sold two thousand shares of the stock short. The broker tried to talk me out of it to his credit, but I was committed, and I was right.

On the way to New York, the company's plane augured in someplace in eastern Colorado. The five company executives, five Andersen partners, three flight crew dead, and the stock dropped like a rock. It finally struck me; the unidentified smell was the stink of unburned aviation fuel.

Some would have been overjoyed at a $35,000 profit on $100,000 at risk. Some would have justified the ghoulish profit, saying it might not have happened. It was just a hunch, and someone might have had only a moment's remorse.

That night the ills I had been experiencing with the insurance deals exploded. I pitched tossed, and found sleep only in snatches, interspersed with terrible dreams that woke me. The dreams came with gruesome creatures yelling unintelligible language, making wild gestures, and pointing at me. They were interspersed with a parade of past victims pointing at me, shaking their heads in disgust.

El woke me several times, genuinely frightened. Most dreams, even nightmares, cease with the coming of the light. Mine continued.

Then things start to happen, which could have just been happenstance. I dinged my car on a post, tripped, and ripped my suit coat. I spilled food on my shirt and tie, ruined a pair of shoes, and dropped dishes at home. All coincidences, possibly, but coincidences are clues to a puzzle unsolved.

El wanted me to see a doctor, but no doctor would cure this. I was finding there were rules for seeing the spots and how to act. I knew the true source of the nightmares and the accidents. I'd violated some practice, and the appearance of the demons, the victims, and the other incidents were demands to make amends. Whatever I had done had disrupted the harmony of the cosmos.

Given a strict interpretation of the law, I had made an illegal trade. Securities laws prevented those with proprietary information from benefiting at the expense of others. You were supposed to call the exchange so they could stop trading until the news was disseminated. It was a law honored more in the breach than in the observance. I could just imagine the conversation.

"Hello. New York Stock Exchange, how may I help you?" a woman's voice would say with a heavy Bronx honk and disdain for anyone not a captain of industry.

"Yes, thank you." A sense of impatience on the other end. "I have some information no one else knows about a company that will cause the stock to drop."

"Hold please."

"Office of market supervision, may I help you?"

"Yes, I hope so. As I told the operator, I have information on a company that only I know. When it gets out, it will cause the stock to drop."

"I see," the skeptical voice says, "and what is that information, Mister—I don't think I got your name."

"MacIntosh, David MacIntosh."

There would be sounds of writing.

"Exactly, Mr. MacIntosh, what's the information and the company?" Hints of amusement.

"Nerndi Industries, the symbol is…" a voice interrupts.

"I know the symbol," he'd reply tetchily.

"Sorry, of course, you would. Nerndi's top five managers are going to die this afternoon when the corporate jet crashes."

"Indeed." The word *indeed*, being an east coast usage, means *I don't believe you.* "This is very serious, Mr. McDonald." Condescending tone.

"It's MacIntosh."

"Certainly." Dismissal of my name correction. "How did you come by this information, sir?" Condensation mixed with indecision: Call the cops or FBI? Blow it off? Find out more? It was a slow day, so get more information.

"I can see death from violence, disease, or accident before it occurs, and I saw it on these people."

I could imagine at this point the person covering the mouthpiece, saying, "Hey, Frank, get on this line. This nut claims he can see death before it occurs and saw it on the top five executives of Nerndi. Claims they're going to get killed this afternoon!"

In the background, people would be rushing to get on phones, saying things like, "Where is he coming from?" The response would be two self-explanatory words *the coast*, with a rolling of eyes and smiles all around, there being only one coast to an easterner, the home of fruits and nuts—California.

You can see where this is going. Maybe if I called five times and were correct each time, they would have taken me seriously, but once, forget about it. Still, I would have done my duty. Of course, it would have gotten worse after it happened; they would descend on me like locusts investigating my claims in the process, ruining my life and career.

I didn't make the call. I didn't write. I justified doing nothing, saying they wouldn't believe me. I had no obligation to tell and certainly not if will make a fool of yourself. Is it a crime not to tell if people won't believe you and the information will not change the outcome?

It took me weeks of nightmares of demons haunting every moment of repose, days without sleep, every minute a terror, to become convinced of the only acceptable course of action.

I stopped paying the premiums on the insurance and fended off Jorge's increasingly furious and threatening phone calls. I finally donated the money I made on the short sale to a fund for the children of the flight crew. I donated the insurance proceeds to the families of the deceased where it should have gone in the first place. Slowly the demons ceased to be companions, leaving behind a sheen of discomfort and experiential knowledge of wrongdoing.

I didn't tell El what I had done.

I've never been sure of the cause, but I started to feel bound in my life around this time. There was no apparent reason for it. I had a wonderful marriage, and unlike Tolstoy's statement, we were not a fairly unhappy family in our own way. We were as happy as possible when two people committed to one another and worked at it. I was a partner in a prestigious firm and was sought-after in my profession. All the trappings of a good life surrounded me—houses, cars, etc.

But someplace deep within me, I started to feel a need to do daring things to put myself at risk and be schooled by the greatest of all teachers: failure.

We associate risk-taking with the young, but mostly that's just speculative behavior. Appropriate risk-taking requires you to have things to risk, and the young have nothing to risk. So often, the young seeking risk find themselves exploited. I wanted to own the results of my work.

I was facing the consultant's dilemma. Consultants bring unique knowledge and expertise to solve a client's problem. In my experience, we always seemed not entirely to solve the problem, and we drafted our reports so that the client needed to continue to pay us.

In a less cerebral state of mind, I was getting greedy. I watched as the firms we consulted with gained market value, went public, or got bought out. The founders becoming wealthy beyond the dreams of avarice. I guess it was the next step on the California treadmill, but I wanted that.

I was no longer desirous of trading my expertise for a consulting contract.

The other question hidden in most consultants' brains is if they could actually run a company. We had a client in Northern California called ROLM and had just finished a project for them. Shortly after we finished the project, I got a letter from ROLM offering me a VP-level job and a very magnificent salary. It came with bonuses and that holy of holies—stock options.

It was an offer of vulgar prosperity. I almost turned it down. I used a canard of my loyalty to Anderson and my young family to mask the real reason. Faced with the chance to satisfy my disquiet, I was afraid. My fear came from being comfortable in the middle and my guilt and shame at my secret. To take the offer, I had to take on a risk. I viewed risk as dangerous.

I was reverting to type, always in the middle, never on the leading edge. In the final analysis, I was afraid of failure, even though I seemed to be craving the lesson I could learn.

I started to find ways to step over gradually with no risk. Take a leave of absence from Anderson, work for ROLM, and then decide. I was trying to have it both ways, and I would have the safety net at Anderson to fall into with a leave of absence if I failed at ROLM.

When you stand in the middle of the road, what happens is you get run over by cars going both ways.

For all my successes, what took the most significant amount of my consciousness was my perceived failures. There was indeed the risk of failure bringing hard times, but the most legitimate reason was fear of humiliation if I failed. My fear of accepting the ROLM offer was the harvest of the shame I felt about the spots and my perceived victimhood.

The comfort of my soul was between the natural conservative, logical approach to things and the need for a wild jump that seemed illogical. In both of my significant romances, the woman faced the issue and dragged me to the correct decision.

I considered myself a failure due to my curse. I felt I had failed those who died. I didn't understand that what I had done in the past was less important than what I would do in the future.

Failure to see risks in the hunter communities of our past led to death. Humans remember failures more acutely than success, and we began to concentrate on not failing. Then comes the American culture where only success gains rewards; failure was derided and second-guessed with twenty-twenty hindsight, saying you should have known you would fail.

That morphed to, if you failed, it wasn't your fault. It was an external impact, regardless of the virtue that all successful people failed many times before succeeding. Few have mastered Kipling's line, *If you can meet with triumph and disaster and treat those two impostors just the same.*

I feared that I was among them and that further success was not my franchise.

As usual, it was El who initiated the action. I came home one day. She was sitting on the deck overlooking the ocean, ridiculously gorgeous, her beauty blooming with motherhood. She had a massive smile on her face as she nursed Fergus.

"You should take the job at ROLM."

"Really?"

"Yes." I looked at houses up there; they're expensive but not much different than here.

"This place"—she waved to indicate our surroundings—"will go in a second for an excellent price. Ames is begging me to come back with an increased salary, which will cover the expenses, and the stock options are not to be ignored. This is a nondecision."

She was right. Of course, I was the one holding back. She was willing to risk it all, but I was deluded into believing I was protecting her and the family, and I waited to act. I made the excuse that I was about to vest in a large portion of my partner's account at Anderson and didn't want to throw that away. In the end, that was just an excuse to make it seem I wasn't being led around by my wife.

I did all things men do when we don't want to decide. I tried to create a formula for the potential increased value of the partner's account versus the value of the stock options, which gave me more time to make the nondecision. In the end, we moved to Los Altos,

CA, and I was allowed to put the advice from the Anderson years to practical tests on actual products.

Eighteen months after the move, we had our last two children, forever known as the twins. They ended up named Fionna Flora Bruce MacIntosh and Alexander Fleming MacIntosh.

Before they were born, IBM purchased ROLM, and in the merger, all stock options immediately vested and were exercisable. The colossal tax bill, but I was rich! I was contractually bound to stay at ROLM for a year. The former ROLM people were just working out our time.

While the buyout was good fortune for me, as a measure of the new mercenary aspect of my personality, I became regretful I hadn't joined ROLM earlier.

The IBM purchase was the second part of the buyout. Earlier ROLM had sold part of itself, and the money was distributed to the shareholders and employees. I find it hard to believe now, but I was actually upset at what could have been rather than being satisfied I had done as well as I did, given that my contributions to the firm's success had been at best minimal. It was another manifestation of the soul sickness infecting California, of nothing ever being enough.

IBM didn't understand ROLM or how Californians mix their work and lifestyle. Most of the ROLM people had been refugees from exactly the strict corporate lifestyle IBM exemplified. In almost all cases, as soon as their contract lapsed, the ROLM people left, including me.

With the money from ROLM, I paid off the house, set up college funds for the kids, set up a trust fund for El, bought her a Mercedes, and was generally miserable. Perhaps it was the dower reputation of the Scots, maybe it was middle age, perhaps the purchase of ROLM was a marker on the road, but I was dissatisfied.

My mind told me it had been too easy, too fast, and I didn't deserve it. Once again, my middling ways were starting to be my hamartia.

I was also committing an act designed to make me unhappy. Rather than enjoy my success and life in the present, I grew concerned about what came next. Men tend to vest their personal identity in their occupation, and once I left ROLM, I would be unemployed. I feared I would lose my identity.

I was really in the throes of deciding if I wanted to go to work inside the navel of a company again or if I wanted just to sit back and rest on my laurels. I consulted and filled some interim positions with startups needing adult leadership for the next year and a half. It paid well, and I got some stock options.

That concern was soon remedied. Late in 1986, Todd Holmgren, an Anderson alum, called me. Todd had migrated to a place called Microsoft. He invited me to dinner in Seattle.

Like everyone else in technology, I'd heard of Microsoft and its eccentric founders. Intrigued, I accepted. Todd picked me up at SeaTac, as they call the airport. We drove around Lake Washington to Redmond over never quite dry roads under an unbroken overcast. The traffic in the so-called S curves reminded me of LA. It was winter, the days were short, and the weather was oppressive after twenty years of California sun.

I went to dinner with Todd, his colead, and a couple of other folks at Canlis, and the next day, we toured the Redmond campus, another shock. I was in a suit and tie; most Microsoft people looked like a ragbag collection of castoffs. I was thirty-nine, and almost all were five to ten years younger. A good number had a haunted, driven, debilitated look. Some absolutely needed a lesson in personal hygiene. I wondered if I could manage them, given the age and personal habits gap.

My claim to fame was software that corrected errors and learned from the mistakes. Todd and his team wanted to include error correction in their new product, and I was to run a team to do that. I was dithering again, but I opened the job offer on the plane back to California. The proposal was almost obscene: salary, bonus, and stock options on a lot of stock. For the first time in my life, I ordered an alcoholic drink on an airplane.

In Jurassic Park, one of the characters would popularize the phrase, "Life finds a way." El was overjoyed. The woman lived in joy, and there was no place in her life for anything else. She knew, of course, that life was sorrow too, but she radiated joy, and from her came a love of indescribable depth. It filled every corner of our home, infused our friends, and shone like a beacon in any conflict.

She wasn't Pollyanna. She had her downtimes, but they never changed her as they did with me. She just came back with joy. She fought depression in herself and others with joy. Every day I was around her, I loved her more. Her joy overcame my usual placid manner and made me more successful. We weren't two people who married. We were two spirits bonded to truly become one, the yin-yang, the alpha and omega.

Of course, given that I was experiencing joy, the spots had to return. In Greek mythology, when the gods intervened, humans had begun to think of themselves and act as if they were gods.

It's that form of arrogance that leads a person to believe they can accomplish everything and that when good things happen, it's due to their superior being. In the mythology of Greece, when hubris was evident, the gods cast down the imposters through trials and tribulations. It was starting to feel as if the spots were harbingers that I was too hubristic, and I needed humility.

They always seemed to herald a change in my life or brought me back to the earth when my ego became inflated with my apparent success.

It was the type of situation that might lead to the attribution of power to a god or spirit in less enlightened times. My success was due to luck, divine influence, and hard work, but it was easy to give my self-attribution; the spots seemed to be a heavenly sign not to get too full of myself.

CHAPTER 9

One weekend, I stayed in Seattle, and Todd took me to his parish, Saint Jude in Redmond. I met the priest, the son of the old sod, County Clare, Ireland, and was everything a pastor should be. I would have moved to Seattle just to be in his parish.

Todd introduced us before Mass, and Father Lovett's smile and charm filled me with an instant feeling of serenity, warmth, and elation. You knew you were in the presence of a genuinely holy man.

Lovett left to get his vestments, and when he reached the presider's chair, he turned to face the assembly. He raised his arms for the opening prayer, and I almost fainted. There, right in the center of his chest, was a black spot clearly not part of his chasuble. Like an airplane that violates the laws of physics, my emotions dropped into a spin.

I thought the range of emotions from past losses would have inured me to the spot's appearance but not so. The emotional impact of each appearance was growing exponentially. This time, my thoughts ran to the purpose and effects of suffering. Father Altois said that suffering was a way of eliciting God's love. According to Altois, suffering and ministry to the sick and dying allowed them to pass to the Lord with grace. The minister showed love and got love in return. Both parties benefited, the stricken because they were meeting God, shorn of sin, and the minister because they were performing an act of love and godly work.

The question for me this time was what benefit the parish community drew from watching a beloved leader weaken and eventually die. The deeper issue was an old one. If there was a kind and loving God, how could such a deity allow this to happen, especially to one whose whole life was in service to God? It was the same question I posed in my anger when Suzan died, and it was just as simplistically wrong then as it was now.

Suffering is part of life, of course, giving rise to the cliché, "Life's a bitch, and then you die." Suffering comes in all guises; no person is ever free of it. It's the price of living. A world without suffering would be an apathetic one.

How a person handles suffering provides a model for our behavior, either positive or negative. We can never experience the full impact of others' suffering, but we can gain perspective on how we must handle our own. The problem with my suffering was that I had to bear it alone. I went back to one of the wellsprings of my life, *Man's Search for Meaning*, and I found this quote:

> We must never forget that we may also find meaning in life even when confronted with a hopeless situation when facing a fate that cannot be changed. For what then matters is to bear witness to the uniquely human potential at its best, which is to transform a personal tragedy into a triumph, to turn one's predicament into a human achievement. When we are no longer able to change a situation—just think of an incurable disease such as inoperable cancer—we are challenged to change ourselves.

There must be a message of meaning from my suffering, and it became my mission to find it. I was ready to explore and ready to learn. It was scary to stare off into an unknown future with no idea of how that search would end, but I needed to do something to contextualize the spots.

Like the student and data scientist I was, I came to the proposition that I had to find out more. Suffering is too universal to be an anomaly. We tend to shy away from the ugly and distasteful, and suffering is both.

Gilbert and Sullivan had a line in *The Gondoliers*, "When everyone is somebody, then no one is anybody."

The spots were telling me I was not a nobody; I was somehow special. I needed to address my guilt and sense of shame over my possession of this power.

When Jesus cures the sick, blind, and lame in the Christian gospels, he says, "Go and sin no more." A simple understanding of those parables would be that the disabled have sinned, and their affliction is the wages of sin. In the metaphorical sense, the affliction is supposed to provide us with the idea of the mental damage of sin. Those who believe that the sufferers did something wrong are equally in sin.

In another way, suffering can add a perverted sense of value to a person. To convince the world you are suffering is to elicit sympathy, understanding, and excuses. It feeds nicely into the concept of victim and victimhood. In this sense, suffering is a sin because it falsely influences another's emotions and draws from them the energy and force of life.

I've started to wonder if the spots and how I handled them were some forms of ritual suffering supposed to help others deal with stress and chronic unhappiness. In my case, no one knew about my issue, so no one knew I was suffering.

Many people would like to believe that they would immediately know what to do and how to react when faced with something like what I was facing.

My luck with Anderson, Rolm, and Microsoft gave me time to think deeply and seek wisdom. I didn't have to sandwich deep esoteric thoughts in between the realities of life. I had time to contextualize the spots, and from that, I started to create a framework for understanding.

My move to Los Altos severed my relationship with Father Altois, and the local priest was Filipino with an accent so thick I would have been lost if I didn't know the Mass parts. I needed to find someone to act as a guide. I ignored the guide closest to me in common with many married men. I've been lucky enough to have loved twice, both to fabulous women. I had every reason to trust El with my issues. What was holding me back was my fear of criticism and my sense of shame which had been deepening with each occurrence of the spots.

As Frankl said, fate is what happens. You have no control over fate. Your destiny, however, was the result of the choices you made in the face of fate. Your destiny lay in free will and your actions. Seeing the spots was my fate, and I could not control their appearance or the results. My destiny, however, lay with what I did and how I reacted to my fate.

I was dealing with two levels of suffering. The first was my own and its effects on me. The second was the value I was supposed to gain from others' suffering. They were deep and complex philosophical and ethical considerations. Most of us have deliberated on such thoughts, but most of us have never had them become immediate. Society and social norms usually force people to subsume deep thought into the noise and cacophony of everyday life.

Our society makes short work of those who intellectualize moral issues. Instead, it finds excuses for those with no ethics or who choose to evaluate philosophical and theoretical principles so long as the evaluation leads to success. In justice, they shouldn't because they are the foundations of life. I talked to El about my issues. She thought I should tell Lovett the next time I was in Redmond. I was hesitant.

"You don't know for sure if telling a person is ineffective; you're making unwarranted assumptions."

"Hasn't worked in the past. They're all dead," I replied. "I told Jay, and it didn't help."

"He was drunk, you can't help someone who won't be helped, but you tried. You never went to them, not even Suzan, and told them they needed to do something to avoid death in precise terms. So we don't know for sure that the death isn't preventable."

"What happens," I said, "if they laugh at me or just ignore me."

"Who cares!"

"I do!"

"Why?" she asked.

"Because I don't want to look like an idiot or a kook." I was roiling in rationalization.

"What if I tell them they go to a doctor, and he tells him there's nothing wrong? Remember, I don't know mode or time, just results.

The only ones where there was any direct indication of mode were the football player, Jay, and the Anderson partners." I realized just then that I had not told El about the incident with the plane crash or the insurance scheme. Now I had no choice. She sat there looking at me with a questioning look and shock because I kept secrets from her, so I told her.

It was not pleasant. When I finished, El looked like a thunderstorm was about to break. "I don't know if I can live without you, David, but I would rather live alone with the children than have you ever lie to me like that again."

"In any case, I knew, or should have known, they were going to die in an airplane crash." I was chastened, she meant it, and I knew she would do it. I apologized, but given the enormity of the deception, it rang hollow in my ears.

"That's the best argument you have for telling, that you didn't know the specifics. You should still tell people, you might make them aware and alert, and it might lessen the bad dreams. You were well on the way to drinking yourself to death during that time."

"Still doesn't make me feel better. Telling people will make us as popular as a plague." I paused for a bit, then asked, "You think I have a moral obligation to tell people?"

"No, you have a moral responsibility to tell. You are not obliged out of a contract or ethical agreement, which removes choice. You have the power, and that makes you responsible for your actions. I think the bad dreams and feelings are due to your having violated some tenant of behavior associated with the spots. No one is going to sue you in court for not telling them, but they are perfectly right in being angry or hurt because you chose not to."

She looked at me and said, "When you have extraordinary gifts, you have extraordinary responsibilities and have to take extra extraordinary risks. The one thing you don't know—can't know—is how your actions affect others, but that doesn't excuse you from your moral responsibility to act."

In my mind, she was right as far as it went. I had the gift, and I was the one who had to determine what to do with it.

In the end, I fell back on those three psychological havens—rationalization, fear, and avoidance. My rationalization was that life is hard enough without adding to people's worries by telling them they would die before their conceptual time. After all, what was more unsettling than death? Fear came from the lizard brain disease of self-preservation.

El was correct, but I was not ready to accept her perspective. She was thinking in the present, and I told myself my thoughts were of the future and the damage to my reputation. My standing in the world would take a hit if I started to tell tales of death. I could see myself and the family being shunned and ridiculed as kooks.

My fear also came from inside. It was a fear of knowing. Not really of the knowledge but of what the journey to the knowledge would entail. I was afraid of where this could go and what changes might occur if I started to open up and tell people. I knew the gift was too powerful not to portend some change in whoever possessed it. The short sale was using knowledge, and I had no desire to repeat the terror of those dreams.

Abstinence came from making a unilateral choice in a bilateral environment. In the past, I had made decisions surrounding the spots to tell or not to tell only affected only me. Now many others involved the kids, El, Todd, Lovett, and the whole parish. I had no way of knowing the effects of my knowledge on all of them. I was like an artist who abandons his painting, unable to determine all the effects of light in a scene. I didn't know how this knowledge might affect other people. Therefore, I decided that the right thing to do was not to tell anyone.

I didn't tell anyone about my decision, not even El, so I laid one of those cement blocks that build walls of noncommunications in families. If she found out, she would enact her threat, I knew she would view my not telling Lovette a lie, so I was putting my marriage at risk.

My problem to me was so unique that there appeared to be no ethical system that applied. I was intellectualizing my problem. I would have preferred it to stay intellectual, but given its nature, I knew it would eventually force me to make a moral decision to judge right from wrong.

In the absence of a clear ethical principle, people usually fall back on their conscience, to the voice speaking only to them, bringing disquiet if the decision is wrong and peace if correct. Conscience is a derivation of a moral code. Most moral codes, actually no moral code, are so complete to cover all occurrences. My situation seemed to be pushing me to look for answers beyond the Judeo-Christian code. I was, for all intents and purposes, in uncharted territory.

Meanwhile, I commuted to Redmond and cashed stock options. All the time in the air and long airport waits provided plenty of time for introspection. I found myself moving from the emotional riot of youth riot and intellectual violence into the concreteness of age. It was, however, an incomplete movement since I was not dealing with my most fundamental issue.

I had succeeded beyond the dreams of those halcyon years in Wheaton. I should have been satisfied with God's grace, but there was still a drive to know and understand another mark of maturity. One day, flying home from Seattle, I was digging in my briefcase for some report or other, and came across the letter from Gramma Ruth, seals unbroken, years after her death. It reminded me I'd never read the book she gave me either.

The sky outside our hurtling cylinder had turned violently blue with golden-red steaks at the horizon as we crossed Crater Lake.

"*Dear Davie*," it began. Grandma always used the diminutive.

> Since that awful dinner at your parent's house at Christmas, I have struggled with how to tell you more. You may have noticed that your grandfather and I were silent while Anton and Samantha attacked you. It was not from fear of them; there was another reason. It was neither the time, place, nor company for me to bring it up.
>
> Frequently in my life, Davey, I've set my sights on doing something only to have life inter-

rupt my intentions. Had things worked out differently, I would have had a long talk with you
about your visions, but life intervened, and now
my time is nearly run, my strength failing, soon I
cross the bar, and I can't do it now.

Understand please, there are things in the
world which can never be explained even by
science. The rise of secularism, humanism, and
naturalism has made understanding unexplained
phenomena difficult because a lack of belief has
accompanied them. Lack of explanation should
never be a reason for attacks, although it often
is, nor should it be a reason for dismissing ideas
or beliefs. Shakespeare had a right when Hamlet
dispossessed Horatio of his doubts about the
ghost and told him to welcome it as a stranger.

I have failed in a duty laid on me long ago
by generations long past. I should have found
time and a way to tell you what you needed to
know; it might have saved you some suffering. It
is too late for me to do my duty. Soon I'll be at
the last celidah hearth. You should seek counsel.
Contact my sister, Ruth Lovat, in Banner Elk,
North Carolina.

Tell her everything—all of it. You can trust
her. She will give you the counsel I should have.

A Gaelic blessing followed her words: *Biodh a ghaoth
an-còmhnaidh aig do dhruim, agus gum bi beannachd nèimh a' tuiteam
ort fhèin agus ortsa. Is dòcha nach bi am beannachadh a fhuair thu ach
cuibhreann bheag de na tha a 'feitheamh riut.*
And a postscript, *"Read the book I sent."*
Another mystery! Whatever I was doing when I found the letter
was no longer critical. I remembered meeting a woman at Grandma's
funeral who I thought was Ruth Lovat. Grandma Ruth had called

Ruth Lovat, "my sister." My grandmother had no sisters, only three brothers, now dead.

El was intrigued by the letter and pointed out another mystery. There was no address, phone number, or means of contacting Ruth Lovat. El called information; you did that in those days BG (before Google). There was no listing. El was ready to leave for North Carolina the next day, but the romantic image of truth-seekers dropping it all in the quest for answers is picturesque. It was not possible.

We did find the book still in the box, *A Description of the Western Islands of Scotland* by Martin, as El pointed out it was a first edition dated 1716. I remembered that I started to have read it once but was stopped by the text. It was no better now. The style was exceedingly difficult. I now had more respect for Dad, who read this stuff all the time.

As if sensing an opening in my psyche, the spots, seeking to show their domination, started to reappear. The first was Finn Delashaw, one of my team at Microsoft. On his forehead and six months later, he was gone from brain cancer. I didn't warn him; I just started to train another team member to take over Finn's job, which caused some hurt feelings, but I was not about to explain why I did it. I couldn't control Finn's or others' opinions. I resolved my hurt feelings about the harsh things people were saying about my hard-assed attitude, telling myself completing the work was the goal.

Then Todd told me Father Lovett had been diagnosed with congestive heart failure. Josie Labanc, a waitress at my favorite breakfast place, The Village Square Cafe in Redmond, died of a rare genetic disorder shortly after I saw a spot on her neck. One night at the airport, I saw an entire family covered in black and what looked like barnacles. A few weeks later, they were killed in a plane crash at sea in Mexico. So it went. I know there were others, but I was getting to a point where I did not even really notice the spots, or I'd just shrug my shoulders and move on because they were not close to me.

Other than Suzan, I had not been terribly close to most of the people who had spots, or so I told myself. The truth was that each occurrence was making me more anxious, and I was covering that with a blasé attitude. I knew deep inside, a place I didn't want to go, that someone I loved would be marked, and I doubted if I'd have the strength to deal with that.

While the appearance of the spots lacked the vivid nature they had in my youth, they still affected my relationships. I used them as a sorting mechanism. If a person had spots, I shunned them. While my behavior was incredibly selfish and misanthropic, I did not experience the pain of my earlier experience with the spots. I was isolating myself from pain, but at the same time, I was creating fear. What I was ignoring in my fleeing pain was that you have to experience pain and loss to grow as a person. Loss leads to the poignancy needed for compassion.

Compassion is essentially suffering together.

I accumulated losses and pain like a baseball team earns wins and losses, and I was depressed by the losses. I was injuring myself by becoming callous. Callousness eliminates compassion. If you eliminate compassion in one area of your life, you eventually eliminate it in all aspects of your life, and you become unfeeling.

I found myself at a point in life where I had to start making decisions about the future. I was getting older. I had worked hard for many years and benefited more than my modest contributions warranted.

I found myself in the delightful position of being able to stop working full-time to spend time with the wife I adored and the kids as they grew. As fortune would have it, my team's work at Microsoft was left on the cutting room floor as the product was readied for sale. I resigned with no rancor, just fatigue—a ton of air miles when they still amounted to something. El and I decided to take our long-planned honeymoon.

CHAPTER 10

There are not a lot of reasons to go to Banner Elk, North Carolina. I don't mean that in a mean-spirited way, it was just true. Unless you're in the area for the annual Highland games at Grand Father Mountain, attending the college in town, or just touring the southern Appalachians, you wouldn't go there. Indeed, it's not the first place you think of as a honeymoon spot. Banner Elk and the surrounding mountain towns were recipients of the remarkable influx of Scots/Irish who graced these shores in the 1700s, many of whom came in the wake of the battle of Culloden.

The phone book would have passed for one from Glasgow. The region was full of McPhee, Fraser, Buchanan, Buchan, Harpers, and Macleods, but no Lovat. We asked around, but no one volunteered anything. I sensed that they were distrustful of us with our all-over California tans and accents.

El is a real tiger at this stuff and started asking different questions. We ended up looking at the census data in the library. There was no Ruth Lovat, but there was a Ruth L. MacTavish. We asked the library staff if they knew of her, but nobody could tell us how to contact her or where she lived. They sort of waved to the mountains and said she lived in the hills. I got a Shakespearean picture of a wild-haired hag living on the edge of a cliff or even in a cave, summoning thunder and lightning.

A chance to stop for gas on one of the winding mountain roads gave us our first solid lead. Above the door of the station was painted *Rory MacTavish: owner.* A young man, Doug, his uniform shirt said, had copper wire hair, a freckled, fair complexion, startling blue eyes, muscular frame, broad shoulders, and an almost perfect Hollywood image of a Scot, pumped our gas. Men are usually a pushover for El.

Doug looked gobsmacked. One look at her California-tanned legs and sun-streaked hair as she got out of the car, and he would have told us his bank account number.

It turned out Rory was Doug's father and Ruth's nephew. Small towns. It turned out there was no street address for Ruth's house or phone. She was indeed just up there, said Doug, waving toward the mountains towering above us. Everything in Banner Elk is up. We got directions of a sort.

I was partially correct. The house sat, I should say, hung, on the edge of a cliff like the archetypical cantilevered house in the LA Hills. It had a stupendous view to the North and West.

Ruth was as I remembered her, a puckish sprite of what I guessed was seventy or so. I could see incredible depth in her brown, green-flecked eyes behind her wire-rimmed glasses.

There are times when you shake hands with someone, and their power, not muscular power, comes through, and Ruth's stunned me as it did El.

"Ah, ya coome just in time fur ta. Come ye in." I didn't remember her accent being that thick at the funeral.

"God bless this house, and all in it" came a sentence from El, surprising both Ruth and me, and apparently El, who shrugged her shoulders when I looked at her questioningly.

"Why, thank ye, lass. You'd be Elspeth."

Now we were both surprised, I had introduced her as El, and we both got kind of a chill of anticipation that something special was happening. The inside of her modest house was a tribute to Scotland. Plaids, old bagpipes, thistles, and the like. I had, however, to comment on one thing I noticed.

"Mrs. Lovat," I began.

"Ruth, dear. Ruth."

"Ruth, I noticed those large stones standing around the house. Are they significant?" Bad start.

"Nay, nay, they're just bloody stones!" she said coldly, cutting off more questions.

"Sorry. I didn't mean to upset you. They don't look natural, more like a decoration. The stone looked dressed," I said.

Ruth was silent; she obviously didn't want to continue the conversation along those lines.

We'd been standing in what was her family room, and she said, "Come to the parlor."

I'd not heard that term in years. We walked a few steps to a smaller and cozier room.

"Set yourselves doon, pot just boiled, lass, will ya hep me with the tray?"

Soon a complete tea set appeared—teapot, knitted cozy, cups, saucers, butter, jams, cake, and scones, that quintessential Scottish baked good.

"I'll be mother," she said, and soon we had cups and saucers, and I was making a pig of myself with the scones and jam. "'Tis a powerful appetite ya have, Davey, good to see a lad eat so well."

I was embarrassed and should have been. My lap looked like I had been living in a bread truck. Ashamed, I ignored the use of the diminutive of my name.

"The tea is delicious," said El, "as are the scones."

"Thank ya, lass, I make my own scones, canna abide store-bought."

I listened carefully and noticed that the Scottish usage and inflections in Ruth's voice came and went with ease. I got the impression part of it was an act or performance she affected for rubes like us.

"Where does the tea come from? I'd like to get some," asked El.

"Tea cooomes from McLaren's," Ruth replied.

No address, city, state, and phone, I guess we were just supposed to know McLaren's.

I started again. "My grandmother's name with Ruth, but you know that. She gave me a letter before she passed away." I didn't get the rest of it out before she interrupted me.

"Aye, Ruth Macintosh, daughter of Malcolm Gordon and Jeannie MacLeod, in the life we know, that's what she was, which is no more, but what she is still burns but faintly," she said the words with the reverence of a Catholic, saying a Hail Mary or Our Father. It was as automatic as a Muslim saying a blessing after mentioning

Muhammad's name. It was ritualistic but reverential, spoken in a dreamlike tone, something long learned and said frequently, but it was unusual in phrasing and meaning.

"I'm not sure I understand," I said.

"She was Ruth Gordon in the life we know. That's what she was, which is no more, but what she is still burns but faintly." The explanation left me even more confused. I sensed I would get no more answers, and uncomprehendingly, I continued.

"I need to tell you my story. Grandma said you could help me understand, and I could trust you."

She nodded her head in acquiescence. For the next thirty minutes, I laid out the occurrences of the spots. I'd been mentally rehearsing my speech, and I tried to give her all the details and be efficient about it. She didn't interrupt me, but as I watched, I could see her face change, not much, and I might have been imagining it, but there seemed to be a narrowing of the eyes, a flaring of the nostrils, a flexing of the muscles of the neck from clenching, and an unclenching of her jaws.

When I finished, we waited, then she said, "Aye, 'tis a strange and wondrous tale you're telling, Davey. I see it cost you some marvel." The choice of words was unusual. Then she sat for a second before saying, "And, therefore, as a stranger give it welcome. There are more things in heaven and earth, Horatio, than are dreamt of in your philosophy. I thank ya for telling me. I don't know wa' I can do to help for the life of me. I canna guess why your grandmarm sent you to me."

We are being shut down and shown the door.

"But you made a comment about what she used to be and alluded to your knowing her and, well," interjected El. "'Twas the ramblings of an old lady who lived alone too long, too far from town. Think nothing of it." She rose to dismiss us.

I knew she was lying. First, she had been at Grandma's funeral, so there had to have been some connection. Second, the eulogy was more than a ramble; it was almost a benison, a statement of faith based on ancient knowledge, a prayer to a lost relative said with reverence and longing.

I don't often explode in anger, but I was flaring like the flames around an oil well fire as we drove down the mountain. As waves of rage crashed over me, I went faster, tires screeching on the asphalt, closer and closer to the drop-off. El was white as a sheet as we teetered on the precipice of disaster.

"We've come three thousand miles to this armpit of a town to find some old bat, who sounds as crazy as the Mad Hatter, so she could sit there, listen to me make a fool of myself, and then lie to me on top of it!" Finally, we got to the relatively flat land.

El demanded I pull over at a gas station so she could use the bathroom, which shows how scared she was that the horrors of a gas station ladies' room were preferable to my driving. She grabbed the keys from the ignition as she exited and wouldn't give them back for the rest of the day.

"I'm disappointed too, David," she said when I had done what I usually do when I've misbehaved, gone quiet, and sulked. "At least she saw us. She knows a lot more than she said. She knew your grandmother well. She also knows what you're going through. I got the impression this isn't the first time she's heard the story, but she's not talking."

"We are still nowhere for all our effort," I said.

"No, we're in North Carolina on a long-delayed honeymoon. My parents are spoiling our kids. We have not a care in the world. So let's put this aside and enjoy. Maybe when the heat of your disappointment is gone, we'll see it differently."

"Besides, I have a sense we're dealing with something huge and complex. Where did that blessing come from? That's not a normal thing for me to say. There was like...a power or sense of direction that made her say it. How did she know my full name? And the stones weren't natural; they looked like the monolith in 2001 Space Odyssey. I felt different there, freer—I don't know."

El went quiet. This whole thing disturbed her logical scientific mind, and the mystery was deepening.

"I was supposed to be able to trust her. Grandma said to come clean. Called her sister."

"You want to go back and beat her till she tells?" El said, laughing. Her laughter broke my mood. Good women do that to men. They gentle them.

We toured the high and low country and flew home, tired, full of great food, and more in love than ever, but for all that, my dissatisfaction grew. I was more determined to find the root of my problem. It was becoming almost the grail quest. As sometimes happens, more information dropped in my lap.

Dad moved to emeritus status at Northwestern. He joked he was Mr. Chips. Dad had written a book on the influence of Homeric tales on Western thought and politics. While researching it, he accumulated half dozen articles on the ability of ancient peoples to divine the future. He was considering a visiting professorship at Berkeley, and he and Mom were flying out. Dad and I ended up marooned as El, and Mom continued their girl crush. One day we were driving back from UC Berkeley when Dad said, "Your mother found something that will interest you. She wants to show it to you, and we can talk later."

When Mom was going through stuff left by Ruth and Angus, she found a notebook, part of which was an address book. It contained a few English words but was mainly in Gaelic. They'd asked an Irish-born professor of languages if he could translate. The professor said it was Scottish Gaelic but in an obscure dialect. He doubted if anyone still spoke or read it. He had also translated the blessing Grandma had ended her last letter, *May the wind be always at your back, and may the blessing of heaven fall on you and yours. May the blessings you have received be only a small portion of what awaits you.*

Mom also told me the manager of what had been Culloden Farms had called to ask about the four stones they had found in the fields around the house. This was Indiana. There were no stones of that description in the entire state, yet they were tall and gray, just like the ones at Ruth Lovat's house 1,500 miles away. The mystery deepened.

In the notebook, there were five entries in English. One was Ruth Lovat; another was Breanna McLeod Campbell, Isle of Islay, Scotland, a man in Sonora, California, another in Nevada. The final one was Mary Rose McDonald in Opa-locka, Florida. No phone numbers, no street addresses. Now I had some leads I hoped would be more productive than Ruth Lovat, but life intervened.

I decided to join a project group at Stanford Research Institute, and El agreed to do some part-time work at Ames. It was at this particular moment when 'the incident' occurred.

CHAPTER 11

The debacle with Ruth and the incident marked the climax of my intellectual wanderings about the spots. Ruth did what she did, and there was no way I could control her. The incident should have never existed. It was one of those times when good intentions go awry, and people decide to act stupidly collectively.

It was one of those times when people decided they needed to be included in something that was frankly none of their business. The incident should never have even been a ripple on a pond; it shouldn't have been even a zephyr. It became a tidal wave, a howling hurricane nearly sweeping me away along with the family. It certainly changed our lives and views on the world, notably mine, and ignited my search for the truth.

It was a case study on the power of groups and overstimulation on the human brain. Still, in a hothouse of feigned social justice concerns, narcissistic delusion, desire to be included due to lack of personal development, and quiescence in the face of mass action, it metastasized.

Our oldest, Beatrice, was the female lead in what was called the Christmas play in those more innocent days. Political correctness and misunderstanding of the Constitution morphed it into the holiday pageant.

The male lead was the son of an executive at Sun Microsystem who lived several blocks away. We saw a lot of Henly because El was an excellent pianist, and Beatrice and Henly were often at our house practicing the songs. At the end of the opening performance, Henly gave Beatrice a bouquet of roses and made a long speech for a sixteen-year-old about what a joy Beatrice was.

At the reception afterward, Beatrice was gushing with joy, beaming killer smiles in all directions and looking very much like El. Her radiance filled the room. Like El, she lived in joy. I realized then the hard lesson fathers must accept; she had moved from Daddy's little girl to a beautiful, vivacious young woman.

I was talking to Eric, Henly's father, when Henly, Beatrice, El, and Eric's wife, Janelle, came over. Henly was a fine-looking, strapping young man, the very picture of adolescent health and vitality. In addition to having a wonderful tenor voice, he was an athlete of note and a top-level student. His parents were very proud of him and doted on him as parents do on their only child.

As Henly approached, I noticed a black area from his right hip to his foot. I think of all the spots I had seen up to this point; this and the one on Suzan shocked me the most. This was the only son of loving parents, the crush of my daughter, a young man with all the promises of the world. An innocent, and now he was to be struck down before he could fulfill any of the promises. I was sick to my stomach. This was inexplicable. This was truly cruel.

In common with many others confronted with the inexplicable, the first thing I did was question God. The perennial question of how and why? My questions, of course, revealed nothing about God but a great deal about me.

I will never know why I did what came next. Perhaps it was the injustice of a death sentence being pronounced on one so young. Maybe it was frustration. Maybe it was the accumulated weight of seeing the spots over the years and not saying anything.

Years later, I would return to the time and wonder if perhaps I was seeking an answer to one of my questions. If I told someone and if they believed me and sought treatment, could death be prevented? Or were the spots, as Altois said, evidence of fate, not destiny?

In any case, I steered Eric aside and said (not very tactfully, how can you be tactful at a time like that?), "Eric, I know this will sound weird, but in the past, I could see when someone was going to get sick before it happened. So I think you should take Henly in for a full-scale physical exam."

Eric had lowered his head as if concentrating on hearing me, and for a moment, I couldn't tell if he had. Finally, he raised his head and looked at me with a mixture of uncertainty and disbelief. I watched amazement, concern, and anger work through the windows of his eyes, his broad forehead wrinkled and smoothed, his eyes narrowed then opened wide, and he struggled for words.

"Dave, ah, ah, geez."

"I know it sounds odd," I said, kicking myself for the word odd and frankly for saying anything at all, "but there have been seven or eight times in the past when I just seemed to know. I have that same feeling right now."

Janelle saw the serious look on Eric's face. Eric told her what happened, and she started looking at me like I was stark raving mad.

"David," she started with a tone like a schoolteacher correcting a student, "that's a terrible thing to say! I'm shocked and really disappointed."

Using the word *disappointed* rather than *mad* had recently become popular since supposedly, it didn't damage self-esteem or some such foolishness.

She continued, "Do you really believe you can see illness before it happens?"

I was still under the romance that people would respond to logic and reason. I was mistaken. "All I know, Janelle, is that several times in the past twenty years, I have had the..." I stumbled, looking for the word I finally came up with, "sensation when someone was going to get sick. I told Eric out of concern for our friendship." That last was a simple attempt at manipulation. I was hoping to put an obligation on them to act differently toward me.

Janelle started in with her best preaching voice. "You shouldn't go around saying things like that."

I started to defend myself, but she motored on. "People will think you are crazy. No one wants to hear they might get sick, my god. Who would want to know that?" It was an excellent question, and as every second passed, I regretted telling Eric even more. While Janelle had been lecturing me, Eric had told Henly what I had said.

Eric herded the three of them together, and they walked away with backward glances of disapproval. Henly shrugged off the attempts at hugs by Beatrice and El, and they both stood there looking at me perplexed. The hurt cut straight through me.

El and I had not told the children about my—I still can't call it a gift, and I wasn't ready to call it a curse although I was getting there fast, so it was a unique ability. We planned to initiate Beatrice when we thought she was ready to hear the story without judging. However, the incident made us revise that plan.

Beatrice was concerned about her reputation at school. Her relationship with Henly, which according to her, was gone, just gone, unrecoverable in any way. With all the passion of youth, Beatrice declared I had condemned her to spinsterhood. In her mind, she might as well give up and move away.

It got worse when Henly, with a good deal of intemperance, stated that he could not have any relationship with anyone whose father was a nutjob. The nutcase diagnoses seemed to be generally shared by a growing number of Los Altos residents as they heard about the incident.

It probably would have sputtered out but for the insidious nature of the press and its then rapidly growing need to sensationalize. A local woman wrote a weekly doings column for the local rag, and she ran a story naming me, Beatrice, and El but not Eric, Janelle, or Henly. So now more people knew, but it was still localized, or so I thought.

It was after that story the first vandalism occurred. I came out one morning to find my car covered with spots, paint spots. I filed an insurance claim and police report. It must have been a slow news day because the regional paper, the San Jose Mercury, picked up the tale and spread it more widely. The kids were taunted at school with names like spot boy and girl, and, "Hey, see any spots on me?"

Then a local TV station had a segment on its morning show. They cited the police reports and our names and ran a video of our house clearly showing the street number. The show featured a guest, a condescending, prolix fool of a psychiatrist who stated I was making a logical mistake of post hoc ergo prompter hoc. The info babe running the show didn't ask for a translation or explanation.

At the prompting of the host, he went on to say that I must be damaged physically and mentally. Such delusions, he said, could make me a danger to myself and society. When asked for his recommendation, he replied that this sort of delusional behavior was very serious and was best treated by inpatient treatment over a long time. All of this without seeing me and from a thirdhand story. Of course, all our kind neighbors and acquaintances ensured we knew what was said as they rushed to judgment.

The following Sunday, a blood and guts preacher in Cupertino thundered out in his sermon about my devil possession and the danger of the devil in our midst, echoing Jacoby years earlier. That inspired two more episodes of vandalism. One mild, the police had to remove a group from our driveway praying for my salvation. The other was more serious and involved a group who got into the house while El and the twins were there. When they were arrested, they claimed they were going to attempt some sort of exorcism.

Our mail volume exploded with not only condemnations (one guy called it the mark of Cain) but also with letters from people claiming paranormal or supersensory ability. There are offers from people who wanted and would pay for me to come and look at them and their families to see if they had spots. You can imagine how difficult this was for the family. I got a couple of offers to appear on lowbrow TV shows, the kind that features stories about men who divorce their wives to marry their stepdaughters. One offer was from an insurance company that wanted to hire me to look at those applying for life insurance to assess the insured's chance of living.

Even at Stanford Research Institute, I could feel the change. It was distancing, a lack of contact, and short answers left out of the watercooler talk. At one meeting, a guy asked if I saw a spot on anyone, and I wanted to say, "Yeah, on you, asshole!" but I refrained.

The family suffered worse if measured in terms of screaming and yelling. Beatrice found herself isolated and shunned. El was treated with a kind of sick curiosity given to someone married to a profoundly disabled or mentally defective person. The twins were too young to know.

Fergus was getting bullied at school by two thugs, and one day he hauled off and laid both out flat. He got expelled, and we got sued by the parents of the two thugs. Both sets of parents wanted hundreds of thousands for their dear innocent little monsters. Eric and Janelle filed a damage suit for one million for emotional distress. Now lawyers were in the scrum. Finally, the police almost unbelievably opened a criminal investigation around Fergus's fight. Intimating assault and battery charges were being considered.

Then more lawsuits, one from a nutcase who claimed his family suffered extreme emotional distress, loss of work, and loss of consortium (no sex) because of concern caused by my refusal to tell them if anyone was going to die early. When they stopped flying, I added up all the lawsuits. If I lost them, I would have been dead flat broke.

I don't think anything in my life destroyed my faith in human beings like the incident. El had been active in the community and the schools and on the town, planning commission. El was head of the group tending the flowers and trees in the public spaces. We were the very model of the young suburban family. We weren't perfect, but community is supposed to mean something beyond a group of people. I mistakenly believed the community supported its members and didn't condemn them at second and thirdhand stories.

It was hard to accept that those who professed admiration, gratitude, and even love on one hand were only too ready to run from the association at the first whiff of calumny. I made some assumptions about how the world worked and assumed it took on its alternative meaning and made an ass out of you and me.

There are several ways to go in the aftermath of a thing like the incident.

You can get hard-edged and cynical. You can blithely shake it off as meaningless and carry on as usual, which is just endorsing others' meanness. You can rage against injustice, be confirmed as a zealot, gain condemnation, and ultimately wear yourself out. You can run away, confirming everyone's worst feelings about you. Or you can go the most challenging route and do nothing. In doing nothing, you have to adjust. In our society, punishment is distributed to the family and loved ones to an almost greater degree than the person who inspired the reaction, and we never stop punishing.

It was a vital lesson El and I had to teach the children. In love between a man, and a woman, there can be and should be reciprocity of kindness and love. It's not precisely an obligation since obliging one is a demand which can sever a relationship, but there needs to be reciprocation. In love between other people, there can be no implied or actual obligation on the beloved. There is just what you do. You do it without expectation of return, which can be very hard in a society where people seek affirmation from the reactions of others.

The lesson I learned from the incident, which I tried hard to pound into the kid's heads, was that you give with the spirit of love, doing the right thing, but with no expectation that you're building any credit. The reward for good deeds is indeed reaped in heaven, not in the precincts of Los Altos, California, or any other earthly realm. Those who do things only for glory are narcissists and self-aggrandizers.

The other thing I learned, and actually I just fully realized rather than learned, is that probably the most substantial influence on human behavior isn't genes or family but peer pressure. Group identity and belonging are essential to human existence. Standing alone marked you as a shaman or for death. People will give up their moral and behavioral underpinnings to be part of a group. They give up the lessons of academics, religion, ethics, and behavioral rules to be part of a group, even to their destruction.

As the sound and fury of the incident faded, leaving only hard feelings and lawyer bills, another harbinger of change came our way. We got a postcard from Banner Elk. The message read, "I'm gone. Contact Breanna Campbell, Islay, Scotland. I don't have the time to tell you more. Ruth. PS the stones."

The incident forced me to realize I could not bear this alone and that it would have had a tangible impact on innocent loved ones. Second, things were winding down in other areas affording time to pursue the knowledge I needed. Finally, I was mad enough about how the spots had affected me that I was going to break out of my self-pity and remorse and go forward regardless of the cost to me. Finally, everything was in place for my quest.

The real motivator was El, who just simply stated, "We can't go on like this. We have to understand more."

A couple of data points connected. First, there have been Saracen stones at Culloden farms and Ruth Lovat. El went to work and found an obituary for Ruth that listed a law firm as executor. She called and was connected to W. W. MacTavish, another of Rory's sons. W. W., we were told, was for William Wallace, Scots roots run deep. Ruth's estate consisted of some old books, the site of her house, and the adjoining two acres. She was to be interned on the Isle of Mull, the same as my Grandmother. W. W. had been puzzled by that since she, like my grandmother, had never been to Scotland. The estate sold the property to an Atlanta real estate developer named John Hipp.

Hipp tore the house down, combined Ruth's land with other nearby lands, and planned to develop it into housing. When they started to work, they uprooted what Ruth called "her stones" and broke them up to use as gravel. Shortly after that, Hipp's wife was found in a compromising position in their marital bed with a man and a woman. Then a colossal downpour washed out the road to the property. When the road reopened, several pieces of heavy equipment seemed almost magically to fall off the mountain's edge and were ruined. Thankfully, no one was hurt, but the neighbors down the hill filed a damage suit, and the state removed Hipp's permits.

W. W. then passed on the rumors that Hipp had a big secret. He was HIV positive, which he got from his gay lover, his wife's business partner. I wondered if maybe Ruth was up there someplace flinging lightning bolts down at Hipp for the destruction of her house and stones. His whole story rolled out. I remembered Ruth had said there was a lot more to learn.

Back in the real everyday world, we had to make a tough decision. As the controversy of the incident cooled, there were juicier scandals to exploit; we had to deal with its residual damage. Although I tried to apply my philosophical school of 50 percent Spock and 50 percent Marcus Aurelias and have as much compassion as I could as had El, we both resented the way we were treated. I think most of those who had weighed in, except for those pursuing lawsuits, would have had a hard time remembering what the fuss was about, but would have readily condemned us for feeling any resentment or hard feelings. The resentment mostly lay with me. Every man's a hero in his own story. I saw myself as one who took a considerable risk to help someone, only to have my kindness shoved his face and my family subjected to abuse.

I knew Christianity's precepts about forgiveness and could imagine old Epictetus discoursing, "What did you lose? No slave, you lost nothing," or Marcus Aurelias saying, "Make sure that the power within stays safe and free from assault, superior to pleasure or pain, doing nothing randomly or dishonestly, and with imposture not dependent on anyone else's doing something or not doing it."

Spock would simply say, "It's not logical to be resentful since you can't change anything."

I had made the mistake of confusing acquaintance with friendship. The incident showed El and me and the kids we had fewer friends than expected, and acquaintances were conditional on our perfect behavior. These were hard lessons and presaged societal changes just beginning to unfold.

The kids were far more sensitive to it than we adults. Children tend to measure their success in raw numbers, not in the depth of attachment. Blows to self-esteem at a young age can be damaging, but they don't have to be, they can't be avoided. The vital role of parents, and for our ability to be full-time parents, I thank God, is to help the formative personality sort out the real from the imagined, true from false, the signal from the noise, and the noble from the ignoble.

Of course, parents have to be engaged with their children and have some sense of ethics themselves. But unfortunately, it seemed like many of the parents I was seeing were only too anxious to rid themselves of the nuisance of the complex parts of parenting, dumping it on the schools or counselors. It seemed that in California, hedonism was required for citizenship.

I believed the kids should stay in Los Altos schools and face down the sniggering. But, of course, that's easy for me to say I wasn't taking the abuse, or so I thought. El sort of agreed but cautioned that each child was different, and we had to be careful to watch them as people, not as a group. She felt things would be okay if I didn't talk to anyone about the spots. The kids were divided, so we decided to wait a year before deciding whether to move or go the private school route. I chose, and El agreed, that this was the time to seek more knowledge.

CHAPTER 12

Even though we were approaching the end of the century and the Internet was around, the world was still largely unconnected, and finding information, particularly obscure information, took real work. It was possible then to live with no digital footprint. A few years later, I could go to a search engine and pull up hundreds of articles about people who could see things in the future and other manifestations. I went to the library and found some serious studies underway about exceptional abilities, paranormal, and supersensual experiences. By serious, I mean scientifically. A doctor at San Francisco University named Oren Mayotte had a grant to study such things, and I made an appointment to see him.

With the incident still fresh in my mind, I was nervous about approaching him. Academic studies are published in journals and presented at conferences. If the subject was topical or controversial, it sometimes became a news item. If anyone in Los Altos read the journal or saw a news story, they would instantly know it was me, and the whole thing would get fresh fuel. However, I was growing tired of my fears, so I came clean with the entire litany of my experience.

He didn't interrupt once. He sat in his chair, chin slightly lowered, fingers steepled, his index fingers at the tip of his nose, eyes looking down as if deep in thought. He broke his reverie, looking up, smoky blue eyes looming large behind his round wire-rimmed glasses. "What was the reaction when you told people? I'll bet it hasn't been favorable." His voice was a deep rumble from his chest, almost out of place with his whipcord body.

"You guess right," I said. "It has ranged from assault to disbelief, to devil possession, to anger, to disappointment. The only people who have accepted my story are my wife, parents, and paternal grandparents. Even the lady who was supposed to help me blew me off."

"The reactions are a little more extreme than normal, but the substance of the revelation is similarly extreme," Oren said.

"Have you ever had anyone else with my issue?" I asked.

"We've had lots of people claiming the ability to tell the future. That's the most frequent claim in extra, supra, or supersensory abilities. You are the first who claims to see the future in the form of death. Certainly, we have had people who had visions and manifestations but none related especially to death."

"Do you believe me?" I asked.

"Yes, but…"

"Always the scientific but!" I said with a laugh.

"You're taught that in research school, like a lawyer's first word, is no. We start from the standpoint that whatever a person claims as an ability is true, and then we seek to duplicate their experience in measurable and observable ways. Falsification is the opposite of verification. With falsification, if you fail, you strengthen the theory."

"The falsification concept," I said. "See if what the person says can be falsified."

"Yes, that's the best way to approach this. People who have these abilities are absolutely convinced they possess the power, so starting out by making them prove their powers is not a fruitful path. We assume they have it and then present situations that either prove or disprove their assertion. Your particular ability poses some complications in testing it since you don't know time, causation, or mode, and I see issues with medical ethics arising. That, David, is the hard part." He looked at me for a reaction.

"I understand the problem of duplicating the experience; we have the same issue in data processing, and my wife is a geographer, so we are familiar with the workings of scientific proofs. But most of the time, the death occurs quickly after I see the spots, and I think the longest has been six months between the events."

"We also have an issue with some of our subjects. Many of our subjects cannot produce the phenomenon within the strictures we place on the experiments and fail to complete the study. We had one case where the experiments produced counter results disproving the claim; the person claiming the power most of the time refuses to accept our findings."

He looked at me to see if I was following. "We had a lady and year or so ago who claimed she could detect and cure disease without touching if the person was there but covered with a sheet, for example. We asked her to explain her technique, and she said that if she could pass her hands within two feet of the person, she could tell. So we created a trial with four healthy people covered with sheets and had her stand two feet away. She had no sensations, which was the correct response. Then we substituted four hospital patients with various disease factors. Again, with the sheet, she got no stimulations even though they had a disease. Then we substituted cadavers, no responses." He was sort of smiling.

"She got them all wrong."

"When we reported the findings, she said she got no feelings because she had cured them. Remember she claimed to be able to detect and cure, which was patently not true. Some of the sick people died within days of the test. Then she claimed the observation of her work interfered with her. Being generous, we took one healthy person, two sick, and one cadaver and did not observe her, just asked her to identify the sick ones. She identified the cadaver as the one who was sick, hardly overwhelming. Regardless of our findings, she left convinced of her ability, and she advertised we had clinically proven her powers. We had to threaten a lawsuit to stop her!" He shook her head in amused remembrance.

"I guess it must be some sort of mental fixation people get into. I would be delighted if I didn't have these visions. I guess that is as good a word for them, although it has negative connotations," I said.

"True, many of those who claim special powers form a mental picture of themselves as blessed. Rarely is the power to see or predict death, making your case interesting. If you think you can cure people, you can look at yourself as an admirable person. No one wants to give up the idea of being admirable. You, on the other hand, see death but not healing, sickness not recovery, and you say it's 100 percent correct you don't know timing or method."

"I can make some assumptions," I said. "The locus of whatever will happen is the spot." He was putting me at ease, more so than I expected. "Sometimes it's almost instant. With Shamus, it was thirty minutes later, the football player, forty-five minutes, Jean's father several months, Caesar, several months." I looked at him to see if he was getting my point. "In the case of disease, it's different. For example, Henley's parents took him to the doctor, and he checked out just fine. It's very confusing."

"I can imagine," he said. "Do you have to actually see the person? Do the spots appear if a person is videotaped or if there was just a picture?" He leaned forward. His chair squeaked and picked up his pen to make a note.

"I don't know. All the spots so far have been seen in person."

"Well, that might be interesting. Let me make some videos of people. Then we can meet again and see. Okay?" We parted with the next appointment three weeks out.

The path to knowledge continued to be revealed. Father Altois had retired and moved to the Mount Calvary monastery near Santa Barbara. While he was still in LA, I visited him several times, and we exchanged letters. He never mastered email. One day, a letter came from the monastery. I first thought it was an appeal for money, but it was hand addressed. The Abbot, Peter Spurgeon, related that Father Altois had been diagnosed with dementia and wanted to see me. The Abbot stressed that he thought it was important that I visit Altois.

I called the Abbot and arranged the visit. El and I flew down to Santa Barbara on a Thursday to visit Altois for several days; it was likely to be the last time he would be able to remember us. The monastery sits east of Santa Barbara on the upslope of the mountains. It has beautiful views and acres of gardens.

I was taken by surprise when Altois came into the garden to meet us. It had only been a year since I had last seen him. Never a big man, he had shrunk and looked wasted. He leaned more heavily on his cane. His limp was far worse than I remembered, his back was humped, and he had to raise his head to talk to you. His eyes, however, still sparkled. With him was Abbot Spurgeon.

"I asked the Abbot to come and talk to you, David, he's much more learned in the areas of suffering than I am, and I thought he could help. I hope it's okay."

While I was still very sensitive about having my secret widely known, I was on the hunt. I agreed that knowledge from any source would be helpful.

For all the sunshine in California, some places can be downright cold, even in summer. Santa Barbara, like Monterey, is one of them. The four of us sat at a table sheltered from the wind. El and I had jackets on, the Abbot (a heavy sweater), but Altois had a cassock, and he soon showed signs of being cold. The ever-thoughtful El had brought along a blanket, which she wrapped around Altois with a touching tenderness that made my breath catch. Altois looked up at her with a benign and loving expression. He patted her hand in thanks.

"How are you, Father?" I asked.

"I'm dying. That should be obvious, David." His no fools' attitude had not faded. "You should know that. I must have a spot on me?"

"No, I don't. I only see disease, violence, or accidents, and I don't see spots where the cause of death is part of the normal practice of living."

He stopped me from going further.

"It's not something I fear. Frankly, it's long overdue. I've suffered enough, I've given enough, and the Lord is calling me," he said without remorse, and I truly believed him. He fumbled around under the blanket, producing a cigarette and lighter.

Altois noticed my disapproving expression.

"I'm dying, David, this isn't going to make any difference. If you're shocked by this, you'll be apoplectic when I tell you I smoke pot sometimes. It helps me feel more alert." He looked at us both. "Cool dude!" he said in a weak imitation of a pothead.

"Time's short," he began. "I wanted to talk to you further about your problem." He made air quotes around the word.

"Okay."

"First, everything you have, including the spots, is a gift from God. That being true, the spots have to be part of God's plan for you."

"It's hard to see any plan or purpose to knowing when people will die."

"Hard for you, not for God," Altois replied. "God's wisdom is so infinite we can't conceive it. We only see hints. So inadequate is the human language we can't even express it, and if we could, our words would limit it. The mystery is so great as to be beyond human understanding."

"The term we use is that God's blessings are transcendent since they move from the supernatural to the natural," said the Abbot.

"If that is true, how does a person know if he or she is living according to God's plan?" El asked. "You aren't getting Calvinist, are you?" she added with her tinkling laughter.

"You two take this on the road? Two of you beat up on an old man?" His eyes smiled at the exchange.

"Might be an idea, but you have to stay alive," El fired back.

Altois flipped his hand at the remark dismissing it. "God's plan is the one which makes you happiest."

"So God's either a devotee of emotism or a utilitarian ethicist," I said.

"The boy reads, I'll give him that," he said in an aside to El.

"God wants us to be happy. He created us in his own image to be like Him, but he gave us free will so we could make bad choices to provide a comparison between evil and good so we can learn."

"Free will enables humans to make their own choices. Foolish choices bring the most devastating consequences. While many in the midst of those free will consequences blame God for them, the responsibility for unwise choices is their own, not God's," said Spurgeon.

"Sounds like you've been reading Irenaeus," I replied.

"I liked you better when you were just a dumb computer nerd," said Altois. "I guess this is my fault. I got you thinking about the philosophy behind suffering. It was easier when the parishioners were illiterate, and the priest had all the knowledge. You know the good old days." He did a Groucho Marx imitation, pushing his white eyebrows up and down, which got a smile from El and me. "You know the world was not created to be totally happy. Suffering produces endurance, endurance produces character, and from character hope. Not only for the sufferer but also for those around them, and it moves everyone closer to God. That was the meaning of Suzan's death, by the way."

"Our friend, Thomas Merton," said the Abbot, referring to a Trappist monk who was prolific in writing about man's relationship to God, "said death contributes something decisive to the meaning of life. Without death, we have no idea what living means, and the absence of suffering is apathy, which is equally destructive."

"Suzan's death was like the incident with the six-year-old in *The Brothers Karamazov*. She didn't learn anything; she needed no moral lessons. Her death was senseless suffering, a senseless loss," I fired back. Her death was a sore point, not only because of her death but also because of my conduct.

"Brought you this one," Altois said, pointing at El.

I was trapped, and he knew it. El observed me. I could dispute him, causing El to doubt me, indicating she was the second choice, or accept his statement. She indeed was a gift from God.

"Hobson's choice," Altois said.

"Maybe, but you're not so clever, Father," El said. "I know all about David's feelings about Suzan, and his reaction to her death, as well as the fact that he and I would not be as deliriously happy as we are without it, but that doesn't answer the question. What was gained by her senseless struggle and death? Who morally benefited?"

Spurgeon jumped in at this point to try to defuse the tension. "There really are only two ways to deal with the potential loss of a loved one. The first is not to get attached, but then we are only saving the worst suffering for ourselves. The other way is to become so attached that it is impossible to imagine life without the other. In either case, we open ourselves up for suffering. In the first, it's individual suffering that leaves us barren, and in the other, it is the need to survive the suffering from the loss of a loved one."

He looked at us both, saying, "Perhaps the spots, her death, and the incident have forced you to think and believe you're in a specific environment. To find the truth, you need to go from thinking about your specific environment and view the spots and the events in a more general way."

"That explains the suffering and why I have been cursed and why no one else has the problem I have. It's hard not to think you are unique, and the environment surrounding you is specific to yourself when a person is alone. That's the very definition of specific. But it still does not address the value of suffering. If Suzan and the others were sacrificed to improve my moral character, it's hard to see a just God in the suffering regardless of religious faith," I said.

Altois looked at me sternly. "So now you commit Job's sin of presumptuousness, that you know all and can puzzle out God's will and plan with your puny brain?" Altois is getting nasty now. There was a didactic cadence to his voice. "So what's your theodicy then?" He looked at us as we confronted a word we didn't know. "From the Greek theodis [God] and dies [judgment], how do you explain suffering, particularly your suffering, in terms of God's plan?"

I was angry and almost overstepped. What I wanted to say was, *I don't know. Maybe there's no God's plan or God. Maybe this is all crap trying to figure it out.*

A look in El's silent, expressive eyes were pleading with me not to insult him. It was likely to be our last conversation, leaving us at odds that she knew would trouble me forever. I held back.

"I don't know if I can't express a theory yet, Father."

"That's the difference between religion and philosophy. In religion, you just accept it on faith. In philosophy, you spend time trying to find a theory to explain it. You are unlikely to find a theory that explains what you have, let alone develop the ethical schema and epistemology to support the theory. That's where religion comes in. It's just a simple affirmation of faith. You need to have faith that this is all of your good," he said.

"Okay, so let me accede to your points that I was bound to suffer in any case. But there is another part to this that has troubled me for a long time. What moral gains come to me seeing the spots, and what is my moral responsibility to the people with the spots? That's how all this all started."

"We can discuss that tomorrow. I'm tired, the Abbot has other duties, I'm cold, and it's time for my twice-daily round of pills," said Altois.

El and I had agreed we wouldn't immediately discuss what we heard from Altois, and we would wait, and each think about it, then discuss our feelings. We said our goodbyes and drove down the hill to our hotel.

The next day we arrived shortly after 1:00 p.m., and we met Altois in a classroom in the seminary. It was warmer, and the Abbot did not join us.

"So the question on the table, Father, is if I have a moral obligation or duty to tell those who I see spots on about their fate." I began.

"No," came his quick answer.

"Oh, come on, there has to be more to answer than that, Father. It's a big issue," I said.

"Not really," said Altois. "We make it a big question, and we get all confused and unwilling to accept what is right in front of us, but sometimes what seems simple really is simple."

"That flies in the face of the history of thought," said El, "from ancient times, the idea of being responsible has been debated and questioned, and now you are dismissing David's concerns with simplification. I find that hard to take."

"Okay, let's look at it this way," Altois began. "Why do you feel responsible when you see a spot and a person dies?"

"Because I am the one seeing the spot, which signals death, and since I am seeing the spot, I feel I should warn the person of their impending death," I replied.

"But you don't control when you see the spot, nor do you control when the person will die or how at least in the cases you have told me about, you haven't had control."

"That's true," I said, "but I have this ability, and it must be for some purpose. You said that it must be part of God's plan, but what plan and what should I do with it? If it's part of a plan, there has to be a goal or result that is expected. So far, I see no result, but in seeing the coming death, I feel I am called to do something."

"First, I see that you believe the spots are saying something about you and the kind of person you are. You want to help others, so you are taking on the responsibility for the results of the spots. But—and this is a big but—since the spots are the power of unseen forces beyond your control and are part of the path selected for you, how can you be responsible?"

We looked at each other, and then he continued, "To be morally responsible for an action is to be worthy of praise or censure for having performed an act or not performed it. I fail to see how you are morally responsible for not telling people of their impending death. When you have no control over the visions, you don't create them from any action of yours, and the result is fated. You with me?"

"You are right, El. This debate has been going on forever. Aristotle talked about it and declared for a person to be responsible, the action or trait or whatever must have its origin within the agent, and it must be up to the agent's decision to act or not. You may qualify as an agent because you can choose to act, but you fail the test on the origin of the trait." He paused for a second. "Once you see the spot—apparently, any action taken is otiose—the person's fate is sealed."

"If what you say is true, Father," I began, "then God is responsible for evil—the evil of premature death. Aren't we just beating the dead horse of theological determinism?"

"Maybe, but the issue is between the incompatibilist and the compatibilist views of responsibility. The compatibilist believes that a person can be responsible for some things even if who he is and what he does is causally determined by other forces, but we come back to the issue of control. You don't control the spots, so you are not morally responsible, and your actions, for the most part, are not subject to praise or censorship. What still mystifies me is that some of your actions have been subjected to censorious results like the short sale brought on the bad dreams. That still has me wondering about the nature of this thing, but in general, you have no moral responsibility to try to intervene. Now telling someone seems to fall into a whole different class of thought. Put your mind and soul at ease. You don't cause the death."

My mind was whirling, and I couldn't respond, but El did. "So he did nothing wrong regarding his actions surrounding Suzan's death?"

"He did fail in one aspect. Death and the preparation for death are acts of love, and they bring the survivors closer to God and grace. Your departure on your magical mystery tour violated the duty you had to Suzan's family to help them find God's grace in her moment of death. You decided for whatever reason not to be part of the process, and that was morally wrong."

"I had been there for days on end, and I really find that insulting. I loved her to distraction. I considered suicide because I couldn't affect the outcome, and my running away was my way of dealing with the grief."

"But you denied her family the perspective you had on her death, and you left a hole in their lives that you weren't there in their hours of need. Ministry to the dying extends beyond the immediate death of the body. It extends to the family post-death. I will be judgmental here. You sinned by running away."

We went on for another thirty minutes before a novice came to tell Altois it was nearly time for Nones, the part of the liturgy of the hours prayed at 3:00 p.m., which seemed to signal a natural end. He invited us to stay, and we did. The prayers and readings were in Latin even though Latin was no longer the language of the Church. I was full of emotion to be sitting in that austere church, listening to the monk's chant, knowing it would be the last time I would talk to Altois, and knowing that in his mind, I had sinned. I was almost moved to tears.

We said our goodbyes to Altois and the Abbot. It wouldn't have been an authentic Catholic experience if Abbot had failed to ask me to volunteer some time to help get their computer systems working. To which, of course, I said yes. We left with Altois's variety on the Christian view of the death experience and my part in it. My purpose in knowing of the coming death was that I was supposed to have my behavior and thoughts conditioned by the pain and suffering of others and that any ministry I gave to those dying would bring me closer to grace. It was not a very encouraging or hopeful outlook pre-staging as it did a lot of suffering for me.

I had my next appointment with Oren Mayotte at USF. He had created an experiment to test my abilities. He and I walked through a series of patient rooms as if on a tour of inspection. I had a clipboard with numbered sheets corresponding to the patients I would check if I saw a spot. I protested that I couldn't see the whole body, and presumably, all the patients had some illness or wouldn't be in the hospital. He agreed about the weakness of the experiment but asked that I give it a try. He was working on other tests.

When we had finished the walkthrough, I handed Oren the sheets and waited for the results. Oren was blown away. Of the fifty patients, I marked thirty-five as having spots. Only half the patients had a terminal illness. The additional ten were ostensibly healthy.

"Remember," I said, "I only see the spot. I don't know the method, means, or time so that those last ten could be fine now, and the terminal issues will occur later."

"We're running up against medical ethics," he said. "I can't have you sitting in a clinical meeting with a patient, nor I can ask them to strip naked. We will monitor the patients you identified as sick, but we had as healthy. We will see how this works out over time."

"I'm not sure I can see the spot unless I see the person face-to-face. There seems to be some need for me to face death."

Just then, his assistant came in with some files. When she left, I said, "Track her. Something is going to happen in her back, and she will die from it."

He looked at me with a steady glance and some anger. "Okay, but we don't know when it could happen. It could be years."

"True, but now you know what I go through. That young woman will die, and if the past holds, it's 100 percent sure it will happen. You work with her every day, and now you possess this information. How are you going to treat her now that you know?" I asked. "I have the same issue all the time. Do you tell her, would she change anything, would she even want to know? What benefits do you and she and everyone she touches get from her demise and your knowing beforehand?"

We parted without a plan. I think Oren was troubled by the knowledge I had given him about his assistant.

I went back to my life. Three months later, I got a call from Oren. "You remember Persephone, my assistant?" There was sadness and resignation in his voice. "She was crossing Nineteenth Avenue three days ago and was struck by a car running a red light. Severed her spine, instant death. We are very interested in continuing to work with you."

I was noncommittal; I was getting tired of all this.

I started to refuse invitations. I stopped attending meetings concerning my project at SRI. I hated going out of the house, I hated going to the store, I hated shopping in any case, but now I had another reason for my antipathy. I wasted time I could have been researching my visions, seeing if there was an explanation or context, I could have been reading Martin Martin's book. I grew short-tempered and unwilling to be involved with the monotony of the research.

I excused myself that I wasn't feeling well, but I was heartsick, questing for answers that seemed forever just beyond my grasp. I was troubled by the news of the consequences of my visions, impotent to either understand or ameliorate them. I grew more frustrated daily. I was grateful I didn't have to work nine to five. I started to withdraw from my involvement with the kids, and of course, they noticed.

I was losing interest in everything because everything placed me in a situation to see the spots. After all the years with my silent companion, I still knew nothing with any certainty. Where did the power come from? Could its forecast be changed? What was I supposed to learn? Was I supposed to suffer for the benefit of society? Mostly, why the fuck me? Of all people—me?

What had I done? It must have been something. I moped around the house. I read a lot, but that grew old fast, and I continued to sink into a morass of my misery.

One day, El came home and found me still in my bathrobe and underwear. Unshaven, unshowered, or groomed, eating hot dogs from a plate on my stomach as I lay on the couch. The remainder of other meals and snacks strewn around me, watching a daytime soap opera. It would have been easier if I had been in bed with a goat.

"David Joseph MacIntosh!"

You know you are in trouble when your spouse starts using your middle name. The color rushed to her neck, cheeks painting, her rosy pink, fire blazed deep in her green-flecked hazel eyes. Her breath came in short, gasps, her breasts rising and falling. She was hot! I flashed back to the first time I had seen her. She was mad then too. She noticed my approval; my robe had fallen open.

"That's disgusting," she spat.

"What?" I replied with feigned innocence.

"I'm yelling at you, and you're getting a boner!" She was having a hard time not laughing. I pulled my robe closed and waited.

"Why are you lying on the sofa, watching trash on TV, half-dressed? You look like a slob out of some British sitcom. What's wrong now?"

"I'm tired of seeing death," I said. "I'm tired of having to go through life with the fear of seeing spots or being the grim reaper and of knowing people will die and not be able to do anything about it. Look at what it did to our lives here when I tried to help. It's a curse."

"Oh, boo-hoo!" she volleyed back. She was furious. "So now you're going to play the victim card? Oh, poor me, I'm a victim. You can't expect anything from me." Her eyes flamed with passion and turned green. It was scary. "You're not a victim. You're making yourself a victim. You are making victimhood a way of life. You have something, and what you do about it is up to you. You're not going to lay around here like a slob. Get up, go shower, clean up. God, what a mess you are!"

She stood there, towering over me, arms akimbo, breathing hard.

"Join me?" I asked.

"Join you what?"

"Please?" Both of us collapsed in laughter. I couldn't stay mad at El, and she couldn't stay mad at me either.

"You smell like a goat! Maybe that's the answer. You have this ability, don't shower, wear sackcloth, live in a cave, and have people reach out to you. You could be famous."

"Better idea. I'll be like that Indian guru in Oregon. We'll set up a cult, and people will come from all over the world to give me money to find out they're going to die, and it could be huge."

"Get showered, cult boy. We have to go to the diva's performance."

The diva in question was Beatrice. In addition to acting, she had developed a truly remarkable singing voice for one so young. Her vocal coach said her voice was like someone pulling cotton candy as she moved through the notes, seamlessly blending one to the other. Her choral group was putting on a concert that night. The diva would be the featured soloist.

She and her coach selected a piece from Vivaldi's Laudate Pueri, Nulla in Mondo Pax Sincera, which roughly translated as, *There is no true peace in the world without bitterness.*

How appropriate, I thought.

The whole family trooped off with resulting grumbles from the twins and Fergus.

I heard Beatrice sing and listened as she and El practiced, so I knew how difficult the music was. Here was my oldest about to sing to nine hundred people! It was enough to burst a father's heart with pride. There had to be a fly in the ointment, really an ass in the crowd.

The MC was a miserably named guy, Duns Scotus Thackery or DS, as he preferred. His parents must have hated him to stick him with an odd name like that. He and his wife were very wealthy. It was her money, and he loved her for it. They were major supporters of the arts. The price of accepting their money was his insistence on being the emcee at every performance. He stunk. He never found a shopworn phrase or worn-out line he didn't love and repeat, stringing him together in endless banality.

He came out on stage showing he was one of those who can make good clothes look bad, waving like he was on the Johnny Carson show. Then he went into a miserable imitation of either Ed Sullivan or Richard Nixon or both. His pomposity continued as he reminded us of his generosity, how he and the *little woman*—I could feel El's nails digging into my arm—had funded this or that. I looked at Fergus, who had his mouth open, and was pointing his finger at his throat like he was going to vomit.

The program came to the piece featuring Beatrice.

"I ain't too good with Ey talian," he said with what I think was supposed to be a backwoods Howard Cosell, "so I'll butcher the name. It's by a guy named Vi Valdi. So here's Beatrice MacIntosh singing nullah in mondo pox."

The conductor's baton flashed down to prevent further insults to the music, and the strings began a crescendo arpeggio by way of an intro. Then the director nodded to Beatrice, who stood there in a long, shimmering gown bathed in a light from above.

She opened her mouth.

What came out wasn't notes, tones, or pitches; it was the music of the angels. My first sensation was a chill on the back of my neck, and the second was El's fingernails driving even deeper into my forearm. I looked over, and tears were running down her cheeks.

Even Fergus and the twins stopped fidgeting and sat transfixed. The notes poured forth, and Beatrice stretched each one to its perfect point. Her range was amazing. As I watched her, the notes floated above us all; the only word was heavenly. Two and a half minutes into the piece, there's an orchestral bridge. Many people started to clap, only to have the director wave them silent again. At four minutes, there was a pause, and the audience started again, only to be waived off again.

Beatrice stood there, eyes closed, lost in the music, singing from the spirit. After the second bridge, two very brief pianissimo parts set the stage for the finale. It's much more difficult to sing softly than loudly, but Beatrice somehow made those ghostly quiet notes heard throughout the audience. She finished with a series of swoops and declinations.

Often when a crowd has been stunned by excellence, they sit momentarily, letting the beauty wash over them. In our audience, Fergus, who had a voice like a rutting elk, broke this dreamlike feeling, bellowing, "Way to go, sis!" then the thunderous applause started rising to a standing ovation. The director motioned to the orchestra to stand, and as one, they bowed to Beatrice, one artist to the other. Beatrice executed a perfect curtsy in return.

DS, of course, returned to the stage, no doubt feeling deprived. "That was really wonderful, Beatrice. I didn't understand a word of the Italian, but you did it very well." He was about to speak again when the twins stood and yelled, "It was Latin!" invoking nervous laughter.

"It all sounds the same to me!" DC said with a goofy look. His playing the dumb hick was getting tiresome. So he switched and suddenly got very serious, sophisticated, and self-centered. Finally, after he'd gone on too long, he said, "There's a reception afterward. I'm sure you'll want to meet our artists. Just be careful to stay away from Beatrice's father, David. Unless you want to find out if you're going to die soon."

A few people laughed most incomprehensibly. I was furious.

"Fucking asshole," said El.

When she used words like that, it was time to stay clear. I frankly didn't want to stay, but I couldn't deny Beatrice her moment, and honestly, I was happier for her success than I was mad at DS. Few people noticed me. How could they with the forces of El and Beatrice there? DS never missed the opportunity to network, and while I was at the refreshment table, DS was talking to a crowd next to me.

"And that Bea! Wow, what a babe! In that dress! Hard to believe she's only seventeen! Wish I was a few years younger, you know?" he said in a leering way.

I put down my watery punch and grabbed DS by the shoulder. "That's my daughter you're apeing after like a sex-starved teenager. I could never figure out, DS, if you were as dumb as you appear, but now I know. You will not talk about my daughter like she's a piece of meat, asshole!"

I never mastered the art of the stage whisper; a lot of frustration and repressed anger was coming up. You can only sit on stuff for so long before you damage yourself, and it was long overdue for me to stop being the reasonable, stable, mild-mannered Clark Kent. There was a pause in the babble of conversation,

"Geez, Dave," he began immediately, adding to my irritation by calling me Dave. "You seem a bit overwrought tonight. I was just complimenting her, and by extraction you, and you treat me like I'm a bad guy. You need some help, buddy." He turned back to his group.

I stood there for a second. He just put me down in front of others, diminished his culpability, and recalled the incident vicariously. I'd been bested, and it felt like crap. My cheeks were burning, and my anger was still unresolved.

I was struggling with myself. If I continued the argument, I looked like a nutjob and risked further put-downs. I was becoming a victim of my concerns about how I appeared to others. I still hadn't learned that you couldn't control what other people think or feel about you. They will believe and feel as they will. You can only control your own impressions and what you do.

So no matter what I said, DS would believe what he did unless someone or something changed his mind.

I walked over to El. "What was that all about?" she said, inclining her head toward DS.

"He's going on about Beatrice. Saying stuff, I thought inappropriate for a married man of his age to be saying about a teenage girl, so I called him out."

"Looks like it didn't go so well," she said.

"No, he told me I needed help, and his comments about Beatrice were compliments to you and me, pompous ass!"

"Well, no good deed goes unpunished, I'm catty, but his wife tells me things are not well between them. They've been separated for several months."

"Since we're candid, that makes me feel better. I hope that smart ass ends up on his ass."

"We should round up the kids, pry the diva free of her adoring public." El laughed.

"She deserves it. She was incredible tonight."

"There's a guy from UC Berkeley here talking about a scholarship."

On the way out, we saw Eric and Janelle, Henly's parents. Since we were still parties to a lawsuit, we had been advised not to talk to them, so we steered our brood away. However, they both looked stressed and made it clear in their actions they wanted to speak to us.

"David, El, can we have a word?" said Eric.

We stopped.

"We're dropping the lawsuit," he said.

I was about to say something ungracious like *you should have never filed it in the first place*, but I held back, judging there was more coming.

"We wanted to tell you that you are right, David." His voice caught in his throat. "Henly had some issues at basketball practice with his right leg, and docs found some kind of growth in his hip joint." He was close to tears, and in a grief-choked voice, he continued, "They operated, but the thing exploded. That's how the doctor described it, and now the cancer is all over his leg." He was shaking and couldn't go on.

I stood there at once, feeling their deep grief for the young man and his parents.

"They took it," said Janelle, speaking for the first time. "The leg, they took the leg. They expect he will have a year at most to live."

"You saw it first. If we had just listened and had some tests done, it might have been enough to catch this. If we had done the complete physical when you first warned us, he might be alright," said Eric.

"You don't know that," said El.

I was about to say that intervention had never had any effect before but held back.

"Have you ever tried to reverse the process, David? Do you know if you can control it?" They were grasping at straws as all parents would have been,

"It's not like I pray, and the spots appear. They just appear. There are times I go years without seeing them. I have warned others in the past, and so far, it hasn't changed the outcome."

If possible, they looked more crestfallen. I was about to go on when El jumped in.

"But David is going to try to help," she said. She and Janelle were hugging as if the pain would flow out of Janelle into El.

I knew it would do no good, and I resented El prolonging these people's agony.

"Yes, I'll try to help," I said in a failing voice.

With exquisitely bad timing, DS came blundering up with the grace of an elephant. "Oh, look, the lovebirds are kissing and making up!"

We looked up. He stood there with his wife and two daughters.

"Fuck you, DS," fired El and herded our kids and Eric and Janelle out the doors, leaving me momentarily behind.

"In case you are too stupid to get it, DS, that was a putdown, not an invitation," I said.

I didn't talk to anyone on the way home. I was angry and wondering what I could do with Henley.

Later, that evening after the kids were in bed, El and I were sitting in the living room with Chopin's Nocturnes playing.

I said to El, "What made you offer my services like I'm a witch doctor or something? Am I supposed to dance around the bed shaking a rattle or something?"

"It was something to give his parents some, however faint, hope. It's hope, and they need hope, even false hope. Imagine what they're going through."

"You know, El, I have concluded that one of the worst things in humans is hope. Hope indicates a lack of something. That something can only be satisfied in the future. We have no control over the future, and we only have limited control over the present. I know that sounds bloodless and cruel, but I wonder if I'm not prolonging their healing by holding out the possibility that Henly's cancer will be reversed. El, I really think this was a one-way street. I see. They die. I don't think once I see it is reversible, it never has been."

"It has changed over the years. Maybe it's a growing, evolving thing? The point is you don't know, no one does, it's worth a try, David, and I know you will."

I hated it when she was right.

A couple of days later, I went to see Henley. One look told me that nothing was going to save him. In fact, I thought a quick death would probably be a blessing. The black spot extended from his deformed hip, up to his body to his neck, and black tendrils reached toward his brain. It was almost as if I could see it growing.

Before coming, I visited a store that sold items used in natural healing and had with me a chalcedony on a chain for him to put around his neck. I knelt by his bed, bowed my head, and prayed Christian prayers. My mind was saying, *God, spare him. He is innocent. You've given me this curse. This cannot be justice or mercy. Take this cup from him and give it to me.*

I knelt there, hoping for some feeling, but there was none. I stayed longer, emptying my mind to allow the voice of God, but there was nothing. Prayer often fails to give comfort because we don't mentally shut up long enough to hear the answer. That wasn't the case here. I quieted my mind, but there was nothing there.

I rose and touched all the spots. I said, "I hope the stone may do you some good, Henly. You're a fine boy, and I'm sorry you have to bear this cross."

I've been seeing the spots on and off for more than twenty years, seen friends killed, and people struck down for no good reason. I was death or at least a harbinger of it, and I hated my role in the world. So not for the first time I considered the idea the world might be better off. Indeed, I felt I would be better off if I weren't around. It got worse.

Beatrice, being Beatrice, wanted to run over and be with Henley, but first, she had some words for me and not good ones.

"Your impossible, Dad. Your delusions ruined my life at school. No one talks to me. I'm called death girl. My class thinks you're nuts. They love Mom, but you're unwelcome anywhere. I hate it, and I hate you!" She stormed off. I was crushed. I know she didn't mean it. She hated not me but the spots and their effects. Still, when you feel defensive and depressed, words strike like poison darts.

CHAPTER 13

I'm not a constantly upbeat person, but I try to be steady, to hold in check the wild emotional swings, but I was starting to spiral down again. I had to assume this would be with me forever; that was a weight I increasingly did not wish to bear.

I had developed coping mechanisms for the occasions when I saw spots on relative strangers and those no longer resulted in long bouts of depression. Over the years, the spots had changed, and I started to realize that I might see them on those I loved and were close to. I had no mechanisms to deal with that and was fearful.

I started entertaining the great rationalizations of every suicide. They would be better off without me. I had no right to subject them to the effects of my affliction. They were innocent. I was being punished for some sin. I started to worry that one of the kids would develop the same curse. After all, it had just appeared to me one cold day. Then I would have to bear even more shame. I didn't enjoy the social distancing. My eyes were full of tears, my heart heaving with infinite sorrow. It wasn't all for me, but most of it was. I was cursed, and I dragged the family into the terror of my curse.

After Beatrice's explosion, I had moved out onto the deck, which faced east. I often found the view, the beauty of the lights of Mountain View, and the hazy outline of the mountains across San Francisco Bay calming. But I sat there slumped in a chair, wrapped in the cloak of misery, head down, heart lower. All I could see were the endless experiences with death with no means to prevent it or stop it.

"She didn't mean it, David," said El, sneaking up behind me to gently knead my shoulders. "You're like iron, sweetie. You need to relax. She'll come around."

I was so full of self-pity all I could do we shrug my shoulders and continue to hang my head.

I heard footsteps on my right. I looked up to see Fergus inching his way toward me. He wasn't hiding, just being careful in his approach.

"Dad," he said quietly.

I didn't respond.

He continued, "Did you get this thing from Grandpa?"

"I honestly don't know where it came from, Fergus. I've spent my life running from it and the reality of it. I never considered where it came from."

"Does it run in families? Am I going to get it? I don't think I want to live with something like that. It's awful to know that others are dying."

"Fergus, son, we start dying the day we take our first breath. Dying is part of life. There is no avoiding it. It's a known thing, so shouldn't be feared."

"Wouldn't you be afraid if you know you're going to die? Or Mom? What if you saw this thing on Bea? The twins or me? Wouldn't that make you afraid?"

I need to be careful here. It was the first time Ferus had to address death, and he was scared. I needed to not add to his disquiet by talking about El or me dying. I remembered how I felt when Shamus died.

"I'm upset when I hear of anyone dying. It's worse when I love the person, so, yes, I would. I'm afraid, but I have to tell you your mother and I are sure she or none of you has the spots. You are all gonna be around to harass your poor old, tired Dad for a long time."

"That's not true!" came the strident voice from the other side. Beatrice was back. "It's all bullshit, Fergus. If he'd seen Henley ten years ago before cancer got there, he wouldn't have known. It's all bullshit. He can look at you all he wants, but he has no idea if you're going to die if the disease isn't there!"

I made a mistake. I was dealing with an emotionally distraught young woman whose first big love was dying, and horribly, shattering her youthful belief in immortality.

"That's not true, Beatrice. I don't know the full parameters of this thing. I've had situations where I see the spot, and death is almost instant, others where it was a period before they get sick or were killed."

"You'd seen Henley before that night at the reception, and you didn't see your so-called spots."

"I can't explain that," I said.

"See? More bullshit. Why can't I have a normal father, not some freak who thinks he can see the future!"

I was about to explode. All the anger, frustration, fear, and self-hatred were rushing to get out. A few things can make a person explode faster than disrespect from someone they're supposed to have control over. When that person is a teenager who would have nothing without you, combining a preexisting feeling of anger and frustration can be devastating.

El had come back on the deck and wisely stepped in. "You're not fair, Beatrice. Your father's hurting over this. He's had to carry this burden all his life with no one to talk to. He's not a freak. You should apologize."

"The fuck I will!" Beatrice screamed, shocking us both with the crudity and vehemence of her response. She stormed off, leaving wafts of anger and breaching the dike of my depression.

I fell into the land of self-pity and self-hatred. What I feared for years that the spots would destroy the family was actually happening. My anger was so deep that I didn't hear the screaming match between Beatrice and her brother and sister over her conduct. Instead, I was lost in my world of cruel self-doubt. I was worried that what you fear most happens frequently, almost as if you are willing to have it happen.

I had adopted the habit of turning on music when I went on the deck. It was playing softly in the background during the exchange. As Beatrice stormed off again an aria from Handel's Agrippina came on. It was Ottone's lament, "Voi che udite il mio lament," which I called the woe is me aria, as he mourns that everyone had deserted him, and he truly was alone. At that moment, he and I could have changed places.

I was surprised at how long the icy embrace of the anger stayed around the family. We crossed the Rubicon. Things were vastly different afterward, between the children and me and between El and me.

"David, we have to get to the bottom of this thing. We're both scientists and rational skeptics, but you have proven to me we are dealing with something beyond our current rational view."

"I know a part of me, right now it's a big piece of me, says, 'Don't approach this, and it will destroy you and those you love.' But another part says, 'Go at it, find out.' Knowing is better than not knowing. But I also feel I have no right to drag you and the kids through this. It is a personal thing. It's really lonely being unique."

"But it makes you so special, and you have to find the balance between the two. You're going to be out of phase with the world, but didn't William James define genius as perceiving in an unhabitual way?" She took my hand, looked at me with her penetrating look, and continued. "As for me and the kids, I'm in and have been since I said, 'I do.' The kids are just going to have to grow into it. It will be a good lesson for them in how to deal with those who are different."

"Okay, lover, here we go, in for a penny, in for a pound. I'm thinking I'd like to talk to Oren Mayotte again about some questions. Then I guess we start working on the list Grandma left?"

"No, first den, third section, third shelf, get the book out and read it. Then you need to get one of the best resources you have working for you."

"Who?"

"Your father, he's a scholar of ancient literature. He has to have access to academic sources with some knowledge of this."

The plan started to take form. We were set up to undertake it—no need to work. Parents nearby to watch the kids. I made an appointment with Oren, and he asked me if one of his colleagues, a psychiatrist, could join us. I was nervous and didn't want to be analyzed, but I agreed so long as my confidentiality was maintained, not only my name but also any description that would lead people to identify me.

He agreed.

"David," began the colleague whose badge proclaimed him to be Thomversy. "Oren and I often talk with those who come here to be tested, so we can get information, no wrong word, impressions of how the special ability affects them psychologically. It can't be easy to have something like this."

Alarm bells ran off. "I don't claim it. It exists. You can find plenty of evidence that in every word I said and every time I saw a spot, death occurred, focused exactly on the spot. There is no claim. I predicted Persephone's death, as you know. For us to get anywhere, we need to move to the understanding I have this ability." I was hotter under the collar, and I should have been, but I was still reeling from the incident with Beatrice.

Oren intervened, "Simon, I think the word *claim* is inappropriate. We have enough proof to give David credibility, and part of the problem we are having is with language to describe it. Let's start by agreeing that David has these manifestations?" He looked over at me questioningly to see if I agreed.

I nodded.

"I'm sorry I used a poor word," Simon began again cautiously, "when we deal with people who come here, we have to separate the charlatans from the real. Sometimes there are people so convinced they are special and fight so hard against proof it's easy to be jaded, and of course, our mandate is to start with the premise that they possess the powers they express. This curse must be very wearing. How do you feel?"

"You're not going to ask me how I feel about my mother?" I parried using one of the oldest jabs about shrinks.

"I was planning on getting to that later, but how do you feel about her?"

I couldn't tell if he was serious or not, so I took the noncommittal route.

"She's a real piece of work." I paused for a moment to organize my thoughts.

"I've been dealing with this for over twenty years. It's exhausting to feel constantly out of phase with the world. One of the ironies of life is we all think of ourselves as individuals, unique one-of-a-kind, and that might be genetically true. Still, society submerges our individuality and makes individuals seem like eccentrics, which makes them feel isolated. I felt like there was a missing spoke in my wheel or maybe an extra one."

"Do you feel this active tension, as you call it? Is it harmful?"

"Tension tires you out. It's exhausting. Even materials like steel can't stand tension all the time. Eventually, they break."

Simon asked, "If everything in the world was guaranteed to be in harmony and the world was predictably perfect, wouldn't that be a sterile world?"

"Interesting question," I replied, trying to sound like I fully grasped what he was saying, which I didn't.

"David, you survived this because your life is deeper than you know. Our lives always have a spirit of the divine in them. But, of course, I use the word divine, not necessarily to indicate God. Still, there is something beyond ourselves and our sensations, allowing us to find the strength to survive despair, which otherwise would engulf us. Somewhere you have summoned that divine spark, a reserve, to tide you over when sensations destroy the false conceit of facts."

"Here we get back to the irony," I replied. "While I may have touched the divine spark, beautiful phrase by the way"—Simon nodded his head—"the rest of the world, everyone else is still working off the facts, and if my impressions don't match the facts, then I'm wrong. It can't be that I'm right, and everyone else is wrong, can it?"

"Why not?" said Oren.

"Why not what?" I said.

"What if your ability was given to you to allow you to show others' experiences and knowledge they need to know? To show them if they think they know, they really don't, that you know is not to know, and vice versa?"

"Sounds like a lot of doubletalk talk to know is not to know!"

"Did you ever think about how new things get explained?" asked Simon. "How can what has not yet been encountered be comprehended, understood, embodied, faced, or adapted to? What is yet to be encountered must be comprehended if we are to survive. We, as humans, are capable of a set of paradoxical abilities. We know what to do even when we do not see why we do it, and we know how to represent what we have not yet experienced."

"David," said Simon, "there are times a person for some reason is either given or decides to seek new knowledge, to bear the trials, withstand the slights, endure the condemnation to bring that knowledge to be interpreted, to be experienced by others. You may be one of those. They have a special name."

"Nutjob? Right?"

"Hero is the right word," both said in unison.

"Heroes," Simon continued, "are those who lead the way to new knowledge. It can be things like…" he stumbled, but Oren picked up the tag-team effort.

"Pasteur and germ theory or Curie and radiation."

"Or Terman and semiconductors," said Simon. "He can also be a hero in the social sciences, people such as Descartes, Spinoza, Jesus, and Mohammed."

"The Buddha," added Oren.

My neck was hurting from going back and forth between the two of them.

"What holds society together is myths, the stories which bind us and help us move from the physical facts to those transcendent to life. So often, myth represents experience we can't define with words. In an attempt to understand, people name. The act of naming bestows structure in a chaotic world. Words limit and define rational facts, but they cannot define what appears at the edge of rationality. The hero shows how that experience can be interpreted." Simon went on professorially.

Oren jumped in. "Remember, the ancient Jews had no word for God because any word they used limited the unlimited."

I was whirling. "You're saying that I'm some sort of John Wayne figure or Captain Kirk going where no man has gone before?"

"We use the word hero promiscuously and incorrectly. Not all heroes are men or women of action. A hero can be a good father or person who simply pursues knowledge far from the norm. They can be a person who finds a way to express knowledge to others previously unlearned so they can grasp it. Think of St. Paul in his letters explaining the Christian ideal."

"Are you saying I was cursed with this to show others a path to new knowledge or way of living? That I'm just an example?"

"It's possible. We just don't know. Frankly, we have never seen anything like this before, either in detail or generally. We're convinced it's not pathological, and we aren't sure if it's a psychological illness, but we can't explain it. We are preparing a context that might help you view it," said Simon.

"One of our graduate students did some digging and found this ability has a long, legendary history. It's mentioned in several books, including *A Description of...*"

"*The Western Islands of Scotland* by Martin," I interjected. "I have a copy. But unfortunately, I haven't read it."

We all laughed and ended the meeting.

I now had three perspectives. The first, from Jacoby, was that this was the work of the devil and a pure curse. The other, its polar opposite, was the Christian ideal mixed with Frankl that suffering and handling suffering is an example to others. Third, I was a mythical hero, Beowulf, Roland, and Siegfried seeking new knowledge or higher planes of existence. I rather liked the last one, although I still leaned toward the cursed concept.

I didn't feel like a hero ready to be heroic. I'm not sure any hero ever set out to be courageous. Heroism just sort of happened to them. The guy who overcame evil and got the girl. So what kind of hero was I supposed to be? What were the parameters, how should I act, what should I do to gain the knowledge to make me a hero, and a hero to whom? Did a hero need an audience? Who would be mine? My rational training and theory were now a detriment since I was dealing with something that defied logic.

The project at SRI was winding down, and I was frankly glad. It started well but soon bogged down in the inexorable sluggishness of bureaucracy and self-seeking. The guy who directed the program was one of those subjective idealists who gave California its reputation. He was scrupulous in ensuring that no one got any credit for the work, and everyone was rewarded regardless of their level of participation. I was reminded of the dodo in *Alice in Wonderland* everyone deserves, and everyone must get prizes.

It wasn't a case of me having an inflated sense of self-worth. We had guys on the team who showed up late, or didn't show up at all, had lofty excuses of how their genius flowed best at home or the beach. Other people consistently failed to meet deadlines but never apologized for making the rest of us wait. Finally, a guy who spent his time whispering in corners in a conspiratorial way. He was always around telling stories, each more fantastic than the next, about his past successes.

Dad was ensconced at Berkeley, so he and Mom were built-in childcare. Dad had inherited over a million from Angus and Ruth, and they were financially secure. Dad was nearby for consultation. In addition, the spots seemed to be taking a break, so I wasn't under a great deal of psychological pressure.

One weekend, we had dinner with Mom and Dad, and I told them about my talks with Oren and Simon and the concept of being a hero seeking new knowledge. Mom was supportive, and Dad went into professor mode, with his endless questions and long periods of silence.

"I agree with Oren and Simon," Dad said. "I also agree we use the word promiscuously. But a hero really is a person seeking new knowledge. So how do you think the hero concept applies here?"

"I haven't had time to give it a great deal of thought, so I honestly can't frame it yet," I replied.

"Good answer. It may be that you can only frame it from the standpoint of the endpoint, just as Ulysses or at least as Tennyson framed it for him in the poem Ulysses."

Dad continued, "Order can be a representation of the explored territory. It is what we know, is constructed out of chaos, and it exists simultaneously in opposition to chaos [the new chaos]. It is the known in conflict with the unknown. The appearance of a hero threatens the established order, and his action patterns can upset society itself."

"Perhaps, but I would at least like to find out if it's evil or good."

"It's neither," said Mom.

"How can seeing death not be one of the other? If I see it and tell people and they change the way they live, it's good, but if not, it's evil," I replied.

"No, the spots are external. You don't control them. We have discovered some folklore on this. We will share with you that this is an involuntary ability. It is not of your will. They cannot be good or evil. They just are events. Good or evil is determined by free will. Epictetus said evil lies in the malicious use of moral purpose and good the opposite."

"It can't feel very good to be able to see death. Couldn't it be a manifestation of some non-corporal evil force?" asked El.

Dad pulled his chin while he was thinking. "It's possible, I guess. But if we assume this non-corporal evil has intelligence, similar to that we attribute to God or the good, then it's logical to think that evil would have in mind some gain, so far there's been no gain for evil."

"If it destroyed David, it's gained, or if it makes him do bad things, then evil has captured him," she replied.

"I guess that's a risk, but so far, David has resisted. He made a couple of false starts, the short sale, but he pulled back. There is a force here that we can't explain behind this. The hero's quest—and I mean heroes, plural, since you will both be part of this El—is to find that force and see what it means," said Mom.

"How?" asked El.

"David, when he has the sightings, feels isolated and alone, he gets depressed, he feels and perhaps it's true, and he's the only person in the world having this experience." Mom paused for a moment, then continued, "A soul in isolation is like an ember in a fire without the coals around. It gets colder, not hotter. I think St. John of the Cross said something like that."

I had used that line before and thought it was my original creation, but now I found out I had plagiarized. What was really new was Mom quoting Catholic mystics or Catholic anything.

"I'll dig into the library here and back in Northwestern to see what there is on this matter," said Dad. "You read your grandmother's book, and she rarely did anything without a purpose, start running down the leads from her address book."

"Remember this," he carried on. "Everything we know, we know because someone explored something they did not understand, explored something they feared. Consciousness might be considered the organ or function of humankind specializing in analyzing and classifying unknown events. The unknown is man's greatest fear and greatest friend, and it constantly challenges individual facilities for adaptation and representation, pushing us to greater depths and more profound heights."

"I'm convinced this is not a curse," said Mom. "Good people aren't cursed."

We parted that evening, the kids bouncing off the walls from all the sugar Mom had stuffed them with, and El and I started our new journey. We started it with a new revelation. To me, it appeared as if Mom was wearing a black kufi, and Dad had a spot as big as the one I had seen on Caesar on his chest. I was going to need those new coping mechanisms soon.

CHAPTER 14

Martin Martin's book continued to be a difficult read. The difference now was my dedication. According to the book, the Highlands and Islands of Scotland were places full of wild superstitions and unexplained happenings. There was a long history of seers being able to see the future, and some ended up being burned as witches. There were tales, with little or no fact surrounding them and considerable disagreement. There was no empirical research to back them up. I hoped to find more from the people in the address book.

We found the man in Sonora, but it wasn't easy. I was starting to wonder about these people. None of them seemed to have telephones. I called directory information. No luck. We then went to the census data, and it showed sixteen McPhees of any spelling but only one with the three initials G. A. M. There was no phone number or address.

El suggested calling a local Scottish organization to see if he was a member. The Caledonian society only had a PO Box number but no street address. We went on a similar search for the lady in Florida and found a similar lack of information, only a post-office box.

We sent a letter to McPhee and the lady in Florida. El insisted on trying to find a lady in Islay, Scotland. A fortnight later, we had a letter from McPhee telling me I could come anytime and giving directions.

The first thing that struck you about Gordon Alexander Malcolm McPhee was that he was black. My slack-jawed look when we met was returned not with offense but laughter.

"Happens every time," he roared in his full-throated laugh.

His modest house sat on a hillside outside Sonora overlooking a small lake. His den, where we eventually settled, was full of all things Scottish. He offered, and I accepted some uisge-beatha, Scotch Whiskey for sassenach.

"Aye, it was Dad in the merchant marine in the war doing convoys between Canada and Liverpool when he married Mother." He pointed to a picture of a gorgeous black woman in a nurse's outfit. "She were a nurse in the Royal Navy in Liverpool, looove at first sight." His brogue came and went.

"She was a gorgeous woman," I said, wondering why I used the past tense. She could well be alive, but he didn't correct me.

"Aye, they made a bonnie pair. Dad red-bearded and maiden fair, and she so dark and beautiful."

I told him part of the story of how I came to contact him, and I told him I was trying to find out how the names are all connected.

"I didn't know your grandparents at all, David," Gordon said, looking down as people do when they know something, but they're not saying. I pushed a bit with, "Was your father's family from Islay?"

He brightened a bit. "No, they came from an area called the Black Isle," the name awakened romantic vistas and stories of Robert Louis Stevenson, "although I donna know why, 'tis not an isle 'tall." He smiled. "Like I say, I don't know why my name was in her book, maybe it was Dad, his name is the same as mine without the Malcolm."

I was smiling, and Gordon said, "You'd be smiling, something funny?"

"I'm reflecting on the irony of a white guy of Scottish descent, sitting in a room with a black man speaking with a Scottish brogue, in a state named after a legend, in a town named for a Mexican province. Truly a melting pot!"

We both laughed.

I hadn't brought the book, so I couldn't check to see if the name was Gordon's father. I decided to edge closer to the fundamental question. "Did your father ever say anything about seeing or knowing the future?"

Salespeople, con artists, and sociopaths, who may all be the same person, are excellent at determining by observation when something has struck home. I wasn't that good at it, but at my question,

Gordon's lips compressed, the skin on his cheekbones tightened, and his eyes narrowed. I could almost hear the silent groan; here it goes again. He swished the last drops of Edradour around his glass. Gordon thought he was giving me a poker face, but I could see that he was mentally working on something, then he said, "Why would you ask such a thing?"

My inquiry trapped me. I could've lied and said I was writing an article or some such, or I was studying paranormal activity, but if a lie is to be believed, it has to have some element of truth and be something the hearer wants to believe. So the lie I would have to tell would be belabored; the truth was the only way. Gordon's expression became more inscrutable as I told the tale. I could see he was struggling with himself.

"Have you told anyone your tale?" The word tale came to me with a negative connotation, and my mind flared at the thought I might be called a liar. "Yes, my wife, my parents, and a few others, including Ruth Lovat."

"Wa was the—"

I interrupted him. "Sorry, I did slip once. I told someone in Los Altos I thought their son would get sick, he did, and he died."

"And the reaction?" he said, with a bit of anger at being interrupted.

"You can imagine," I continued. "At various times, I've been treated as either devil possessed, demented, addled brain, mentally unstable or deluded, or all of those. It's been hard on my family, and the kids have been shunned, and so on. The incident in Los Altos was almost an auto de fey."

"There is no room in a narcissistic, solipsistic, naturalistic, and secular society for anything that might require belief outside of oneself or that order as we see it is not absolute. It's a road to madness. We are speeding down hell-bent." The Scottish accent was gone in a flash; the reserve, something I said, touched a nerve. He had something to say. His face glowed with passion, his voice precise. This was not a random thought; he'd had it for a long time, waiting to express it.

"I never had anything like you describe, David, but my mom and Dad argued about things he claimed to see, or when he claimed to see things before, they happened."

"Is your father..." I stumbled.

"Nay." The brogue was back. "Wa' twenty year ago, must've been, he repainted one of the bedrooms with his brains. Gordon McPhee, he was in the life we know. That's what he was, which is no more, but what he is still burns but faintly."

The image was gross, and Gordon said it without humor. I did not miss the use of the same benison Ruth Lovat used.

"He couldna' deal with what he saw, with his inability to do anything. It wasn't shotgun killed Da', it was his powerlessness."

"My condolences on your loss."

"Aye, I miss him terrible. He was a good man trapped in a cycle. Today there be drugs to treat depression, and I imagine PTSD from the war too."

I made ready to leave, feeling very unsettled.

Finally, Gordon said, "It's a strange story you tell. Be careful who you tell it to and pray you be the last one to have it. It can't make life easy."

As I said my final goodbyes and thank-yous, he thought another question. "Did you ever try to profit from it?"

"Once or twice," I replied, "but had guilt about it, and I had such terrible dreams I had to stop and make amends."

"I heard Dad say the dreams were as terrible as anything and made him feel he had no strength. His head would spin for days afterward."

With the tragedy of Gordon's father in my mind, I started to drive home more disquieted. In the old days, people who claimed to be seers were burned. Now they killed themselves with shotguns.

The California gold country and the foothills of the Sierra were in the process of being ruined by the pell-mell expansion driven by overpriced Bay Area real estate. The sun was going down, and it was right in front of me. The rays made it impossible to navigate. I pulled over and waited for the sun to set further. The golden rays silhouetted the coastal range and shimmered off the bay and San Joaquin Delta. Finally, the sun dropped far enough to let me drive.

As I approached the San Mateo bridge, San Francisco was to my right, standing clean and impossibly beautiful. At the western end of the bridge, I drove through Foster City, a place waiting to become gumbo in the next earthquake, before hitting the sclerosis known as Highway 101.

El and I were on the deck at home, and I reviewed the meeting and new information. First, I could see people's future. It was people, not cities or society in general. Second, others have had it. Third, Grandma and Ruth Lovat knew a lot more than they were comfortable telling me. Fourth, if you try to profit from it, you get punished. Lastly, in the past, it was viewed as witchcraft, and people were burned for witchcraft. The difference was that today the burning took the form of social ostracism.

We were stuck. We'd had no response from the woman in Florida. We had yet to locate the fellow in Nevada or the mysterious Breanna of Islay.

El had not been idle. She hadn't fully identified the man in Nevada but had narrowed the search to the Walker River Indian reservation. She said she was waiting for a call back from the tribe to see if Clifford W. Jones was a member.

Six weeks passed. I had not retained the inquiry top of mind when I took a call from Ramona Del Cohen. I had no idea who she was. I assumed which, of course, was an opportunity to make an ass of myself; she was soliciting the local synagogue. I put on my tough-guy act.

"I'm not a person who responds to phone solicitations, Ms. Del Cohen." I barked.

"Good, because it's Mrs., and I'm responding to your solicitation for information." The phone is a remarkable instrument. One of its most singular achievements is its ability to transmit emotion. Perhaps that's why my tough guy act doesn't work; I'm not a tough guy.

Mrs. Del Cohen was vice-chair of the Walker River Indian Tribe. I wasn't going to guess at the fascinating genealogy that created her last name. There were nine Joneses on the tribal rolls. Amazingly, none related to any of the others. Of Clifford W., there were three. I finally narrowed it down by an age guess. Given the ages of all the players in my little drama and contemporaries, I guessed Clifford would probably be over sixty. There were two. I had a funny feeling it was the first one, not due to anything said but because of tiny inflections and emphasis people add to verbal communications.

Del Cohen gave me the idea she had had some experience with the Clifford Jones I was targeting. Again, no phone number but an address on the 'Rez. It took three weeks, but we got a postcard. I was welcome to visit him any day except Sunday after 9:00 a.m., followed by a set of minimal directions.

There are places in this country that will always be remote. Walker River Reservation was five hundred miles from lonely and three hundred miles from nowhere. We had an early version of GPS, cumbersome and not precise, but it could get you close.

The Sierra Nevada poses a granite barrier to and from California. Perplexingly the Sierras is a double-crowned range, a fact which shattered the weary hopes of settlers and railroads for decades. First, the Native Americans and the mountain men found the passes through the range. Roads would eventually follow these historic routes. In the gap between the summits lies the great jewel of the Sierras, Lake Tahoe, a place preternatural in both beauty and scale. More a land-locked sea, the lake captures the eye from his first glimpse to the last view. So popular has it become that Tahoe became a noun, a verb, and an adjective. My rhapsodic description of Lake Tahoe came from my route to the Walker River, Highway 50.

After passing through the incongruity of Sacramento, the road climbs steadily until it descends into the south end of Lake Tahoe. Following the lakeshore, you pass the pornography of the casinos before surmounting the range again and dropping into Carson City. Carson City is one of those questions in Trivial Pursuit or trivia tests when asked to name state capitals. Places like Jefferson City, Montpelier, and Juneau.

I found the reservation, and the GPS got me to the road where Jones lived. There were only a few houses. They were really like small ranches. I had few choices, and those disappeared when I saw the mailbox saying Jones in bright brass letters. Standing next to it was a man seemingly waiting for me. At first glance, Clifford was about sixty-five or so, very erect, with none of the old man lean that's so often part of age. I estimated him at six feet tall, with broad shoulders bespeaking a life spent in manual labor. His hair was still dark with only a few hints of gray, and he was clean-shaven.

Clifford's skin was tanned, his eyes widespread, deep-set, and dark. He smiled shyly like he might have been ashamed of imperfect teeth.

"Nice to meet you, David. I know you like David, not Dave, just as I prefer Clifford, not Cliff." He began removing one of the awkwardness of introduction. "I hope El, Beatrice, Fergus, and the twins are in good health?"

How did he know everyone's names? El had been researching Jones and might have given her name but not the children's. Clifford might've found some information from news articles but knowing the kids' names was interesting. I almost felt déjà vu when I remembered that Ruth Lovat knew El's name.

Clifford's house was painted dull ocher with red composite shingles. There was a chimney at one end of the house and, if I counted correctly, were likely three bedrooms and one bath. There was a small tiled entrance hall exiting into the living room. The fireplace was at the north end of the room. A hallway led to the bedrooms, and across the living room was a small dining area with the kitchen to the right.

I could see the backyard through a large window lighting the dining room. It was apparent Clifford held court in the living room. To the left of the fireplace was a comfortable chair radiating the fact it was his. Behind it were bookshelves. A small rollaway table stood nearby, which could fit over the seated person. Clifford sat down and adjusted the chairback's position.

"Hurt my back working at a sawmill we used to have down the way." He lazily swung his hand in the air giving no precise direction, just an indication of away. "So have to be careful about how I sit."

I took the chair closest to him, as his voice was soft and mildly singsong as native voices can be.

My tactic with Clifford was different from the one I used with Gordon. First, I brought the book. El and I kept it in a clear case and used cotton gloves to handle it. Second, I would be open and see what happened; finally, I would really probe Clifford even to the point of being offensive. I wanted to know all I could. I was running out of leads.

There is a word for those who obsessively plan out every detail as if there is no cosmic interference: insane. Plans exist only until placed in action. More often than not, plans that come together result from getting a few things right, followed by a confluence of likely events. I should have known from the greeting my plan was trashed.

"Clifford, thanks for taking time to meet me. I appreciate it and won't waste your time," I began.

"David, I have nothing but time. I retired. In this country, retiring means I have nothing left to contribute, so helping someone is a gift to me," he replied with a hint of bitterness about his enforced status.

"Thank you for letting me intrude on your solitude then," I said, smiling.

"I'm grateful for the company. It can get very lonely when they put you out to pasture."

I took Grandma's book out of the box after putting on the gloves. I brought spares, but to my surprise, Clifford pulled a pair out of the drawer of the rollaway table next to him.

He winked at me as he did it. I had put a small piece of paper as a bookmark for his name. "As you can see, most are written in Gaelic, but there are a few names in English. Yours is one of them. Did you know my grandmother?"

He pulled a book from the shelf. "Your last name is MacIntosh, correct?" He thumbed through the M section, running his fingers down the pages, lips moving in some pattern, helping him sort the names, the same way people do when looking at a dictionary.

"No, I don't see her. There are no MacIntoshes at all in any spelling."

"Please try Gordon, MacTavish Lovat, or Campbell."

"No one by any of those names either."

"All those people are listed in her book, but none knew her. How did the names get there? Ruth Lovat, before she passed away, knew more than she was telling me. She was at Grandma's funeral, and Grandma called MacTavish her sister. Gordon was more open, but I still had the feeling I was not getting the full picture. It's like there's some deep dark secret only a few can know. It's very frustrating."

"What secret do you think they held?"

"I think there have been many people who've had the issue I'm struggling with, but no one wants to talk about."

"So there's something about you, or you have some ability that is unique and perhaps dangerous or can cause upset?"

"Maybe I should tell you my story you can get a better handle on the dilemma."

He agreed but first insisted on making tea for us. He spooned the leaves into a pot. The smell was exotic but not cloying. I commented on it.

"Get it from McLarens," he said in a voice that indicated I should know McLarens. Over tea, I held mine as I had not mastered drinking tea and simultaneously talking. I unreeled my story. He listened, not censorial but with interest. His eyes never left me, only to blink, which felt disturbing.

When I'd finished, I took a sip of tea. "So you see death, and you're upset about that?" he said with a gleam of humor in his eye, his mouth curved in a smile, completely disarming my tension.

"I don't want to make light of what you say, David." He reached over and patted my knee in reassurance. 'I have some idea how haunting it can be to know of death and be powerless to deal with it. Maybe I can ask some questions."

I've always admired those who realized and followed the Socratic method to gain knowledge. But unfortunately, in the modern world, what passes for wisdom is revealed only by a long soliloquy inviting no response.

Clifford was a skillful questioner asking probing questions in a way neither offensive nor hectoring. After questions about when the spots started, what I saw, the environment when I saw them, he moved to a usual question. "Have you ever intervened with someone you saw spots on?"

After seeing the spot, I told him I got Suzan to do a baseline physical, which found cancer and a couple of people without being specific, and what happened after my direct intervention with Henley.

"What did you expect as a response from Shamus or Henly's father or your professor?"

"I don't have a real compelling answer. I guess I expected everyone would believe me for no other reason than it with me telling them."

"Do you think people like to hear bad news or ill tidings?" he probed.

I suddenly felt stupid. Of course, people don't want to hear bad news, although the media seem to provide nothing else. In a flash, I realized the more dire, the greater the resistance.

"No, I guess not, and they will shoot the messenger once they hear it."

"Why do you feel it necessary to tell people? After all, it does no good, and the spots seem, from your description, to be fate's hand. Yet you seem to feel telling them will change fate's outcome. Kind an attribution of a godlike power yourself, isn't it?"

I was rude here. "Isn't seeing spots a godlike power?"

"Perhaps, perhaps not, but those who are godlike will see a problem and take some action within their power to alleviate the problem or at least try. Unfortunately, you apparently have no power to change the outcome, so all you do is frustrate yourself with your impotence."

We've been talking for quite a while. It had been around one o'clock when I arrived, and now the sunset was beginning to close in. As I looked out the dining room window, I had a spectacular view of the sunset. The air was incredibly clear. The day had been absent of the dust stirred up by the winds common to the high desert.

As the sun slipped down, it painted the mountains a light gold, darkening as the light failed, painting the edges of the few marshmallow clouds gold and the undersides a rosy pink.

A single ray of light blazed straight at Clifford's house through a gap in the mountains. As it crept across the yard, it lit up a stone standing in the backyard, and then it transfixed the house to another stone I had not noticed in the front yard. Instantly Ruth Lovat's warning came to mind.

Remember the stones.

As Apollo's chariot left the sky, shadows lengthened fast, the air-cooled, and Clifford excused himself to put the kettle on for more tea and start a fire. Just as the kettle boiled, his non-native wife appeared. She introduced herself as Delores. I helped her carry the bags of groceries to the kitchen. The fire was pine, and both it and the tea had powerfully pleasant odors.

Dolores excused herself. "You and Clifford have much to discuss. I'll leave you to it." She waved off my protests. "Thank you, David, but I know how it gets with Clifford. Either way, I know you won't want to drive back to Los Altos tonight, so I made a reservation for you in a hotel in Carson City under your name."

While gracious and thoughtful, this was a bit disturbing. I had never told Clifford the exact day I was coming. He had said any day but Sunday, so how did she know I was there? I had seen no evidence of a phone. She also knew this conversation would last a while.

I thanked them profusely for the kindness they accepted graciously, with none of the annoying "no problem" or "it's nothing," phrases which pass for courtesy today.

"Clifford," I began, "it was impressive to watch the sunlight on those stones in the yard. It must mean something to you that they are placed with such care."

He'd been raising his cup to drink. He stopped, peering at me over his rim, steam fogging the reading glasses he had put on.

"Those are nothing, just a garden decoration, nothing special," he said.

I felt the need to discomfort him. Despite the gracious manner, he was blowing me off. I felt the need to get in control.

"I'm sorry, Clifford, for my rudeness. That stone"—I waved in the direction of the western one—"aligns with the last beam of sunlight. The light goes through the house and hits that one." I indicated toward the eastern stone with a jerk of my thumb over my right shoulder. "And I bet if I stayed till dawn the first rays of dawn would do the same thing in reverse."

"You have a good eye, David." He was struggling with an explanation. "We natives have a reverence for the cardinal directions. The stones are there to mark them as part of our cosmology."

"You're telling me your house is inside a spirit wheel or circle?"

His face took on the guilty look of a school kid who'd been caught stealing other kids' lunches. "Yes, it is. I'm often consulted by those who seek the old wisdom, the wisdom of the Moomooanu Tusoopedakwatoona." He used words in a language I had never heard. So I assumed it was either Paiute or Shoshone.

"You're on intimate terms with the supernatural?" I was getting more formal and less precise as I tried to get the upper hand. It was like I needed to demonstrate my superiority further.

"David, for natives, there is no sacred and profane, no celestial and temporal. We have a unified cosmos a disturbance of the harmony can be and is destructive to the well-being."

I remained silent as I should have in the face of his mild rebuke.

Clifford continued, "The cardinal directions have been vital not only to Native Americans but also any people with a naturalistic, animistic metaphysics."

I now realized to my shame that I carried with me the supposed superiority of the Bay Area. I assumed he was uneducated, and I was the superior intellect and reasoning person. I was humbled at every turn of what I thought would be a meeting held on my terms. I apologized. I wasn't even sure why I was apologizing. "One of the characteristics of white people," this is the first time I'd ever thought of myself as white as he. I guess the words would be a person of color. I was shocked at my ignorance, "Is it they rush to deny or denigrate anything they don't understand? It's counterproductive and stultifying."

"Clifford, we are getting off to a bad path due to my ignorance, but I'd like to get back on track if you're still willing to talk to me," I said humbly.

"David, I will always talk with you. You aren't the first person to come here and give offense from a lack of knowledge. I don't get mad at those who are uninformed. They can't help their callowness. When I get angry, it's with those who stay ignorant intentionally."

There was my graceful way out. "I want to learn, and you've been the first to try to teach me. Let's continue please."

"David, there was a man on the reservation a hundred years ago or so named Wovoka. Have you ever heard of him?"

I shook my head.

"Of the ghost dance religion?" said Clifford. "White people called him Jack Wilson, but his birth name was Quotze Ow. Wovoka means woodcutter in our tongue."

"I read a little about the Battle of Wounded Knee, which had to do with the ghost dance."

"It wasn't a battle but a slaughter. Field artillery and repeating rifles against a bunch of frozen Lakota." His voice took on the hard edge of someone reliving great injustice, "But the winners write history, and no winner wants to be remembered for a massacre. Losers have to live with that history."

"Wovoka had great power, the faux Indians would say big medicine, but he wasn't a witch. He saw the future. He also could change matter and predict; some say he could change the weather. He saw a new way for Indians to live with the whites by forging the old ways with the new."

Do you think it worked?" It was an obvious question. The reservation was not emitting an aura of prosperity or success as most would define it.

"No," he said, "it didn't. Perhaps it needed to spread more or to have better teachers. It's interesting. It came at the end of the century and could almost be called a millennialist movement."

"You believe Wovoka had." I was stumbling. I didn't want the word supernatural, it seemed wrong, but I wasn't spinning out new words.

"Special powers?" he asked.

I shrugged my shoulders in agreement or at least acceptance.

"Yes, he had special powers and insights, but not because he himself was unique; he had them because he was listening to the Moomooanu Tusoopedakwatoona, the wisdom of the elders, that formed his, our world.

"In the Christian world, he'd be classed with the mystics like St. Teresa of Avila," I said.

"I'm impressed. You don't strike me as a person who deals in mysticism."

"I don't. My world is software and systems. Not a lot of mystery. However, in everyday life, most people don't have time or the inclination to deal with mysticism. That paints them as weird."

"I think you found out about that perception recently," he said, smiling.

I nodded in agreement.

"What Wovoka did was to preach because he had no choice, the spirits directed his actions, he could do nothing else without incurring wrath. As you Christians define it, free will has little meaning or utility with us. We are more fatalistic."

"It's hard for me to accept that something in my life is fated out of my control. But like many people of my generation, I was brought up to believe I can accomplish anything, I controlled everything, I had a destiny, so fatalism is sort of anathema.

"That's one of the major sources of contention, past and present, between Indians and Europeans," Clifford added.

"I still find myself wondering about the moral and ethical aspects of the spots. Do I have a moral duty to tell people even if they don't believe me and the knowledge will not change the outcome?"

Clifford was quite a teacher and had spent a long time thinking about morals and ethical systems. He swished his tea around his cup.

He looked up. "David, a moral decision is based on an evaluation of right and wrong, good or evil. Defining a moral decision requires two things in decline today, a willingness to judge and second, an ability to discriminate one from the other. Your decision must be based on a code of belief to avoid driving you nuts. It must be integrated."

"I don't mean to be rude, but it's getting late. I'm frankly tired; this has been hard work," Clifford continued, "and I've given you all the insight it can for one day. So feel free to see me again. I enjoyed our talk. You have an unusual problem, and you will be closer to me when you move to your house in Lake Tahoe."

"What place in Lake Tahoe?" I asked, puzzled.

"The one you're going to buy on the way home," he said, eyes twinkling.

I drove away, reflecting on the conversation on my formulation between fatalism, free will, and destiny and how I had gotten this power. The hotel they reserved was right on the road to Carson City and easy to find. Strangely enough, the manager was Clifford Jones.

As I walked to my room, I passed a well-dressed man and a woman who had working girl written all over. Major breast enlargement, tight short dress with a plunging neckline. As she passed me, I noticed that she had a large black spot across her genitals.

Who dies of venereal disease these days? I thought.

Was I getting jaded? That was an unkind thought and dismissive of her coming suffering. Yes, she engaged in an illegal profession, and to many an immoral one to boot, but did she deserve my censorship, my lack of empathy?

I was assuming again. I'd seen no indication on the man, so perhaps either he got treatment, or maybe it wasn't venereal disease at all. I knew I needed not to complicate my already confused brain with more quandaries or judgment calls on who deserved a spot and who, in my opinion, didn't. I called El to let her know I would be back the next day, and I tried to sleep. I didn't. Pitch and toss all night as I ran my mental recordings of the meeting. Was I ever to make peace with my gift, or was I to end like Gavin's father? Driven to insanity?

A minister would have told me I need to have faith, and from faith would come revelation showing me how to understand the meaning of the spots. To have faith is the hardest of all things. It's easy to have faith when all of life is bright and sunlit with promise and the ripening fruits of human endeavor. It is easy to have faith and talk of character, morals, ethics, and value judgments when the results cost you nothing. Instead, I found my faith challenged once again as I realized the spots were something inexplicable in human terms and in terms of our definition of what was real.

Like insincere evidence of character, faith is a fragile edifice built by people with no stress. Then like the biblical house built on sand, it falls in the first storm of adversity.

The following day, blurry from lack of sleep, unshaven and rumpled, I drove down from the mountains. I had forgotten about Clifford's comment. When I reached South Lake Tahoe, I decided to drive up the western shore and take I80 back to the Bay Area. It was just a whim, some sort of rebellion against the conventional—or was it?

I made a turn, and there before me was a bay off the lake where the water was green or appeared to be. A few houses dotted the shore, but my eyes were drawn to one. It stood separate, higher on the slope; the road took me above it. I could see a green metal roof, useful in a heavy snow environment, decks on three sides, log construction, and it appeared pristine. I thought I saw a road down to the shore, but it turned out to be a driveway to the object of my wonder. I stopped and stared and started to turn around. A man appeared from the side pushing a wheelbarrow. He waved, signaling me to stop.

"Are you looking for directions?" he asked, his voice betraying long years of smoking. He had a bluish cast to his lips, his breathing was labored, and he seemed thankful I provided him a chance to take a break.

"I was driving up the road saw your house and the bay and thought this road would take me down to the shore."

"No way to do that. All these drives are down to the houses."

"You have a beautiful place here. It takes your breath away," I said.

Thanks, I'll be sorry to leave, but I'm in no shape to keep it up; the winters are brutal. No, I need sunshine and warmth for the time I have left."

"You're selling?"

"Yeah, just haven't listed it yet. I hate realtors. It's such a hassle with all forms and stuff. You interested in buying?" he said a twinkle in his eye and a note of pleading to save him from the rack of realtors.

"I hadn't thought about it. I live in Los Altos, so this would be a summer place."

"Most of the other houses are summer places and rentals. Only a few are full-timers. If you feel like it, take a look around."

I parked, and we introduced ourselves. He was Tom Denglise. He and his late wife had owned the place for forty years. He took me on tour. It was slow; going up and down stairs left him gasping. He was really sick. The place was fabulous. The windows facing the lake were floor-to-ceiling, as he explained special ordered to keep out the cold. All the principal rooms faced the lake and were arranged in an open plan. The place just flowed, and it felt like a family needed to be there.

The finish details were impressive. Floors of polished hardwood, French doors leading to the 270° decks, stairs from the deck down to a boat dock. Huge kitchen, which El would love, an enormous master suite with fireplace, massive stone hearth in the living room, a den with yet another fireplace, and a Murphy bed. The final straw was four more bedrooms; each kid would have their own room.

I fulfilled Clifford's prophecy. I bought the place on the spot, cash, wrote a check, big one, in earnest money, and promised to stop in South Lake Tahoe and engage an escrow firm to handle the sale. We shook hands, and I knew Tom would not deceive me. He gave me some pictures to take home.

I reversed my whim to drive the entire lakeshore and stopped in South Lake Tahoe, getting the process underway. I debated whether I should tell El then or when I got home. I elected to wait. I wasn't sure of her reaction and thought it would help if she saw the pictures. Also, I hoped the kids would gang up on her. It wouldn't have been me if I didn't have some misgivings. I worried if I were taking advantage of Tom, he would probably get more money if he chose to go with a realtor-sponsored sale. I was once again second-guessing myself.

I didn't need tricks with El/ She always sensed my attitude and feelings. She was so integral to my life and thought that I could not conceive how I existed before. She didn't second guess. She questioned, but only for information, never for condemnation. We argued no two people living intimately can avoid it. Our credo was never arguing in bed, drunk, or tired. Never go to sleep without telling the other person you loved them and praying thanks for loving each other every day.

When she saw the pictures, her response was the essence of El. "Hope you bought the place!"

The kids were over the moon. They could now stick their noses in the air and say, "We're going to our place in Tahoe this weekend."

The solution to a problem changes the problem. Since I had a dock, I had to have a boat, actually two, one sail and one power. There was furniture. Tom left a lot, but the kitchen needed refitting, and the kid's rooms needed customization.

The joy and excitement of a new house pushed away my desire to guest for further information. I had a wonderful family, a one in a million wife, four healthy kids, houses, cars, wealth, and admiration. Of course, the snake of unhappiness had not slithered far and now decided to ruin my happiness.

El and I worked hard on our marriage for different reasons. I worked because I was convinced I would never find anyone else. I loved Suzan to distraction, but she had died. I was lucky enough and bold enough to love El because nothing other than boldness would've gotten her. I was not going to have the marriage end because of a lack of effort. El worked at it because it was her very essence. She loved, simply, but totally without reserve. The person who earned her love was paraphrasing The Bard quadruple, blessed, first physically, second emotionally, third by the support, and fourth because she made you want to be a better person. Not a person with more money, a bigger house, nicer car, no it was in the things that mattered. In many ways, she was like Mom, and I was kind of like Dad.

Anton and Samantha, Mom's parents full of years and accomplishments, passed within days of each other. Mom was bereft, and

I think she had to take her mortality into account for the first time. One day she asked me if I ever saw the spots on the family.

"I saw one on Suzan, another on Jean's father, but no one closer. I don't want too either. The thought gives me the willies. No, Mom, I don't see one on you or Dad." I was, of course, lying.

A depressed person cannot hear the logic or appreciate the reassurances extended to them. Sometimes we can see what we want to see or what not to see. I had pushed out of my active mind the spots I had seen on them her question opened a whole new era of depression. I tried to console myself, and it didn't work. I started a long descent into the dark place in my soul where no light penetrates.

The skinny hand of depression pulls levers of isolation, catastrophe, self-pity, pathos, anger, and defeat. It spreads its ugly hands wide to draw in your loved ones. It eats at your brain, releasing all the demons buried deep inside to romp and dance. The monsters attack and overpower the good things you've done, leaving only a dirty taste for your life and accomplishments.

Depression's voice whispers the great lie of worthlessness.

I fell downward with no arresting my fall. I withdrew, failed to leave the house for days, and would not answer the phone. I had no drive or curiosity but plenty of anger. I started to fear and hate myself for the knowledge I had. To see death is surely no blessing. Once again, I painted myself as a victim, which only made things worse.

I've been depressed before, but nothing like this. I'm unsure if it was because the subjects were my parents or just seeing death constantly had worn down my resistance to the invasion of negative thoughts. I understood why Gordon's father killed himself. As I recovered, I realized the spiral started with three actions. First, Mom had asked. She didn't want to know if she and Dad would die; she wanted to know if they would die of natural causes or some other vector. Second, I lied. Third, I didn't give her the full details.

It seemed whatever force controlled this thing seemed to change the rules. This was the first time I had seen spots on anyone close to me other than Suzan. My lying was a factor in my depression. It's hard to live a lie. Mom had asked, I lied, and now I was in depression. My summation was if asked, and I had to tell. If I didn't tell, I would be racked with depression. Now family, spouse, and children would not be spared. The pressure of seeing the spots was increasing.

In my intellectual wanderings, I began to wonder if my success in attainments in life were a condemned man's last meal. Had I been given a taste of the good life early, so I would see them taken away later? My greatest fear was if the spots would make increasing behavioral demands on me, would the rules and punishments get stronger over time until the only relief would be death. I wondered about my relationship with El and the kids. We were a close family because we did not lie to each other or keep secrets, except in extreme cases and not for long.

Human relationships can endure almost anything except falsity. Lies and secrets impose costs. They are two of the levers depression pulls to destroy peace of mind. Truth is never easy. It takes a strong character to be truthful. That's why it's so often not part of people's lives. Lying seems easy. It's harder to lie, and lying does no one any good, especially the liar. The truth is its own virtue, lying is a web of further lies, and deceit is never a virtue. Lying is an exercise in pain. I had come to realize that most of the terrible thing people do is the result of unrelieved pain.

I had seen spots on Mom and Dad. How long before I started to see them on El and the kids? I wasn't sure I could handle knowing, and it appeared as if not telling them was no longer an option. To not tell condemned me to horrible dreams and deep depression. Then the image of the sword of Damocles appeared. I did know if I saw them, I had to tell them. The spots still seemed to have given me a pass on my conjugal family. Or had they? Now I began to understand Ruth, Gordon, Clifford's, and my grandmother's reticence to tell me anything. They thought they were sparing me or that I needed to discover the edges of this by myself.

That first year we owned the Tahoe place, we used it sparingly. On the following year, we decided to spend the summer there. It was a great time generally, and Mom and Dad came up. Dad was moving slowly because of what he called a minor breathing issue. I knew the truth. My sister, Eleanor, came out, as did Peter, who struggled with his demons from Army service. We took long hikes, swam, ran the propeller off the boat, wore out the sailboat's sails. We camped out under the stars. The kids didn't seem to miss Los Altos, although Beatrice and Fionna were constantly fighting over the phone.

One day we were on an all-day jaunt in the mountains around Heavenly Valley ski complex. We had been hiking for three or four hours and stopped to take a lunch break. We were in a beautiful high alpine meadow strewn with gigantic boulders. The ground was covered with lupine, mallow, and other plants I couldn't identify. A few small evergreens tenuously held onto life in the small dirt-filled crevices of the rocks. The meadow was dotted with stone rings marking the places past hikers had made fires. There was also the foundation of an old shepherd's hut.

The view was spectacular, Tahoe blue and huge gleamed in its majesty. Yet only a few hundred feet above, Freel Peak and Job and Job's Sister and Monument Peak still wore shawls of white. Under the copses of pines, the ground was soft, littered with pine needles. As we stopped, we saw another family group nearby.

The other couple had five children with them, all younger than ours. Three were theirs, the other two friends. The adults were as Irish as I was Scottish. He was Liam, she, Asieling. Their children were Patrick, John, and Mary. The other two kids were Hector and Helene.

El and Asieling soon found a common interest. Soon they were chatting away as they set up the picnic. The kids had been complaining noisily of being tired, suddenly found reserves of energy, and raced around jumping off rocks, playing tag, and hide-and-seek. Liam and I talked briefly, and in a man's way, communicated all we needed to know about each other in a few sentences.

I couldn't have engaged them more fully. I was distracted. As I looked, each appeared in duplicate. Next to each, dressed exactly like them, moving with them, except the copy was covered in a shroud. At first, it was gray, then it darkened. On the youngest boy, the darkening was the slowest. This was a whole new method of manifestation. I know Liam thought I was an idiot or a pervert because of how I was staring. El came over and told me I was rude. I tore my gaze away.

I think El knew that something critical was going on with me, but there was no way to have the discussion. If I made a guess, it would have been that death was coming soon, it would not be instant death, and the youngest boy would be the last to die.

I was in a quandary. One of the lessons about the spots I think I was supposed to follow was that if I knew I had to tell, otherwise I would be tortured by dreams or demons. My warning could potentially save their lives, but only if they took my advice, and then again, maybe I was wrong. Even after all my experience, I still had the vain hope that the spots would not dictate fate this time. I didn't know how to tell them so they would believe me. There could be no expectation that they would instantly believe a crazy story by a relative stranger and act correctly. What should I do?

I excused myself, saying I had to go the bathroom. I walked far enough away to be out of sight and leaned against a tree heedless of the sap sticking to my shirt. Finally, I slumped to the ground. My conscience was screaming, *Tell them!*

Then the voice of caution demanded attention, telling me, *Remember Henley? You can do no good.* The third voice, clinical, constant in tenor and volume, saying, *This is another chance to learn the dimensions of the condition.* The voice of caution and cynicism said, *You owe them nothing. How do you know? They could be child molesters and deserve to die? You don't need to get involved.*

Then yet another voice found expression with a quandary as old as time or at least *Star Trek.* If I save their lives, how does it change the course of history, or does it?

These and other thoughts rippled around my brain. I had a good deal of self-hatred because I knew the event was coming but try as I might, I just could not get by the idea I was causing it. I was running up against one of my male characteristics. Was I not in control, or was I? I seemed to have no control over the appearance of the spots. This appearance showed me that I didn't have control. I didn't know these people. I knew nothing about them, and they nothing about me, yet here were the spots.

I wasn't in control. Much as I hated the spots, only isolation of the most severe kind would prevent me from seeing them. People's lives were what they were. I had no control over anyone. I could cajole, advise, try to avoid things, but it was madness to think I could control anyone after they had been emancipated.

Fergus came looking for me. "Dad, Mom's worried about you and says we need to get going to finish the hike. Besides, that Patrick kid is a pain in the ass."

"Okay, thanks for coming look for me. I guess I was lost in my thoughts." We walked back to the families.

"Liam, which way are you going from here?" I asked.

"We are planning to be out four or five days, so we're headed east, over the pass, then down to Heavenly Creek before we start back. Why?"

"It looks like a big storm brewing west and south. We've hiked here before and know how vicious those storms can be."

"Thanks for the concern, but we're experienced hikers and have all the storm equipment and clothing. I think it exciting to camp out during a mountain storm."

We exchanged good wishes, handshakes, and hugs.

El knew something was wrong. She always did. "David, what's wrong?"

"Nothing," I replied in a clipped, no-nonsense tone for which I was instantly sorry. I set a blistering pace; everyone was straining at the eight thousand-foot elevation. The kids asked me for breaks to slow down, but I was unrelenting. I needed to burn out my anger, fear, frustration, and powerlessness, but I made them pay for something they couldn't understand because I had not shared the root of my anger.

It might've been exhausting for them, but my anger was increasing, and finally, I had exhausted my breath, my muscles, and my conscious thoughts, so what remained was anger and stress.

Then the twins cracked. They were the youngest with the shortest legs, they virtually had to run to keep up, and they rebelled and sat down on a rock. Seeing this, everyone else stopped. I went on for fifty yards before I realized they weren't there.

"Get up!" I commanded. "We're almost at the car, you weenies."

"Dad, we're really tired. You have longer legs, and you been pushing us hard. We need to rest a bit."

"You have the rest of your life to rest, toughen up, and get moving. Now!" I bellowed like a demented drill sergeant.

"Honey," began El, "they're children, you've been storming around like we have the devil on our tails. Lighten up."

They were right. To some extent, there was a devil after us—the devil of the spots. I just knew something in the mountains would kill Liam, Asieling, and their family. I didn't want to be around when it did.

"We need to get going. There's a storm coming, and we don't want to get stuck up here. The car is only a mile away, over that ridge." I was still speaking in a command style of language, brooking no arguments.

"Yeah, but we have to go through the valley of death to get there," said Beatrice, "there are a lot of hills and valleys to cover." She was right. There was a steep decline and an equally steep rise to the ridge, and another down ramp, even more experienced hikers gathered strength before tackling it.

"You go ahead. I'll catch up," said Fergus.

"We all go together; you know the rules," I replied.

"You and Mom can go. Beatrice and I will take care of the twins. They're totally whipped," he said.

I looked at them. Fergus was right; they sat there bedraggled, sweaty, almost asleep from exhaustion. The family was rebelling. Instead of trying to work it out or failing that be honest, I used a masculine technique. I yelled more. I harangued them for their weakness, staying up late, and eating habits. I told them I was ashamed of them for their weakness. Then I moved apart to stand alone like I was some rock of strength betrayed by those I lead. It was a shocking display of ill-temper, arrogance, lack of care, and general assholeness.

I didn't want to tell them the truth because they would want to go back and help Liam. I didn't want them around whenever what was fated happened.

I treated my children as pawns in a big game, putting them at risk by exhausting them and El while we still had a dangerous country to cover. I was running from my own devil and making them pay for it. I had never treated them this way. Like all parents, I had had to yell at them, the kids, not El. Yelling at El was dangerous. However, this was different. For them, there was no apparent reason for my behavior, and I was unwilling to listen to reason. I was a dictator. I stood off to the side for what seemed a long time. It was long enough for the sweat to dry, chilling me and for my legs to tighten up. Tiredness began to rise from my feet toward my head. I finally sat down on a rock.

"Honey, what's wrong?" asked El as she put her hand on my shoulder. If you're trying to scare us, you succeeded. The kids have never seen you act like this, and they're afraid."

I shook my shoulder and said nothing. El stood by me for a few minutes, unsure what to do. I ignored her. Then she walked over and sat down with the kids.

A family divided. It was metaphorical but reflected the actual event. Everything I did was increasingly driven by the spots, their effects, the possibility they would appear, my desire to avoid them, my quest to understand. The rest of the family had no such issues.

We had told them about the spots, we had to in the wake of the incident, but they could only have a glimmer of the impact this curse had on me. I was convinced that at this point, God was punishing me, I was immoral, and I was violating more of society by not telling everyone.

My feeling of being cursed was counterweighted by my fear of humiliation, being made fun of, not being believed, rejection, and isolation. I was subjected to constant tension rooted in fear with no release, at least not a healthy release. I hated myself. I had suicidal ideation more frequently. I had an understanding wife, to be sure, but I was trying to be a rock of stability and afraid of being seen weak, so I hadn't shared the latest twist of my haunted psyche with her.

I was driving a wedge in our marriage. After I sat for a while, I got up. I was gonna move them. As I did, I stumbled, my cramped muscles refusing to move, my stiff ankles refused their duty, and down I went. The kids laughed, and that humiliation set me off.

"Get the fuck on your feet and on the trail now, lazy asses!"

No movement.

"Did you hear me? Get up, you lazy assholes, get on the fucking trail now, or so help me. I'll go on without your lazy asses, and you can find your own way home, goddammit!" I was yelling like I was trying to be heard in a windstorm.

Beatrice, El, and Fergus looked at each other in wonder, and the twins started to cry. I shouldered my pack.

Eight thousand feet of elevation, steep inclines, descents, rocks, and tree roots can make any degree of anger fade in the welcoming arms of exhaustion. I stormed down the grade and up the far side before it hit.

The family was dots far behind when the tiredness took over. The combination of a rock sticking out of the trail, a declivity to one side, and a tree root reached out and caught me. I stumbled, my pack changing my center gravity, and I went down hard. I let out a scream that echoed and redounded off the rocks as a witness to my angry foolishness. Then in the grip of total exhaustion, frustration, and anger, I could do nothing but lay there pounding on the insentient ground as the pain in my leg, knee, and ankle screamed.

I lay there long enough for the family to catch up. As he passed, Fergus said, "Sic temper tyranus."

El gave him a withering look of reproach for using the same words Booth used after killing Lincoln. But he was beyond caring, and he was administering punishment. El threw Beatrice the keys to the car and told them to go, then she sat down with me.

"Well, you managed to scare the hell out of us. Now you've sprawled in the dirt, screaming like a madman. After your performance, you're lucky we even stopped. You have acted weirdly before, but this is the first time you've ever been an asshole." Coming from El, this was a severe rebuke.

I sat up. "El, I really don't need this now," I said dismissively.

She reached over and pushed me back down.

"Nonetheless, you're going to get it. The kids think you're a raving maniac. You violated two of the basic rules of the family, and hiking, going off alone, and doing anything in anger." She was right, of course. "Now you have fallen and hurt yourself."

I was on my back, my upper body elevated by my arms. I looked down, and my lower leg was bleeding from a long gash, my ankle hurt like hell, and swelling, making my boot too tight.

She ministered to me in her usual quiet, competent way, no longer criticizing, but her anger was expressed in extra pushes or shoves of my damaged leg. With her help, I got up and sat on a rock with her.

"Okay, David, what's happened?"

"El, the spots are changing again and getting more definitive," I explained about the avatars mimicking Liam and Aishling's family, how they were covered in shrouds which started as gray but then got darker, of how the one on Hector's body was the last to turn dark. A vision of an ill-defined creature had appeared in my mind, its features askew and flattened screaming at me, then it was gone. I told her I knew that Aisling and Liam and the children would die on the hike they were on.

"That's why after you had walked off and returned. You tried to convince him a storm was coming, and they shouldn't go east."

"Yeah, and I know I can't stop what's going to happen. At least my warnings have never had an effect before, but I had to try," I replied. I sat with my head in my hands, crying from physical pain and frustration and my stupidity in punishing my own family.

The winds were rising as the storm I predicted approached. Clouds were scudding like old-time sailing ships across the incredibly blue sky. The mountains were moaning, and the words of "They Call the Wind Mariah" was playing out. Folks were out there dying. El held me as I sobbed and tried not to cry. I was racked with grief, self-loathing, and filled up with emotion.

The dam I erected to hold the tumult was overtopped, and it all came pouring out. Eventually, it passed, I cried myself out. My foot and ankle still hurt. The gash on my leg was crusted with dried blood. El got me on my feet, and we limped the rest of the way.

"The kids will know I was crying," I said.

"That's what you're worried about? Crying? You scared them half to death, and you worry about them knowing you cried! You're the limit. You really are. You should be worrying about how you're going to tell them what happened. This has gone too far. You can't ignore it."

She was right.

We got to the car just as the first drops of rain plopped into the dust. Petrichor filled our nostrils. Beatrice was behind the wheel, Fergus was shotgun reading a book, the twins were in the very back asleep. El and I climbed in the middle, Beatrice looked at her mother for permission, then started the car, and we drove off. It took us an hour to get home, and as we drove in, Mom and Dad's car were there.

Oh joy, I thought.

Now I had to explain to them as well as my family about the spots. I tensed, and El could feel it.

"It will be okay," she said softly in my ear, which looked like a kiss to which the twins reacted with "oh gross!" My foot and ankle hurt like the devil. The one drawback of the house was lots of stairs, which were agony.

Fergus stayed outside to clean out the car, Beatrice unloaded and put away the gear, and the newly energized twins went off to do whatever they did. El and I greeted my parents, and I headed for the shower. Tom apparently had had a disabled wife because showers had rails and seats. I crawled in and sat down. My foot and ankle were the size of a football, black and blue from the toes to the bottom of the calf.

The shower refreshed me, giving me a chance to relax, but the tension was still there as I contemplated how to explain my actions. I got out and stumbled into the living area. Mom had made a light dinner. El was showering, Beatrice on the phone, Fergus and Dad were arguing cordially about Moby Dick and its portrayal of insanity. I felt Fergus was questioning my sanity and using Ahab as a proxy. I was that sensitive. I could hear the twins outside trying to coax a raccoon family down to the deck.

CHAPTER 15

I sat there in a beautiful setting, glistening lake out the windows, fire in the hearth, the family, gathered around; I should have been happy. My foot, ankle, and knees hurt terribly despite scotch, ice, and aspirin. I was miserable. I had just acted terribly to my family, more ogre than father. I'd let my distress color my relationships in the process contributed to their alienation from me.

I was sitting there, looking at my father, who was aging rapidly. You have to get older, but you don't have to age. He was aging.

My mother, who none of us thought would ever slow down, was missing the spring in her step. She moved more slowly and deliberately as if she was thinking her way through every action. She would stop at times and just stare, then proceed. It was as if she was gasping for some spark to drive her on. If I had to guess, I would have said she was in the early stages of Parkinson's or Alzheimer's.

Everyone came in for dinner. I was served where I sat. I took that as a mark of exile. As I sat there, I was watched by six pairs of eyes, all bright and shiny with anticipation and hope from the family of raccoons we now owned.

The storm I predicted roared through the mountains that night. My ankle was no better the next day, and I went to the ER, only to find out it was broken and would likely require surgery. I guess that was just punishment for my sins. The family was glued to the TV when I got home, and I didn't need a newscast to know why.

A search was underway for a party of hikers. A friend of one of the kids had received a cell phone call, but there was no voice, but the person could be heard crying. There were pictures of Liam, Asieling, and the children and a number to call with information.

I called and reported we had seen the hikers the day before.

The police came to the house. I showed them on a map where we had seen Liam and his family and where they were heading. One of the officers asked, "Did they seem okay when you last saw them?" I got concerned the investigation would make the connection between me and the incident and dredge up all the issues. Fergus volunteered to go with the search crew.

Several days later, the searchers found them. They apparently sheltered under a rock overhang. The storm loosened the rocks, and a slide trapped them all. A cellphone was found. The last number called was to the friend who had heard crying. The youngest boy, who had had the flickering, lighter shroud, was found about fifty feet down the slide face. The coroner confirmed he had survived the initial slide but died of injuries and exposure.

They all turned to me. Dad figured it out, El already knew, Mom seemed clueless, Beatrice and Fergus were bright enough to connect the dots, and the twins were blessedly ignorant. I had to tell them, and I did. I didn't know where to start, so I did it from the beginning. I watched the story unfold. There was disbelief, then anger.

"Here we go again. I can't have a normal life with a normal father. I have to have a man who can see death! You knew they were going to die, and you did nothing! You ran away. That's why you pushed us so hard on the trail. You were running away from their death!" screamed Beatrice.

"Dad, those kids all died. I didn't like them, but they're dead, and you knew. You knew and could have tried to stop them, to warn them, but you didn't do anything," said Fergus.

"I did warn Liam, and I tried to get him not to continue their hike, but he didn't listen."

"Oh, bullshit!" yelled Beatrice. "You should have stopped them!"

"And how was your father going to do that? Tackle them, tie them up, beat them insensible, and drag them back to the car? He tried to warn them," said El.

"I don't know, but you should have done more than warn them." Beatrice's argument was shredded by El's logic, but logic loses in the face of emotion.

"I warned Eric, Janelle, and Henly, and looked at what happened," I said. "Remember, I don't know time, place, or method, just that it will happen," I continued. "You beat me up when I warned them as being a nutjob because of the reaction, and now you are beating me up because I didn't do more? I can't win. Maybe you do need a new father." I was exhausted, hurting, and under pressure from my family, so I started to burn the earth.

"I least I could have friends and not have to worry my dad is going to pronounce them dead every time I bring them home. It would be nice to have a normal family."

I was stung and walked or hobbled out of the living room onto one of the decks and then thought better of it and retreated to the bedroom, where I sat in darkness, in the agony of self-pity and hatred. Not for the first time, suicide raced through my head with all its lies of peace.

In hedonistic California, stories like this have a short shelf life unless the victims have some unique hook that will interest the ravening hordes like the daughter being pregnant by her abusive father or one of the kids being gay in the closet and fearing to come out or such. This one seemed to have no hook. Then someone found it.

It came up on an investigative show. The reporter identified me as the person who had seen the deceased last, and I was the same person immolated in the incident, and it started again, the recurring nightmare. The old stories were unearthed, comments made, and judgment passed. Luckily, California was even more self-centered than it had been at the original incident, and the story passed the system with the trouble and pain of a kidney stone.

Time passed, and things calmed a bit, but Beatrice always seemed to have bubbling away under her skin a good deal of anger about my ability. The incident in the mountains did renew my desire to find out all I could about my curse. After the surgery on my ankle, I had plenty of time to read and study. The book Grandma had given me had a chapter devoted to "the sight."

One weekend, when Dad and Mom were over, Dad took me aside.

"David," Dad began, "when you first told us about this, I didn't know what to do. As you remember, we sent you the doctors trying to eliminate all the physical problems, and there were none, so I let it drop.

"Over the years, I tended to think it was merely coincidental that you seem to know these things, but as they continued, I realized there was something really going on here. I started doing some research, and it turns out there's a long history of people being able to see death. I decided not to tell you what I found out of fear it would increase your turmoil. The endings of these stories for the person who sees death are not positive. There are a series of Scottish legends about Highlanders who could see death. I've known about this for some time. I suspect your grandmother also did. We probably were wrong not to tell you."

"I know that Ruth Lovat knew also, and Gordon, his father, had it," I replied. "I think Clifford knew it too and perhaps had the sight also. What still confuses me is how all of them connected. I'm not sure I can take much more of this. It's ruining the family, stressing me out, and I just can't continue."

"David," Mom spoke, "I'm your mother, and you are a lousy liar. I can tell you are lying from a million miles away." The mom I knew was back in her straightforward way. "I asked you if you saw spots on family, and you lied. You don't think I see what's going on with your father and realize I have some disease of the mind?"

El was now in the room. She and I looked at each other, and Mom continued, "You saw spots on us, but I bet this is the first time they appeared on close family members, right?" She nailed it is always.

"Yeah, Mom, you both have spots. You both have something wrong, which will be fatal. I didn't want to admit that you won't always be here. Telling people doesn't seem to do any good, so why tell? Do you want to know?" I looked around, my eyes fierce, and I was on the attack.

"Does anyone really want to know?"

"I would," Mom replied. "It would help me plan and help me make plans for the future. To me, it's the right thing to do." She looked around at all of us. "You can speak for yourself, Joseph."

"I've never given a lot of thought, to be honest," said Dad. "On one hand, it would help with financial matters to know when one was going to die. On the other, it would change how people lived their lives, therefore, what contributions they would make to the world."

"What the world needs are fewer two-handed intellectuals, so they can't say on the other hand!" fired Mom, paraphrasing Harry Truman.

Sometimes answers or clues appear just when you need them. One now appeared. It was a note; actually, a postcard marked Port Askaig, Scotland, UK. It was written in a beautiful copperplate script with the message, "When you're next in Scotland, please visit me," signed Breanna McLeod Campbell.

I guess we were going to Scotland but not just yet. Until my leg healed, I wasn't going anywhere very fast. In the meantime, we had to deal with tropical storm Beatrice and hurricane Fergus. I loved my kids, but I sometimes wanted to strangle them in their sleep. Beatrice had always been the most impressionable and volatile of the four, which is why she's a good actress. She was more profound than her surface emotions, but she always seemed to be playing a role.

Her feelings were never very far away, and they could be very intense, and when Beatrice sang, the emotions of the music found an incredible instrument in her. She lived the music.

We had a habit of having family meetings when big decisions arose. We had one now. We talked about the spots and my inability to affect the outcome. Beatrice sat next to El, arms tightly folded across her chest in that classic defensive posture.

"You've had this since you were thirteen, and you did nothing?"

"Yes, but when it first started, I was young. I really didn't know what to do. When I told the pregnant lady, the reaction from her husband scared me to silence. This is not an easy thing to bear, honey."

"So no, then," she snapped.

"I didn't try to intervene until the Henley incident," I replied.

"So you let these people you saw die when you could've saved them!" She's wound up now. "You're nothing better than a murderer." She shouted with violence and passion of youth, untempered by wisdom or experience.

"Honey," I said, trying to put oil on a raging sea, "it's not that simple. I tried to get Liam not to go the way they were headed, but he wouldn't listen. I tried to tell others, and I was laughed at or made fun of. In no case did my warnings change what happened. I don't think I can change the outcome. I'm no more a murderer than a guy who watches an airplane crash."

"But you know you should have tried harder, the same with Henley!" she screamed at me in full anger mode. Now tears streamed down her face, nose running.

"You're so smart. You could have convinced them you didn't try. All you did was yell and shout at us." She was on her feet now. "You killed Henley. I loved him, and you killed those people on the mountain just as if you shot them. I don't want to be around here anymore."

I shouldn't have let her get to me, but I was sensitive, very intolerant, and conflicted. I was angry at Beatrice for being such an idiot. I wanted to match her anger with my own. Anger returned is never equal; it's escalating and leads to terrible results. Better anger is met with silence than more anger.

Violating one of the rules of family meetings, she started to leave. "Beatrice, you know the rules no one walks out of a family meeting. Get back here."

"I don't meet with killers." I felt El's nails bite into my arm.

Fergus was a different matter. He didn't rage and scream; he was a thinker. He concluded that I was on shaky moral grounds. His formula was based on the premise that I had had options as to my actions in every case, and I could have told them or tried to stop the people with the spots or done nothing, a choice. That choice, according to Fergus, was mine to make. I had free will and could make choices. Since I had options, I had a moral responsibility, and I acted immorally, not trying to help the other person avoid death.

The damage I caused hung on. Beatrice stayed mad for a long time, she withdrew from any activity where I was involved, and all her answers were short and sarcastic.

El, as always, encouraged me to give her space and time, "She's eighteen, has lost her first love, and she's your daughter."

"I think you were there at the birth. She's a lot like you too."

"You've been a bear since the incident with Liam and Aisling. It's reflecting on her, and she's mirroring your distress."

"You're failing in your wifely duties. You're not making me feel better," I replied with a smile.

"I have a feeling you aren't going to feel better, sweetie. You're going to have ups and downs on this. You can't avoid it unless you become a monk or a hermit."

Summer never really ends in California; it just changes shape. School started, and we had college applications in SAT and pre-SATs to do. I got a major consulting contract with Lockheed. Eleanor's husband passed away, and she entered an order of nuns, fulfilling Suzan's insight. Her order was the Sisters of the Sacred Heart of Jesus (RSCJ). We all went to St. Louis for her final vows.

It was the first time in many years the whole family was together. Uncle Fergus had passed away, a significant loss, but the funeral had been legendary. Dad's two sisters, Mary Stuart MacIntosh and Flora, came with their husbands, and even a couple of their adult children showed up.

Mom and Dad made the trip, although Dad was on oxygen. My younger sister, Daphne, and her family were there but not her husband, and most surprisingly, my brother, Peter. Peter had enlisted in the Army right after high school to the dismay of Mom and Dad. He served in Korea and Europe and was part of the Grenada and Panama operations. In the process, his young, unformed mind became institutionalized.

He formed opinions about everything, but he had no experience outside the Army. He'd become one-dimensional. I was concerned for him since he was now twenty years into the service and had no idea what he could do on the other side.

He made his maladjustment apparent when he introduced us to his fiancée. I'd seen plenty of sailors' wives, and the woman he introduced us to was the Army equivalent. She was rude, crude, uneducated, and totally out of place in the setting. She was thrice divorced, all from Army members. She had custody of the four kids she had from her former husbands. She and Peter had met when Peter was an instructor at Fort Benning.

Of course, during a time when we should have been joyous, the spots returned. It was a spot, this time no avatar or shroud. If I had to guess Peter's girl, Lurine would die of cancer of the ovaries or the uterus and soon if the darkness of the spot were predictive as it had been for Liam.

I felt that I needed to tell Peter and the effect was dramatic. He rounded on me in anger. He might be institutionalized, but he was big and strong and used to aggression.

"You're still doing that stupid thing you did in high school, telling people you can predict death. I've seen you all look at her like she's trash. You're so high and mighty."

"Pete, you're my brother, and I love you. If she dies, all those kids are gonna be yours, man. You can't take care of yourself, let alone four kids." I smiled at the last part of my response, hoping he would take it humorously. It failed.

"Just because you got rich doesn't mean you know everything. You don't know her, and you barely know me. This is the first time we've talked for years. Everyone has someone but me."

"Lousy reason to get married," I said.

"I'm lonely, brother. Almost twenty years in the military, and I watch you and the girls get married, and I don't. You all are so perfect. Not a lot of women want to marry a soldier."

"I'm sorry you're lonely. You know you're welcome to come and stay with us any time. We have the place at Tahoe now. Being lonely makes you vulnerable you have to be careful, and if what you say about women and soldiers is true, you need to be even more careful."

"I've been careful. That's why I'm still alive."

"Have you really checked her out? Three divorces, all from soldiers, kind of a warning, don't you think?"

"Maybe," he grumpily replied.

"I'll take that as a no. She's not making a lot of points here. She's drunk and loud in a religious ceremony. It shows a lack of control. Don't you think?"

He looked at me angrily. "She's pretty raw, I admit that, but she's not had time to get cultured, with the kids and all."

Peter had started talking as if he was less educated, his syntax and placement of words were poor, and he was rationalizing.

"Where are the kids now?" I asked.

He looked at me like I had asked the question that opened all the doors of wisdom, wealth, and power. He got up and walked over to his intended. I watched as he took the glass of wine from her hand, had a few words with her, watched her flush, and her overly made-up face crack from the smile of a drunkard to a mask of fury.

Then she lashed out at him. He took her by the elbow and steered her out of the room. If the tone of their voices and the length of time of the argument were indications, quite a battle was going on.

Peter made their excuses and left. All of us breathed a sigh of relief. Peter notified us later that the engagement was off. Lurine died of cervical cancer. Maybe the spots would allow me to do some good after all. Out of the investiture was born the idea of periodic family reunions.

As spring arrived, El and I planned the trip to Scotland. We decided to tour. I invited Mom and Dad, but Dad's heart condition precluded air travel, and Mom's declining mental capacity had advanced to the point she would require special care. Dad did provide us with a lot of genealogical information.

While the calendar may have proclaimed spring, London was wet and cold. I put the ankle to the test, and it gave me trouble and slowed us down. After touring all the typical spots in London, The Tower, St. Paul's, the changing of the guard, Harrods and Fortnum & Mason, we took the Royal Scotsman to Edinburgh and spent a couple of days tramping up and down the Royal Mile.

From Edinburgh, we trained to Inverness, rented a car, spent some time learning to drive on the left, and went to the traditional lands of the MacIntosh, to Culloden to commune with the ghosts of the lost cause. While London had been cold and wet, it was nothing compared to Scotland. The first thing you notice is the wind. It's constant with an edge, and a twinge of ice flows from the far north. It wicks away body heat. It's like a demon and has learned to harm in various ways. You button up your coat; it finds a way around the barrier. It bounces off rocks and climbs up women's skirts and, of course, my kilt. I got a new respect for women after wearing a kilt in Scotland.

Separate from the wind is the cold. It's wet, sticky, and clings to you even after it drives you inside. It's almost a cloak and, like a cloak, can be oppressive. El did not react well to the cold regardless of the sweaters and other woolens she purchased. After a few days, I stopped wearing my kilt; it was beautiful, but its disadvantages outweighed the beauty.

It's not far across Scotland, but the route we had to take to get from Inverness to the ferry to Port Askaig was long, complicated, and beautiful. We eventually found our way to Kennacraig. We had a two-hour ferry ride to Port Askaig on the east coast of the Isle of Islay. We had no real plan as we got off the ferry except to get out of the bone-chilling wind. We had no address for Breanna Campbell, no phone number. We only knew she was on the island.

We saw a sign a few blocks off the ferry: *McLaren's*. We headed there. One of the incredible sensory experiences announced itself as soon as we opened the shop's door. The large rectangle had shelves along the walls reaching above my head. The shelves were stocked with large metal containers, and in front of them were smaller paper bags labeled *Orange Pico, Jasmine Dragon Pearls, Irish breakfast*. There were green and black teas, white teas, tea from China, Sri Lanka, India, and Thailand. As you moved through the store, you moved from one teahouse to another like a traveler on the road. They didn't assault the senses as much as massaged them.

In the rear was a counter like a bar. On it was a scale and to the left was a cash register. From behind the scale came a woman's voice. "Welcome, you are travelers, may your travels be blessed." At the last words, a small, white-haired woman stepped into the clear.

She had the most beautiful complexion I had ever seen. Her weathered skin had a rosy inner glow. Her brown eyes were clear and bright under her white hair. She had to be seventy, but her face was unmarred by age spots or wrinkles except for a few tiny crow's feet. She looked the picture of health.

"I hope I look that good at that age," murmured El.

"Have no worry about that, lass. It's a beauty ya are and a beauty you will always be."

El was not the blushing type but was close now.

"'Tis tay ya be needing after the boat ride. Come along then." The woman waved us toward the seats. As we did, I got a better view of her. She was quite short, no more than five feet. Behind the counter, she stood on a raised platform. She wore a long tartan skirt, which I recognized as MacLeod of the Isles. We sat down, and she fussed behind the counter back to us.

When she turned around, she had two small teapots and two cups. "For you, lad, looking peaked from the ride, typhoon, and for the lass Kunming with coconut for the skin. Enjoy."

"Look at me forgettin' ma manners. You'd be David and Elspeth MacIntosh. I'm Heather McLaren."

I almost dropped my teacup. "How did you know who we are?"

"It will be a mystery until you meet Breanna. I'll say no more now, but 'tis not a bad thing."

We've gotten initiated enough in the English tea culture to let it steep or mash a bit and remembered it was loose tea to use a small filter on the saucer. Heather was right, and the typhoon gave me a lift. Finally, we asked how to find Breanna Campbell.

"We had a card from her a few months ago asking us to call when we were in Scotland."

I paused to sip tea, and El jumped in.

"There was no address or phone, just a postmark at Port Askaig. We met a lady in North Carolina named Ruth."

"Lovat. She was Ruth Lovat in the life we know. That's what she was, which is no more, but what she is still burns but faintly."

I was spooked. Heather's words were the same mantra we had heard in North Carolina.

"Her name was in my grandmother Ruth's address book..."

"She was Ruth Gordon MacIntosh?" asked Heather.

"Yes, did you know her?"

"No, she were a coostomer." But there was more to it; I could tell from her voice.

I continued, "The address book my grandmother left me when she passed was in an ancient Gaelic dialect with some names in English. One was Ruth in North Carolina, another man in California, and a Native American in Nevada."

"Aye, that would be Clifford Jones, such a dear man," said Heather.

"How we go about finding Ms. Campbell?" El asked. "Does she have a phone?"

"Nay, no phone, but she lives down the road there." Heather waved her arm so she could have meant any direction.

The cold and traveling tired us out, and we asked Heather if she could recommend a hotel. She recommended a B&B she coincidentally owned. She made a call, and ten minutes later, a strapping 6'4" man walked into the shop. He was the Hollywood picture of a Scot. Even in the cold, he was bareheaded, showing off a fine head of red hair. His shoulders were broad and tapered to a narrow waist. His complexion was ruddy and weathered. His kilt was in a tartan I didn't recognize, and above that, he wore a gorgeous white cable-knit sweater, dark-green knee socks covered large muscular calves.

"'Tis ma nephew, Lachlan Harper," Heather said, as she introduced us. "Runs the inn, he does and does a fine job too."

His hand was like holding a ham; it made mine look dainty and El's Lilliputian. With introductions finished, I shouldered one of our bags, and El picked up her small bag. Lachlan scooped up the other two bags with the ease of great strength.

The weather had not improved. A raw cutting wind stormed in from the Irish Sea, carrying a taste of saltwater and snow. The harbor was riven by white horses whose tops the wind turned to foam. Baskets of flowers hanging along the sidewalks swung in dangerous arcs; signs stood out at impossible angles. The temperatures had to be in the forties. The windchill made it feel like the twenties, and El and

I struggled to button coats and get gloves on while Lachlan strode ahead, impervious to the weather.

"Aunt says you're special guests and to give ya turret room. You will luv it, has fireplace and a sitting room. Good place to cuddle doon on a parky day."

I took two steps to his one. El was jogging. Luckily, the place was only a few blocks away. It was a Victorian-style house painted dove-gray with red and white trim. On the second story, left side was a turret. The place had to be a maintenance nightmare, but it looked like it had been recently painted and scrubbed. In the front was an immaculate rock garden with heather of various colors tucked in the crannies of the rocks. A giant wisteria climbed the lattice at the entrance. I stopped just after we passed through the garden gate.

I had looked at my watch on the run to the hotel. While it was about 2:00 p.m. and the sky was not pellucid, it was dark, but the darkness didn't keep me from noticing the stone. It was about five feet tall, gray, rectangular, and on the eastern side of the house. The edges looked as if they had been worked smooth. I was willing to bet there were three others around the house. I realized the house was not parallel to the street but angled, so the front faced the stone.

Remember the stones, Ruth had said.

The weather worsened during the rest of the day, and we were glad to be indoors. The wind screeched around the edges of the building. In between gusts, we could hear breakers crashing on the shore. The windows rattled, and doors shook in their frames. We had tea, one of England's best contributions to civilization, with scones, jam, and sandwiches. After tea, there was sherry for the ladies and whiskey, heavy full and peaty for the men.

Our room was everything Lachlan and Heather had said. Comfortable, warm, with a peat fire going, romantic, very relaxing. Both the oppressive weather and long travel had tired us more than we knew. We were soon fast asleep under down comforters about a foot thick and sheets of white cotton that felt like silk.

CHAPTER 16

The following day, the sun made a brave attempt at being seen but failed, leaving the sky battleship gray. The wind had lessened a bit, but the harbor was still a series of spume-tossed waves racing down the wind. The morning ferry came in, with waves breaking against the sides with explosions of foam and spray.

We had a typical English breakfast of eggs, toast, fried tomatoes, tea, and scones. We had purchased a map of the island, and we learned the town near where Breanna lived was about forty miles south. There was no car rental place, but Lachlan made a few calls, and a local cabbie named Dermot Sullivan agreed to drive us around for the day. It wasn't tourist season, and he was glad for the fare. Dermot was as Irish as Paddy's pig and relentlessly garrulous. According to him, he knew everything about the island, but I had the feeling he was giving the Yanks what he thought they needed to hear.

Islay is a large island. Port Askaig is on the northeast corner. Most of the population live on the littorals, mainly on the southern shore. There are numerous whiskey distilleries on the island. A major road artery cuts more or less diagonally from Port Askaig to Port Ellen on the southwest coast. It passed through several small towns, one of which was the hamlet of Leorin, where we might find more information on Breanna.

Dermot drove like a maniac, smoking, talking, and gesturing with his hands. I hadn't seen anyone drive like that since the first time El and I met. The road was narrow by US standards but in generally good shape without much traffic. The speed signs posted the road at sixty miles per hour, but the speedometer showed one hundred. I hoped it was in kilometers.

We reached Leorin, and Dermot said, "You can stop here if you like, but a wee bit more. We could tour some o' the stills and shebangs in Port Ellen. They make a fine whiskey here not as good as Jamieson mind but good nonetheless."

We decided we would rather stop, and he said, "You can see 'tis early, no one's about. It's teatime ya want, then the lads and lassie will be around to tell ya what you seek."

It looked like no one was around, so we let Dermot have his way.

We worked through Port Ellen and headed out of town toward Ardbeg on the road called the A846. In England, an A road is supposed to be a fast highway just a bit below the M routes, the freeways. Apparently, speed was not a factor in Scotland as we had discovered the A roads were usually less wide than suburban streets in the US and frequently featured sheep and cattle being driven from one side of the road to the other.

As we generally motored east, I saw a sign pointing to the right, indicating a stone circle. I asked Dermot.

"Oh, aye, a standing stone once part of a stone circle. Claims to be older than the one in England…"

"Stonehenge?" I asked.

"No, the other one, Avebury, summa local queer folk say there's doings there during the year. All that's there is single stone standing, some say others are buried."

"Doings?" asked El from the backseat.

"Aye, ya know, dances and such, harvest celebrations. Claim the Druids built them an' claim special power in rocks. Don't tell me you're interested in such things. It's all doss," he said as he made the sign of the cross.

"No, really just a question," I said, not buying Dermot's off-hand dismissal.

"Aye, usually a bunch of American hippies come twice a year, dance naked the police ha' a real time with them they do."

"Must be pretty tough to dance naked in this weather," said El from inside her layers of wool.

After visiting the Ardberg distillery, we drove back to Port Ellen. We picked up info on the ferry service and hotels if we came back. We also discovered an airport but couldn't find out if there was regular service. We started north, and around four, we reached Leorin.

"'Tis either the post office or the local where you'll find what your need," said Dermot.

The post office, which was inside a newsagent, was closed, so we walked to the local pub called the Old Shepherd. The process of consolidating pubs into giant chains was well underway in England, but the Shepherd proclaimed itself a free house, meaning it was licensed by the government but owned by the landlord or house, as he was called.

In America, we would have called it a dump; ten thousand miles made it quaint. According to the sign, The Good Shepherd was founded in 1789. Two centuries of progress had raised the road, so the door required two steps down. The door itself was of ancient wood planks rough sawn on the outside and studded with colossal iron bolts holding the hinges.

Like other buildings we had seen on Islay, there was a double entrance to contain the effects of the weather. Through the second door, we were confronted with a long passage ending in a large room with a bar. To our right was a stairway leading up and to our immediate left was a small bar, known as a snug.

"Wh'ere a wee bit early for tea," said Dermot as he went down the passage shouting, "house there."

His cries were met by a large overweight man in a semi-clean apron. He appeared in the dim light to be about sixty, his face showing a few days of beard, his hair sticking out here and there. His deep lines showed long years of hard work, and his eyes narrowed by scar tissue at the edges featured a deep fissure between them as if he were constantly concentrating. He kept his hands wrapped in his apron as if we were trying to wipe them clean.

"Welcome ta the Shepard, a bit early for tea ya are, and the lads haven't arrived yet but snug's ready." His manner of speech was almost like some of the old English novels, and I wondered if he wasn't acting a bit.

The snug is called a snug because it's snug. There was one table, a booth really, and opposite a small bar with two stools. The wood on the walls was dark with years of smoke and human touch. The bar featured the standard pull handles, signaling that the house pumped the beer from the kegs below, not driven by carbonation as American beer is.

I guided El to the table as the landlord bustled in. I ordered a double whiskey and a large sherry for El. It was cold outside, but it seemed even colder inside due to the stillness of the air. The house's name was Aaron, and he had an accent that made him sound like a walking Burns poem. I had difficulty understanding anything. Luckily, Dermot could interpret as he drank the whiskey I'd bought him.

Aaron asked what brought us to Islay and this out-of-the-way place, and we told him we were seeking Breanna Campbell. He looked back and forth at us with a look that seemed to question our sanity.

"Yud be seeking Breanna, is it?'

I replied yes.

"She's nought aboot, over ta Oa tending to wee bairn whose poorly," said Aaron.

"Is there a hotel about where we could stay? I mean, she lives here about, right?" asked El.

"Aye, she lives up the way," Aaron said, waving his arms generally to the north. "No, lass, the only place wid rooms to let is The Rose down road a bit."

At this point, two men walked in who were likely farmers if I read their clothes and boots correctly.

"God bless all here," said one, taking off his flat cap stomping his feet. He headed to the large room in the back. The other man, taciturn and more roughly dressed, followed closely.

"Most of the people around here area farmers and peat cutters," said Dermot.

I hated to be like a typical American in a rush. I had a feeling that things would reveal themselves in a pattern of time not suited to Yankee hurry, but I had Dermot to think about, and if we were to go back to Port Askaig, it was a long drive. Then three more men walked in dressed in tweeds, rough work pants splattered with mud. They scraped their heavy boots, then walked down the hall.

"Maybe we would find out more if we join them in the common room," El said.

Dermot agreed and led us down the hall.

Beyond the snug, the walls were wooden to mid-chest with translucent glass above nearly to the eight-foot ceiling. I noticed much of the glass was bull's-eye, the thick center roundel indicating age. The common room opened to the left of the hallway, the bar running across the narrow side of the rectangle. There were no stools at the bar, but the rest of the room was filled with tables that looked aged and not by human artifice.

A large fireplace with a large inviting fire was on the far side of the room. The snug was warming up from lack of size, but the common room was cold, but the fire was pouring out heat. El shivered as we entered, we sat at a table a bit removed from the fire, and I went to the bar.

"Owt again," said Aaron.

"No, two doubles," I said.

"Yanks would you be?" asked one of the men.

"Yes, from California."

"Not many come here," said the other one.

"She's a good un, the lass, drinking whiskey," said a third man "'tis it's few that love ta whiskey."

"Would you be tourists? If you are ya be a bit off your path, most stay south by the works." The first man was short with powerful shoulders, big rough-hewn hands, a face like boiled leather with sparkling blue eyes.

"We are in a way," I replied, but before I could finish, Aaron jumped in.

"They come to see Breanna." There was a kind of clearing of throats, shuffling of feet in discomfort when people collectively know something and are slightly embarrassed by it. I had a brilliant thought.

"House, please give all around on me."

The attitude brightened immediately. It got better when El, warmed by the fire and whiskey, took off her coat and came to stand next to me. Nothing changes taciturn Scots into the chatterboxes like free drinks and a pretty girl.

"She's no here, Breanna, she's over to the barin," said one of the men, a sad-looking guy in a worn tweed coat, pants patched at the knees, unruly gray-brown hair that looked permanently wind-tossed.

"You think she'll be away long?" asked El. "If we could get a hotel, we could wait. We've come all the way from California."

"Hotel it is?" replied the one with the powerful shoulders whose name we discovered was Donald. "Nay hotel around 'cept The Rose."

"Shame on you, Donald Barton, ta send the lass ta the Rose. Not fit for your lambs or rams," said the sad-looking man, whose name was Reggie.

"What about the proofs?" said the third, Paul. "They're all high and mighty, a B&B it is." He snorted.

"That'd be the place for you to wait till Breanna gets back. Aaron, why don't you call them? The lass looks worn out. It's the cold, lass," said Reggie, clearly smitten by El. After buying another round of drinks on me, Aaron moved off to the phone.

We moved to a table by the fire. Gay men were not in as much fashion as they are today. I had heard the term poof applied to them by several British colleagues. Given Paul's intonation, it was clearly not a form of affection.

"How do you get in touch with Breanna?" El asked. "She doesn't have a phone, and we have no address."

"Ifa was you, I stay quit of the witch," chimed in the fourth man. "She's naught but trouble with all her ways."

"Stop that talk, McKenzie, you don't know she's a witch and naming calls ya daft bugger," said Reggie.

"You can say what you like, Reggie Harper, but remember Jamie Overton. She shows up, and all sorts of bad things happn," shot back McKenzie.

"McKenzie is the local wet blanket he is, time for a party. McKenzie shows up to tell you it's a bad idea. No fun he is," said Donald.

At that point, Aaron came back. "I talked to the head proof." He looked around. "What's his name?"

"Gareth Neucombe," said Paul.

"Aye, he says if you've not had your tea to have it here, they'll come down to pick you up if you're staying," Aaron said.

We told him we were staying, and Aaron returned to the phone to confirm. I ordered another round. Some others had joined us, glad to have free drinks. We were warm, cozy, and full of whiskey.

"So what happened to wee Jamie?" El asked.

"It's all rumors and tales that McKenzie had naught be telling and troubling your pretty head about." He was patronizing her, which can be very dangerous, but El refrained from ripping Donald's head off.

"She's now't good, 'tis evil that's with her and that other one, no good," said McKenzie as he rapped the table and made a move with the fingers across his forehead.

We chatted comfortably warm by the fire until we heard two more sets of boots in the passage. The leader was a man dressed well in wool and a raincoat. He had a fedora in his hand, and heavy work boots on his feet. His neck was long and slender, supporting a round head with a dense beard and a full head of black hair.

"'Tis not fit for man or beast outside or will be, wind's rising, storms coming in, be surprised if we don't have snow before morning," he said. He ordered a whiskey. I heard Aaron call him Doc.

"Local doctor?" I said to Donald.

"Nay, lad, works for the government, weather forecaster."

The other man coming down the hallway, his steps less confident, his tread lighter with a longer stride. He entered the public and stopped, framed in the door. He was athletically thin, about 5'10", dressed in dark green wide whale corduroy pants, his feet in midcalf green Wellington rain boots. He had a beautiful turtleneck sweater on and draped over his shoulders; sleeves empty was a Barbour oiled cotton coat.

"God bless all here," he said cheerfully.

"May the devil take the low road," replied Aaron. "Drink, Gareth?"

"White wine" came the response, which caused some elbows to be exchanged by my companions. Gareth was genuinely uncomfortable with the men in the common. He was nervous, constantly signaling his importance with glances at what I saw was an expensive watch. He never took the Barbour off his shoulders and never sat down. He held his wineglass by the broad base, never touching the bulb or the stem.

I settled with Dermot and bought another round. We went out to transfer baggage to Gareth's car. Gareth was silent most of the time except to return our introductions. In the car, the radio was tuned to a classical radio station which was playing the Sea Interludes by Britten.

Gareth's place was eight miles farther south and looked like a shipwreck on a clean beach. It was huge and modern, two stories, white paneled, pitched shingle roof, and many lighted windows. He drove up the driveway, which felt like cobblestones, and stopped at the walk to the front door. The front door was two arched doors made of tongue and groove planks that looked like oak. The hinges extended almost to the division and were wrought iron in the most fantastic designs. As we walked up, the door opened, and a very tall man welcomed us.

"Welcome to Edoras," he said.

I smiled, remembering Edoras was the seat of King Théoden in *The Lord of the Rings*. I couldn't resist, so I replied, "Hail, Théoden, King!"

He laughed. "No, my name is Philip. Good of you to make the connection and visit." He was a man who took care of himself. He was very fit, broad shoulders, narrow waist, blue jeans tight, and resting on his hipbones. We moved away from the door, and he hefted two of our bags with ease and moved with the sinuous grace of a dancer.

"Please come to the parlor," he said with a melodious voice that spoke of a cultured upbringing. He was definitely not Scots.

We entered a very tastefully decorated smaller room, fireplace crackling cheerily. A couch was opposite the fireplace, fronted by a coffee table and straight-backed chairs at each end. It all looked costly, as did the deep pile carpet on the floor. The walls were covered with wallpaper of broad dark green stripes alternating with narrow bars of tan and smaller bars of red. Very lush, and it reminded me of a private club I once visited.

Gareth came in. "Welcome to our house. I'm Gareth Neucombe, and you've met Philip, Philip Hollister. May I offer you sherry or perhaps some whiskey?"

Philip said, "I'll bring tea in a moment." He looked to Gareth. "Kettle just boiled." With the emphasis on just.

Gareth, El, and I sat down, and Philip brought some registration paperwork.

He asked, "Did you have your tea at The Shepherd, or are you starving?" His smile grew larger when he heard we had not had tea.

"I have a lamb roast in the oven. Goodness, I forgot to ask, you do eat flesh?" It was an odd way of asking if we were vegetarians and frankly made my skin crawl. I never thought of meat as flesh, and flesh had a barbaric connotation.

Phillip got up to tend to the kitchen returning with a tea set.

"Gareth will be mother," he said, and left.

Gareth was a refugee, or perhaps escapee might be better. He told us he had been deeply involved in the theater in London, as an actor, director, and finally as a playwright. His tone and references indicated he had garnered fame or at least semi-fame, and I should know his work. I did, however, get a strong feeling of profound alienation and hurt. He was running from something. Given the long, loving, lustful looks at Philip, there was no doubt that he was gay, on an island of uncompromising landscape and belief.

Philip's dinner was as good as anything we'd eaten on the trip. The lamb was tender, pink, and juicy. The new potatoes firm, asparagus crisp. As a desert, he served a traditional English pudding flavored with rum and currents.

As dinner finished, Gareth got down to the question. I think it had been there all along, but his manners dictated he wait some period before beginning the interrogation. "What brings you Islay? It's not exactly the tourist season?"

"We came at the invitation of Breanna Campbell," El said. Her response drew a disapproving, uncultured snort from Gareth, and I knew we hit a nerve.

"Do you know her, Gareth?" I said.

"I'll get sherry and brandy," said Philip. "You smoke cigars, David, El?" He smiled, and we knew something was coming. He walked off, and, Gareth returned his attention to us.

"Never met her, but you can't live here long without hearing about her. Some of the hayseeds like McKenzie at the pub think she's a witch with all sorts of magical regency."

"McKenzie seemed almost cowed by her. Not afraid but respectfully wary. He seemed to know a lot about her various activities," El said.

"Alex McKenzie is a gullible old fool. He's a peat cutter who spends days in the peat hags alone except when the foreman comes to count the cuts and pay him. Spend too much time alone in the wind, rain, fog, and murk your only companion a flask you come to believe almost anything." Gareth lit his cigar.

"She seems to be some sort of doctor. Apparently, there's a sick child she's tending to?" I asked.

"Bah, she's no more a doctor than I am. The baby's mother, who's a drug addict and a slut, has slept with half the island and, I'm sure, has no idea who the father is. She drugged, smoked, and drank right through her pregnancy, and now everyone is amazed the baby has all sorts of problems? Please, the world would be better off without both of them. Bad seed all around."

I watched as El stiffened, her maternal instincts and caring nature aroused by Gareth's cavalier dismissal of human life.

"You don't mean that, Gareth," she said, trying hard to control her voice, "surely the child is innocent, did nothing to deserve its condition, and you wish it dead? Sort of heartless."

Gareth rolled his cigar around in his mouth, one eye squinting from the smoke. "I think not. What's heartless, Elspeth, wonderful name, by the way, is that the kid will be on the public dole for life, and the mother will continue to reproduce, adding more people to the welfare rolls, when a simple snip, snip would save us all a lot of money and trouble. This lunatic Breanna runs over there with witch-craft and potions or whatever, giving hope. If the doctors can't save the baby, let it die. It's the way of nature."

El was fired up. "I know you are our hosts, and I appreciate it, but that is the most cynical attitude toward human life I have ever heard." Her cheeks were getting red, and her voice quavering with emotion and outrage.

Gareth drew on his cigar and took a sip of brandy. I got the impression he was toying with us, then he continued and convinced me, "You and David have had privileges all your lives, which have blinded you to the reality that the world is a hideous place. If you were less privileged, you would agree my opinion is fully justified."

"Privileged?" I said.

"Yes. It's all around you, and you have been living it for so long you don't or can't see its effects on you. It's inculcated in you by years of being privileged you have no other perspective, nor can you consider one without challenging your worldview."

"Gareth, that's pretty insulting," broke in Phillip. "He gets this way sometimes. Don't take it personally."

"Hard not to," I replied. "But, Gareth, you condemn us as priv-ileged but so are you. I hear traces of Oxford in your speech and the trappings of a posh public school, Eton?"

"Harrow, old man," Gareth replied, a bit surprised to be chal-lenged so intimately.

"You indite us for privilege, yet you live it every day as we do, so I'm not sure your argument will hold water or is even relevant." I took a drink of my brandy, and I looked at Phillip, who had a big smile on his face.

"Perhaps to defuse the tension," said Philip. "I should show you to your suite. You must be tired. We have two, one next to the mas-ter and another at the other end of the hall, any preference?" Phillip asked.

"We'll take the second one," El said quickly, before I could say anything.

We said good night to Gareth, and Philip led us to our suite. "You have to excuse him really. He burned itself out in London. He came here to recoup and found the attitude of the locals challenging to say the least."

The suite was beautifully and tastefully decorated. It had a large bedroom and bath and an equally large sitting room. The bed was so high off the floor my butt was only halfway up the mattress. There were two movable steps to help people get into the bed. The sitting room was separated by French doors and featured a couch, armchairs, coffee table, and armoire, which I found contained a TV and a well-stocked bar.

El looked out the windows saw two large trees, the branches scratching softly at the sides of the house like scratching a person's back. I came up behind El wrapped my arms around her.

"I love you," I whispered into her fragrant, lush hair.

"I hope you don't mind my deciding on the suite. I couldn't bear being closer to Gareth after his remarks about that child."

"You think he and Phillip are lovers?"

"He and Philip aren't sleeping together yet."

Soon El and I were snuggled deep in luxurious sheets and mounds of down comforters. El's rear end never did get warm until she shoved up against me.

The next day dawned, sort of. The sky remained leaden, low, and oppressing. The wind held steady from the northeast, soughing as it rounded the corners of the house, driving the lowest layer of crowds like ships before a storm. It was like the day couldn't make up its mind if it wanted to stay in bed.

We decided to go outside and walk around the grounds as we always did back in California and found out how foolish we were. The wind made a wreck of El's hair in a second, slashing locks across her face. It found every unprotected hole and seam in our clothes bringing icy fingers to caress our skins and probe deep into our bones. We hurried to the back door and the warming cocoon of Phillip's kitchen.

"Tea?" he said, dispensing the universal English remedy for everything from colds to cancer. He poured from a giant teapot into heavy china mugs with real handles.

"Gareth worked into the night...on what, I'm not sure. He won't be down till much later. He said for you to take the VW, tour a bit unless you hear from Breanna, and we'll see you for tea, say four-ish?"

We didn't hear from Breanna, but we discovered more about the island's south coast. I picked up a more detailed map of Islay.

We had tea in the parlor, featuring Philip's homemade scones, small sandwiches, and other snacks. It was sociable, close, and easy, and Philip was chatty and expansive, but Gareth did not appear.

After tea, we went to our suite to wash up have some time alone before dinner. I, of course, was worried about hearing from Breanna, but I had found a copy of *The Financial Times* that peach-colored savior and settled in. El called Mom and Dad.

Gareth joined us for dinner. The English eat late, and Gareth's face looked like a thunderhead about to break. He was snappish with Philip, barely civil to El and me, which was rudeness in action given his apparent good breeding. His mood did not improve when Philip brought a message from The Shepherd, "Breanna would have us for tea the next day."

"Must've gotten her broom fixed," fired off Gareth with a sardonic laugh.

I hope the baby is better. Sick kids get to me," said El.

"No loss if it doesn't." Gareth was looking for a fight, and El was just the person to give it to him. "Witchcraft should be left to Macbeth."

"You know there are numerous studies by the National Institutes of Health, among others showing nonmedical intervention can promote healing and improve patient outcomes. Apparently, Breanna doesn't charge for her services, so what resources are wasted?" El took a breath. "What's the harm?"

Gareth made two mistakes. He underestimated his opponent and tried to fob her off by patronizing her. I couldn't figure out if he had an agenda he wanted to talk about or was just being bloody-minded. El was a scientist and used to dealing with sophistry, and she was looking at it right now.

"I can see this is distressing you, dear lady, you're a mother, and of course, you would approach it from a sentimental perspective. I didn't mean to offend," he said.

"We passed that line a while ago," said El.

"Gareth, El is a geophysicist and worked in Ames Labs. Her work is largely responsible for the GPS," I said.

It's always funny to watch a verbal bully deflated. Gareth's eyes narrowed. His rigid posture seemed to soften, if only for a second. He was nonplussed at having violated the rules of hospitality and having walked into a minefield. He stopped talking and started to sulk.

"Gareth," I said, "we don't know what Breanna does or doesn't do, but we know when people are sick, their healing is improved, and mortality lessened by being in a therapeutic environment including relevant cultural and behavioral elements. If Breanna can make the milieu surrounding the child more helpful, what's the harm?"

"Dear David," Gareth began. His words painting him as a patronizing ass. "There will never be enough resources to treat all the world problems. I'm sure *you* would agree." He paused and fixed me with a gaze so bold in its invitation, its intensity, and its obvious desire for argument. It was uncomfortable. It made me feel he was trying to draw me into a conspiracy.

"That may or may not be true," I said, "but the point at issue"—I was proud of my phrase, it sounded so English—"is that the baby is sick, a woman is providing care that might help the child, who is innocent, get better, for no charge."

"Perhaps, but the child is the result of the sins of the mother," said Gareth.

"That doesn't make it guilty or deserving of death? What kind of mercy is that which condemns the innocent?"

"The same kind which condemns innocent men to death from AIDS because of who they love, in the nonsense that Christians believe there is Exodus 20 verse 5," Gareth said in a self-satisfied aggressive tone designed to play the trump card.

El looked at me. "Thou shalt not bow down thyself to them, nor serve them: for I the Lord thy God am a jealous God, visiting the iniquity of the fathers upon the children unto the third and fourth generation of them that hate me; Euripides made the same point in one of his plays."

HIV/AIDS had ripped through the gay community like a threshing machine. It was one of those plagues which came along and changed perceptions. In this case, it caused many deaths and had a political and social impact. The AIDS crisis and the carefully creative way it was reported and framed united the gay community, made them political players of considerable power, and brought many people to their side. It was, along with abortion, the root of future social movements.

"Gareth, that's not a correct usage of the Bible. First, you condemn it as nonsense, and then you use it to justify a position that is at odds with the fundamental concept of Christianity. That passage is about those who worship false gods, including the gods of intellect and reason. Really, your distaste overbears your logic," I said.

"That's a conflation of the worst kind," said El. "AIDS has nothing do with the child's condition or Breanna's involvement."

"That child and her slut mother are consuming resources that can be better used, and Breanna is just perpetuating the myth of some preternatural power. Next she'll be claiming, she speaks for that other mythological obscenity, God!"

"You don't believe in God?" I asked, "even a little?"

He reached over and patted my hand like a parent to a child. "Of course not, how simpleminded. Believing in an all-powerful creator with all knowledge is foolish and believing that same being is one of mercy or justice is the height of superstition and mental failure. All religion does is try to make people believe in paranormal events and actions, and of course, that is the height of foolishness."

"Really..." both El and I replied almost in unison.

"Please don't tell me you believe in that mumbo-jumbo spewed by old men in black robes and rosary beads? Heaven help us!" He was positively gleeful.

"We do, and if you are a nonbeliever, why did you just invoke heaven?" I said.

"Just a habit, old man, habit."

"Here is the real issue," he began, "the logic behind atheism is unassailable. If God or the supernatural power were good, it or he would want all his creatures to be happy, and if he is almighty, he could do whatever he wanted, but we are not happy. Therefore, God is not omnipotent or omniscient. Otherwise, there would not be suffering, and gay men would not face pointless suffering because of who they loved. It's that simple." Gareth rolled his cigar in his mouth before taking a sip of his brandy.

"Logic of that statement is doubtful, to begin with," I said. "It's the same conundrum C. S. Lewis dealt with in *The Problem with Pain*," I said, "and he pretty well demolished the idea of God failing because of the existence of suffering. Even in atheistic and polytheistic cultures, the existence of suffering is acknowledged, either as a punishment for hubris as the Greeks had it or a path to knowledge, as Homer phrased it. Or as a necessary item of existence, as Freud said, or more importantly as a path to meaning as Frankl discovered during the greatest terror the world ever saw. I have come to believe that the absence of suffering is apathy."

"At this point," El began, "we know you don't believe in God, or that Breanna has powers. Mercy doesn't exist because injustice does, one might ask what you believe in?"

Philip snorted in surprise. Gareth seemed bemused as if no one had challenged his beliefs before. "So what do you believe?" Gareth fired at us. One of the most irritating habits of speech and rhetoric of the modern world was to respond to a challenging question by asking another question. It was like a fencing move, the thrust, and parry.

"Let's answer one question at a time," El said. "David asked first—what do you believe?"

"Only what science proves and what I can feel. No God's will or supernatural jabber."

"There is no faith in your life?" I asked.

"No, faith is a cheap way of not knowing."

"But what you believe proven by science requires you to have faith that the scientists who tested for truth did everything right."

"I think that's a given," Gareth said, "the scientific method eliminates all variables and all inconsistencies."

"Only so long as the execution of the method is sound and the hypothesis well stated," said El.

"Isn't the job of a scientist to make sure all that is correct?" said Gareth, asking a leading question.

"It is, but all scientists are not as pure as the method. Some faced with the intense competition for grants and research funds stray from the method." El sipped her wine and continued, "Besides, science is never final. We are always looking to disprove something, so the statement that science is settled is never correct, and science is full of pulpil just as philosophy and humanities are. Those factors lead science to be less pure. The pressure to shade the edges is growing, not vanishing."

"I appeared to have been bested. Congratulations, dear lady." He toasted her. "But we still don't know if Breanna actually has the powers attributed to her."

"No, and we may never find out. Experiments to determine wellness or improvements in wellness are notoriously hard to construct," said El.

"Another question, if you don't mind?" Gareth said, nodding at us both. "What particular quest that would bring you to Islay and Breanna in particular?"

It was a question I had dreaded, but so far, the ultra-polite English had avoided asking. I was with a doubting mind, an insightful chronicler of the human condition, and a world-class skeptic. I was not before a sympathetic audience for a tale of mysterious powers.

"We're tracking down a family legend about one of my distant relatives, and that led us to Breanna," I said, using one of the stories I had cooked up as covers. It didn't work. Before I finished, I felt stupid. It was going to engender more questions, not fewer. *Hadn't thought that through had ya, dummy*, my mind said.

"Tell us more," Gareth prompted. "Scottish legends are fascinating, silly nonetheless…he didn't finish his sentence. Now I had to improvise, and I decided to tell a partial truth.

"There's a legend that one of my ancestors long ago had some ability as a prophet and made quite a name for himself."

"What kind of prophecy, I wonder," said Philip. "There are legends around Ireland and the islands of seers, and on the continent, some people believe in seers to this day. It's mostly coincidence when it comes down to it in most cases."

"I suspect the same thing will prove to be true, but we had to check it out," El said, laughing.

"Well, those fools at the pub, Breanna and her niece, will be the ones to tell you about that foolishness." Gareth laughed.

The next day Philip told us Gareth was working upstairs and we could take the car to tour and meet Breanna. "Aaron at the pub will be able to direct you. Give him a big kiss for me. I suspect he's not out of the closet." He laughed.

Overnight it had turned colder. The north wind brought thoughts of ice floes and polar bears. We drove down to the south coast and purchased yet more woolens that would end up at that Tahoe house. In Port Ellen, the wind had flattened waves and pushed against the retreating tide. Gulls hung suspended in the air, boxed the compass, and sailed far to the south. The wind kicked up specks of the water left from previous days' rains, so we had to flick the wipers on and off constantly.

People huddled in deep coats with hats and gloves, shoulders hunched forward, heads down against the wind. Every banner and flag snapped like rifle shots. As the weatherman said, it was indeed a miserable day, not fit for man or beast. The air was full of the smells of the sea and a working harbor.

It was too cold to shop. Small miracles do happen, so we retreated into a tea shop and sat by the window watching fishing boats and the ferry fight to gain their moorings. Around two, we left and drove north, the wind buffeting the car

At The Shepard, Aaron poured over our map. "Nay, nay, 'ta road's not here. It twa the park and here." He pointed to the floor, meaning The Shepard. "Ya, canna miss it if ya take first turn to the right going north. Then just climb up 'ta bloody hill, ya find her place soon enough canna miss."

I knew two things, there were no signs announcing roads or turns, and it would be easy to miss, which is usually what happens when you can't miss it. Mc Kenzie was there. "A see the poof gave you the kraut car, and that fine big one sitting in the garage. It's rough, the track."

It was getting dark, and I had seen no indication of streetlights, so finding the track would be difficult. Mc Kenzie had divulged that the road to the park was eight miles north and that the track to Breanna's was short of that. We started north at 3:00 p.m., and after we had gone four miles, I used the broad shoulder, what the Brits call a layby, to determine where we were. We still missed it, and soon there was a sign for the park, two miles short of the eight miles we expected, so I used the park road to do a U-turn and headed south.

I drove four miles and then turned and started north again. Just after, I saw what might charitably be called a road at the edge of my headlights. I edged off the highway onto the rough gravel and rocky surface. The road started to rise fast and to twist. The only good thing was there was no traffic and no turn-offs.

Up we went, the car rocking on the ruts and occasionally giving a bone-jarring jolt as we hit a rock, and there were a lot of rocks. We were two miles up the track when it took a wide sweeping turn around a slight rise, and then we were looking at hills to the north in the far distance over a valley, but between us stood a magnificent house.

CHAPTER 17

As we approached, we noticed the long axis was north-south. We swung around the Southend and onto a drive to the front, which faced east. It looked to have three wings of two stories each. The front had a massive arched door with a Porte-cochere, and all the paving was stone. The Porte-cochere had stone pillars of single gray stones and enormous wood beams supporting the roof.

The door was massive. I guessed a good eight feet wide, made of timber planks eight to ten inches wide. The hinges came from the side and formed curves, loops, and fanciful designs across three-quarters of the width. There was no doorbell but a huge black iron knocker which I raised.

I had the vision of the booming echo resounding off the interior and a creepy butler shuffling to answer the knock like an Addams family movie. Before the knocker could connect, the door flung open, and El and I gasped.

There standing before us was the mature vision of our daughter, Beatrice. Same reddish-gold hair, cornflower blue eyes, slightly longer nose, small ears, same longish body with shorter legs. The lady at the door was fuller in figure with a more rounded face, but she could have been Beatrice's twin.

El was standing there, mouth open in amazement. I reached over and pushed her lower jaw up.

"Ms. Campbell?" I asked.

"Nay, I'm Fionna, ma aunt is Breanna. Welcome you are, welcome to our celidah hearth."

"Thank you, I'm..."

"'Tis David and Elspeth from the states," she said in a high but pleasing soprano, "Ma sister's Elspeth 'tis a popular lassies' name here

305

about. Come ya in, come 'tis not a fit night for man or beastie. Ach, ah see Gareth gave you the car and that great Land Rover sittn' in the garage. Dinna be so timorous," she rattled on, "come to the fire and get a warm."

We went down one of the wings to a sitting room; a fire burned cheerily in the grate. Next to the sitting room was an eating area and a table covered with a white tablecloth. The merry sound of a tea kettle on the boil greeted us.

"Let me take your cloaks. Aunt will be doon shortly. We just returned from seeing to the wee bairn who's sickly."

We stood by the fire. "I hope the child is okay," said El. "We heard terrible stories about what's wrong."

"Ay, 'tis a lot for the wee lass to bear, but she's a fine bonny child, and when we left, she's nursing like a newborn calf."

Fionna excused herself to go to the kitchen to make the tea. She returned with two armloads of plates. El stayed by the fire, and I rushed to help her.

We moved to the table. I sat at the foot of the table, El on my left, Fionna across from El. "We will, let the tay mash until Aunt comes, then see if she wants to be mother."

I felt her before I saw her. It was as if some tiny zephyr entered the room with a scent of roses, primrose, heather, sage, peat smoke, and salt air. It was almost as if she just appeared. There was no noise of feet, the rustling of fabric, no heel taps on the stone floor, but there she stood.

She was tall, and I expected it was not the effect of shoes. She wore a gown of green that brushed the floor and went up to her neck. It was piped in white at the cuffs, hem, and neck. She wore no jewelry save the silver pin, which held the Stewart tartan shawl around her shoulders.

All my life, I had been told gentlemen stood up when ladies entered a room. I jumped up so fast I knocked over my chair. El also stood, though not as clumsily as I. It would be obvious to describe Breanna's movement as feline; it was more like she floated. I never saw a movement of the hem of her dress or the contact of shoes on a floor.

All the time, at least to me, she was preceded by the whiff of the perfume of nature, fresh, and breezy. As she moved next to me, I noticed her face was unmarked and bore no makeup; it glowed almost as from within, a light of health and happiness. Her dark hair fell below her shoulders and gleamed in the candles like a well-oiled tail feather.

"Bless all here," Breanna said in a pleasant alto voice, melliferous, and almost like a chant.

"David, I've long hoped to meet you," she said, extending a finely shaped hand that expressed a firm handshake.

"Thanks, Ms. Campbell. I've looked forward to meeting you also. Mmay I present my wife..."

"Ah, the lovely Elspeth, of course, much has been spoken of you. Your loveliness precedes you," Breanna interjected. She could have heard rumors about El from folks on the island, but what she said next, combined with Fionna's appearance, floored me.

"I hope that Beatrice, Fergus, the twins, and Joseph and Elise are in good health?" She had no way of knowing all that. We had never talked about the kids, and most certainly, we never mentioned my parents.

"The children are fine. My parents are having some issues, Ms. Campbell," I replied.

"Please call me Breanna. I dislike that feminist necklace term, Ms.," she replied.

"Fionna, would you please be mother?" Breanna said with a wave of the hand and arm that was so graceful and effortless but in no way dismissive or superior.

She brought her other hand up and clasped them both. Not quite in a traditional prayer posture, her right hand held by the left in a manner Catholics use when receiving Eucharist. Her lips moved silently, then her hands parted, and she held them out over the food. It seemed the tea blossomed from the pot full of fragrance and joy.

"McLaren's?" asked El, before receiving a nod of affirmation from Breanna.

"I'm not sure what Heather does with her tea, but the effect on people is almost magic. You should take some home." She spoke with an odd lilt to her voice faintly Irish, a trace of Scots. Still, there was another sliver of accent, an emphasis, a dragging of vowels or consonants, and a form of construction hinting English might not have been her first language and might still be a part-time mode of speaking.

We had tucked into the offerings.

"Ay, warms the heart to see such an appetite," said Fionna.

Both she and Breanna had tea and a single crumpet. El and I had mounded our plates.

"'Tis the cold I'm thinking," she said with such grace that what might have been a reproof was made humorous.

"So am I the witch Mc Kenzie and the others at the Shepard described, or should I go and snaggle my teeth and paint my skin green?" Breanna said, smiling brilliantly and showing rows of perfectly white teeth.

"Do na' forget the pointed hat and brewing kettle," chimed in Fionna.

We all laughed, but I could hear the weariness of their having to dispel the rumors.

"There are also those who seem to believe you have special, ah, ah abilities but who aren't sure. You do have a reputation as mysterious," I said.

We talked on, occasionally laughing until Fionna called the question.

El and I had decided before we arrived how this would go. I started, "My late grandmother..." I never finished the sentence.

Breanna and Fionna almost chanted, "Ruth Gordon MacIntosh, she was in the life we know, that's what she was, which is no more, but what she is still burns but faintly." It was the same blessing or mantra or eulogy we had heard from Ruth Lovat.

"Did you know my grandmother?'

"No, I doubt it," said Breanna.

"I wondered because I have heard your eulogy if that's the right word for it from Ruth Lovat, Gordon McPhee, Clifford Jones, and Heather McLaren."

Breanna waved her hand like she was shooing away a fly. "'Tis naught but a custom." This was the first time she had broken character and returned to her Scottish roots. I decided not to pursue it. I was after a bigger truth.

"I went to Ruth Lovat, and the others to try to understand my gift, curse, or whatever it is, of seeing death before it happens. There have been some elements that don't seem to make any sense." I nodded at El, who produced the address book. I sipped tea, and I started to wonder if it was enchanted because I was beginning to feel very warm and relaxed and willing to be more open about the spots.

"My grandmother had this, and we found it after her death. It's in Gaelic but a dialect so old and obscure that a native speaker couldn't translate it. My grandmother did not speak Gaelic. I'm certain she was never in Scotland. Yet at her funeral, there was a Catholic priest and several others from Scotland. She was interned on the Isle of Mull. Her last letter to me contained a long goodbye in Gaelic. There are several names in here in English, yours among them."

El handed the book to Fionna, whose face clouded over, then she gave it to Breanna, whose face became stony and hard-edged.

"'Tis no wonder ya couldna translate it, not only 'tis it in the old tongue but also it's in code." At this, Breanna put her hand on Fionna's and gave her a sharp look and mouthed no.

"It's a wonder you have come so far in search, and I have no answer for you. It's a mystery, but there are more things…"

"In heaven and earth than are dreamed of in your philosophy Horatio." I finished the Shakespeare. "My grandmother wrote that to me in her last letter. Ruth Lovat said it, and now you."

"Shakespeare was a clever man, likely a Scot, and had a fair dose of the old wisdom," Breanna said.

"It may well be true about more things and all, but it's a damned nuisance having this ability that seems useless and morally dodgy," I said.

"Tell me about what you think is so dodgy, about your ability; in fact, we have waltzed around it; what is your ability?"

"It's straightforward," I began, but it wasn't simple. "Since I was thirteen, I have on numerous occasions seen spots on people that heralded their death. In the last few years, it has changed, and the manifestations are shrouds, and in one case, it was like identical people were standing next to the ones who were to die. It's never natural death. It's always accidents, disease, or violence. It's been 100 percent accurate. I just never know the time or the exact method. It's not constant." I stopped to see their reaction as I was talking faster with more passion than I usually did.

Breanna exchanged a quick but knowing glance with Fionna over her teacup and nodded as to say go on.

"It's very distressing to know something like that and not be able to intervene. The few times I tried to warn people, it made no difference to the outcome, but it made the family and me the objects of ridicule."

"I can sympathize. The locals around here ascribe all sorts of power to us, some of them quite fantastic, and they react with anger if I don't perform like a trained animal or get the result they want. Others react in fear and loathing like Gareth, then there are the censorious ones like McKenzie."

"I even thought that since I had to have this, I hate to call power, and is not a gift, so I call it a curse. I might as well profit from it. So I purchased insurance on some people and even sold a stock short once."

"How did that work for you?" asked Fionna.

"Not well, I made money but had the most terrible nightmares and even daymares if there is such a thing. They weren't like most bad dreams. It was like I was looking through a fabric, and terrible things were yelling at me. It was unbelievably bad until I gave up the money."

"That's really terrible. Did you change your behaviors?" asked Breanna.

"Yes, I no longer try to use the information in any way. I even lied to my parents when they asked. I saw spots on them. I have terrible guilt feelings about not telling people, but I know it will make no difference, and I always live with the fear of being made fun of and being written off as a nut job."

Breanna was silent. She had steepled her hands with them over her nose, her thumbs on her jaws. It was a reverential posture. I couldn't tell if he was praying for concentrating, Fionna was busy refreshing the tea, and El sat there in silence, then Breanna spoke. "I should think you learned two lessons, don't lie about what you see if asked and don't use it to your benefit."

"Agreed," I said, "but what is it? Is it real power? Has it occurred before? How are or where you grandma, Ruth, Clifford, and Gordon connected if you never met?"

"There is much modern science or inquiry can't explain, David. You have something unique; I can see how it's very distressing. It's dangerous to have such an ability in a non-believing world."

"It's a pain in the ass frankly, excuse the French," I said.

"If you really are a seer and can see death, you need to remember, *L'homme n'est ni ange ni bête, et malheureusement celui qui veut agir l'ange, agit la bête.* Man is neither angel nor beast, and unhappily whoever wants to act the angel, acts the beast."

"Pascal," said El, "but wasn't he talking about those who would think themselves angels because they pursue reason and that the pursuit of reason leads to passion which reduces a person to an animal?"

"True, but in this context, David apparently has been given the power normally associated with angels, but if he misuses it, he will become a beast. Dualism splits humankind into matter, spirit, evil, or good which is metaphysically flawed. A person's spiritual and mental health depends on the right order and balance of the whole being, body, and soul. David, you need to find a way to make the power you have compatible with the rest of your life. Otherwise, it will destroy you."

"That's the problem I'm seeking to solve, but I find I need to understand what it is and where it comes from, then I will be better able to deal with it."

"Maybe," Fionna said. "When Shakespeare wrote his lines, he didn't say Horatio would understand Hamlet's ghost just he needed to accept it." She had totally dropped her Islay hayseed accent and phraseology. "There was more there than expected. Somethings are beyond knowing, beyond inquiry others inquiry brings harmful implications."

Breanna bought the meeting to the end, pleading tiredness, and as we drove away, I realized we had been there for three hours, and we left with not much more knowledge than we had when we arrived. I was troubled that I hadn't been able to gain the understanding I considered so vital.

Back in California, things were about the same. I guess it's an element of self-aggrandizement to think that things will change when you're away. Most often, we were reminded by a lack of change how minuscule our impact is on the world.

We all had such a good time at Eleanor's investiture, and we made it a biannual event and picked a central location of Jackson, Wyoming. El and my sister, Daphne, did all the work. Peter got leave on his way to Korea and spent it with us. Mom and Dad continued to fade, the lights were dimming, and it was a race to which would go first. Dad's congestive heart failure was progressive. Mom's dementia slowly ate her mind. In her moments of lucidity, she was aware of their pending joint end, and I wondered if they were planning a collective exit.

I continued to visit Clifford. He was the only person who tried to help me understand, and he was such a fount of wisdom that it would have been criminal to ignore the resource. I had asked Clifford if it would be okay to bring El along, and he readily agreed. Over dinner prepared by Delores, Clifford broached the subject of my suffering overseeing the spots.

"The real elephant in the room, David, is the amount of suffering you do when you see the spot on someone. I bet it's a lot, and it's not lessening with the years or the recurrences."

"You're 100 percent correct, Clifford," said El, jumping ahead of me. "He really suffers, and it's deep and long-lasting. I really worry about him and his mental stability.

"I've contemplated suicide more than once," I said.

I was embarrassed to bring up such a sensitive subject, but it was true, and there was no reason to deny it. Besides, I'm sure Clifford knew.

"What do you think the meaning of suffering is, David?"

"I have wrestled with that for a long time, and I have various perspectives, none of which satisfies me or gives me peace," I replied. "There is the Catholic perspective which I got from Father Altois, there is the humanist perspective, and then there is my synthesis."

"It's a very complex subject and caused a lot of debate over the years," said Delores, "and I'm convinced it's one of those eternal questions of human existence that will always resist a global answer."

"My dad has quoted a line from Dryden many times. We, by our sufferings learn to purge our bliss," I said.

"True that!" replied Clifford. "However, it's pretty narrow and focuses only on the negative effects of suffering, not the positive power of the experience. It ignores, for example, that when we suffer, we are forced to focus on weaknesses. Suffering can reduce the rise of autotheisim."

We looked at him with questions in our minds, and he answered them, "It's the tendency of those with no other direction to think of themselves as gods, so it's self-god."

"The Greeks would have called it hubris, and in their cosmos, it would have unleashed punishment on those so arrogant to think themselves gods," I replied.

"There is no doubt that suffering is part and parcel of human existence, it's too widespread not to be, but suffering is also part of the mystery of humankind's existence. Through suffering, we discover ourselves, our humanity, our dignity, and our mission in life," Delores added. "I think it was your friend Frankl who said that the only unendurable suffering was suffering without purpose."

"The problem you face, David, and by connection you, El," said Clifford, "is that your suffering seems incurable and unending, giving you few opportunities to consider it ennobling rather than degrading. Psychologically there is a point at which suffering stops having value. At that point, the positive aspects of suffering are outweighed by the negative effects of mental deterioration, physical illness, and eventually self-harm. That led to the fate of Gavin's father and Hugh Miller and the others who had the same issues as you."

"Father Altois linked my suffering back to the redemptive suffering of Christ on the cross and said that my suffering was opening the path to salvation. That was right before he told me I had acted immorally in my reaction to Suzan's death. That charge of immoral behavior sticks in my craw. Frankly, I don't think I was immoral at all. I had a choice of actions. I could have dumped her when the cancer was discovered, I could have distanced myself during her struggle, but I didn't. I hung in there and suffered with her."

"You need to realize, David," said El, "that when Altois said that he was in pain himself and dying and was harsh in his judgments. You are the most moral person I know. As you have gained wisdom about your ability, you have tried to help and prepare others for their fate, unsuccessfully as it turned out, but their actions are not your failure, and they are theirs. The fact that you continue to recriminate yourself is a testament to the wisdom and kindness you have discovered via your suffering."

After we returned from Scotland, we started importing tea from McLarens, and Heather blended something special for us. I'm unsure if it was advancing age or awareness, but I felt more comfortable with my affliction, but I still wanted to understand it more.

A year after we'd been in Scotland, Dad passed away.

We often mark our time by the end of eras and Dad's marked the end of a phase of my life. In the immediacy of his death, I didn't have time to grieve because I was too busy dealing with the details. As days passed my grief grew stronger, and I found myself angry that he was no longer here, but at the same time, I realized that his death was just part of the scheme of things. I thought back on the times I could have been more loving to him and the times I caused him distress and beat myself up for what I perceived as my failures to be a good son,

In his office at their house, there had been a chest. It could've been an old sailor's chest. Made of dark wood, it had taken a mellow patina as it aged. The wood seemed to glow in the soft light. It was reinforced with brass hoops and had brass handles and locks. In all the years it had been around, none of us ever looked inside. We used

314

it as a seat or ladder to get books but never opened it. Now I did. It was a treasure trove and a revelation at the same time.

The first thing I pulled out was a giant scroll showing the entire genealogy of our clan stem back to the thirteenth century when we secured our lands around Culloden. We had secured them by judicial combat, Scot fighting Scot was kind of an old obsession, and the saying was that Scots preyed on their knees and on their neighbors. Beneath the scroll and some supporting documents was an expandable file with academic papers on Scottish folklore and legend. In the final layer were books—extraordinary books.

They were all in plastic cases; almost all were first editions. One had a note to me telling me to read the marked pages. It turned out to be Boswell's story of Dr. Samuel Johnson's trip to Scotland. The marked pages told of Johnson's discovery of seerism among the Scots, particularly in the Hebrides. There was another first edition of Martin Martin's book, and I still hadn't read the copy of Martin Grandma Ruth had given me. There was one more interesting than the rest written by someone using the nom de plume of Theophilus Insulanes. His real name was Donald MacLeod. Even though I'd floundered around researching the issue, Dad had done the work. There was also a letter to me.

David, the death of Shamus, started this project. I had wanted to tell you about the research for years, but the time never seemed right, or we were all too busy. What you have is called the sight or the second sight, the first being the ordinary sight of a human and the second sight of the seer. It has a long history. I suspect it was known in prehistory. Things like the sight are part of the mythology of human existence and are not often written down but passed verbally.

Given people's reaction to seers, I suspected this was a very closely guarded secret and probably wasn't talked about to outsiders. Nevertheless, there is a connection between people who have the sight. I never understood how or what the link was, but my mother was somehow connected to many others who maintained old traditions. I asked her several times, and she always shooed me away.

They're very secretive, and your grandfather was aware she had some connection but was not invited to be part of the choir or whatever Ruth was doing.

I remember a few times Mom would be gone for several days, usually in early spring and late fall. I also remember her getting cards from someone written in a language I had never seen. She always told me it was Polish and was for the farm down the road. Unfortunately, I never got to do all the research I wanted; you know what Frost said, so I collected this for you. Hopefully, it will be of some use to you.

Love always,
Dad

CHAPTER 18

Since the advent of the spots, I always wondered if I would still feel real emotion. Would they so jade me that emoting would take more and more stimulus? As I sat in Dad's now-and-forever empty office, tears poured down my cheeks for this man of learning who cared so much. He collected this treasure trove to help me on my way.

Mom was living with El and me, and we had plenty of room with Beatrice and Fergus in college, but it was a shame to watch that bright mind and sharp wit degrade to someone who couldn't remember where the bathroom was or what to do there. We had part-time help, but we knew there would soon be a time when we would have to put her in a "place."

About five months after Dad died, she left us. I mean, she got up and walked away. We searched high and low and finally had to bring in the police. They found her sitting at a picnic bench in a regional park. The policewoman who found her said she had a look of peace and contentment, not one of a person who died of exhaustion or exposure. The only thing that was strange was that she had a blanket like those used in hospitals for newborn, and it was cradled in her arms like it held a child. Her last act was to connect with my dead brother.

Her passing turned on the emotional machine again. A few weeks after her death, I was okay because I had things to do. She and Fergus had kept a secret for years. She had selected what she wanted to be read at her funeral. It was not so much a remembrance of her as it was a direction for the rest of it. When Fergus read Christina Rossetti's *When I Am Dead, My Dearest*, I was overcome with loss and grief. I cried unashamedly and copiously, thereby answering the question of the degree of jade in my soul.

When the funeral was over, I began to live my life without them. I was overwhelmed by loneliness and loss. There were nights, just before Morpheus claimed me, I would see them hand in hand waving at me, and I wanted to join them. Several times I passed the room Mom had used, and, in my imagination, I could hear her voice and smell her scent. Once, our twin Fionna said something that sounded so like Mom in tone and phrase. I ran to see if Mom was there.

Alexander, the other twin, was very much like Dad, bookish, learned, quite capable, strong-willed with an inquiring mind. I could almost see him down on Culloden Farms like Dad quoting Renaissance poetry to the cows. When I was working on a complex problem for a client, I would see a vision of Dad when no solution came, doggedly reading his books and reminding me more study was likely needed.

The losses stayed with me far longer than I felt they should, but El summed it up.

"Who says there has to be a time limit? I think it's wonderful you have such vibrant memories." She was right, of course, but there were times, in the early morning, the bushes and trees indistinct in the pre-light, they would speak to me, "Let us go, David. It's okay. We are free and happy."

Their passage affected how the spots impacted me. Before, I struggled with them, like I didn't want to see what I had to see. It was an unwelcome intrusion into my happiness, and I resented them. After Mom and Dad passed, I started to see the spots differently with less trauma. They became almost a natural part of life. However, Mom and Dad's passing did not remove the problem that haunted me initially; the contradiction between knowing a dark secret and the suffering it would bring and the need to stay silent for personal preservation.

I had struggled for years over the morality of my position. Over the years, different people advanced different views of the moral quandary. The first was that no one was obligated to tell a person distressing or even offending news. To do so, cheapened the effect, and the knowledge reduced the negative impact and thus the learning from suffering. There was a note of truth in that formula. Since the time of Homer, man has come to wisdom through suffering.

The second part of the formula was that since my divulging the information could not change the outcome, my intelligence was useless, and I needed not complicate things.

To me, this argument is flawed. Wisdom might come from suffering, so could much ill. Most people accept bad news in the same way, and death is undoubtedly bad news. To gain wisdom, one must contemplate the situation or see a direct link to a cause. For example, science showed that smoking led to a whole raft of illnesses, including long, painful, disfiguring death, yet people did not gain the wisdom to stop. Some did, others did not.

I started to read the books Dad and Grandma had left me, and they were no more accessible to read now than the first several times I started, but this time, I was incentivized to read and find the answers. One of the books was by a pastor who spent a considerable amount of time researching the sight and came to believe it existed and was not contrary to Christianity.

It turned out the sight was a long tradition in Scotland going back hundreds of years. There had been people who could see the future; there was a great deal of imprecision about who these people were and even if they existed. The penalty for having the sight in those unenlightened times was death, most likely, but the punishment was social death in the civilized world, so not a lot had changed. I also learned the sight was most often found in men, though, there were some notable cases of women, but most had been men. I also learned it could skip multiple generations.

Many of the seers I read about were very unhappy, and many killed themselves in anguish. Nevertheless, I was determined self-murder would not be my fate, so I had to dig in and understand my gift.

Two years after Mom and Dad had died, a card arrived. Always a card. *David, please visit me again. Breanna Campbell.* Again, no address or phone. We booked our trip almost immediately; it was summer, and maybe the temperature would be above 40°. This time we went directly to Port Ellen.

The first day we were in the post office, I asked one of the clerks how to contact Breanna.

"'Tis Breanna, is it?" "Most who wish to see her leave a note with Mrs. Adair at the next shop but one."

Mrs. Adair ran a general store of sorts. She was a bright white-haired septuagenarian with rosy cheeks, bright-blue eyes, and a permanent smile, which did nothing to hide her less than admirable dental work.

"Ay, Breanna, be ya kith or kin?"

"Neither, we met her two years ago, and she invited us back," said El.

"'Tis many who seek her, leave a note here, and she'll get it," said Mrs. Adair, patting a pile of letters and large envelopes on the stool next to her counter. "It might be a time, though. She's busy wa wid the celebrations."

"Celebrations?" I asked.

"Ay, 'tis the summer festival up to the park, you'll see the caravans. Come from all over they do."

Two days disappeared with no word, we'd gone out exploring, and I kept leading us to the distillers lining the southern shore Ardbeg, Laphroaig, Lagavulin, and Cola Isla. On the third day, without hearing from Breanna, we explored the far western side of the island and followed a guidebook we had found to prehistoric sites. We got on a farm track leading us to what was called Cultoon. It was a rough track and long, but we finally got to where the stone circle was supposed to be, but it wasn't visible from the car. We got out and hiked up the rocky terrain, generally headed west. About two hundred yards off the track, we found it.

Cultoon is the only complete stone circle still in existence on Islay, according to the guidebook. There were three stones upright, and twelve more lying on the ground or partially buried. In all, it was an ellipse of one hundred twenty feet by ninety feet. The signs indicated they dated to 2500 BC and were believed to relate to druidic worship. We walked among the stones, amazed at how difficult it must have been to get them to that location. Strangely, given that the outside temperature was in the '60s, the standing stones seemed warm to my touch.

El went back to the car to get the camera. It would be romantic and magical to tell you I was transported to some other dimension or place. What happened was almost as incredible.

I felt I was being pushed to the center of the ellipse to stand still and close my eyes. As I stood there, all my tension and concerns faded. I felt at home. My mind recorded voices speaking a language I didn't understand, but somehow, I understood them. The voices were warm like a mother talking to a child. I have no idea how long I stood there. Finally, the hold on me lessened, but I was left feeling at peace as if the world and I were in harmony. I was drained but happy. The Navajo talk of being in beauty's way, and perhaps that's where I was.

Then El was alongside me. "I hope some of the pictures came out. That was amazing!"

"Why?" I asked.

"You were standing there with your head partly thrown back and motionless, then a smile started at the corners of your mouth then spread to become the most beatific smile I have ever seen. You looked so incredibly peaceful. Every so often, you would move your head like you were cocking an ear to hear something." She was breathless, smiling, and joyous.

"But the best part was the God beam!" A God beam was our description of the times when rays of sunlight break through clouds and illuminate small areas like a spotlight. "A beam stayed on you for thirty to forty seconds; your face was so beautiful and angelic. I hope I got some shots of it. I've never anything like it. It reminded me of the description in Matthew of Jesus's baptism."

"Were there angels?" I asked in all seriousness.

"Not that I saw," she replied, laughing, unsure if I had asked a serious question.

Now that the experiences were over, I was a bit shaky. I wrapped my arms around El,

"Oh, my love," I whispered into her hair. "My love, my love, my love" was all I could say. I was still shaky, so El drove, and she kept looking over at me as I sat there with a one hundred-mile stare.

We retraced our steps and drove into the town of Portnahaven, stopping at a local pub called the Grapes. Unlike the Shepherd, this place was well populated. It was getting colder, and after my experience, I needed a drink. El and I ordered whiskey and sat sipping it quietly in a corner.

"You'd be the Yanks, that's aboot," asked one of the men. He was noticeably short and of indeterminate age. His face was weathered, and he had a unibrow which partly concealed his eleven on his forehead. His clothes were shabby and dirty, and there was a distinct smell of animal dung about him.

"Yes, we're from the states," said El.

"'Tis Breanna you've come to see no doubt like all the other furiners." This was said in a way indicating non-approval.

"We were here a couple of years ago," I said, "to see her, and we've come back to visit our friend."

"She's no friend, that one—a witch is what she is," said a nasty-looking man standing at the corner of the bar. He was large and overweight, his face a mask of disdain. "Ought ta be in jail that one and the young witch too."

"Shush now, Duncan Thomas, such talk'll scare the lass," said the bartender.

"Ah know what I know," said Duncan, "she's dark spots aboot her; she's a badun for sure." Duncan took a drink. "Remember wee Jamie?"

We had heard something about Jamie before, so he asked what had happened.

The more garrulous of the two men, Alex, he of the shabby clothes, said, "Ay, he wasn't a Scot, Jamie, but a bonny lad for 'tall. Bought farm down road, raising sheep he was for the new crofters."

We must've looked perplexed, so Will the landlord added, "There's a group of people over to the coast," he said, waving his arm generally west, "will only weave wid all-natural wool, takes a particular sheep.

"Ay," continued Alex, "doing right well he was, couple distilleries found a peat bog there, and he set to cutting peat for them."

"Alex works the peat for the workings," added William.

"He needed to expand and starts to build a bigger barn for the beasts and when the trouble started." Alex sipped his beer. "He finds some great flat gray stones near the barn, so he hires men to get them up, so they use them to build the barn." He sipped his beer again, stretching out the tale. "Well," he said, looking at the dregs of his beer mournfully. His voice and manner improved when I signaled Will for another round. "They just got the first of great rocks up, and who shows up? Breanna."

"How many of these stones were there?" asked El.

"Don't rightly know, lass," said Alex, "several, I think. Anyway, Breanna—"

"Bloody witch," interjected Duncan, who I could see needed a refill.

"Breanna, all high and mighty like tells Jamie not to cut or move the stones. They're sacred like."

"Fooking hag," said Duncan.

"Duncan, that'll be enough o that kinda language with a lass present."

"Wee Jamie ignores her, and they cut up a couple more stones, and he's building a great fine barn, and the sheep get sickly. The wool gets sticky and smelly, so he canna sell it, then beasts start to die."

"All of them?" I asked.

"Ay, but not all at once, takes a few months. Government man says don't know what's wrong says maybe put beasts in different pasture, they still all died. Jamie was smart. He bought insurance on the sheep, and they paid off he bought more," added William.

"But Jamie kept cutting the stones and building the barn when his lass—he married a local, Leah MacDermen—gets killed when the cutter blade of Jamie's automatic peat cutter snapped. I always said machines kill people. Canna do better than a good peat spade."

"How terrible!" said El.

"Aye, and she be wid child too," said Duncan, making the sign of the cross. "Bloody witches," he added for emphasis.

"Wee Jamie sold farm moved Ireland. Broken he was, finished."

"You think she cursed Jamie?" El asked.

"What else ya call it? Evil things come wid that woman," said Duncan.

All there nodding in agreement, as were four or five others who had walked in during the tale.

"Someone asked her about it, and all she said was remember the stones," added Will.

El and I gathered our things, bought another round, and left. We drove toward Port Charlotte and then around the end of Laggin Bay and turned south toward Port Ellen. We were surprised by the number of what we call RVs, but in England, they are called caravans, all seemingly headed north.

We had not heard from Breanna, so we took our time the next day. We were in the hotel dining room finishing breakfast when she entered. Again, I was struck by how she moved, gliding, not walking, every muscle and joint in unison, with no hint of a gait or age. The waitstaff seemed to know her. As she passed, they stood respectfully aside like she was royalty. Others in the room noticed, and eyes turned as she and Fionna transited the room.

I stood and took her outstretched hand. "David, good of you to come. Hello, Elspeth, I hope your time here has been fruitful?"

She declined both the chair and tea, pleading a busy schedule, but would we care to come at noon the next day? We, of course, would. Then like smoke, she wafted away, leaving most people wondering what happened. It might've been my imagination, but it seemed we received just a soupçon of additional deference due to Breanna visiting our table.

We took the rest of the day just to hang out. In the London papers, I saw that Gareth Neucombe, after years in exile, had written a new play that he was going to produce and direct. It dealt with a man's journey to knowledge. I commented to El that all Gareth needed to do was to star in the play, and he could really blow smoke up his own ass. Teatime found us near the ferry docks. As we sat in the bow window of the tea shop, we watched the caravans rolling off the ferry. Our waitress, who was also the owner, overheard our comments.

"Aye, they all be comin' for the doings up north, not a farthing do they spend here. Most of them furriners too, I'll have naught to do with all that nonsense!" she said with real anger and feeling.

"Is this special? Does it happen often?" El asked.

"Every bloody year they come, the furiners."

I was beginning to feel that a foreigner was anyone not from Islay. "Such doings, go on I've heard, I've heard dancing, singing lots of drinking, foolishness. I say furiners!" she said as a Parthian shot.

The rest of the day was spent walking, shopping, and looking. I didn't mind shopping with El. She was eminently practical and aware of my short attention span for such things. She glanced, and if she found something, there was none of the usual comparisons, usually three items, one of which worked. We always delighted in our chances to be together in companionship, placing no demand on the other. It was companionable and could exist in silence without hurt feelings, feelings of abandonment, or neglect.

The next day was the summer solstice. In recent times, pagan imitators claiming ancient wisdom and provenance claimed the day. Really, they were desperately seeking to infuse meaning into lives centered on the self, which found no justification beyond individual choice.

We joined the heavy traffic headed north, leaving ourselves plenty of time to get there by noon. We passed the Shepherd and saw Aaron had moved tables outside to catch some of the traffic. I thought I saw McKenzie sitting there with some visitors. It was an interesting flow of vehicles. Registrations from Germany, Spain, Ireland, France, quite a few I didn't know. Traffic was slow, giving us plenty of time to find the turn to Breanna's house. Unfortunately, the Scottish Road improvement had not made it this far; it was still rutty and empty.

By day, the house was even more impressive. The place was enormous and looked like it had just come straight up out of the earth. By night I had not seen them, but there they were, huge gray-black stones, about seven to ten feet high, five to six inches deep, maybe four to six feet wide. One was directly across from the main door. I could see another one to the south and knew there were two more. We used the knocker and Fionna appeared.

"David and Elspeth! Welcome you are, welcome you'll be in weather fair or foul. Blessings on ye," she said, almost chantlike.

"Blessing upon you, Fionna, and all who reside here," replied El.

"Come ya in, Breanna, be back in a bit. She had doings to tend to."

We entered the house, and for the first time, I saw the foyer in daylight. It was overwhelming in its immensity, soaring up thirty or more feet. The heavy beams bore all the marks of being hand-hewn. I put my hand on the stone. It was warm to the touch. We walked into the kitchen dining area where we had tea two years ago. Down the hall, I could see out of a window another of the stones. I nudged El and nodded in that direction.

After we had dropped off our coats and the other material we had brought, Fionna took us on tour. We entered the southern wing to a great room with a fireplace on the east wall, stairs to the second story, and the entire south wall was windows and French doors leading out to a large garden.

"Aunt's room is just above. That's the garden for herbs and such," she said.

"Last time we were here, there was a baby in trouble. I hope they're, okay?" El asked.

"Aye, right as rain she is, fine bonnie barin and my goodness wa a set o lungs! They don't know everything, doctors."

We moved back to the central atrium, which soared up forty feet with essentially a moon or sunroof in part of the ceiling. As we passed the west wing entrance, Fionna waived airily, "Down there are the bedrooms four up, four down, my own wee room just there." She indicated to the first room on the right.

I noticed high in the atrium, flags and tartans. So I made a note to ask about them, we entered the north wing, and the breath came out of our lungs.

The floor was entirely of stone, closely fitted with no grout lines. The far end was floor-to-ceiling windows maybe eleven feet high, and the view was spectacular. Some distance away was a hill a bit higher than ours. In the deep valley between the hills, just a glimmer in the broken sunlight, ran a creek or burn as they are called in Scotland.

The hillside was covered with heather in full bloom. Patches of white, blue, green, and pink played across the land, interspersed with a few trees and shrubs. Sheep or perhaps cattle grazed and here and there, and we could see small groups of people, who appeared to be gathering firewood. I immediately flashed on the opening scene of Hardy's Return of the Native.

In the center of the room was a circular fire pit set down two steps. It was about ten feet across and not ornamental. I looked up and saw a large opening for the smoke. "This is the aite coinneachaidh," said Fionna in Gaelic, but it sounded like gibberish to me.

"That's a lovely sounding word, but what does it mean?" asked El.

"Gaelic doesn't always translate exactly to English, so I guess the best translation would be meeting place."

"What kind of meetings? It would be a great place for weddings and things like that!" El said, enthused with the uniqueness of the space.

"Nay, nay, it's the place of the bal tein." Before she could continue, Fionna tensed for just a second before saying, "Aunt's back. We best go meet her."

I looked at El, and she at me. We had heard nothing.

"This is an amazing place, Fionna. I can't figure out if it's old or new," I said.

"A dinna know really," she said, "'tis always been here."

It was midsummer. The light lingered long on the Islay hill-sides. In the hollows, it was dusky. As we walked back to our starting point, we could see an endless row of headlights headed east into the hills and disappear. Beyond the hill, I could see the diffused lights as if there was a town there, but I knew it was parkland. We walked back to the center and into the south wing.

Breanna was standing in the great room. "Welcome back, David and Elspeth, and blessings on you." She looked more tired, her formerly ageless face drawn, her complexion paler. She was nervous, too like a cat when a dog was nearby.

Fionna seemed nervous, and for the first time, I noticed she had bags under her eyes.

"And on you, Breanna," I said, "this is an incredible place you have."

"It's comfortable for us," she said.

We sat around a large coffee table in the great room. "Breanna, thank you for taking the time to talk to us again. It's very gracious. A good deal has happened since we were last here."

"David, strange it is, and stranger still it will be. I was not fully open with you the last time, so I owe ye." Her language was taking on a Scottish brogue, which I had never heard her use before. It wasn't the tongue of one who is uneducated, nor was it posh as she spoke. I had images of farms.

I unrolled the scroll Dad had made. "My father passed away a few months back." My voice caught in my throat.

"His ember burns but faintly," said both women.

"Thank you," I said. "Before Dad passed, he collected a large amount of information on Scottish legends and folklore and had this made." I handed the paper to Breanna.

She and Fionna huddled around it, pointing to various people muttering and what I presumed was Gaelic.

"He also had collected some books, including another copy of Martin Martin's book on the folklore of the Scottish Highlands. You remember my grandmother gave me a first edition."

"I suppose he also had the book by that blowhard, Samuel Johnson, or really his mouthpiece Boswell," said Breanna. She rattled off the names of some of the other books Dad had saved for me.

"Then there is this," said El, taking an envelope out of her purse. "Elise, David's mother, wrote this to me, and even David has not read it." She handed copies to the three of us. We read in silence the description of my birth. I read, and I watched Breanna and Fionna glance and nod to each other.

"Wednesday's child," said Fionna.

"What?" said El.

"David was born in the wee hours of Wednesday his poor brother on Tuesday. Wednesday's child is full of woe according to the old reckoning."

"And encaul too," added Breanna.

"Is that important?" asked El.

"Well, 'tis said a caul is a sign of good luck. It was a center-piece of Dickens's *David Copperfield*," said Fionna. "In this case, the Wednesday's child belief may be canceled by the caul."

"There is something else about being born encaul," said Breanna. "In mythology and Christian iconography, there is often an almond shape surrounding the blessed or divine person called a mandorla. Mandorla is Italian for almond. In some cultures, it's called a fish bladder, but it signifies the source of all things. To be born encaul is very rare, to begin with, and in ancient times such an occurrence would be taken as a sign of connection to divine powers."

"David had an unusual experience at one of the stone rings," said El.

"Oh?" the two of them said together. "Which one?"

"I think it's called 'Cultdoon over by' Port Charlotte," said El. She described what happened, adding her impressions, and I watched Breanna and Fionna grow more focused and ill at ease.

Breanna took the lead. "Well, David, the time is come to tell you some things. Some of them you've guessed or found by your efforts, and we're going to tell you more. Some of what I say will sound outlandish, some perhaps blasphemous, some downright silly. Take it as you will. I can't control that, but I will tell you the truth as I know it." She paused, waiting for our acquiescence, which she got.

"Over the years, you have been troubled with what you see and what happens, and you have tried to find explanations, and I think failed as you had to. The reason you have failed is you were looking at the problem with the wrong set of eyes and trying to understand with the wrong parts of your brain." She had an intense look, which comes when one speaks the truth.

"I'm not sure what that means," I replied.

"There are things in the world, which don't respond to logic and can't be discovered by searching. They have to be lived and felt.

You are at the point where your research, reading, and doctors' visits have left you at a standstill. I'm sure someplace in all of this some minister or priest has told you this is the result of sin, the devil and questioned not only your sanity but also your moral compass."

She was, of course, right. On the first visit, I had partially told them my story without detail about Jacoby or the doctors in San Francisco and my conversations with Father Altois. Still, she seemed to know the path I had taken, I was impressed and wondered how she knew so much, but I was also spooked to think she was somehow watching everything I did.

"You're right. The first person I told the full details to was a psychologist who was also a Baptist minister, and he brought in the devil. A priest now gone who I dearly loved, questioned my moral compass. I did consult with some doctors who think I am a mythological hero seeking new knowledge. The books are confusing and very troubling."

"What we have to say," said Fionna, "may add to your discomfort or give you some peace. We will see. When you were last here, we told you your grandmother, Ruth Lovat, and we two were sisters, not in DNA but belief."

"I would appreciate having that explained," I said, "to my knowledge. My grandmother never was in Scotland, didn't speak Gaelic, and didn't know you at all, yet you claim sisterhood but sisters in faith. What faith? Grandma was a Catholic."

"David," began Breanna, "these eilean, our word for island, are places where people have lived for thousands of years." She paused searching for the right words. "In the early days, people rarely moved, and the people of the islands, the eileanach, began to develop unique beliefs. As the earth changed, the eilenach discovered doirlinn, causeways allowing passage from one island to the other, and belief began to spread." She paused to sip tea. "It was a belief based on nature. It was animistic. I hope you understand that animistic faith is different from polytheism."

"We have a basic understanding of the differences," said El. "One places spiritual content and elements in natural phenomena and objects, the other attributes divine power to physical beings."

"Yes," said Breanna. "That's a good and straightforward way to say it. One of the elements of the faith was reverence for the dead. When people died, they were buried in cairns where their spirits would spread into the rocks and soil. So the spiritual nature of the stones would increase over time.

"The word *sith* is confusing in Gaelic and can mean peace, mound, or even fairies, for example, ban-sitean and the fear-sithean or the people of the mound or people of peace. So the spirits came to be called sluagh sith, which translates most readily to people of peace. Fionna, why don't you take over? I'm more tired than I realized."

"Since the spirits were in the natural world and the everyday object of people's lives, it was believed the sluagh sith would and could influence and interfere with the lives of the living. It also came to be believed that the sithean wanted to communicate with the living and not be walled off. In the world of these early people, there was no difference between the spiritual world and what we would call the secular.

Gone was the country bumpkin, and this Scottish Beatrice was lecturing us like a professor. I could only imagine what our Beatrice would make of this. We were nodding our heads. I'm not sure if it was agreement or sympathy, but I was fascinated, and I must have smiled.

"Are you smiling at our silliness or in agreement and revelation, David?" asked Fionna.

"Neither. I was just imagining our daughter sitting there and lecturing us. You look like her and sound like her!" We all laughed.

"To go on, you may have heard of the Druids?" Fionna continued. "Most people know something about them, most of it incorrect. The Druids were descended from this earlier faith and took it in their direction, but the root faith of the pre-druids continues, and your grandmother, Ruth Lovat, and the other woman in the book were all adherents to the faith, as are Breanna and me."

Breanna picked up the narrative. "Our belief and faith, if you will, stretch back almost before time. Before Columba and the coming of the Christians, before the druids—"

"About the time of Stonehenge or Avebury?" I interrupted excitedly.

"Those newcomers? No, when the land was young, and those who passed stayed in the land and *the stones*. You might call them Druids, but the Druids built on the ways of those ancient ones. As civilization advanced, it displaced people of the faith who moved to the heather and bracken, but the belief has continued unbroken for millennia."

Fionna picked up the tale. "One element of the faith is that there are holes in the fabric of life and death. Through the holes, the living could gain glimpses of the future, but only those whom the sithean found capable. The ability to see apparitions of the living and the dead is called *da shealladh*." She pronounced it *daa haloo*, "the second sight."

"The taibshear," which she said as tysher, "means he who is specter haunted, and this part is important because it is most often seen in men. The taibshear show the living what will happen to the person represented. It can be to see the mode of death or some other symbol such as your spots. It takes skill to understand the meaning, and the meaning of the prophecy is not known until it happens and when it's too late to change."

We all took drinks of cold tea, which Fionna instantly refreshed. This was heavy going.

"Since this showed up, I have wondered about several things," I said, "maybe you have answers. "Why me? Is the sign changeable? If I tell a person, can the death be prevented? Do or can I cause the spot or the death by bad thoughts or bad feelings? Will it ever go away, permanently?"

"You," said Breanna, "have also wondered if you have a moral responsibility and if you are a moral agent. These are questions you wrestled within your conversations with Father Altois."

"How did you know about those conversations?"

Breanna looked me straight in the eyes in a confrontational way. "It didn't occur to you that I might have some of the gifts of sight? I don't have it the same way you do, but I know things, and there's a connection to you, similar to—what are those things—modems.

Those of us in the faith have some ability to know things. Your grandmother had it, so did Ruth Lovat. Your grandmother communicated with me as did Ruth Lovat, not with letters but with our faith via the taibshear connection."

"You are saying David's grandmother, Ruth Lovat, and you are some sort of connected sisterhood, leaders of the faith?" asked El.

"The early Celts and later druids had female and male priests and divines as did the Norse. Our faith, which existed before the first druid was thought of, transmits via the female priesthood only. Yes, we are and were all priests or priestesses of the faith. We call ourselves gairn a-mach."

"That explains the address book that David's grandmother had," said El.

"It wasn't an address book although it looked like one, and it was supposed to be destroyed when the gairn a mach pass. It was the rites of the faith like a Catholic lectionary or a grimoire," said Fionna. "It's written in the tongue of the old ones, and it's pregaelic. That's the reason you couldn't translate it. It's coded purposely to prevent outsiders from reading it. If the ceremonies are not done correctly, the gairn a-mach can become a taibhsearan, haunted by the taibhs, and the curtain of the world can be opened."

I was challenged in everything I believed about spirituality. "You believe this happens? I mean, this is hard to take. That there is a parallel world of spirits and diviners, alongside the established religions, and that there is a secret female society that communicates without writing or electronics and has done so for thousands of years. Don't you think that sounds just a little silly?"

"David," said Breanna,. "You are living proof of its existence, and besides who established those other religions? Compared to the faith, they are all parvenue. Those other religions were created from the bones of other faiths, especially Christianity."

"How can you say that!" I was getting pissed off.

"Well, let's look at Christianity. The Easter Celebration is when?"

"It's the Sunday following the full paschal moon."

"Right," said Breanna, "and the paschal moon is the first full moon on or after the spring equinox, which is March 21. In our faith, equinoxes are the time of balance as the world swings from dark to light, and the spring equinox is called Alban Eiler or light of the world. What is it Christians call Jesus the light of the world?" She looked at us but felt we needed more convincing.

Fionna picked it up. "How about Samhain, one of the Celtic fire festivals. It happens in the current calendar between October 31 to November 1. During those days, there are Christian festivals like All Hallows Eve and All Saints Day. At Samhain, we believe the barrier between the world of the living and the world of the dead is the thinnest and that knowledge can flow each way. In February, we have the festival of Imbolic or the beginning of spring, and the farmers know it has lambing season. Most religions, like most things, are evolutionary, not revolutionary, and our faith is the foundation of belief from the wells of time."

"There can't be many believers, can there? I've never heard of it, and I live in California, where every new thought becomes a religion."

Fionna got up and walked to the windows and pulled aside the curtains. There across the valley were the three cylinders of light, and lights glowed behind the hills like an unseen village.

"Those lights are the druid sign and really shouldn't be there. All those other lights beyond the hills are those who come to celebrate Alban Haruin, the light of the shores or midsummer's day. Shakespeare built on that celebration in his play.

"What made us cautious of you, David, was the way it manifests itself. We have never heard of it being in spots, nor appearing to anyone so young, of it taking breaks, and being only focused on disease, violence, or accidents," said Fionna. "The men we have known to have the sight have seen avatars. Most see the avatar once and never again because death always occurs quickly. Furthermore, you are different because death occurs at various times, and you do not know the method, again a unique manifestation."

"Did they only see fire hanging, or did they see accidents or disease?" I asked.

"You are the first to see disease and to see it constantly even after the first appearance. I imagine that has presented some challenges," said Breanna.

"I wish I weren't unique," I said.

"Most of the men affected would say the same thing," added Fionna, "some choose suicide as a route out of it. It's never been easy to bear."

"Most have not had the support of a woman of your parts, Elspeth," said Breanna.

Before we got too far in the weeds, I decided to get some questions answered about our hosts. "Breanna, before we go a lot further, I'm interested in you two. We've been to Islay twice, and you two are held in awe. When you came into the hotel dining room, the staff treated you like royalty. I expected them to bow and curtsey. We have heard you called witches and accused of foul doings. Everyone knows of you, but no one seems to know you."

Breanna sat for a few seconds organizing her thoughts.

"Those stones you visited are called Druid stones, but that's not correct. They were here long before the Druids or Stonehenge. The faith that made those stones isn't BC or AD. It goes back to the basement of time and life. The power of the spirits of all who have passed is centered there."

"Those stones and the ones surrounding the house contain great power, but they cannot be touched with metal tools. They had to be worked with stone and wood. Once erected, they dare not be changed or moved except by nature." She stopped, seeming to wonder how much further to go. "What you experienced in the Cultoon circle is an example of the power residing there and only available to those who believe or who have special gifts."

"Does your position—I guess, is the word—flow in families? For example, Fionna is your niece," said El.

"Breanna is not my aunt. We use that word because it reduces questions."

"The word for our relationship is *oileanach*, which doesn't translate well to English, but in your Catholic faith, it would be like *catechumen*," said Breanna.

"I have been wondering at the relationship. Breanna, you look so young," said El.

"Tonight is my eightieth solstice and Fionna's fifty-fifth."

"No way you are eighty!" I said, genuinely in shock, "You move so gracefully. You don't look more than thirty-five or forty," I said, stumbling at the age and knowing what women get testy if you're wrong on their age.

"You were both born on June 21?" asked El.

"I said it was my eightieth solstice, not my eightieth year." She left that enigma to hang there.

I asked, "How do you maintain contact with the others?"

"When you tried to profit in the ring, you heard voices or sounds, correct?" asked Fionna.

"Yes, they were terrible voices and visions in dreams even in the daylight, but I don't know what kind of voice I heard at the ring. It was in a language I think might have been Gaelic." I thought for a second. "You use the rings to communicate?"

"No, the rings are places of sacred power. Our faith communicates through the unity of the earth in nature. Perhaps the simplest way to say we connect with the continuity and leave messages, it's not telepathy," added Fionna.

"So you got a message of David's grandmother passing as did Ruth Lovat?" asked El.

"Yes, both bodies had passed their embers, what Christians call the soul, continue to exist in the continuum along with millions of others so they…"

"Glow dimly," I finished.

"What you experienced at the ring were the tabilths," explained Breanna. "Those who have your condition have an indwelling of the tabiliths."

"I can see why you said this might be difficult," I replied.

The horrible figures you experienced when you tried to profit were the tablishears of the demon form. Your profits rent the fabric between the worlds, letting the tablishears through momentarily. Once you made it right, the tears were healed."

I thought for a minute before speaking. "I have had a hard time reconciling the spots and my Christian and Catholic faith. I wonder if seeing the spots and taking no action violates some duty to help the dying prepare for death and attain grace."

"The sight of the seer, *an da shealladh*, has been part of human existence since before the current newfound concept of God was formed by the academics of the thirteenth century," said Breanna. "It is derived from nature and the need to make nature and man coherent."

I excused myself to use the bathroom, and as I was coming back, El was on the way, and we kissed.

"We are finally getting the answers," she said.

CHAPTER 19

I came back to where we had been sitting, and a fire was burning in the fireplace. I would have sworn there was no wood or peat in the fireplace before I left. Now firewood was burning brightly. How it got laid and lit that quickly was another mystery.

When El came back, we resumed our conversation.

"I get the feeling there is something much more complex involved here, something that would be dangerous."

"You would be correct. It's so strange that it was the reason Ruth, your grandmother, Clifford, and others were so cautious in our contacts with you," said Fionna.

"Have we satisfied your concerns sufficiently?" I said with not a little bit of bitterness.

"David, I know you are frustrated by the long process, by the things which the sight has led you to do, and by our purposeful deceit, but you must remember it was not long ago when people were tortured and burned for the traits you show and for our belief. You have experienced some that directly, have you not?" said Breanna.

"Yes, and it was none too pleasant. It almost destroyed our reputation in Los Altos and was really hard on our kids."

"What you have, David, this *an da shealladh*. The second sight is more than that," said Breanna. "The seer's sight is a well-known folkway in Scotland, and while most would set it down as folktale, it's real and has been around for thousands of years. You have two ancestors we know of who had the sight. You're named after one of them; the other lived in the time of Henry VIII."

"Ruth Lovat, my grandmother were—what do I call them—priests, ministers, fountainheads or maintainers?" I asked.

"We have no hierarchy, we just are keepers of the faith, and no one has tried to develop titles," said Fionna.

"Like the faith, we just are," said Breanna.

"It's confusing," said El. "People like to have structure, to know the flow of power, and to whom they are responsible. So something amorphous is hard to comprehend."

"Indeed," replied both ladies.

Fionna continued, "I don't expect we are going to give you much comfort on that score you are involved with something large and wonderful."

"Remember what Samuel Johnson said after his trip to the Highlands where we are unable to decide by antecedent reason, we must be content to yield to the face of testimony."

"Is it animist, naturalistic?" asked El, surprising me.

"I've been reading up on things like that, David," she said almost smugly but not really. El was never smug.

"I think," began Breanna, "that animist would fit but naturalistic, not naturalism. We don't believe that all spiritual events occur from nature. And we believe the good is revelatory. Also, we would characterize it as dualistic."

"Why is it not naturalistic? I mean, it's based on nature?" said El.

"Not really, we ascribe to each person a soul which is central to each person, but that soul doesn't indwell in inanimate objects," replied Fionna.

"So this an da shealladh curse I have is part of my soul? Is my soul fouled in some way? I asked. Like many people, I had a hard time staying focused on what appeared to me as esoteric discussions. Like many Americans, I was conditioned to short-term answers easily obtained.

"What you have is not a curse, David," said Breanna, leaning forward and putting her tea down. "It feels like it and can be very traumatic, but it's a calling from God to fight evil. It's a great weight to bear, but it is nothing you can't bear. The Faith gives you the strength to handle the stress and pain," she added.

"I wish The Faith didn't have such a high opinion of me," I said with a wry expression.

"You don't mean that David if you don't have the strength, you will use the sight for evil and damn yourself forever," said, Fionna.

I was silent.

"David," began Fionna.

Breanna rested a restraining hand on her arm. "David," said Breanna, "to fully understand or at least glimpse what we are talking about, you need to know that good and evil, spelled with capital letters, exist and not just as relative concepts but as real tangible things. Moral absolutes, things that are always right and always wrong, exist, and evil constantly seeks to destroy good."

"I can accept the idea of moral absolutes, things like the Ten Commandments you mean?"

"Yes, that is a good distillation of the concepts of the Faith. Most are shared in some way or another universally. Another is the Golden Rule of Christianity which verbalized Aristotle's golden mean in personal terms and was also one of the foundations of the ethics of the faith," said Fionna, as she continued to move from Scottish bumpkin to philosopher and prize student.

"If it is so ancient, why have we not had more instances of it in the general world?" I asked.

"There have been many examples, thousands, think of Joseph's dreams in Genesis, Elijah's trances, St. Therese of Avila for example," said Breanna.

"So how did good and evil get created? You haven't mentioned a God or anything," I asked.

"We believe there is a spirit that controls the universe. We have no name for it. Much as the ancient Hebrews had no name for God. He was what he was. Good was not created. It was and is the natural state of affairs. It's a truth revealed to people by life and maintained by people doing good and being in harmony with the earth and the faith. Many indigenous people had a similar concept of harmony as a goal," lectured Breanna.

"If the good is revealed, I sure would like to have it reveal something to me or reveal itself. all I have gotten is tragedy, anger, hatred, fear, and terrible depression. Is that what good is supposed to feel like?"

Unlike a lawyer who never asks a question they don't know the answer to, I made a mistake, and I was not ready for the reply.

"Good is and has been revealed to you by the very emotions you name, and that's how those called to do good learn the wisdom of the good," Fionna said. "Just as the Good has been revealed to me."

"Wisdom comes from suffering. The old Homeric codes?" I replied with less than overwhelming enthusiasm.

"Homer expressed the ancient Greek experience with the faith," Breanna said. "Can you read those poems and not see wisdom being gained by the various plagues and misfortunes? Either they gained wisdom, or they died. Job in the Bible is a perfect example of revealed good."

"I don't see I have gained any wisdom from this thing." I emphasized *the thing*, denoting disgust.

"Don't say that!" the three woman chimed in. "You are gaining wisdom. You need to open yourself to its revelation."

"How?"

"In a thousand ways, you have learned from every experience of the sight. What is remarkable about you, David?" Breanna rushed to say. "Is that you have only used the sight a few times for evil and that you immediately did good to heal the rent you made in the fabric. While good has always existed, evil is created by man. What separates the two is the fabric, which is just a term of art because there is no other way to express it. Man's arrogance and his choices created evil. While the good is revealed, evil wins its converts by adumbration. It hints at suggestions of alternatives. It's as relentless as a virus, ruthless as a terrorist and a changeable as the wind, always seeking power and control."

"Can't good or the controlling spirit control evil and strike it dead?" I asked, hoping for a simple answer but knowing it would be more complex.

"Not really," said Breanna, "good and the faith aren't anthropomorphic. They do not act as a man would act. Good depends on those who do good and cleave to the faith to maintain good and fight evil.

"So good maintains the fabric."

"Yes, but evil can rend it and seep through holes made when man makes evil decisions or falls prey to evil's lies," added Breanna.

"When you tried to profit from the sight, the horrible creatures you saw were the talibshears or the specters of those corrupted by evil. Your actions tore holes in the fabric and let some evil through," added Fionna unhelpfully.

"The sight is a sign of favor or disfavor in the faith?" I asked.

"That's up to you. You are special. You have this ability. Good exists, as does evil. No one polices you saying do this or don't do this except the sense that you are doing the right thing. Christians call it a conscience. For us, it is the immanent Good. You seem to have an unusual strain of the sight in that you get warning of good or evil," said Breanna.

"The thing has been going on for years. It has nearly driven David mad," said El.

"Yes, that's the burden of the sight, but its value too."

We had talked long into the night. The long Scottish day was slowing ebbing, and night crept up from the moorland. To the north, the lights of whatever was happening in the park created a barrier to the encroaching darkness. I could faintly hear music, mostly drumming, wafting to the house. Occasionally either Fionna or Breanna would glance a bit nervously toward the north.

"Sounds like quite a party up there." I nodded north.

"Hardly a party," snapped Fionna.

"'Tis the solstice, tis a critical festival to us," she continued.

"I'm sorry, I meant no offense," I said, chastised.

"David," began Breanna, "Christianity displaced paganism with a powerful message of a transcendent God of love and the promise of future resurrection and eternal life and for the last 1,500 years pushed out the concept of an imminent religiosity and sublime experience. It will not and has not totally eliminated the older religions it disparages."

It was quiet for a moment, and we continued to hear the distant music sounds before Breanna continued.

"Since the development of Christianity, primarily male-dominated Christianity, and its desire and willingness to punish belief straying from orthodoxy, human minds have been closed to the old ways, but the shadows are still there and leak through in the form of taidh and sithean manifesting itself in *ah da shealladh* or other powers.

You are living proof of the vitality of the faith. It's not devil worship, and those folks over there"—she waved generally to the north— "are not going to break in diableries. It's an old way of looking at the world and our place in it. We believe in the eventual divinity of humans, but only after successive lives have been led and experiences gained, moving them closer to God. So I maintain the ancient faiths are the truly established religions."

"What you are telling me is I'm a doorway between the living and the dead and, the spirits of the dead are working through me?"

The two women nodded in agreement.

"To what end are they working, and to what end am I the agent?"

"We don't know the full intent of sithhean."

"This is my destiny to be the bearer of death notices? Somehow that fills out my place on earth, and in the heavens, it seems like I got the short end of the stick."

"Of those who have had the sight, none of them ever thought of it as a gift. It takes a strong person and personality to bear the weight of the gift, just like Frodo was the only one of the fellowship who could bear the ring without being corrupted," Fionna said, referring to the Tolkien classic.

"As you found, you can never profit from it or lie about it to gain advantage or to discomfort others if asked you have to tell the truth, or the sithean will haunt you. It has always been thus," said Breanna.

"Can I cause the spots by my thoughts?"

"No, you are not the cause of the death. You only see it," said Fionna.

"I have no idea of the method or the time of death, just that it will happen."

"That's what is so different. You see the spot near or around where the disease or accident will occur, so you know something will happen there. For example, you saw the spot on Jean's father's nose, and he died of cancer of the vomer, a rare thing. Sometimes it will be obvious like Shamus and others subtle like the family in the mountains."

"If I had convinced Shamus to leave with me, he wouldn't have died, and if I could have convinced the family to go a different way, they would still be alive."

"Wrong. First you are second-guessing, and that is senseless, once the spot appears, that is the person's fate. You might delay it, but it will happen. Second, you don't want to break the chain of events and deny those who should gain wisdom and knowledge. You've never been successful convincing someone with the spot you're right, correct?" asked Breanna.

"No," said El, "and I've watched him try. David was right in the incident, and Henly died three years later of cancer. We ended up with twenty-five lawsuits, and we almost had to put the kids in private school."

Fionna carried on. "All those with the sight find the same thing today. In the older days, when the world had more faith before the arrogance of science and the world accepted things that couldn't be explained readily, the seers of the world were accepted and even honored. Today, none of us talk about the faith because we would be written off as nuts, fools, and even dangerous. That's why everyone was so hesitant to tell you about it. You also need to be prepared for this to follow in your family. There are a few occurrences of the sight passing father to son. More often, it will skip multiple generations as it did with you, so be ready someone else might have it and will need your guidance."

"There as so many questions I would like to ask, but I can see you two have had busy days, so if you answer one more question, we will leave you in peace."

"Okay," they both said together.

"We heard a story about a sheep farmer and peat cutter on the Oa who moved some stones after you told him not to and a series of misfortunes followed him. What happened?"

"That's really more than one question, but fair is fair, so we will answer it," said Breanna. "The island has been occupied for twenty-five thousand years and is the center of the old faith. When the Druids became the ascendant part of the faith, they ruled all of Britain, but the Romans pushed them back on the islands or the Druidhneach. So things went well for a few centuries until the Norse and then the Christians arrived." Breanna took a drink of her tea.

"The earlier faith practitioners built stone circles, cairns for the dead, and erected standing stones to make places of worship and to act as calendars if you will. When the Druids became ascendant, they built stone circles. The circles existed so the festivals of fire and light could be done at correct times. Since the faith believes that spirits inhabit all-natural things, the stones they used were sacred. Subject to some rules. I will let Fionna talk about that. She's more expert than I.

"The stones were monolithic, solid and of one piece. They cannot be worked with any metal. They were placed in particular locations and shaped at the tops to resemble the hills around them. They were places of great power. Over time, some were cast down, others broken up for building material, and some fell in the bogs.

"We know the location of the circles, and we know which have been profaned and which not. The ones on Jamie's land had fallen over but had not been touched, but they also must not be moved from the site, or the sithean will not be able to find them again. Jamie did not believe us. He moved some, broke a couple up to build a barn, and then his peat cutter hit one of the stones with its steel. When sithean cannot get back to their world, they become dangerous, and they will do damage to the living."

"That explains comments at the pub that you had always been here and about the use of stones in the house.

"The house is a circle site, and the stones outside needed to be left in place. Since stone is the one thing in abundance here as a building material, we needed to be sure none of it came from broken, scared stones, so we had to touch each of them. It would not do to seal up a sithean in the walls.

"The house does appear to be that old," said El.

"Parts of it that have been here since before Columba, and there has always been some sort of structure. This hill is one of the most sacred sites of the faith, not just this hill but the hills around here," said Fionna.

"So that is what is going on over there?" I said, nodding my head toward the window and the lights beyond the hill. "They come from all over the world and stay here a week."

"Most of the people we talked to think you are witches and that this is some sort of hippie thing," said El.

"We don't advertise it or tell much to the locals or anyone in the towns. We find that witch curse all the time, and people are afraid and intolerant of what they don't understand and mostly refuse to try to understand. You know the history of witch burning and inquisition, which has been part of humankind's legacy. It's not that we threaten anyone's faith or belief. It's that we are different, and that irritates people."

"People make a big deal of being individuals, and if you were to challenge them, they would aggressively deny they aren't, but they herd together and act as packs, and that's dangerous to us and those who follow the faith," said Fionna.

"My dad used to say if you want to know the IQ of a mob, take the lowest IQ in the group and divide it by the number of people in the group. It sure took hold in California during the incident. As El said, we almost were run out of town, and we still will likely move."

"We run into that here, with people like Gareth who didn't believe in us, the Christian God or anything. That's why he burned out. He had no belief system to maintain him in the troubled times we all have. A few hundred years ago, he was one of those who would have led the witch trials."

It was growing late, we had come at noon, and it was now past eleven. I could see that there was something else on their minds, so we took our leave. On the way down the hill, El asked me if we should drive up to the gathering.

I said no, and we had enough to think about, so down the lonely ridge we went, and out on the highway south for Port Ellen.

I drove through the gloom of the midsummer night. It was somewhere between needing headlights and not. It was almost metaphorical for what I now had to consider.

Like most people of the Christian faith, I had been brought up to believe that we had free will or the ability to choose between courses of action unimpeded, but here I was being told that my free will was limited.

Even if I saw the spots, I had the ability not to tell unless asked, so my free will extended partway, but my curse was part of my fate since I couldn't affect it in any way other than by my death. It was also part of the fate of those with the spots since they had, apparently, no ability to change the course of events, although they might be able to put off the ultimate end.

My fate overrode human destiny, and my fate was sealed, directed by a supernatural power beyond my understanding. That fate interfered with the destiny of others, or was their destiny their fate, or was their fate their destiny? My mind whirled with all the permeations of what we had heard.

"Do you believe what they said?" asked El.

"Yes. In all the years I have had this, there has never been a convincing explanation, and the reaction from Jacoby all those years ago sort of confirms the concept. He thought it was the work of the devil. Breanna and Fionna talked about the Christian churches and their desire to punish strays from the path of dogma. The fact that he was so powerfully affected indicates to me that this explanation is the correct one, however weird it might seem."

"It's hard to believe. We are both scientists, trained, and cleave to hard facts and the idea of disproving a hypothesis. Still, here we are on a lonely road on an island in Scotland, learning that one of us has something for which there are no hard facts and which life has shown is a fact and it's impossible to disprove. Hard for my rational mind to get a handle on this, and it must be an insurmountable challenge to yours."

This wasn't helping. I focused on other aspects of what we had learned, so I didn't respond beyond the typical married male grunt and nod. El noticed, however, that I was sufficiently distracted that I was driving on the right side of the road, and she made me pull over. We switched positions, and she took us the rest of the way, for which I was grateful.

CHAPTER 20

The next day, I penned a note to Breanna and Fionna, thanking them for taking time with me and being so forthright, hoping we could stay in touch. I left it at Mrs. Adair's store, and El and I started our journey back to the US.

I was still troubled by the experience in Scotland. I knew what I had, but I was still struggling with my responsibility. There was a story I had read about a fellow named Hugh Miller, who had the sight and struggled with it to such a degree that he committed suicide. I researched Miller's story and found that it was pretty well known. In reading further about Miller, I found he had been a pillar of the romantic view of Scotland.

As the story went, he just could not live with seeing the death of others, playing out like a TV rerun in front of his eyes.

He had foreseen his father's death in the form of a spectral hand and arm unattached to a body at the same time his father's ship disappeared. He had several experiences, witnessed by others, when he was suddenly unable to walk, claiming that the furies had hold of his legs. He seemed to take responsibility for his sights as if he were the source of them.

Suffering forces us to deal with our weaknesses, especially those that brought on the suffering. Miller accepted personal responsibility for something he had no control over. He had no choice but to see the visions. Still, his suffering did not lead him to wisdom about handling the grief. I was determined that I would not fall into the same trap.

I spent a good deal of my ample time reading up on the ancient religions and faiths of the Highlands and the Western Islands and the second sight. I read those great men of letters and science like

Samuel Johnson, Robert Boyle, and Samuel Pepys were interested in and studied the concept of sight.

The natural upwelling of interest in Scottish tradition and folklore was during the Romantic period of the nineteenth century when England rediscovered the Scots after the long repression following the Jacobite uprisings.

Many Scottish religious figures collected and wrote extensively on the folklore, and many talked about the second sight. It turned out that everything I had learned on Islay was true. You couldn't profit from it, and you couldn't avoid seeing it. It was always correct, and it was primarily found in men. My unique twist was my vision and death were disconnected often by many years.

This last was curious to me. In Western society, it is a sort of common belief that women are more spiritual than men. Yet according to my reading, *an da shealladh* was a connection through the fabric between the two worlds, so it would seem logical it would pass to women. Some women had the sight, but the great majority were men.

The years passed, and the kids grew and went to college, graduated, and started lives. Beatrice went off to be a teacher in Appalachia. She said it was penance for living so well while others had nothing. Fergus grew up to be a strapping man well over six feet with copper hair and fair skin, making him look like a recruiting poster for the Black Watch. After college, he went off to the Navy for six years.

The twins (Fionna and Alexander) were virtually inseparable for most of their lives and went to different colleges. Alexander ended up at Harvard and Fionna at Chapman. Alexander was a real handful at Harvard and proved that the most challenging thing about the Ivy League is getting in. Once in, unless you quit, you would be kept in. Fiona went to Chapman into prelaw, became a devotee of conservative politics, and Chapman's law school was one of the leading conservative schools in the country.

El and I fell into the rhythm of middle age but not into the trap of empty nesters. Because I had been able to retire early, we raised the children and learned to communicate and watch each other grow. So when the children left, we still had the commonality of being able to communicate.

As we got older, I began to see spots on more and more on our friends. Diabetes, cancer, kidney disease, heart problems, and in increasing numbers dementia and Alzheimer's.

Since no one would believe me if I told them outright, I would get into a conversation about estate planning when I saw a spot. Then I would try to steer the conversation. I didn't recommend strategy but approached it from the aspect I was planning for our estate and talking about how I didn't want to kick the bucket and have El not know where the will was or who the lawyers were or where the money was.

It fell on deaf ears with most men, but when I talked to a wife about such things, I usually heard later that she had encouraged her husband to being more forthcoming about estate issues.

I thought about creating a partnership with some doctors researching cancer and dementia and other diseases. If I saw a spot on someone's kidney region, I would alert the nephrologist, and they could contact the person and get them into some sort of fake study. It wouldn't save the person's life with the spot, but it might give the doctors insight into diseases and their progression. It, of course, was a foolish idea since no doctor in their right mind was going do that, but it showed how troubled I was about the spots.

At one point, El and I took a tour of the Holy Land, and while at the Temple Mount, I saw a small tour group. Eight or nine of them had spots on their arms, legs, bodies, or heads. A thunderbolt struck me, and I knew they were going to be the subject of a terror attack.

I thought for a brief second about trying to convince the group leader the group was in danger but rejected it because I would have probably been viewed as a terrorist myself.

Two days later, while they were waiting for their bus in Bethlehem, a car bomb detonated, and seven were killed. I was crushed, and I knew it would happen but could do nothing. However, my bad feelings were short lived. I had the empathy and compassion expected, but I did not fall into the spiral of depression as I had in the past. I used a technique of cognitive behavioral therapy called the three Cs. Where confronted with an unhelpful thought catch it, check it for accuracy and then challenge it.

I did that with the tour group and realized that I could have done nothing to change the events and that I had no part in them, so it was self-defeating for me to accept any responsibly. It was as if a new light was shining on me.

The children married. Beatrice married another teacher named Andreas Higston, whom she had met in Appalachia, and they moved to an Indian Reservation in North Dakota. Eventually, Beatrice and Andreas would have four children, two girls, and two boys. Beatrice insisted that the children have the MacIntosh name in their names.

Fergus's experience in electronic warfare netted him a job at Lockheed after he got out. He married a lady he met at work. Helene Duverneau was never going to be Scottish, and she didn't take the MacIntosh name, but agreed instead that the boy children would be MacIntosh and the girls Duverneau.

So life went on. In my reading, I learned that sometimes those with the sight could determine if their sons would have it but have the son stand on the father's feet. I tried to do it with Fergus one day when we were out, and I saw a woman with a spot, but Dad or not, he wasn't going to humor me.

If one of the boys had the sight, I thought it might be good to prepare them, but there really was no way to know without them having the experience, and it could skip a generation or even several as it had in my family.

How do you prepare someone for something like that? In the modern world, rationality was supposed to be replacing emotion and mystery. Modern media streamed endless facts and behaviors; scientists dispelled any phenomena that had no hard facts. Faith slipped away in the constant hammering of supposed facts. Everything needed an explanation. Nothing could be taken as belief. Aquinas says that no explanation is necessary to one who has faith. To one without faith, no explanation is possible.

Even if they ran tests against me, it would not have proven anything since the sample size would be too small to have much relevance. Of course, if you took all the people in history who had the sight, they would likely fit comfortably in a hotel ballroom.

There were two other things different with my version of the sight. Most of those historical sighted persons had some portend of the manner of the subject's death. They would see an avatar with a rope around their neck, indicating hanging, bathed in fire, or wet and covered in seaweed to drown in an ocean. All I saw was a spot. Other than the smell of aviation fuel with the Anderson partners, I did not have any indication of the method of death.

The other issue that began to fill my thoughts was a staple of hundreds of science fiction shows. What happened whenever a person interfered or changed the march of time? The sad fact is that if most people hadn't lived, their contributions would not materially affect the world, but what if somehow you interfered with the train of human development that led to Beethoven, Solzhenitsyn, Steinbeck, or Salk?

Homer's central theme was wisdom came through suffering, and it seemed to be a concept that had transcended all cultures and religions. For example, Buddha thought life was suffering. If the idea that wisdom came out of suffering was universal, then it followed that suffering was a fundamental element of human existence. What was important was not that you suffered but from what you learned from it.

But suffering damages mental and physical well-being, and there comes a time when the wisdom gained by suffering is outweighed by the damage done. At which point, suffering became degrading, not ennobling?

Perhaps the real meaning was that death or the realization of death contributed something decisive to the meaning of life, and it should have come earlier when the person could have enjoyed the joy that comes from finding meaning. But it also troubled me that most people, including myself, saw death as something waiting to ambush them.

If one focused on death as an inconvenience instead of a part of life, then death became more authentic but life less real. So not focusing on death allowed people to focus on life, and the real challenge was to get people while they were healthy far from their deaths to find meaning in life and avoid the meaningless existence that came from the personal pursuit of wealth and power, leading to loneliness and sin itself.

With its constant inputs and attempts at sensory and physical stimulation, the modern world made us so tightly wound that we left no room for meaning. Instead, we assigned meaning to material and, therefore, forfeitable things.

One of the concepts I gained from the talks with Breanna was that the mind could only see what it wanted to see. In the old days, the mind was ready to see different things than today when all answers could come from a TV or computer, and the knowledge imparted cost us nothing, so it meant nothing. In the final analysis, I came away with the idea that suffering, including my own, was a door through which we passed to get to a mirror, allowing us to see ourselves more clearly.

I was like a stone garden wall that had been upset by a hard winter. Through the gaps in the wall, visions of the future could intrude on the present, or in Breanna and Fionna's faith, the sithean could make known the future. It would be hard, if not impossible, for a modern person to grasp the idea of the juncture of future and present. In the end, I came to peace with my mental gymnastics. I was fated to have the power, there was nothing I could do to make it go away, and I was likely to pass it to future generations. I was not responsible morally because the affliction was a determining factor. Moral responsibility came from choices and judgments made where the person had the possibility of doing otherwise, and I had no such freedom.

I also got to peace with suffering, which was one of the great things of my life. It was not that I became hardened to suffering quite the opposite, but I saw it in the context of an existential part of human life, which could not be avoided. Every human would suffer at some point, and some more spectacularly than others, but all would suffer.

When I saw an amputee or someone disfigured by burns, I offered a silent thanks for not only being that person, but I also tried to have compassion for what that person had gone through. It made me more grateful for the blessings of my family, my life and success, and my ability to find a workable solution to my plight.

Life became sweeter, and happiness seemed to flourish. I took nothing for granted because I knew that there was someone who had tried what I did and failed and suffered through a bankruptcy, jail, or ruin for every one of my successes. Life was sweet except that it seemed upside down. Men, as they age, are supposed to get either better-looking or at least distinguished. Sure, the spare tire shows up, the hair gets thin, wrinkles appear, and sex is sweeter because it comes less often.

Women are sometimes thought to get less attractive due to various physical differences, childbirth, and other things. In my marriage, I was at least in my own mind aging faster than I should, and El was getting more and more beautiful as time passed. Or maybe it was just my old man's eyes seeing the one with love.

Every five years, El and I tried to get the entire family together. It was quite a gang. By this time, all the kids had kids, and El was reveling in being grandmother El to a herd of children. Beatrice had four, Fergus and Helen had one, then adopted two more. Fionna married another lawyer, and they had four more children. Alexander didn't bother to marry. He and his girlfriend had three kids before they thought about marriage. Alexander ended up working for a Wall Street Bank, something he swore he would never do, and his girlfriend worked as a literary agent.

Then there was my family. Mom and Dad were gone, as were the parents and their siblings, but my brothers and sisters were there. Daphne, Eleanor, and Peter. Between them, they had another eight children but only two spouses.

Peter had recovered somewhat from his PTSD and worked for CSX in a middle management position. He eventually married a lady from work named Darlene or Dolly, and they had two children. Daphne had three children, divorced, and remarried an airline pilot who couldn't keep his hands off the flight attendants (male or female). He got fired, and she divorced him, taking their two children with her. She then remarried, and within six months, her third husband died of a heart attack. She married again and had one more child before hanging up her spurs.

So we were looking at forty people. We tried to move the reunion around, so it was convenient for the greatest number. Undercutting all the joy when we got together was my concern that someone might be carrying my affliction. Of course, my children knew about it, as did my siblings, but the grandkids were blissfully ignorant. I quickly got the reputation of being a bit crazy since I would ask questions to see if I could glean any hint that one of them had the sight or a connection to the old Celtic faith.

One night at the third reunion, the bumptiousness of the day had quieted. I was sitting in front of the fire in the house we rented in Jackson Hole with an Ardbeg Scotch when Eleanor sat down next to me with a glass of wine.

"We having Eucharist?"

"No, we aren't in the fourteenth century. Nuns drink wine outside of Eucharist, David, just like I'm not here in some impossibly starched habit looking like Audrey Hepburn in a nun's story."

I remained silent.

"David, I've overheard some of the questions and comments you asked and made to the children, and it seems to me that you are seeking an answer to a problem that has plagued you. It seems to be a spiritual issue, and that's my area." She stopped at this point and waved her cross at me. "Is there anything I can do to help?"

"Sis, that sounds weird. You are both a sister of an order and my sister, ironic?'

"Yeah, so call me S-squared," she said, laughing, and when she did, I realized that all those years ago, Grandpa saw something because she did look like Eleanor Parker.

"You're much more perceptive than you used to be. Yes, I had something on my mind that has been there a long time since Wheaton. I haven't told many about it. El and my kids but not the grandkids. I'm gun-shy about talking to religious people about it. The first religious guy told me I was devil-possessed, and the other told me I was morally irresponsible. It left a bad taste in my mouth."

"There is no doubt you were possessed by the devil at one point with some of the stuff you used to do me, and Daphne could have only come from the devil!" She was smiling as I asked what precisely. "Oh, the time you nailed Daphne's gym shoes to boards and then tried to use them to walk on water, or the time you stuck chewed bubble gum in the pocket of my coat. It took me weeks to get that off me!"

We both laughed.

"I know that you can't give reconciliation as a sacrament, but I will tell you if you promise that you will never tell anyone else without asking me first, Deal?"

"Of course."

I was just about to get started when El and Peter came in and sat down, and I was not going to talk about this to Peter, so I had to wait.

Eleanor and I decided to drive up to a hot spring south of Jackson a few days later. Neither of us had any intention of getting in the water.

We stopped and walked up a hill to get away from the dust of the unpaved road and get a better view. The scenery around Jackson is nothing short of spectacular, and we were looking south over a small river with part of the Gros Venture mountains around us. To the north, the mountains were snowcapped even in the midst of the warm summer day. The verdant slopes of pine, ash, and aspen carpeted the hills, while below them in the river bottom was long prairie grass and smaller brush trampled here and there by elk and deer slaking their thirst. Yet it was all a peaceful place that made the heart glad in response, and trouble seemed far away.

Eleanor and I sat at a picnic table. The yellow jackets buzzed around before realizing we had no food. The background of our lives was birds and insects in their ordinary pursuits, and it was a perfect place to unburden.

"We were rudely interrupted last night before we could get into this great mystery of yours," started Eleanor.

"I wouldn't have minded if El stayed and listened as she already knows, but Peter is another matter. I just don't know how he will react to things, and this is so strange that I can't run the risk of starting a family dispute."

"Peter is dealing with a lot of issues from the PTSD, which is a very long-term thing, and those folks do have unusual reactions to inputs, so your instincts are probably right. He came to me a few years ago because he needed to tell his story, and I hope I helped him. I sure pray for him every night."

"Okay, so here goes," I said, starting off the tale. I did not hold anything back. I just let it go while I was telling it time passed, and we ate the sandwiches we had purchased at a gas station/sporting goods/deli/grocery store. I told Eleanor even more than I had told Breanna and Father Altois. I talked about the depression I fought through. Eleanor had developed over the years from being a noisy, intrusive nosey girl to possessing one of the great skills she did not interrupt. Still, she never gave the impression she wasn't actively listening.

When I finished, she looked at me with a mixture of questioning and compassion. Her eyes fixed on me, mouth set, her shoulders, and body fixed and tense. What I had said affected her. "That's one hell of a story, David. It's too detailed to be made up. Too many facts match what we felt, but the scope is incredible. No wonder you didn't want to talk to anyone."

She had heard some rumors when we all lived in Wheaton and remembered the commotion the night Shamus died.

"There is so much about this that is strange and inexplicable. Grandma spoke Gaelic, and there were many people from Scotland at her funeral, but she had never been to Scotland, and I never remember her speaking Gaelic. Then there was the connection to Ruth MacTavish in North Carolina and Breanna in Islay. They were united but had never met. There was the uncanny resemblance of Fionna in Scotland to Beatrice and Beatrice being an old family name the Scottish Fionna's family. Yet there can't be any genetic connection because our traditional lands were so far apart. There are others, but you get the idea."

"Not everything can be explained, David. I have learned that in my religious life, there are, and I believe, there are powers beyond the imagining of humankind that can affect the living. How do and how did you feel when you told the story?"

"You know I felt a bit relieved, especially when I knew that the other person was not going to run for butterfly net and straitjackets."

"They don't use those anymore," she said, smiling, "they just drug you into somnolence and keep you there. Mental health via pharmaceuticals."

"First, there is a need in humans, a fundamental need, to tell things to others," she said. "If you can't tell someone else, the secret can eat you up. The problem, as you noted, is that you have to be careful who you tell things to, so they don't exploit you, shun you, or judge you. Though to find a good ear with this kind of a story."

"You mean because it has so many unexplained elements?"

"No, because it requires someone to believe in things different than what they hold as beliefs in their minds. That is why Jacoby reacted so badly. In his seminary training, he was taught that sickness or distress was inexorably linked to past sins. This faith that Breanna and Fionna exposed challenges almost two thousand years of Christian teaching, so some push back is to be expected."

"Okay, that explains Jacoby and perhaps Father Altois, but what about the nonreligious who heard the story?" I asked.

Eleanor thought for a minute while watching a truck motor by on the road below, trailing a cloud of dust. "People think in the form of rubrics, short cuts that let them explain things without all the deep thought that might go into learning a new thing. Think of them as rules of thumb like 'red sky in the morning sailor take warning,' and when a concept works against the rule, they reject it sometimes with great anger."

"I guess you're right. They weren't bad people except for the ones who sued us for emotional distress, but it sure was difficult to have your community overnight turn on you."

"Yeah, but I will bet you there were a lot of folks who felt sorry for you and wanted to comfort and support you, but the peer pressure was too great, and they were weak in their beliefs. Most people believe they are strong and independent, but they are just creatures of mass society in reality. Don't blame them or hold grudges."

It had grown late, and we knew that activities were planned, and we needed to get back. So we stopped our conversation after I said, "What's strange about this is that in all the research about the McIntosh line, I find that two others had the sight, but they seemed to have been accepted and believed because science hadn't yet destroyed faith."

"Not true," said Eleanor, "but we can talk later."

The next day, Eleanor told a white lie. I guess nuns can tell them, and everyone believed that we were going to visit one of her nun sisters who was working on the Wind River Reservation but was in Jackson for a few days.

What we did was to drive north toward Teton National Park, but we stopped at a wildlife art gallery where Eleanor convinced one of the employees to let us use a meeting room for free.

"So let's get back to your little problem," she said, smiling. "Here you are, a trained scientist married to a trained scientist, living in the middle of the electronics capital of the world, and you have something that defies explanation by any of your rational senses. You are struggling against two things. One, you want to force the sight through the hole of rationality. Second, you are working against your personality. That's a lot of tension in anyone."

"What do you mean working against my personality?"

"I have known you for all of your years, and I know the kind of person you are. I know you have made mistakes, but you are a person who is sensitive and affected by the unhappiness of others and a good person. That means that you naturally want to reach out and help people and do so via your knowledge. In this case, you are possessed of the ultimate secret for most people knowledge of their deaths. If they knew they were destined to die via disease, accident, or violence, they would change their lives, but you can't tell them because they won't believe you, and worse, they will attack you making you feel worse. That about, right?"

"I guess you are right. When I see the spots, I usually react with depression or misplaced anger, so that is the tension surfacing."

"Depression is a tough nut. Lots of people are depressed but don't know the reason or what they can gain from it. It's not all bad to be depressed."

"That's a unique perspective."

"Not really, depression or melancholy is a form of suffering, and you know that suffering is an essential part of human existence. Depression is a saturnine emotion, and it makes a person gloomy. Viewed in perspective, it changes the time frame of reflection and helps to look at the events of a long life in a distilled manner, helping you discover your essential nature. It's not something to be afraid of once you understand what it is intended to do. The anxiety of depression is that it will never end, that life will never be joyous again."

"Boy, is that true the first few years of this experience. I was convinced that I would go through life with a black cloud over my head, and life would be one long experience of gloom and misery. I worried that as I had more and more experiences that they stopped bothering me as much, and that made me jaded and callous."

"No, neither. You just found a way to deal with it and to move on. The best way out of depression is to stop fighting and focus on living. There are a few other things that you knew but have probably forgotten about. First, you were born on a Wednesday."

"Yeah, so what?"

"The old saw is that Wednesday's child is full of woe. It's an old rhyme that supposedly tells fortunes. Tuesday's child is full of grace, so our departed brother…"

She and I both stopped and made the sign of the cross. "Was born on Tuesday and certainly was in grace since he could not have sinned. On the other hand, you waited till Wednesday, and guess what? As you see, your life has been full of woe. The other thing was that you were born with encaul, and that is supposed to give people special powers and good fortune."

"Sis, you're a Catholic nun and a rational person. You don't believe all of that old wives' tales, do you?"

"I don't make it a practice to run my life by them, but if you study the ethnography and history of them, you find that like all rules of thumb or explanations, they have a basis however tenuous in fact or behavior. It might be confirmation bias, but something leads to the saying. Besides, I believe you have the sight, and that flies in the face of my religious learning, so who is to say they old sayings and beliefs don't have merit?"

We talked on, and I knew that Eleanor understood what I was going through. She was wrong about one thing. While the spots had caused misery and distress, most of my life had been blessed with good health and good results. Maybe the good side was compensation for the bad times. Whatever it was, I had made it through all the evils of the spots without suicide or losing sight of who I was, and that was an accomplishment.

Up until now, we had seen no evidence that any of our children or grandkids had the sight, and I breathed a sigh of relief that I did not have to deal with explaining it to another person. I remembered, however, that my study had told me there was no set time for it to appear. In my case, it had been at thirteen, so it might yet still occur, and it did skip multiple generations, so it was still possible it would pop its ugly head up.

On the last day of the reunion, I was in the bathroom of El and my condo. A couple of the grandkids and great-grandkids were playing in the living room. I had the door open, so I could hear them and my shirt off as I shaved.

"I'm going to go watch Grandpop shave," one of them said.

I heard little footfalls behind me but didn't turn to see which one of the kids came in. Then I heard a voice say.

"Grandpop, do you know you have black spots on your back?"

About the Author

This is Dennis Gibb's second novel, the first, *Exordium*, was published in 2014. After graduating from college, Dennis served for five years in the Army and is a decorated Vietnam combat veteran. After leaving military service, Dennis spent almost five decades in the investment industry, acting as financial advisor to Native American communities in the lower forty-eight states and Alaska. At age seventy-three, Dennis was incarcerated where self-evaluation inspired him to author this novel with its themes of guilt, shame, truth, lies, loss, isolation, and fear of death.

Dennis currently works at a small college in Washington State where he has created and manages a program assisting incarcerated veterans to return to society.